A MIGHTY WHI...
DESERT PEOPL...
OLD DREA...

JOSHUA—Heroic in ...ttle and driven by a vision of a promised land, he is the greatest warrior the world has ever known . . . but the taste of blood threatens to turn him from a man of principle and honor into a merciless killer.

PEPI—Son of the cruelest sorcerer in all Egypt, he has embraced an uneasy peace over the mighty swords he forges, but he may soon have to make a heartrending choice to pick up arms once again— this time against a friend.

THE MINOTAUR—Bold, brash, a ruthless pirate of the ancient seas, he challenges the old ways with his stealth and cunning, threatening to become the one enemy the Children of the Lion cannot conquer.

KETURAH—The blind beauty married to the sword-maker Iri, she will be stolen from the arms of her beloved and put on the slaver's block to face a destiny of shame, danger . . . and redemption.

THEON—Inheritor of the secret that can destroy them, he will become a master spy for the Children of the Lion . . . only to be snared himself, not by a sword, but by a woman's charms.

Volume XI

THE SEA PEOPLES

PETER DANIELSON

Created by the producers of
Wagons West, White Indian,
and **The First Americans.**

Book Creations Inc., Canaan, NY · Lyle Kenyon Engel, Founder

BANTAM BOOKS
NEW YORK · TORONTO · LONDON · SYDNEY · AUCKLAND

THE SEA PEOPLES

*A Bantam Book / published by arrangement with
Book Creations, Inc.*

Bantam edition / January 1990

*Produced by Book Creations, Inc.
Lyle Kenyon Engel, Founder*

ISBN 0-553-28300-6

Published simultaneously in the United States and Canada

Bantam Books are published by Bantam Books, a division of Bantam Doubleday Dell Publishing Group, Inc. Its trademark, consisting of the words "Bantam Books" and the portrayal of a rooster, is Registered in U.S. Patent and Trademark Office and in other countries. Marca Registrada. Bantam Books, 666 Fifth Avenue, New York, New York 10103.

PRINTED IN THE UNITED STATES OF AMERICA

OPM   0   9   8   7   6   5   4   3   2   1

This book is dedicated to all of the friends of the Children of the Lion, in all Lands.

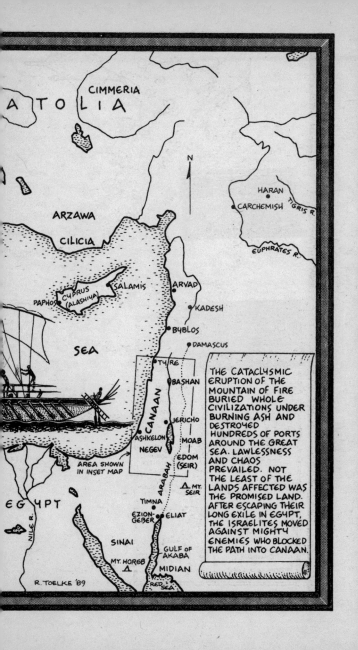

CIMMERIA

ANATOLIA

ARZAWA

CILICIA

HARAN
CARCHEMISH
TIGRIS R.

EUPHRATES R.

CYPRUS (ALASHIVA)
SALAMIS
PAPHOS

ARVAD

KADESH

BYBLOS

SEA

DAMASCUS

TYRE
BASHAN

CANAAN

JERICHO

ASHKELON
NEGEV
MOAB

EDOM (SEIR)

AREA SHOWN
IN INSET MAP

ARABAH

△ MT. SEIR

EGYPT

TIMNA
EZION-GEBER
ELIAT

NILE R.

SINAI

MT. HOREB △

GULF OF AKABA

MIDIAN

RED SEA

R. TOELKE '89

THE CATACLYSMIC
ERUPTION OF THE
MOUNTAIN OF FIRE
BURIED WHOLE
CIVILIZATIONS UNDER
BURNING ASH AND
DESTROYED
HUNDREDS OF PORTS
AROUND THE GREAT
SEA. LAWLESSNESS
AND CHAOS
PREVAILED. NOT
THE LEAST OF THE
LANDS AFFECTED WAS
THE PROMISED LAND.
AFTER ESCAPING THEIR
LONG EXILE IN EGYPT,
THE ISRAELITES MOVED
AGAINST MIGHTY
ENEMIES WHO BLOCKED
THE PATH INTO CANAAN.

Prologue

As the last light faded in the western sky, the people gathered in the lee of the tall cliffs could hear the harsh cries of the gulls in the distance. The tang of the Great Sea filled the air, waking memories of faraway places: Greece, Crete, the islands.

For as long as a man might hold his breath the sky took on a curious coppery intensity, then darkness washed away the color.

Suddenly the Teller of Tales appeared before them, his features thrown into high relief by the blazing campfire. From under beetling brows the sharp old eyes scanned the crowd. The people were of many lands, headed in many directions, for tonight the oasis sheltered three separate caravans, newly arrived from far-flung cities, bound for many foreign lands.

"What sort of tale shall I tell you tonight?" he asked.

"Tell us of the coming of the Sea Peoples," voices cried out.

"*Tell us of the pirates on the Great Sea,*" others called out.

"*Tell us of the wanderings of the Habiru, under Moses, and their arrival in the Promised Land.*"

The old man's white beard hid his thin smile. "*I shall speak of all of these.*"

From all sides came a murmur of appreciation. The Teller of Tales turned his back to gather his thoughts, and when he again faced the people, he was ready to cast his spell.

"*You have heard,*" he began, "*of the great cataclysm that occurred in the isles of the Great Sea*"—with a sweep of his hand he motioned to the sea, which lay just beyond the dunes—"*and caused such horrible damage and suffering. When the eruption of the Mountain of Fire destroyed the island called Home by the great sea trader Demetrios, its dark cloud blotted out the sun and buried all the nearby lands and islands under burning ash. Civilizations were destroyed, and many thousands died in agony, their lungs seared by the poisoned air.*

"*The same explosion sent gigantic waves out across the sea, to bring destruction and devastation to a hundred cities; to silt up river estuaries and ruin the sea bottoms of a hundred ports; to change forever the world beside the sea.*

"*Now, as old civilizations died, new ones grew up to take their place. People settled in places where their faces had never before been seen. First they captured the ports; then they moved inland, exhorting their brothers from across the sea to join them. Others came, as well, privateers who robbed ships and interrupted the flow of goods around the sea.*

"*Not least of the lands affected was the Promised Land of the sons of Jacob, a land where strangers now*

2

reigned. After escaping their long exile in Egypt, the Israelites moved toward the land their God had given to their ancestor Abraham of Ur so many years before, but mighty adversaries blocked their path.

"Not only the Canaanites stood in their way, but the warriors of Edom, Midian, Bashan, and the new city-states settled after the arrival of the Sea Peoples. To reenter their land, the Israelites would have to challenge all of these, plus the fierce, implacable tribes descended from Ishmael and Esau, the dispossessed who bore them a grudge of many years' standing."

His eyes pierced the darkness, and his voice lowered slightly. "Hear now of what happened when Moses, the great leader, grew old and could not lead his people into the Promised Land. Hear of how a new generation arose to take up the fight and how a new commander seized control—a single-minded soldier named Joshua."

He raised his spidery hands, and his voice grew in strength. "Hear of the new wanderings of the people called the Children of the Lion—among the sons and daughters of Israel; among the cities of the plain; among the pirate chieftains of the sea lanes; and among the cruel and fearless new tribes that now ruled the lands beside the River Jordan.

"Among," he said, "the Peoples of the Sea . . ."

CHAPTER ONE

On the Great Sea

I

She was two days out of Lemnos, bound for ports on the Canaanite coast, and for all the eye could see, she was like many other trading vessels plying the sea routes around the Great Sea. She was under fifty feet in length—a "round ship" rather than a "long ship," or galley, and yet she bore forty feet of yard and nearly seven hundred feet of sailcloth aloft. Her sail allowed almost infinite adjustment for varying winds. As round ships went, she was the finest afloat.

Ladon, captain of the vessel, stood forward of the steersman on his raised perch, looking with pride on his ship. It was his first command. A month before he had been given the position by Demetrios the Magnificent himself, in a commissioning ceremony at the secret island hideaway Demetrios called Home.

That Ladon had shared the honor with six other new captains did not dampen his pride. It was an honor to graduate from a mate's rank to that of captain on a ship belonging to the greatest privately held fleet in the history of the world.

He looked over his ship with pride. The *Nemea* was a coastal trader, neither very large nor very fast, but she would last many years. She was ready for action and soundly built, and the lead shielding below her waterline would foil the shipworms that were the bane of most freighters.

Above decks were the sail (two spares were stowed below), the fragile steering oars, and the brushwood bulwarks that protected the wine-filled amphorae from the ocean spray. Below, she bore consignments of mace heads made of stone, ivory, great earthenware pots, fishing nets, ingots of copper and tin, logs of exotic and expensive wood bound for Egypt, and containers of aromatic resin.

The cargo was worth a king's ransom, and Ladon looked forward to trading it. As captain he would now be entitled to a larger share of the profits than he ever had in his six years with Demetrios's fleet. He might even be able to build a house back at Home or maybe buy a slave to share his bed.

The *Nemea* carried some surprises: One was a secret and potentially wildly profitable cache of bronze swords, spearheads, and arrowheads. They were made according to a secret casting process developed for the Great Sea trade by Seth of Thebes, Demetrios's distant kinsman. Both Demetrios and Seth had been born to the Egyptian branch of the Children of the Lion, and each was born with the distinctive birthmark common to all males—and to at least one female—in the famous family of arms makers.

After old Seth's death, Demetrios found his notes and had put Seth's apprentices to work deciphering them.

Thus, Demetrios's armory had become a major supplier of bronze weaponry throughout the world around the Great Sea.

The other distinctive difference about the *Nemea* was the new duties of the crew.

Decades before, a staggering volcanic eruption at the site of Demetrios's original headquarters had caused incredible devastation around the Great Sea. Fires and enormous columns of red-hot ash had blotted out the sun, and towering waves had destroyed entire ports and wiped out whole populations.

Now, once-great Egypt was a weakened nation, trying to regain its strength, and Crete, once the region's most impressive sea power, was a shadow of its former self. New entities had moved into the area, changing the balance of power around the Great Sea forever.

Nameless foreigners drifted in from strange parts of the world, capturing ports left ill defended in the wake of the great devastation, then moving their brethren into the newly conquered lands.

These Sea Peoples, as the vanquished and fearful called them, had already captured much of the Greek mainland and flowed from there to Anatolia and the islands before spreading to the Canaanite coast, where they had quickly overrun the ports of Tyre, Arvad, and Ashkelon.

The sea-lanes had been similarly affected. With no great Cretan fleet of warships on patrol, pirates were causing havoc in the shipping trade. When a ship was sunk the shipper was traditionally held responsible and had to make it up to his suppliers out of his own pocket or risk losing his reputation and livelihood.

For a long time Demetrios's mighty fleet had been spared the pirates' attentions. But recently even his ships had been among those missing and unaccounted for. Again and again his rich and powerful trade network had been disrupted.

As a precaution, the crews on all Demetrios's vessels now included small contingents of highly skilled warriors, expert with bow and sword, ready to repel boarders. The fighters looked like ordinary crewmen, suntanned and naked; but on a moment's notice they could disappear belowdecks and come up fiercely armed.

Ladon turned to the steersman. "We're losing the wind. Two degrees starboard."

"Aye, sir," the steersman answered.

Ladon's mate, Pauson, immediately barked orders to the crew to adjust the sail. Slowly the tubby ship turned; the sail filled once more, and they could feel the pull of the wind as the boat moved forward.

Ladon beckoned his mate. "We're in Cypriot waters, Pauson. This is Minotaur country. Last we heard, the Minotaur had thirty ships on the water. Better alert the men."

"Very good, sir." The mate grinned. "This crew is not your peaceful kind, sir. I think that most of them secretly wish someone would challenge us, so they'd get a chance to fight."

"I don't share their eagerness," Ladon said with a frown. "We're not in business to fight; we're in business to make money."

"True, sir. Nevertheless, sir, if we did sink one of the Minotaur's ships, we'd have done the whole fleet a favor. I mean, the fewer of the bastards there are . . ."

"Yes, I agree. But I'd rather get safely to Tyre and unload our cargo first. It's a rich load, and the sooner the credit goes into Demetrios's accounts, the better I'll like it."

"Yes, sir," Pauson said. "Although . . ."

7

"Yes?"

"Sir, when I was in port over on Chios, the gossip in the taverns was all about the Minotaur. Most of it was blather, of course—the business of his being one of King Minos's bastards, for instance. Probably about as royal as I am, sir. But there was mention of his having an 'invincible' galley, which could catch anything on the sea, under oar or sail."

Ladon smiled indulgently. "Sailor gossip."

"Yes, I know, sir," Pauson said. "When I first went to sea the old salts had me believing the one about Medusa, the woman with the snakes in her hair. I used to have nightmares about her."

"You must have come aboard the boats about the same age as I did, innocent and naïve. Well, it didn't take much to knock that out of us. But always there lingers the suspicion that one of the old boys, white haired and toothless, might just be telling the truth."

"Of course those of us who take to the sea tend to be a bit on the imaginative side. Lots of wishful thinking, you know. Part of our mind actually wants to see Medusa or sea monsters."

"Or pirates with boats that can travel twice as fast as a galley at full stroke. You're right: We are a damned silly lot of bastards. If we had a lick of sense we'd be on dry land right now—"

He got no further. From atop the yard the lookout sang out, loud and strong: "*Ship ahoy! Ship ahoy!*"

II

The captain instantly stiffened. He shot a hard-eyed glance at Pauson and said, "Arm the men." Then he craned his neck to squint up at the lookout. "Tell me more, lad! Longship or round?"

"Long, sir!"

"What nation's banners does she fly?"

There was a pause as the lookout strained to see. "None, sir. She bears the black sail!"

Ladon's eyes narrowed.

"It's furled but clearly visible. And, sir—she's making good speed!"

"Good lad," Ladon called up. "Keep an eye on her. Tell me of any changes."

He looked around him now, watching the crew appear on deck bearing bows and swords and wearing helmets. Disdaining body armor or any clothing other than the helmets, they preferred the freedom and mobility of nudity. Ladon watched Pauson distribute quivers of arrows to the archers gathered amidships. How good would they be in a fight? No doubt there would be one: The black flag was the emblem of the Minotaur.

The mysterious pirate seemed to have appeared overnight, and in command of a sizable fleet. One day there was nobody of that name; the next day the inns and taverns of twenty cities around the Great Sea buzzed with rumors and tall tales about a pirate named the Minotaur after the legendary half-man, half-bull bastard son of the famous lord of the Cretan Labyrinth.

At his first appearance, the Minotaur's corsairs had overtaken a three-ship convoy of Greek vessels, plundering their cargo and sending the ships to the bottom. A single crewman had been allowed to escape, put to drift in a leather-sided coracle as a warning that a new and dangerous enemy of free shipping was loose.

After being picked up by a passing fisherman, the lone survivor had been questioned by authorities on Rhodes.

He had told of the cool demeanor of the Minotaur—a huge, powerfully built, hirsute man with a black beard. After his two sleek galleys had overtaken the convoy, the Minotaur himself had arrived in a ship of curious design. It rode high in the water, and the crew of burly rowers sat on a high platform behind protective planking. The Minotaur had monitored the transferring of the cargo, his practiced eyes apportioning it expertly among the three ships. His word had been accepted by the crews without argument, and the discipline had been that of superbly drilled sailors.

Moreover, the captured crewmen had been treated with firm fairness, although it was understood from the moment of their capitulation that they would wind up as slaves on a rower's bench. They had not been abused or mistreated in any way, and even the witness, marooned in his coracle, had been handled more gently than he, as a sailor with many years' experience, had had any reason to expect.

Since then the mysterious brigand had taken more than thirty vessels. When the Minotaur had finally struck Demetrios's fleet, he had done so with a vengeance. A dozen of Demetrios's vessels had fallen to the Minotaur's assaults in the last two months, forcing the powerful shipper to call a secret meeting and formulate a new defensive policy.

Now, the secret weapons having been distributed, Pauson returned to the low poop deck and squinted at the vessel gaining on them.

"You can see the black sail clearly now," Ladon said. "It's one of his, all right. But why only one? The usual pattern calls for at least two galleys to flank the victim. I wonder if he's changed his tactics and is spoiling for a fight." He sighed. "Tell the men to shorten sail and drop anchor. We'll stand and fight, if that's what everybody wants. Perhaps the pirates will get a little surprise they won't like."

Thus it was that the *Nemea* met the attacker, her crew lined up: swordsmen at the ready, bowmen with their arrows nocked, waiting for the first sign of action.

The unexpected maneuver seemed to confuse the pirate captain. As he drew alongside the *Nemea* and his rowers turned their oars skyward, he studied the armed men along the rail and stood for a long moment, hands on his hips.

"Ahoy the *Nemea*," he said at last. "You're outmanned; you can't get away. Submit, and you'll outlive the day. What say you?"

Ladon, standing on his own deck, looked him over. This was not the Minotaur. The man was tall and yellow haired, and spoke with the barbaric accent of the Circassians. Ladon frowned as the enemy crew aligned itself. He counted them. "Perhaps they use a different kind of arithmetic where you come from. The way we count in my country, we've a man for every one of yours, less one or two. We accept the odds. And where I come from, we kill our game before we eat it. Those are the rules you'll be playing by today."

"That's telling 'em, Captain!" one of the *Nemea*'s men sang out, only to draw an angry curse from Pauson.

The pirate chief threw back his head and laughed. "The minnow challenges the shark! Listen to that, men. We'll get a bit of entertainment with our day's exercise." There was a loud laugh from the pirates. "Prepare to board!"

Ladon's face tensed. He held up one arm; the bowmen raised their bows. "So be it," he said in a taut voice. "Men, wait for a good target. Until they're atop the rails."

"This is rich." The pirate captain let out another belly laugh, drew his sword, and offered Ladon a mock salute. "Well blustered, Captain, but before you doom your entire crew to death, you'd do well to wake up your lookout. Apparently he's gone to sleep on you!"

Ladon clenched his fists and looked up; his lookout, stung by the criticism, now whirled around in his wicker basket and spotted another vessel. He pointed out to sea, to their rear. "Captain, ship ahoy!"

Ladon turned, and for the first time he felt fear. A galley, half again the size of the one that lay alongside the *Nemea*, was headed straight for them. It rode high in the water, and Ladon could see a vast, churning forest of oars dipping and pulling in perfect precision.

In the bow stood a tall, black-bearded man, broad of shoulder and chest, with huge arms crossed over his hairy breast.

"The Minotaur!" someone said with stunned awe.

Ladon's jaw dropped. "No ship can go that fast," he muttered to himself. "It's impossible."

Too late he called his bowmen to attention. The enemy was already tossing grappling irons over the top of his mast and swinging across the chasm that lay between the two ships.

"Prepare to repel boarders—" he shouted, as arrows began falling on his men from the Minotaur's ship.

Ladon saw Pauson stagger and fall, an arrow protruding from between his shoulder blades. As the captain turned to see whence the arrow had come, the first of the boarders reached him. A blow to the head drove him to his knees. Then there was another, and he knew no more.

* * *

Ladon awoke to a bucketful of frigid water splashed over him. "There, now!" someone said affably. "Well, boys, it looks as if our sleeping prince might just consider coming out of it and joining the rest of his little playmates."

Ladon sat up quickly and was jolted by a stabbing pain in his head. He raised his hands to explore the lump above his temple but found that his hands were shackled.

Where am I? He looked around. He was deep in the guts of a galley, his bare bottom resting on a rower's bench. His ankle was shackled to a chain that ran the length of the galley's rowing well. The men on all sides of him were strangers, filthy, long bearded, and hollow eyed.

I've lost my ship! he thought, quick tears of shame filling his eyes. *I've lost the* Nemea!

He raised his hands toward his face, but the short chain caught them up. His hands could be lifted no higher than the oar before him.

He looked up at the pirate standing above him. "Did we? . . ."

The pirate looked down at him. "Your boys put up a good fight," he said sympathetically. "I'll say that for them. Good luck, my friend. Pull hard and you'll get fair treatment. That's all we can do for you." He grinned, gave a salute that did not seem totally scornful, and disappeared.

Through the beams under his feet Ladon could feel the footfalls on the deck as the pirates transferred the priceless bounty of the *Nemea*'s hold to their own vessel.

He had failed. Even if he ever got free, he would never hold a command again.

13

III

No survivor from the *Nemea* was allowed to escape to carry word of the pirates' deeds; yet it was less than a month before the news reached Demetrios. In the spacious receiving room of his lavish mansion on the acropolis of the island's single, unnamed city, the great trader met with a select group of advisers.

In the center of the floor of the enormous columned room was a vast map of colored tile representing the Great Sea, its surrounding landmasses and its islands. Slaves had been detailed to keep up with the various comings and goings of Demetrios's fleet, and tiny models of ships bearing his colors were arranged over the floor.

Demetrios, barefooted and dressed simply in a linen tunic of flax grown on the island, stood in an empty patch of sea, directing the activities of a slave. "Now, boy, move the two galleys by your foot to the port on the western coast of Corcyra."

The child did so, then tiptoed off the raised map as Demetrios spoke to the men around him. "That's the approximate location of the fleet."

The advisers murmured among themselves, but no one spoke out.

"Well?" Demetrios demanded. "Do you see a pattern? Can you derive some picture of the Minotaur's activities?"

A former sea captain named Agis spoke up. "Sir, the black markers specify where our boats have been taken in the last six months, right?"

"Right," Demetrios said with a nod.

"And between Crete and the mainland is where a fishing boat saw the *Nemea* last."

Demetrios nodded.

"All right, sir. I'd say we have enough of a pattern to allow an educated guess as to where the pirates are based." Agis stood up and walked to the edge of the map. "They sank the *Nemea* after unloading her. One of her timbers, with her name burned onto the beam, floated to shore on Carpathos. But then the pirates have to get their own vessel back to port and unload quickly, before they are spotted."

"Ah," Demetrios said. "I see where this is going. You think we ought to investigate the area between Rhodes and Cnidos."

Agis folded thick arms over his barrel chest. "That'd be my first guess, sir."

Demetrios looked around him. "And a good one. Unfortunately I've already combed that area. If the Minotaur was on one of those islands, I'd have found him by now."

Agis studied the map intently for several more moments. "A pirate galley with her black sails furled would be too conspicuous to sail into an open port loaded down with someone else's cargo. We'd have heard about it by now. If the cargo's been dropped anywhere near the Lycian coast, it would have been managed a piece at a time, using vessels that don't look like pirate ships."

Demetrios beamed. "Listen to that, my friends. That's an experienced seafarer talking. The Minotaur must have normal-looking cargo vessels in that area—ships onto which stolen cargo can be divided and loaded so that the contraband can be sold in nearby ports."

"Gods!" Someone gasped from the far right of the room. "You mean he's organized enough to decide to raid a ship in a particular patch of water and station other boats nearby to carry the booty?"

"Admittedly, it's incredible, but the Minotaur is no ordinary pirate."

"Right you are, sir," someone said. "Imagine getting any two pirate crews or captains to agree on anything, much less coordinate their activities."

"We must treat this fellow as a resourceful and dangerous enemy," Demetrios said. "He's outsmarted us for quite some time now." He fixed his eyes on each man in turn. "Does anyone else have any suggestions?"

A new, younger voice chimed in. "I do."

A smile of affection lit Demetrios's leonine face. "Theon, I didn't see you come in!"

He watched the speaker step out of the crowd. Theon, son of Seth and his beloved wife, Mai, both of whom had died a few years earlier, was tall, bright-eyed, and well built. His stance was aristocratic. His beautifully modulated voice carried a ring of authority. "A thought did occur to me, but it may not be well developed enough to bear the critical discussion I'm likely to get from these experienced and intelligent men." His words, which took in all the council members, was accompanied by a deferent bow. "If you don't mind, I'll discuss it with you when I make my private report; then, if you don't think my notions too ridiculous, we can present them to this distinguished assembly for their thoughts and reactions."

A general murmur of approval greeted Theon's words. His courteous behavior was highly appropriate for a lad of twenty, no matter how brilliant he might be, speaking before his elders.

"We will discuss the matter as you say," Demetrios agreed. "Meanwhile, I'm sure I join all our friends here in welcoming you home from your long and, I'm sure, profitable journey.

"I am very grateful to Theon for taking this past year to complete a survey of alternative boat-building techniques. Great strides are being made in the shipwright's trade these days."

"I think you'll be pleased with some of the designs I've brought back," Theon said, moving aside to make room for a short, powerfully built young man with strong, dark features. "Allow me to introduce one of the men who's going to be building ships for us from those designs. Meet Crantor of Massilia, a shipwright of outstanding skills who has come to live with us."

Demetrios shot him a sharp glance. It was a violation to bring an outsider into Home without his first being investigated and vouched for by several other members. Even then the practice was to admit a newcomer only by stages. And the approval of Demetrios had always to be secured first.

Theon looked at the shocked faces and gauged the enormity of his error. He offered a somewhat more perfunctory bow and said, "Demetrios, I'll await you on the terrace. It's good to be back."

And, as assured as ever, he took his leave.

From the terrace they could look out on the harbor spread below them. It was circular, with deep-blue water, and its narrow opening was commanded by a pair of fortresses.

"Magnificent," Crantor breathed. "But I can't understand how a place like this can have remained secret for so long. Why doesn't every sailor on the Great Sea know about it?"

"It had no access from the sea," Theon explained. "The harbor is a collapsed crater, and until a generation ago it was walled in from all sides. Before Demetrios came, there was a volcanic eruption, causing the wall to collapse and the sea to rush in. Since then the area's reputation for volatility has kept people away. Only

17

Demetrios had the good sense to realize that there is little chance of an eruption in the foreseeable future." He smiled. "It also helps that we keep the waters near here well patrolled, so nobody gets too close."

Crantor looked down at the town on the hillside, at the busy waterfront, and at the buildings around him atop the acropolis. "It's sensational. I can't imagine how so much was built in so short a time. And you say the architect was your father?"

Theon sat down on the wall and let his legs dangle. "I suppose Father's reputation isn't known as far west as Massilia. Anyone east of Rhodes has heard of him, though. He had Babylon more than half rebuilt before the Hittite invaders destroyed it."

"He was obviously a man of great talents. I guess you were very proud of him, eh?"

"Yes, I—" He stopped. "Here comes Demetrios," he said. "Sir, may I present my friend—"

Demetrios strode right up to them. "You're too old to call me sir," he said fondly. "So this is your shipwright, eh? You stirred up quite a ruckus back there, Theon. You know the rules. What prompted you to defy them and bring this gentleman here?"

Theon bowed again. "I can only plead mitigating circumstances. Hired assassins were after Crantor. The best way to get him out of harm's way was to bring him with me. Besides . . ." He turned to Crantor and nodded.

The shipwright turned his back and pulled his robe aside. On the boat builder's bare back was a red blotch: the unmistakable outline of the paw print of a lion.

"A fellow Child of the Lion," Theon continued. "I thought that this would override the rule about strangers. Of course I'd gotten to know him fairly well and think him a good man—and the best shipwright east of Sardo."

"Well, my friend, I thought the world had exhausted its store of surprises for me." Demetrios gave a chuckle. "How did the Sons of the Lion get to Massilia?"

"I don't know, sir," Crantor said. "Any legends about our family have disappeared. All I know of the Children of the Lion is what Theon told me on the voyage here. It's fascinating."

"Indeed it is. You'll hear more by and by. But for now, welcome to Home. Theon, has Crantor been assigned quarters?"

"No. I was going to—"

"Never mind. Crantor, go upstairs and tell the head servant—the bald fellow—that you're to stay in the guest quarters here in my house. He'll find you a room overlooking the garden. Have the caretaker send two of the girls in to give you a bath." He grinned. "That ought to keep you occupied until dinner. I'll want to talk with you more then."

"Thank you, sir." The shipwright bowed to both of them.

Crantor left, and Demetrios turned to Theon and held out his arms for an embrace. "Now," he said, as they sat down side by side on a stone bench, "you had a report for me. And you had an idea about what we ought to do about the Minotaur?"

Theon sat back against the railing and looked at him. "We have to put our own man among the pirates. It's the only way."

Demetrios frowned. "I've thought of that, but all my best men are too well-known."

Theon looked steadily into his eyes. "Send me."

IV

Demetrios was not easily shocked; but now he looked at his young guest in amazement. "No, I won't hear of it!"

"You'll have to," Theon said. "You have nobody else you can trust for the job. Nobody who knows what questions to ask, what to look for."

"I appreciate your offer," Demetrios said, "and it's a brave suggestion. Your courage matches your brains and resourcefulness."

"You think I am too young? Come, Demetrios. When my father was my age—"

"Seth was different."

"Certainly he was different. At my age he had no experience of life at all. He was a late bloomer except for his intellectual brilliance. Where were *you* when you were my age? Wasn't this when Akhilleus picked you out of the crowd?"

"Well, yes, but . . ." Demetrios grinned. "I see I'm going to have to hear you out. Proceed."

"Thank you," Theon said. "My report, incidentally, is written on fifty scrolls. Your house overseer has it. It's nearly complete, except for what I'm about to say now."

"Fifty scrolls! You're thorough, I'll say that for you."

"You pay me to be. Shall I send for them?"

"No, no. I'll study them at leisure. I gather you're about to summarize them for me."

"Demetrios, I've been hearing about this Minotaur all over the Great Sea, in every port. And even if you discount the stories by half, as with all sailor stories—"

"Make that two-thirds."

"Even then, we have a problem. As fast as we can put ships to sea, he can destroy them and seize the cargo and

20

crew. His force grows with every raid. Every vessel he captures provides him a new hold of rowers."

"I doubt he's sinking every ship. He's probably sinking the round ships and keeping the galleys."

"No. I learned that he's not stealing galleys. He's building them."

"Building them?" Demetrios said. "But that's impossible."

"If we can build them, why can't he? I estimate that by the end of the year he'll be making as much money stealing as we do from our legitimate trade. And he doesn't have to maintain a network of agents like ours in every port or influence peddlers in the capitals."

"Or pay our network of spies, either," Demetrios said.

"That's my point. All that money can be put into building ships with which to attack us." He looked Demetrios squarely in the eye. "Even this mysterious 'invincible ship' we keep hearing about."

"Then you've heard of it?"

"Who hasn't?" Theon asked. "But nobody admits to having seen it." He smiled. "That's one of the reasons I brought Crantor back with me. He's not only a Child of the Lion and a superb shipwright himself, he also thinks he knows who's making ships for the Minotaur."

Demetrios leaned forward. "He does? Who is it?"

"A man he studied with named Memnon of Salamis."

"Memnon. I've heard of him! I tried, through intermediaries, to buy a ship from him years ago. When he turned down the deal, I wished I'd done the negotiating myself. My negotiator was young and green."

"As I gather you think I am."

"No, not at all. Don't take offense where none is intended, Theon."

21

"But I still don't understand why you oppose my undertaking this task. If I'm not too young or too green—"

Demetrios laughed. "All right, all right. I'll consider it, although why you should want to go into danger like that, I can't imagine."

"We must have a man inside the Minotaur's organization, Demetrios. To find out who he is and what he's up to, to learn what we can of the structure of his operation; how he manages to be everywhere at once and to have cargo ships available to take away stolen booty."

"Yes, on that we agree."

"There's another reason, easily as important as the others."

"You believe our most pressing needs include finding out about the Minotaur's 'invincible ship,' " Demetrios said thoughtfully.

"Exactly. You've no idea how much fun it is to talk with someone who can keep up with my wild leaps into the dark."

"Oh, yes I have," Demetrios said. "Until your father came to Home it was a lonely place." He smiled. "As it's been during the time you were away."

"It's good to be here. I mean that."

"It's good to have you back. So why in the name of the gods do you want to leave us again, much less go into danger?"

"It's the only logical solution, Demetrios. Either you send me, or you send Crantor. And we don't know him well enough. I'd trust him to build a ship, or I wouldn't have brought him here, Child of the Lion or no. But whether I'd trust him to remain silent under torture if he were captured—"

"And you? How does anyone know how he will withstand torture?"

"I know myself and my weaknesses. I endure pain well. And I'm as hardheaded as my father."

"I can see that. You also have your mother's skills of persuasion."

"I hope so. We have to get a look at their new ship design. Anything that can overtake our galleys and bring them down like a cheetah chasing a gazelle—"

"I know. But—"

"Demetrios, your spy will have to be someone who knows shipbuilding. Who can draw plans from the model. And do it quickly." He pressed his palms together. "Anything I see, I can draw. I see details that the average man wouldn't notice. Most important, I'm not well known around the Great Sea and won't be recognized as one of your relatives."

Demetrios sighed and got to his feet. "I seldom won an argument with Seth, either."

"Then it's settled?"

"No. But I'll consider it."

Theon threw up his hands. "What am I going to do with you?" he asked in mock exasperation. He rose. "But you'll have to make up your mind soon, or you won't have any fleet left."

Demetrios watched him leave. It was indeed a delight to have Theon back. He had missed the young man's intellectual companionship.

How can I let him go? he thought. *This time, if he's gone too long, I may never see him again.*

Demetrios's mistress, Rhodope, came out on the terrace. "I could not help overhearing," she said. "So the young bird wants to fly. Are you going to let him?"

He looked at her, golden haired and blue eyed, still

young and fresh in her early forties. He had bought her in the Knossos slave markets two years before the destruction of the city, and she had been with him ever since. She had effortlessly worked her way into his heart with her beauty and intelligence and spirit. He could not stand to look away from her for even a moment, for fear she would disappear and he would never see her again.

"In my youth," he said, "I told myself not to get too attached to anyone or anything. I thought that if I never came to love a friend, a woman, a place, possessions, I would never be hurt by their loss."

"The vows we make in youth are not so easily kept when we grow older, are they?" she asked softly.

"No," he said. "Come to my side, please."

She joined him before the rail, and they looked out over the bay. His arms went around her, and her blond head nestled just inside his arm. She pressed her face to his chest and hugged him close. "I don't know about the boy," she said. "But I will not leave you while I live. You can count on having me here beside you, though the world itself may disappear."

"The world is safe," he replied. "It is I that will disappear. You have little time left with me, you know."

"Are the physicians so omniscient, then?"

"On the contrary. They are quick to reassure me. But it runs in my family for a man to know the number of his days. I am the son of Sinuhe, who was the son of Ketan. My grandfather and his twin sister had this gift. I seem to have inherited it. My heart is rotten, worn out. Feel its irregular beat through my skin. I'd give it a year at most before it fails me altogether."

"Then let us fill your last year with the best life has to offer. Love, friendship—"

"Ah, Rhodope. I have to let him go. He's right. As usual, the boy is right."

"Keep him with you a little longer."

"How can I? I have responsibilities. All the people of Home, all the people around the Great Sea depend on me."

"Always you think of others. Think of yourself this once. Please, Demetrios!"

He held her close. And when she put her face up for his kiss he could see her eyes were wet.

V

Theon called for Crantor a little before sunset. "Come," he said. "Demetrios thought you might enjoy some wine with us on the terrace before dinner. It appears we're going to have one of our more spectacular sunsets." He grinned. "I think he's just trying to show off his view."

Crantor stepped into his sandals and adjusted his chiton. "How did he take your idea of infiltrating the Minotaur's organization?"

"He huffed and puffed," Theon replied. "But he'll give in in the end. I know his ways. I know how to get around him."

"You mean he indulges you. After one brief meeting, there's one thing I am sure of: Your friend Demetrios can't be gotten around by anyone. He won't do anything he doesn't want to do and doesn't think is right."

"It doesn't matter," Theon said lightly as they walked around the front of the big house toward the terrace. "He'll realize it's a good idea. And he'll let me go because I'm the logical choice."

"He could send me. Nobody knows me."

"That isn't true. Memnon knows you. That is, if you're right about his being the pirates' shipwright."

"Your point's well-taken," Crantor said. "And there's no doubt in my mind that he is. When you've been raised by a single shipwright you can recognize his little touches everywhere. I inspected the one galley of the Minotaur's that was abandoned after an engagement with the Cretans. It caught fire, and the crew went overboard. The Cretans managed to board and put the fire out. I examined the trim. It was one of Memnon's, all right."

"But you say this was a normal galley."

"Right. It was old but splendidly built. Thirty oars. A modified *aphract* design, with no built-in bulwark to protect the rowers, but with a wall added."

"Thirty oars. Perhaps ten *epibatae* to do their fighting and looting for them. The same number of ordinary seamen. The *kybernates* to pilot the ship, and the *proireus* to enforce his orders. The *trieraules* with his flute to give the time to the rowers, and the *keleustes* and the oar master to keep them to the mark. What does that come to? Gods, that's fifty-five men. No wonder our round ships are no match for them," Theon said.

"It's worse," Crantor said. "On the Minotaur's boats the ordinary seamen are trained to fight, too." He stopped for a moment as they reached the terrace, dazzled by the colors spread out in the sky. "When you said you were going to have a sunset tonight, you really meant it, didn't you?"

"Ah, there you are," Demetrios said. "Greetings, Theon, Crantor. Boy, wine."

A boy brought cups and filled them with fine-tasting wine. "Demetrios," Crantor said, "I'm doubly honored. This is wine of Cos!"

"Your palate is to be commended. Drink hearty! Our friend the Minotaur interrupted our latest shipment, so we will soon be reduced to simple fare. But one must give thanks to the gods for what one has."

"We were talking," Theon said, "about the Minotaur and his shipwright. Crantor swears it has to be his old teacher, Memnon."

"Indeed?" Demetrios said. "But what of this new galley everyone's talking about but nobody's seen? What sort of innovation could produce that kind of speed?"

"If I knew, I would build you one like it," Crantor said. "Although Theon comes close to knowing everything I do by now. Give him six months here with me, and he'll have my brains picked clean, and then what use will I be to you?"

Demetrios chuckled. "Theon is his father's son: brilliant, but restless. Seth wasn't the kind to be tied down to a single trade, and Theon isn't, either. I think he brought you here to keep himself from having to take over as our official shipwright. We lost our top man a year ago."

"Who was it?"

"Nestor of Argos. Did you ever know him?"

"I knew of him. Memnon often mentioned him. He was thought long dead. You certainly keep a secret well."

"I hope we do." Demetrios looked him in the eyes. "Of course you understand that in our present situation this is all-important. We'll expect the utmost loyalty if you join us."

"Is there any doubt?" Crantor asked. "Let me set your mind to rest, sir. I'm your man."

Once again the young servant filled the guest's cup to the brim. Crantor looked down at it and shook his head. "I'd better take it easy. I could wind up addicted to this excellent wine. Your health, sir."

They all drank, then Theon said, "You were speculating about the 'invincible ship.' What do you suppose it is?"

"You know that a fifty-oar ship has already been tested at sea," Crantor said.

"Fifty?"

"But I suspect it will have a short life. It doesn't work well. And it's impossible for a galley to be any longer than a *penteconter*. A fifty-oar galley is the limit. Any longer, and it becomes unwieldy, too big to maneuver in your harbor. And you can't increase the length of the beam or you'll create a boat so heavy you couldn't row it at any decent speed. In my opinion, the *penteconter* is too long by half a dozen oars. There has to be a way to get more oars in the water without increasing her length."

"You make the problem sound insoluble."

"In theory it is," Crantor replied. "Yet the Minotaur has something that works, and not only your fleet but everyone else's is suffering."

"And we've got to do something about it—and soon—or I'm out of business," Demetrios said.

"I'm glad you brought that up," Theon said. "I was just going to say—"

"I know. Boys must have their adventures now and then," Demetrios said with a mischievous smile.

"I'm no boy, and—" Theon began; then he saw the twinkle in Demetrios's eyes. "All right, I know when I'm being had. But you have to admit—"

Demetrios laughed. "Come inside. We'll talk about it after we've eaten."

"Another moment, if you please," Crantor said. "The sun's about to plunge into the ocean. Do you have this kind of sunset often, sir?"

"Only when we have honored guests. Look, they're drawing the chain, just like the gates of a city."

"Chain?"

"Another of Seth's innovations. Men on the point are turning a capstan to pull a chain across the harbor mouth. Now we're safe for the night. Nobody can invade."

"But won't bronze—"

"It's iron, another of Seth's innovations. We cover it with many coats of paint to keep it from rusting. The best galley in the Minotaur's fleet would founder trying to run the harbor mouth. And while it was foundering, our men would be pelting it with burning arrows from the two harbor forts."

"I'm impressed. But can't you still be besieged?"

"To be sure. But we have set up a system of signal fires, which can be seen by our own vessels far out to sea. The moment anyone sees three plumes of smoke rising from each of the three high hills of the island, he's to send the alarm through all the ports of the region. Within days we can assemble a navy equal to any challenge."

"Then why do you remain vulnerable to the Minotaur?" Crantor asked as they entered the big dining hall. "If you can crush him just like that—"

"To crush him you must first find him," Demetrios answered. "Thus our friend Theon's little plan."

"Which you're going to take up, I assume?" Theon asked.

In the middle of the room Demetrios stopped. Rhodope stood facing them. "Gentlemen," he said, "this meal is a family affair. So we will break the formal rules about women not sitting with men at dinner. I have a special reason for asking Rhodope, the person dearest to my heart, to join us." He held out his hands to her, and she joined him, smiling. "Crantor, Theon—my wife, Rhodope."

Theon blinked. "W-wife?"

Demetrios put an arm around her, his smile as broad

as hers. "We took the vows this afternoon. They were long overdue, and I decided to formalize what had been in my heart for many years."

Theon beamed and came forward to embrace both of them. "What a wonderful surprise! You couldn't have told me anything more delightful. I've been looking forward to this day since I was a boy. Congratulations to both of you, and long life to your union!"

There was a sudden, poignant exchange of glances between the newlyweds, then Demetrios turned back to his guests. "Now," he said, "let us celebrate our marriage, Theon's return, and Crantor's joining our happy household with a modest feast. We have Copaic eels wrapped in beet leaves and roasted over the coals. We have roasted ox, and the finest fruits for dessert. And, oh yes, Crantor, it's pure coincidence, mind you—we had no idea you were coming— but our chief cook tells us we have a special appetizer. Fresh oysters, brought all the way from the docks of Massilia."

"I've died and gone to paradise," Crantor said. "I thought never to taste them again! Well met, Demetrios! Do we need a contract? Because I'll sign one right now if you want!"

The dinner was followed by easy and relaxed conversation—full of pleasant conceits and displays of wit. When at last Theon went to his room, he was feeling mellow from the watered but still potent wine he had drunk during what had to be one of the happiest evenings he had ever spent.

He lingered long awake on his pillow, thinking of the future. His heart beat fast with excitement. Demetrios had approved his plan. Within days he would be setting out on his great adventure.

Now, in the darkness, he thought of what his father had told him about his own excitement upon setting out for Babylon, where he had found his own fortune.

Theon sat up suddenly. Babylon had been no delightful adventure for his father, had it? To be sure it had started out beautifully. Seth had found a patron—the king—had fallen in love and married, and had undertaken the challenge of redesigning the ancient city.

But it had all ended in the most horrifying disaster, the city in flames, his father-in-law dead, his wife missing and presumed drowned, and Seth himself in ignominious retreat, doomed to a life of guilt and recriminations over his own failure to foresee trouble and prepare against it.

Would his own venture end the same way? Suddenly he worried that he might not be equal to this terrible task he has chosen.

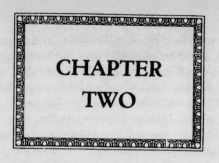

CHAPTER TWO

In the Negev

I

Joshua, son of Nun, commander of the army of Israel, stood atop the hill, shading his eyes, looking north across the Wilderness of Seir. Far across the empty land he could see a tiny speck. At this distance he could make out nothing but movement as the figure worked its way down the long broad valley.

"It's he," he said.

"How do you know?" his lieutenant asked. "I can barely see anything from here."

"I just know," Joshua said. "If it were an Amalekite or anybody from farther north, he wouldn't be coming down this far by himself. They know us better than that. A man of Rehoboth or Beersheba would be surrounded by a caravan or bodyguards."

"It could be a shepherd looking for lost sheep," Caleb argued. It was a game they had developed to test their logic.

32

"No, then he'd be on the heights. At this time of year any sheep would have worked over the bottomlands. Look at him. He's walking in the middle of the valley, as fearless as you please. He doesn't care whether we see him or not. No, that's Pepi, all right. I wonder what he has to tell us about our dear neighbors of the North."

"Nothing we can use, most likely," Caleb said with a grunt. "I sometimes wonder how you talked yourself into trusting a foreigner, an unbeliever, with such a delicate mission."

Joshua waved the objection away. "Stop thinking of Pepi as a stranger. He's spent two-thirds of his life amongst us, sharing our perils and our privations. Again and again he's proven as loyal as any man can be. And he's been a good friend to me."

Caleb snorted. It was no secret that Caleb resented Pepi's long friendship with his commander and lost no opportunity to undermine Joshua's confidence in the young armorer. "An Egyptian," he said contemptuously.

"Better an Egyptian who's a friend—loyal and brave— than a fellow Israelite who blows hot and cold. And don't pretend that we haven't plenty of those. Being a son of Jacob confers no particular virtue upon anyone, Caleb, as you've heard Moses say. All it confers on us is a duty to love God and praise Him. Any of us can fail in that duty, and the man who does is worse than a righteous unbeliever."

"Still, how can you trust Pepi with a delicate job like spying on the Amalekites?"

"I can't trust anyone else, Caleb. You don't seriously think that I could send you, do you? You'd betray us instantly."

Caleb stepped back, his eyes blazing. "Joshua! Surely you don't doubt *my* loyalty."

"Loyalty?" Joshua said. He turned to his second in

command and clapped him on the shoulder in a rough gesture of friendship. "No, no. It is your looks that would betray us, not your heart. You look like one of us. Pepi doesn't. He looks like the Egyptian he was born and bred, for all that his father came from some other part of the world. In everything but his height he takes after his mother."

"Well . . . I see your point. And yes, that's got to be him. It's too tall to be anyone else." He paused. "But how can you trust a son of Apedemek's? Apedemek was a traitor, a sorcerer, an evil man."

"Apedemek wasn't Pepi's only ancestor. Pepi's a Child of the Lion—and on both sides, which is rare even in that remarkable family. And he's a great-grandson of Ketan, and a great-great-grandson of Shobai, and—"

"Yes, yes, and a nephew of Demetrios the Magnificent. He can't stop mentioning that, can he?"

"Why should he deny it? It's something to be proud of. Demetrios is a great man—and he's been a good friend to us. We wouldn't have escaped the Egyptians if Seth and Demetrios hadn't helped us. Come on, Caleb, admit it. He's a good man. He'd be a good friend for you, too, if you'd let him."

Caleb swallowed his quick retort and kept his peace for the moment. "I wonder what he has to tell us."

"Here's what I expect from his report: The only thing that's kept the Amalekites from attacking us is their ongoing feud with the Kenites. Remember, three times they've planned to raid us, and three times the Kenites have saved our hides, however inadvertently, by attacking the Amalekites." He snorted. "When God decides to speak to Moses, He'll tell him not to try to infiltrate Canaan by attacking the Amalekites."

Caleb watched the figure coming closer. Pepi was

recognizable now, and he looked up, saw them, and waved. "How do you know what God will say to Moses?" Caleb asked.

Joshua shrugged. "Every command God has given us has been logical, and we always feel foolish afterward, for not having thought of it in the first place."

"All right," Caleb said peevishly. "Here comes Pepi."

They watched the tall man stride effortlessly up the slope. Despite his thinness, he gave the impression of great strength. "Greetings, Joshua, Caleb!"

Joshua embraced his old friend as Caleb stood by, frowning. "Pepi, welcome back. What have you to tell us? Are our enemies weak and defenseless? Can we march on Canaan at last?" The questions were asked in jest. None of the men had any illusions about the powerful and warlike Amalekites, their nearest northern neighbors.

Pepi accepted a skin of water from his old friend and drank deeply, then splashed some over his head. "Thanks," he said, handing the skin back and wiping his mouth. He left a streak of grime smeared across his chin. "I know what you've been telling Moses, and you're right: To attack would be suicidal."

"Where did you go?" Caleb asked.

"Far in," Pepi said. "I traveled as a tinker, doing odd jobs. I went all the way to Beersheba and beyond: Gerar, Hebron, Mamre, Jerusalem. I saw my mother and Baufra." He smiled. "You have fellow believers in Jerusalem. It's an interesting city."

"Tell me more about the Amalekites," Joshua said.

"Even if you got past them, you'd have trouble with the Amorites and Kenites. And the Hittites have begun to contest possession of the western bank of the Salt Sea with the Kenites."

"Iron-bearing Hittites?" Joshua asked grimly.

35

"I don't think so. If they had iron weapons, they'd have conquered the whole region by now, and they haven't. Farther up the interior there are the Jebusites and the Hivites."

"What of the coast?" Joshua pressed. "Is it all Canaanite? I heard new people were drifting in."

"The Sea Peoples are taking over the coast all the way up to and beyond Ashkelon. Then, farther east, other newcomers have moved inland: the Perizzites, the Hivites, and the Bashanites under King Og. You're going to have your hands full when you take *them* on. Every man is my height or taller. From the stories I heard, Og makes me look like a half-grown child."

Caleb snorted. "Sounds as though you're advising packing up and returning to Egypt."

Pepi laughed. "Not so, Caleb. I'm giving you the most accurate intelligence I could come by. When you resume the march, you'll have some idea about what you're up against."

"Pepi's right," Joshua agreed, ignoring the flash of rage in Caleb's eyes. "You can't go into a fight ill prepared—not when you're outnumbered two or three to one."

"The advantage will be more than that on this side of the Jordan," Pepi said. "By the time you get to where the Canaanites are—the 'Promised Land'—you'll be exhausted from fighting. Better figure out some other way to infiltrate and conquer." He clapped Joshua on the shoulder. "Come on, both of you. Let's get back to camp."

As they started down the path toward the Israelite encampment just outside the town of Kadesh, Joshua said, "Pepi, you're going to have to find a new source of copper before arming the new recruits."

Pepi stopped abruptly. "I thought you were in fine shape with your weaponry."

"We *were*. But while you were away, Moses designated a new unit to be armed and trained. Our young men are drilling without weapons in the hills."

The Egyptian frowned. "Copper's in short supply. Are you willing to march up the Arabah and challenge the Edomites, Midianites, and the Egyptians guarding the mines at Timna?"

Joshua thought for a moment. "Moses once told me that there were veins of copper in the hillsides above the River Jabbok, around Succoth."

"Succoth?" Caleb echoed. "That's in the middle of the area your friend here just finished telling us about, where everybody is as tall as a tree."

"Bashan. Well, that settles it," Pepi said. "All you boys have to do is conquer Bashan for me, and I'll have all the copper I need to make you some nice swords that you can conquer Bashan with."

Joshua gave him a playful shove. "You're no help at all. Do I smell the dinner fire? Come on, you two. I'm hungry."

II

By now Keturah knew the way from her tent to the well and could walk with perfect confidence, her jar balanced on one shoulder. But when she came within ten paces of the well, she slowed and held out her free hand; her sensitive fingers touched someone's back.

"Oh, pardon me," she said.

The woman turned and spoke. "You're Keturah, aren't you? The wife of Iri the armorer?"

"Yes," Keturah replied quietly. "I recognize your voice. You're Matred. I know your children. A boy and a girl."

"Yes, and I wanted to thank you for the doll you made my daughter. It was so lovely. One would hardly imagine that you were—" She stopped. "I mean . . ."

"Blind?" Keturah asked. "You haven't hurt my feelings. The truth shouldn't hurt anyone, should it?"

"Why, no, dear, it shouldn't. I understand congratulations are in order."

Keturah beamed. "Yes. Iri and I are expecting our first child. How proud it makes me!"

"Then you're looking forward to it?"

"What woman wouldn't? Blind women can have babies just like anyone else. It's only my eyes that don't work. The rest of me is in perfect condition. My hearing and my sense of smell are actually better now than when I could see."

"Is this *your* first? You didn't, I mean, back when you were with the Bedouin—"

"Oh, no. My father married me to a man three times my age, and he died almost as soon as the rites had been completed. I came to Iri never having known a man."

"You didn't inherit your first husband's property? What happened to your dower?"

"My brothers-by-marriage divided it among themselves and left me in the desert to die. Their traditions would seem cruel to upright, law-abiding people like you."

Matred snorted. "We have our own barbarians, as bad as any Bedouin. Pious hypocrites—"

"Your people have been very kind to me, taking me in. Without them I'd never have met Iri. There were those against taking in an unbeliever, but Moses spoke up in my behalf."

"Iri and Moses are old friends, aren't they?"

Keturah took the jar off her shoulder and put it on the ground next to her sandaled foot, holding it in place with one slim hand. "Yes. Iri says that his friendship with Moses has been one of the best things that ever happened to him. 'To have the loyalty of a good man,' he tells me, 'is a great blessing. But when the good man is powerful and a source of protection . . .' " She smiled. "Moses is a wonderful person. When Iri and I wanted to get married, Moses performed the ritual, following the customs of your people."

"And you're happy?" Matred asked.

"Oh, yes, we both are very happy. Iri was born with that red blotch on his face, and it's been a burden for him, isolating him. . . ."

"Yes, dear, I suppose that must be so. Poor man. No wonder he tends to be gruff."

"He is?" Keturah asked. "I can't imagine it. With me he's gentle and loving. Any woman would be happy to have a man who's so attentive, so affectionate."

"He *does* have a fine, strong body," Matred allowed.

"Nobody is as strong as a blacksmith. The arms that hold me may be as hard as oak, but the hands are as gentle as a child's."

"That's a happy woman talking." Matred patted Keturah's arm. "So you weren't born blind."

"I was normal until I was almost a woman. Then my vision began to fade. Nobody could do anything about it. The Bedouin thought it was a judgment of the gods. That's why my father sold me to an old man."

"Sold?"

"It's not unusual among Bedouins. And when the man died, his sons took everything he owned." She shrugged. "I should thank them, I suppose. They did me a great favor."

39

"I'm happy for you," Matred said, guiding the woman's steps forward with one hand as they moved toward the well. "Then you're not afraid to bear Iri's child? What if the blemish were to—"

"Why, it would make me very proud. I hope to give him a Son of the Lion. Iri says that having a birthmark on the face as well as the back has never happened before in the family. We'll take the chance."

"Bless your heart. You've got courage. Here, we're at the well. You go ahead of me, and let me help you with your jar."

The Israelite encampment, spread out in neat rows on the northern fringe of Kadesh, was an enormous tent city. The encampment had its own streets, marketplaces, and wells. One of the wells had miraculously gushed forth from the bare rocks when Aaron had struck them with his rod. The God of their fathers had been kind to them, even though He had not yet seen fit to allow them to enter the fabled Land of Promise to the north.

Between the tent city and the northern desert stood the military camp. Here the young men of the homeless nation were sent when they came of age, to drill with Joshua and his officers. Now, as the late afternoon came to an end, the drills ceased; the few, precious weapons were carefully stacked; and the soldiers were dismissed.

Once they had been a ragtag group of civilians; but in the years of wandering through the hostile Sinai wilderness, evading Egyptian patrols and Midianite raids, the Israelites had been beaten into a disciplined and cohesive army under the hand of Moses, who had been a general in the Egyptian army.

But in the last five years Moses and his army had

grown old. An intensive rebuilding of the Israelite military had begun under the guiding hand of Moses's protégé —and, some said, chosen successor—Joshua. Older warriors had been retired and returned to civilian life; new weapons had been forged by Iri and his nephew, Pepi; and the youth of the great encampment had been drilled tirelessly. Now the average age of the warriors of this deadly striking force was half what it had been a decade earlier.

As Iri strolled through the neat ranks of tents he was greeted with appreciation and respect; he grinned and waved back at everyone. That, he thought, was one thing he had always loved about living in garrison: No man cared what he looked like so long as the swords he made were strong and sharp and would hack through enemy necks.

He had been happy here, as happy as a man could be. After years of aching loneliness, he had found masculine companionship and a place in which he could feel at home. He sighed contentedly. There was, it seemed, more to life and to pleasure than he had ever allowed himself to believe.

Finding Keturah had been a miracle—there was no other word for it. And who had done it for him? Moses, his oldest friend in the world. Moses had prayed for him to Yahweh, the faceless, unknowable God of these Israelites, and Yahweh had taken pity on him, giving him someone to love—someone to whom his ugliness meant nothing.

He sighed again, this time unhappily. And how was he about to repay Moses? He was going to seek Moses out and ask Moses to let him and Keturah leave the Israelite camp forever.

Few but Moses would truly miss him. He had a few close friends and had won a place for himself, respected for his metalworker's talents and enormous physical strength. Even now, in his fifties, he was the match of any man in this army. But this was not where he belonged.

Now that he was to be a father, he wanted a secure place for Keturah—blessed, dear, gentle, and loving Keturah—and the child. A place to grow old in, happy and safe and free of the thousand cares of the homeless Israelites. He wanted to take Keturah to the seacoast, sail across the Great Sea, and bring her at last to the island paradise where his brother, Demetrios the Magnificent, ruled supreme.

For so many years he had gotten by on so little and had asked no more. Now Moses's God had given him something wonderful—something to lose—and he wanted only to protect it.

He had wanted nothing. Now he wanted everything.

III

As Iri moved from the military camp to the much larger encampment of the Habiru, he saw Joshua and Caleb coming toward him, with giant Pepi beside them. He hailed the three.

"Iri, wait!" Joshua called. "I want to talk to you. Pepi just returned from a scouting trip up north and has some things to tell us."

Iri stopped and looked up at his nephew. "I'm glad you're back, Pepi. I have something to tell you, too. You're getting a promotion: head armorer."

Pepi looked flabbergasted. "I don't understand."

"You're not thinking of retiring, Iri?" Caleb demanded. "We've got a major campaign ahead of us."

"You don't need me," Iri said. "It's time Pepi took over. He's in his thirties and long overdue for a promotion. In any other army he'd have been head armorer long ago."

"I don't understand, Uncle," Pepi repeated.

Iri smiled. "Keturah is pregnant."

"Keturah pregnant!" Pepi said, delightedly. "How wonderful! I wish I'd known before seeing my mother and Baufra; they'd be so pleased to know. When is the happy event?"

"Not for some months. She's just beginning to show," Iri said.

His nephew embraced him. "But why must you quit the army?"

Iri looked Pepi in the eyes. "I'm no longer needed here. You've been a master armsman for years. Quite frankly, I'm entering a new stage of my life, one in which the rigors of military life are—"

Joshua spoke for the first time. "Iri, you've been first Moses's right arm, then mine, since we came out of Egypt. How can we do without you?"

"You'll have no trouble. It only remains to tell Moses, seek his blessing, and then take my wife, and—"

Caleb broke in. "Moses isn't available. He's been up on the mountain for the last two days."

"Why?"

"Seeking divine guidance about the route we're to take into Canaan," Joshua explained. "I hope he comes down soon. He thinks he still can go without food, drink, and shelter as he did when he was a boy."

"*I'd* worry about him if I were you, Joshua," Iri said sympathetically. "He's begun losing weight, and he isn't the tireless youth anymore."

"All too true," Joshua agreed. "But the matter is in God's hands. He has taken care of Moses and the rest of us for a long time."

"I'd appreciate it if you'd send someone to tell me when he comes down," Iri said.

"Where are you going?" Pepi asked. "Surely not back to Egypt."

"No, no." Iri dismissed the thought with one powerful hand. "No, we're going to book passage with one of Demetrios's ships. I want my child to be born at Home among my kin. It's the safest place I can imagine."

"I understand," Joshua said. "We're in your debt. This was never your fight; it was ours. And to have a good friend like you at our side for over two decades . . ."

Iri, embarrassed, brushed away his praise. "I'm glad to have been of service. Now I'll probably return to making jewelry. Your people's escape from Egypt interrupted a hobby of mine that showed signs of becoming a career. I want to find out if I can be as successful at it as I was as an arms maker."

Joshua stood back, fists on hips, looking at him. Finally he sighed and shook his head in resignation. "If Moses will let you go, I will have to agree. But understand when I say that I hope he doesn't release you."

"He will," Iri said. "He'll give us his blessings." He turned to his nephew. "Pepi, as of now you're the official armorer of the Sons of Israel. And, as such, you're Joshua's . . . well, I suppose Caleb here is his *right* arm, so you'll be his left. Serve him well."

"I will," Pepi promised.

The vision of Yahweh had come and gone, and still the aura lingered. Moses sat on a rock and looked out over the broad land spread below him, thinking.

It was ordained. The Israelites would not enter Canaan from the south. In a way he was relieved. The fierce Amalekites would have killed too many of his people.

The will of Yahweh was clear: They were to avoid direct conflict with the fierce Amalekites and the Sea Peoples; instead they were to strike eastward through the desert, pass through the domains of the Edomites and the Moabites, push northward and strike heavily at Sihon, then at Bashan, land of the giants. A dangerous command. But if it were impossible, Yahweh would not have asked it of them.

Now, perversely, he found himself slipping back into an old habit, second-guessing the commands of Yahweh. His racing mind delved into alternatives. If he were to go back to the Israelite encampment and, ignoring God's commands, draw an occupation force of older men to hold the land the younger had taken . . .

But no. Not only was that denying the clear commands of God, but it was ignoring his own bad experience with the older troops. There was a good reason why God had commanded him to purge the army of the elder generation: The old officers and underofficers had fallen into insubordination and lax ways. They could not be trusted to follow orders or to rule justly the lands that the younger men had won.

And had not God told him that he, Moses, would never enter Canaan? Only the young would be allowed to enter the "land of milk and honey" and reoccupy the ancient lands given to them by God over a century before.

Resentful, he closed his eyes against the sight of the forbidden lands to the north and reminded himself for the thousandth time that if he had been barred by God from the Promised Land, it was his own fault. He and his brother, Aaron, and the older generation of Israel had sinned time and again and defied the will of God. It was these offenses that barred them from Canaan for life.

Moses had prayed for forgiveness, and the right to enter the land of his fathers. He had wept and begged Yahweh to relent, to give him the chance to redeem himself. But it had been futile. His deeds would follow him into the grave.

Sighing, he stood up. He must go down from the mountain and report to his people what Yahweh had told him: that they must now march on the fierce tribes of the east, press on all the way northward to Succoth and beyond, and take the lands of the giants, who held the east bank of the Jordan River all the way up to the Jarmuk and the shores of the Sea of Chinnereth.

Perhaps this was the great push they had been waiting for. Perhaps at last they would reenter Canaan, for the first time since Jacob had led their fathers southward through Sinai toward Goshen. If so, there would be happy feasting tonight to mark the good news.

But Moses would not join in their celebrating with an entirely unburdened heart. He felt bitter tears running down his face.

Forgive! he thought. *Father, forgive!*

IV

When Keturah entered her tent she felt something at once strange and familiar. "Iri? You're home, aren't you? Come now, you can't fool me."

Two powerful arms wrapped around her, lifting her

gently and spinning her around. She could sense his happiness.

"I can't, can I?" he teased. He put her down and kissed her. "Ah, Keturah! You make me feel like a boy again. No, that's not true. When I was a boy I never felt this way—not once—and that's because I never had anyone like you."

"Iri, don't hug me so hard. Remember the baby." But as she said it, she smiled. "Well, not too hard, anyway. If you were ever to stop hugging me altogether, I don't know what I would do. You have me as spoiled as any rich lady."

"Spoiled?" he asked. "Just you wait until we reach Home. You're going to *be* a rich lady."

"Oh, Iri, stop teasing me. Here, let me sit down; I'm a little tired. Come, sit by me." She sat and felt him beside her.

He took her hands. "You never believe me when I tell you I'm a very rich man, and the brother of the richest man in the world. Why, my share of the family enterprises must be . . . incalculable. You're going to have fine clothing, and jewelry I'll make for you myself, and—"

She laughed. "I have enough. A good man who loves me, a safe and comfortable life."

" 'Safe and comfortable.' I'm afraid the camp of the Israelites is not going to be safe anymore. And as for comfort, Moses made the announcement when he came down from the mountain. There's going to be rough travel and fighting ahead. That's why I finally asked him if we could leave."

"But, Iri, your brother's island is so far away. We'd have to leave our friends. It would mean leaving Moses."

Iri sighed. "But I have to think of the baby. Daughter or son, it's going to be born at Home, with experienced midwives in attendance and servants to fulfill your every need."

"Iri, I don't want servants!"

"Keturah, I've been living the life of a poor man for a long time. I'm beginning to grow old, and—"

"You're still as strong and vigorous as my bullock."

"But will that last forever? I've the right to want my child protected and my wife dressed in the finest and most expensive clothing and jewels."

"I don't need jewels and pretty clothes, and I don't particularly want them. All I need is what I have already."

Iri laughed and squeezed her hands joyfully. "That's what you think. Wait until you *feel* expensive clothing next to your skin. You'll never want to do without it again. I miss a bit of luxury myself, from time to time. I remember the food Mai used to prepare, and the feel of soft bedclothes."

"It all sounds very nice, but—"

"Keturah," he said, kissing her hand, "there's no use arguing. We're leaving. With any luck we ought to be on the road tomorrow."

"Tomorrow!"

"We have no choice. The Israelites are going to war immediately. They are marching around the Salt Sea and will come up through Moab. Do you want to make a rough trek like *that* with our baby coming?"

She shook her head.

"That settles it. Moses understands and gave us his blessings. 'Iri', he said, 'you've shared our trials long enough. We are in your debt more than we can ever repay you. If anyone deserves happiness you and Keturah do.'

"So let's begin getting ready. We won't need much clothing, since it won't be long before we're at Home. Then you're going to have anything your heart desires."

"Iri, all the things you promise me, they're wonderful. But if I had nothing but you, I'd already be the richest woman in the world."

He kissed her hand again, and this time she felt warm tears falling on her wrist.

Joshua emerged from Moses's tent to join Caleb before the campfire. "It's settled," he said. "The army leaves as soon as we can muster it." Caleb started to rise, but Joshua put a restraining hand on his shoulder. "I've already sent the message to the unit commanders."

Caleb made room on the ground for him. "Tell me, are we going up against the Amalekites, striking Canaan where it's strongest?"

"You know that the orders Moses gets from God are always sensible and prudent. We're marching up the eastern side of the Salt Sea, just as we suspected."

"Through Edom and Moab?"

"No, we're to skirt Edom. Moses sent a runner to Edom, asking permission to cross their land on the way to Moab. The answer was the loudest, most scornful no you ever heard."

"So instead of facing Edom, which would be bad enough, we'll have to go all the way down to Eilat and around, and then face the Midianites on the way north. They're worse than the Edomites."

"True," Joshua agreed grimly. "And the worst part is that we'll be facing Midian with an untried army."

Caleb nodded. "I would also feel a lot more confident if our soldiers could cut their teeth on a less dangerous enemy." In mock seriousness he raised his eyes heavenward. "God, send us somebody else to fight first!"

"Don't blaspheme," Joshua said, trying not to grin.

"Still, what wouldn't I give just now for a good, stiff fight tomorrow morning, against somebody weak enough for us to beat but strong enough to teach our innocents what a scrap is all about!"

"Amen," said Caleb. "But after Midian, what?"

"Moses says that we're to strike up the eastern bank of the Great Sea, along the Way of the Wilderness, again skirting Edom. But we're to attack Sihon, then Bashan with everything we've got."

"At last a *real* fight!"

"It will be that, all right. Pepi's reports about King Og and his men make them sound like they eat raw lions for breakfast."

"Then we've got to become the sort who devour lion-eaters for dinner the night before."

Hearing a disturbance behind them, Joshua jumped up and whirled around, his hand on his sword. "Who's there?" he demanded.

A subordinate appeared in the darkness, leading a man wearing dirty robes. Even from where he stood, Joshua could smell the perspiration of fear. "Sir," said his aide, "a runner from the forward pickets."

"Report," Joshua ordered.

The runner gasped. "Sir, the forward lines have been overrun by men of Arad! They've taken the forward pickets captive. They only let me loose to tell you!"

"They did, eh?" Joshua scowled. "You didn't just run away from your post and leave your friends to die?"

"Sir," the aide interrupted, "look at his back." The runner turned and raised his robes. He had been whipped until his body was raw and bleeding.

"It was intended as a warning, sir," the runner said. "I heard someone say that this was what we'd get if we came their way."

Joshua and Caleb exchanged angry glances. Joshua's smile was icy. "Well, Caleb, God's heard your wish. Turn out the whole garrison, but keep a token force here. It appears we, too, have a warning to send. And we're going to get our novices blooded."

V

Shortly after dawn, as the young and unexperienced army of Israel stood on the plain north of Kadesh and prepared for the march on Arad, Iri loaded the asses that were to carry him and Keturah in a different direction.

Moses had come out to bless the troops, and now, looking tired and depressed, he lingered with Iri.

"How does one say good-bye to a friend of such long-standing?" Iri asked, grasping Moses's arm. "I can't express my feelings as easily as others can."

"Is this true, Keturah?" Moses asked. "Is he so inarticulate when it comes to matters of the heart that he cannot embrace an old friend who will be devastated by his loss?"

"He hasn't any problem expressing his feelings with me, my lord."

"She's different," Iri said. "But when I try to—"

"Of course she's different," Moses said, giving the young woman a fatherly hug. "That's why we gave her to you. We have no riches to offer you for your years of selfless service, but giving you Keturah will perhaps make up for it."

"The gift is a kingly one," Iri said warmly. "Perhaps more than that. Did your God tell you to give her to me?"

"I do not remember hearing those words specifically," Moses admitted. "But as a matter of faith, whenever any thought occurs to me when I am alone, Yahweh's speaking. At those times I never do anything foolish. And I am a foolish man, I think, without His words to guide me."

"Foolish? Never. But I will always think of Keturah as a gift of the God of the Israelites. And I shall cherish her all the more." Iri pulled Moses to him in a rough masculine embrace. "Farewell, old friend. May Yahweh relent and let your feet cross over into Canaan before you die."

The old man's eyes were damp. "I fear He will not, but I thank you for your kind thoughts. May His hand lie lightly upon the two of you, and may He give you healthy children to gladden your hearts." He sighed. "Please give my best to Demetrios and Seth. But no, Seth, my friend and mentor for so many years, has passed on. Ah, Iri, so many of the people dear to me have died. I can't believe I'll never speak with them again."

"They live on in our hearts. As you will live in mine. Good-bye, Moses. Neither of us will ever forget you."

As Iri and Keturah rode slowly westward toward the sea, the drums of the army began to sound. Joshua had given the order to beat the drums to instill excitement in his young charges and improve their morale. They were predictably skittish and uneasy on the morning of their first battle.

As Joshua surveyed the assembled masses, Pepi joined him. "Joshua, are you sure you want me along? An armorer is more often underfoot than not on a short campaign."

"I want you with us for my own morale," Joshua said,

"and to report on the performance of the combatants afterward."

"I'd rather not."

"I need you. My men are untried. Please watch them and tell me how they do. If the fighting goes the way I expect, I'll be too busy to keep a close eye on individual soldiers."

Pepi frowned. "If you insist, but I'd rather be setting off, to check out sources of copper. Since you won't be coming up the Arabah when you march on Canaan, I thought I'd visit the Timna mines, to see how big a garrison the Egyptians have stationed there."

Joshua paused to consider Pepi's request. At last he said, "I do insist."

Caleb, coming up beside them, said, "I couldn't help overhearing. Joshua, if he can find out the strength of the Timna garrison—"

"No, we aren't to attack it. Not now. Remember Moses's command. We're not to go up the Arabah—"

"—and antagonize the Midianites," Caleb continued. "That was the specific command. Nothing was said about Timna, which is technically not in Midianite territory."

Joshua bit his lip. The argument was compelling, but—"I know what Moses would say: He'd say that the intent of the command would surely be evident."

Caleb's face fell. "Unfortunately, you're right. But, Joshua, there's nothing to prevent us from gathering intelligence on the Timna garrison. And Pepi, with his Egyptian parentage, is our only man for the job."

"Besides," Pepi said, mildly surprised to find Caleb in the role of his supporter, "I'd dearly love to see Timna. Moses has been telling me about its history. More important, I don't relish fighting. Making weapons is one thing, using them is another. The sight of blood makes me sick.

Remember the time the Bedouin ambushed us in the mountains?"

Joshua's color rose. "But vicious people must be dealt with by vicious means. They were trying to kill us—all of us, not just those who bore weapons. We had our women and children to protect."

"I understand. It's just that—"

Caleb snorted. "I seem to remember that you, Pepi, fought just as hard as anyone. You killed a man, didn't you? Gutted him the way you'd gut a fish."

"Yes," Pepi admitted. "I can protect myself. But that doesn't mean that I seek out the opportunity. Afterward I was as sick as a dog."

Joshua looked him hard in the eyes. Finally he put a hand on Pepi's shoulder. "It's your father, isn't it? You're afraid you might have inherited the evil that was in him. You don't want to let your anger and rage come out; they remind you too much of him."

Pepi tried to look away but found he could not. "That may be. Please, Joshua, I'd much rather go to Timna."

"I understand. This isn't your fight. We're lucky to have your services as it is. It's not the armorer's lot to fight."

"What a load of nonsense!" Caleb's eyes flashed in anger.

"Shut up, Caleb," Joshua ordered, ignoring his rage. "This is between Pepi and me." He turned his back to Caleb. "Moses explained that it is against tradition for a Child of the Lion to take sides. I'm grateful that Iri and you chose to leave Egypt with us. I know that we had you only on loan."

"I'm not going to leave," Pepi promised. "You'll have to drive me away."

"I know. You've been a loyal friend to my people and

to me." He sighed. "Go ahead to Timna. This Arad business won't occupy us long. We'll slip in at night, kill a few of the enemy, and rescue the captives. The rest of the army is merely for backup. Afterwards we'll head down the Gulf of Akaba. Why don't you meet us in Selah, in three weeks? At the new moon. Then we'll start subduing the west bank of the Jordan."

"Fair enough," agreed Pepi. Then he added, "Good hunting! And come back safely, all of you."

The two men embraced. Then Pepi turned sharply on one heel, like a military man, and walked away, his head high.

When Joshua turned to him, Caleb was glaring at him with ill-disguised resentment. "What's the matter with you?" Joshua asked.

"You insulted me. You humiliated me before the armorer. A civilian. I'd kill a lesser man for that!"

"Mind your tongue—unless you want to try to kill me." Joshua's hand rested on his sword.

Caleb drew a quick breath. "Joshua, I didn't mean—"

"You're jealous of Pepi and are trying to drive a wedge between us. Start acting like an adult now, or I'll find myself another second in command."

"But you let him get away with everything. He's a coward and a slacker, and he ducks out whenever it pleases him."

"It's not his job to fight. That's our job, and the soldiers' out in the field. There isn't a man here or in Egypt who's Pepi's master in strength."

"Joshua, I spoke out of turn."

"Remember, we can always replace a fighting man; but try replacing a Child of the Lion, particularly when you haven't any money. If he wants to go to Timna, let him. He'll provide us an accurate intelligence report. He may even tell us that they're undermanned and vulnerable. And, if he does, I'll talk Moses into letting us attack the Egyptians and relieve them of their copper mines."

"Pepi's mission is valuable to us," Caleb admitted.

"Now stay off my back about him," Joshua growled. "Alert the men. We move out in ten minutes."

Upon deciding to march against the Arad with the entire army, Joshua immediately realized that he would be sacrificing speed for power. Nevertheless, it was important to strike decisively, leaving the Canaanites—whom Israel would eventually have to fight—with an indelible impression of the strength, valor, and savagery of the invading Israelites.

As he rode at the head of the long column, he prayed. *Oh, Lord, deliver this people into our hands, and we will obliterate their city in Your name. We will take the gold and silver for the treasury of the Sanctuary, and we will destroy everything else, taking no booty for ourselves. We will strike in the name of the One. . . .*

Caleb's words interrupted him. "Joshua, I was talking to the scouts. If we reserved the Fourth Troop to hit from the left flank—"

Joshua opened his eyes, angry about the interruption.

"—we should do all right. Our troops are inexperienced but strong. If the officers set a good example, they'll do well enough."

"Well, then talk to the officers and tell them just what you told me."

* * *

The army made better time than Joshua had hoped. He had anticipated arriving at the Arad encampment shortly after dawn; instead, when the first hint of pink began to light the eastern sky, his scouts rode back to report that they would intercept the enemy positions in a matter of minutes.

Joshua thought for a moment, then told the scout, "Pass the order down to all units: Form battle lines. Have they spotted us yet?"

"No, sir. They're over that next ridge." The young man grinned. "Their pickets are asleep."

Joshua snorted. "Prepare for immediate attack."

"Sir?"

"You heard me. We're going in with a frontal attack."

But even as Joshua spoke, a picket for the Arad army awoke, looked around, and swallowed hard at the ominous sight of a large army moving into place before him. He shook his partner. "Quick! Wake up!"

The other man wiped his eyes and looked where his friend was pointing. And then he saw.

"Get the word back to camp. Those troops are ready for a full-scale assault!" His brow was wet with cold sweat. He could not take his eyes off the advancing Israelites.

"Ready down the line?" Joshua called. He pointed his gleaming sword heavenward.

"Ready down the line!" the answer came.

In the dawn's first light, Joshua's sword flashed downward. The battle had begun.

* * *

The attack should have caught the Canaanites by surprise, but the pickets had roused the forward positions, giving them enough time to send out two defensive units.

Two units should not have stopped that first advance; they should not even have slowed it. But the men of Arad had been fighting the Amalekites over border rights for two years, so the army was ready.

Thus, when the Israelites came over the hill, they found not a sleeping camp, but one half-roused. Surprise was now on the Arad side, and the effect on Joshua's green troops was devastating. The Israelite's attack was slowed, and the counterattack gained momentum.

Battle proved to be much different from sword drill. It was impossible to strike and then run away, and Joshua's young soldiers were forced to stand their ground against better fighters.

This was more than Joshua's inexperienced front line had bargained for, and after a brief, bloody engagement they turned and ran.

Joshua galloped up from the rear with a line of cavalry, outdistancing his own men in his zeal, and rode over the enemy infantry. His killing sword slashed. Attacked, he gripped his horse with his knees and fought with a sword in one hand and a battle-ax in the other. Caleb, riding up behind him, engaged the men on Joshua's left flank.

Joshua dispatched his two attackers and turned to bellow back at his rear-rank officers. "Stop the rout! Whip them back into the lines!"

As he watched, his second-line officers charged their own retreating men, beating them back into line with the flats of their swords. "Follow me!" Joshua bellowed to the cavalrymen. Spurring his horse forward, he charged straight through enemy lines toward the Arad tents.

He slashed through the guy ropes of the command tent with his sword and threw himself from his horse, hit the ground running, and dashed to the camp fire. Caleb came up behind him, and Joshua grabbed his shield and scooped up the still glowing coals. With all his strength he hurled them up atop a tent. The fire caught, and the tent went up in flames—as did the next. Then a breeze came up and spread the flames farther.

Joshua ran for his horse, mounted with one leap, and galloped back into battle, his sword swinging wildly. The enemy infantry, fearful of his sword, parted to let him through. He wheeled and headed back toward his own lines, pleased with the damage he had wrought. Behind him the fire was spreading through all the tents.

The young Israelites who had broken formation were back in their lines. "Go after them, men!" he shouted encouragingly.

But as he turned and scanned the enemy line an arrow whizzed past his head. To his left stood a detachment of Arad archers, their arrows raining down on his men.

Without pause he urged his horse to the left of his own lines and then over the top of the hill. Circling back, he sneaked up behind the detachment. He galloped toward them from the rear, whirling his sword overhead, screaming a battle cry for Yahweh. He watched the formation crumble. A few archers reached for their short swords, but most, panic-stricken, dove out of the madman's path as he hacked and stabbed his way through their line.

Driving the terrified archers before him, Joshua spotted Caleb and the other cavalrymen cutting a wide swath through the enemy's left flank as the rallying Israelite infantry advanced. The enemy line was buckling in the middle, saved from full retreat only by fresh units coming up from the rear.

Joshua heard a commotion behind him, but as he turned to investigate, a spear grazed his side. He saw a squad of pikemen advancing. Just then an enemy soldier lunged forward and stabbed Joshua's horse. The animal whinnied and reared, then fell heavily to the ground, its legs flailing. Instinctively Joshua leaped from its back and rolled to safety, sword in hand.

The pikemen swarmed forward. He turned the first pike aside with his sword and stabbed at the forearm of his attacker. The man's lance fell into the dust, and Joshua stabbed him in the throat. Then, sweeping the sword in a wide arc through the air, he caught the fallen man's comrade in the neck.

Suddenly, Joshua felt new strength flow into his arms, legs, and chest. His eyes glittering with sheer exhilaration, he loosed a great battle cry and plowed through the remaining pikemen, leaving nothing but dead and dying in his wake.

Joshua watched as Caleb, ahead, dismounted and dived fearlessly into the fray, swinging his great bronze battle-ax. But then the enemy surged forward, causing the Israelite right flank to waver and fall back before the Canaanite offensive. Joshua set off at a dead run behind the enemy's front line, dodging Canaanite arrows.

When he reached the Aradians' far flank he came at them, brandishing his deadly sword. He struck twice, and as two enemy fighters pitched forward into the dust he saw a magnificent towering figure standing before him. From the ornate helmet the man wore, Joshua knew he could be none other than the king of Arad.

Their eyes locked in instant recognition. The king

smiled knowingly and dangerously as Joshua roared out a savage battle yell and fought his way toward his foe, hacking through the enemy troops between them as if they were stubborn undergrowth.

The king swept his own soldiers aside and answered with a shrill cry of rage. Hearing it, the men surrounding them cleared a circle for the impending combat.

"Let no one disturb us as we fight!" the king warned contemptuously. "This is between the two of us."

Joshua, in no mood for speeches, lunged and knocked the sword from the big man's hand. He had time only to register the king's shocked expression as he hacked the royal head from its shoulders with a single well-placed blow.

Afterward the heart seemed to go out of the soldiers of Arad. But, to give them credit, there was no move to surrender. They fought until the last man was slaughtered.

To Joshua, the victory seemed to come too easily. The blood lust still boiled within him. And when Caleb came to him and asked in a voice hoarse from yelling, "Shall we go back now?" Joshua looked him in the eyes and shouted, "On to the city! Let us liberate our men!"

"Pardon, sir, but we already have. They were being held here in camp, and they're all right."

"Didn't you hear me?" Joshua demanded. His eyes were those of a predatory animal. "On to the city and burn it to the ground!"

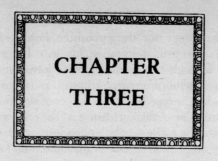

CHAPTER THREE

The Way to the Sea

I

After three hours' travel across the plain, Iri halted and helped Keturah down from the ass she was riding, placing the reins in her hands. "Hold these for a moment, my dear. He won't go anywhere if you've a firm grip. I want to get my weapons."

Keturah's smile was slightly strained. "What need will you have of weapons on a short ride to the sea?"

"It is a short ride, but over a land stained with much blood." He retrieved his sword belt from an onager's pack and buckled it on. Drawing the sword, he flourished it expertly before returning it to the scabbard. "Women never understand the necessity for war or violence, which is as it should be. If we all had to destroy part of our spirit by learning to fight and kill, we'd be animals within a generation."

He stopped, looked around, then tugged his bow from the pack and strung it over his back. The quiver of arrows he hung over the opposite shoulder. Finally, he took the reins from Keturah and helped her up onto the animal's back. As he walked beside her, her leg would brush against him from time to time, and he would reach out to caress her ankle.

"The Shepherd Kings had ruled Egypt with a heavy hand for a long time," Iri continued. "They had to be removed. Poor Kamose drove them out but lost his soul. Most of his men died in his twenty-year war, so he put out a call for mercenaries. He ended up with an army comprised of the dregs of the earth. His supply lines to Egypt had been cut, so Kamose was living off the land. He paid his mercenaries by giving them whatever they could carry away from battle, including women and children slaves. After you hunt down a lioness you have to find her cubs and destroy them, too. To save Egypt, Kamose had to watch the scum he led perpetrate all kinds of barbaric acts on the families of the enemy soldiers."

"How horrible! Now I understand why you speak with sympathy for Kamose."

"In the end, the ghosts of all the people his barbarian army had killed drove him mad."

"The Israelites have nothing good to say about him."

"No, but Kamose wasn't evil by choice; he was evil because of the madness that came upon him. What happened to him could happen to any army commander who is, after all, only a man, a mixture of good and evil, of strength and weakness. That's why Pepi is afraid for Joshua."

He shuddered; she could feel it through the gentle hand that touched her thigh. "Perhaps I could have helped Kamose," Iri continued, "but instead I was abusive and disrespectful. I abandoned him to Apedemek and Amasis, who hastened his demise. If there's a next world and a reckoning in it, I'll have that to answer for."

Keturah reached down and let a soft hand stroke his face. "My Iri, the gentlest man in the world, blaming himself for imaginary misdeeds."

Iri squeezed her brown foot. "I sometimes wonder," he said, "if there really is in me the quality you claim to find there."

"I see in you what a blind woman can see," Keturah declared in a voice full of love. "Let the sighted world see in you what it likes."

Iri felt like purring, but he could not give in to contentment. As they traveled, he scanned the broad plain that lay between them and the sea. They were passing to the north of Sharuhen, a ruined city inhabited by shepherds too lazy to move their stock into the high country where a good living was still to be had.

Soon the couple picked up the ancient highway called the Way of the Sea, which turned at Sharuhen and headed toward the shore. From here until they reached Ashkelon he would have to be extremely wary. There was a new element in the region, people who had settled the old coastal cities. Nobody seemed to know much of them except to say that they were troublemakers. Men called them the Sea Peoples, and they were a heterogeneous group. Some were tall, like the Bashanites who had pushed inland to occupy the lands beyond the Jordan. Some were blue-eyed and golden haired. Some were dark and hook nosed and wore beards of a strange cut.

Iri's curiosity about the new masters of Ashkelon was matched by his caution. He had known Ashkelon's old reputation as a rough seaport bristling with tough sailors. It was risky to expose Keturah to such danger, and it would test his ability to take care of her. But he was prepared for trouble.

Ashkelon, a seaport, would have a trade representative of his brother, Demetrios. And where Demetrios's name was known, there was safety—even if the refuge extended no farther than the four walls of his man's house. If he could get that far, he could shelter Keturah and book passage to Home aboard one of Demetrios's ships.

Home. The word had a secure ring to it. He had never really had a home. A home meant not just a house to call your own. It meant a woman, domesticity, children.

And he was going to have all that at last.

II

The hours on the road passed slowly. Then, just as Keturah was dozing off, she became aware that they had passed into a new world, one she remembered from her childhood. "Iri, I can smell the sea!"

Her remark broke into his reverie, and he patted her leg. "We've been riding within sight of the sea for quite some time. The wind must have changed now."

"I can hear the seabirds, too. Can't we stop and go down to the water's edge? I haven't been this close to the sea in many years."

"How I'd love to do that with you, Keturah, but it's too dangerous. We must be off the road at sundown and inside the walls of Ashkelon. I'm not taking any chances— not with you along."

"I appreciate your worrying, Iri. But the thought of wading in the seawater, smelling it, and feeling the wet sand under my feet . . ."

"As soon as we're safe I'll let you do just that. But

now we must get into town before dark. It's not far, if I've understood the directions correctly."

Iri saw the disappointment on her lovely face. He shook his head. Any other time but this he would do anything in the world to indulge her smallest wish. But the road was dangerous—more so than he had admitted to her—and he knew how perilous their situation could be if they were locked out of the city gates at sundown. For the first time in his life he had begun to feel fear, because now he had something to lose. His concern for her safety ate at his guts and had prompted his decision to move the two of them to Home, where Demetrios's fleet would stand between danger and his beloved Keturah.

He looked at the dear, delicate bare foot with its golden bangles and jeweled toe rings, and imagined the joy she would feel walking along the sand and feeling the waves splash her feet. He could almost hear her delighted, silvery laughter.

But there would be time for that later. Once, during the wanderings of the Israelites, he had made contact with one of Demetrios's trade representatives and had asked about the new Home. He had been told that there were white sand beaches on one side and black volcanic-rock beaches on the other. On Home Keturah could wade in safety. He would watch, make certain she did not wander out too deep, and keep her from all harm.

Two hours before sundown they came within sight of Ashkelon. The city wall perched above the water antedated the Hai conquest of the region. The tent city outside the wall was, Iri noted, everything he had expected, housing a rough group of evil-looking drovers and caravan workers, their faces scarred, their bodies warped and maimed from incessant labors and warfare. *Cutthroats!* he thought disapprovingly, and prodded his small packtrain forward, glaring at the men as they passed.

At the gate he unloaded the asses and sold them, bargaining in the broken Canaanite tongue he had picked up in the course of the wanderings of the Israelites. He came away feeling that he had been cheated, but he had enough money to hire men to carry their belongings to some hostelry inside the gate.

But when they entered the city they found that most of the inns had no vacancies. There was a large caravan in town, and an important slave auction was in progress.

After their third rejection, Iri stood looking up at the slowly sinking sun, wondering if they were going to find any lodging.

"I could find something for you, sir," said one of the bearers, resting beside his heavy burden. "What's it worth to you?"

Iri paused. "To the first man who provides me with a place we can stay, a bonus of twice what he's being paid already. Does that sound rich enough to you?"

"Yes, sir!" the fellow said. "But this is no place for you and the lady to wait. I'll take you to the central market, and you can wait there while I scout around. It won't be rich folks' accommodations, I'm afraid, but I think I can come up with a room in somebody's house."

"You find it, and the bonus is yours," Iri said.

The bearers shouldered their loads and set out once again with Iri and Keturah—her tiny brown hand clutching his in total trust—bringing up the rear. The sun was nearing the top of the city wall.

The central market was four times the size of anything Iri remembered from Egypt. Apparently there was only this one, whereas a comparable Egyptian city would have a market in each quarter, to accommodate each different social caste.

In one corner of the marketplace the slave auction was in progress. Iri sat Keturah down on a smooth stone slab and stood by her as the bearer disappeared down the street.

He had never seen a slave auction; in Egypt, quiet negotiations were discreetly held within the homes of the only caste that could afford to own slaves. As he watched, the auctioneer brought out a new lot of male and female slaves from a building behind the platform. Buyers crowded around, eager for the chance to bid, while the auctioneer and his brutal-looking, red-bearded assistant led the slaves up onto the platform.

The slaves were a mixed lot; Canaanites, Syrians, half-Hittites, Alashiyans, and hybrids stood miserably together.

Slavery, Iri had long ago decided, was a strange, uncivilized custom. Cheap labor was a boon for traders, contractors, and other businessmen requiring extensive labor. But the most successful arrangement, Iri believed, allowed the laborer to be paid on the basis of how hard he worked.

Now he watched, frowning, as two towering, blond-bearded men were auctioned off like oxen. The bidding was brisk: The Northerners were tall and well built, and would provide many hours of labor to an owner who fed them properly and did not abuse them.

"What's going on over there, Iri?" Keturah asked.

"Nothing," he lied. Keturah knew only the tongue of the Bedouin and the tongue of the Israelites and could not understand the bidding. He watched with anger and distaste as a family—husband, wife, and two children—were led onto the platform. For some perverse reason he could not take his eyes from them.

In response to a shouted demand from someone in the crowd, the red-bearded assistant stripped all four of them, and they stood before the crowd wearing only the chains on their ankles. Iri winced at their frightening vulnerability. The woman was ordinary looking, small in the bosom and short legged; no one would hire her for a dancer. Her husband was of average height and build, his face flushed with shame at the open display of his family's nakedness. Someone shouted an obscenity from the crowd, and the man whispered something to his family; they straightened their backs and tried to stand proudly, staring their viewers down.

The children, the poor children.

But it became worse. The auctioneer, having failed to get an offer for the family, was separating them. The husband and wife were going to be torn from one another and sold to different owners; the children were going to be ripped from the bosom of their parents.

The husband knew it, and a look of despair twisted his features. The woman glanced at her man, and as tears came to her eyes, she bit her quivering lip.

The children did not understand. They looked up at their mother, trusting her to save them.

Iri stifled the impulse to step forward and call a halt to this barbarism. But he had not the money to buy them—the first offer for the father was far more than Iri had in his purse. His guts churning, he watched the family divided forever and sold to four different men.

"What's happening, dear?" asked Keturah. "I hear a commotion."

"Nothing," Iri said. "It doesn't concern us."

His stomach was sour. He tried to swallow down the bitter taste in his mouth. But his heart told him: *It does matter! It does.*

III

"Look at the bastard, will you?" Metinti of Ashkelon said. "He is the ugliest son of a bitch I ever saw."

Silbel of Gaza sent his gaze in the direction his friend indicated. "I wouldn't say that too loudly if I were you. He looks tough."

"Nothing but muscles," Metinti argued. The two sat on the high step above the city well, looking not at the auction but at the red-faced man and the blind woman who sat at the bottom of the stairs amid their pile of baggage. "He looks like the sort of freak they exhibit in Damascus. He'd make a good one at that. He could double as a strong man, lifting a half-grown bullock in both hands."

"True," Silbel allowed, "but who's going to chain him and exhibit him?" He shrugged. "However, I see something that's more worthy of notice than the red-faced lout."

"What?"

"The blind woman with him."

Metinti nodded unenthusiastically.

"Well, yes, she's nice to look at."

"Look at her fingers and toes," Silbel continued. "Jewelry of gold, my friend."

"True. And unless those gemstones on her rings are fake . . ."

"And there's just the two of them."

"What about the bearers?"

"Hired help," Silbel said. "They're cowardly. You holler too loud, and they'll take off for the hills."

70

"What about the one who disappeared a few minutes ago?"

"A cheap hustler who hangs around the gate. One day he plays the cutpurse, the next day he begs. Throw a coin at him and he'd roll over for you like a trained dog."

Metinti frowned. "Let's think before we do something rash. Anything you have in mind will involve dealing with the red-faced lout, and he obviously dotes on her." He snorted. "Who but a blind girl would put up with a face like that!"

"That's a wicked-looking blade at his waist," Silbel pointed out, "and he gives the impression of knowing how to use it."

"Tell me what you've got on your mind."

"First we follow them to their lodgings."

"Here comes the bearer. He's probably found them a place to stay."

"Good. Follow me."

The bearers shouldered their burdens again and set out in the gathering darkness. Iri, still holding Keturah's hand, took half the first bearer's bundles under one powerful arm and kept pace with him. "Tell me," he said, "do you know a trader here named Balu of Tyre?"

"Balu?" the bearer asked. "Seems to me I remember the name from somewhere."

He was stalling, Iri knew. But that did not matter. If he had found them safe lodging for the night, that would be enough. He would leave Keturah in their room and go searching for Balu himself. It ought not to be difficult: A representative of Demetrios's would be well-known in a small seaport like Ashkelon.

The incident at the slave market continued to sicken

71

and depress him. He wanted to be far away from a place in which families could be cruelly separated and no one saw anything wrong with it. Iri shut his eyes for a moment, trying to banish the memory. But the moment his eyes closed he could see the scene more clearly. Would he forget the bravery of the wife, the humiliation of the husband as his family was destroyed, or the weeping of the children?

Why didn't I do something? he asked himself again. *I could have found the money somehow. I could have drawn on credit with Balu.*

But he had been paralyzed with fear that any move to help the family would have called attention to himself and, more importantly, to Keturah. How strange it was that he, who had always been so fearless, was now unmanned by the very thought that something might happen to his wife.

Ah, to be in Home already, where he would not have to face such terrible decisions. To be safe under the great sheltering wing of Demetrios's mighty empire.

"Here we are," the first bearer said. "It's this house on the right."

Soon they were settled in rooms above a livery stable. The house was patterned after the Egyptian fashion, with a flat roof. Access to the upstairs rooms was from the roof, which was reached by a steep, narrow flight of stairs. Inside, the rooms were pleasant and well kept, and the landlord, for an additional fee, promised to bring up lentil stew. Iri paid everybody but the first bearer. "How would you like to earn a little extra?"

"Doing what, sir?" the bearer asked. "If it's legal and won't get my head put on the block—"

"Never fear," Iri said, laughing. "I want to ask around for Balu of Tyre."

"I'm your man, sir," the bearer said. "If anyone can find him, I can."

"No, no," Iri said. "What I need is a reliable man to stay here and protect my wife until I return. Ashkelon has turned into a tough town in recent years."

"Oh, yes, sir, it is indeed. So much so that I hesitate letting you go out in the street by yourself."

Iri shook his head. "No, I'll be all right. The thief hasn't been born who can get the better of me in an alley fight. I made this thing"—he patted the sword at his side—"and I can use it. No, that's not the problem. But Keturah is the most important thing in the world to me. If anything were to happen to her . . ."

He paused, the horrid spectacle of the slavers breaking up the little family flashing in his mind in all its shocking brutality. He shuddered and his fists clenched involuntarily. "If you keep her safe there'll be a fat bonus for you. I have money on deposit with this man Balu. I just don't carry it around with me."

"I understand, sir, but I didn't bring any arms with me. Just my knife here"—he flashed a wicked-looking dirk, which looked equal to most tasks—"and nothing else. Now if I had something a bit more formidable at hand—"

"Can you use a bow?"

"Yes, sir—"

"One of the big longbows the Bedouin use out in the desert?"

"Yes, sir. I did military service up north in my youth."

"Then if you'll look in that big parcel in the corner you'll find such a bow and some arrows. There's also a club I carved from an acacia wood. If you'd prefer cracking heads, then that's the thing to use. I'm leaving you in charge." He turned. "Keturah!"

"Yes, dear?"

"My darling, I'm going to leave you here for a bit. It won't be more than an hour, most likely."

"No, couldn't you—"

"I have to find Balu as quickly as I can. In the marketplace someone mentioned that a boat named the *Corinth* is one of my brother's."

"Iri, can't I come with you?"

"Stay here and rest. I'll not be gone long. The innkeeper is going to bring up some stew. You'll have no other visitors. This gentleman who found us the room will see to that. I'm leaving him here with you while I—"

"Please, Iri. Besides, I had hoped to sponge off before dinner."

"I can wait outside on the roof, sir, so the lady can have some privacy," the bearer offered. "From there I can watch the door."

"Splendid," Iri said. "Then you'd better take the bow with you, after all. The more menacing any prospective intruder thinks you, the better. And guard her with your life."

"Yes, sir!" the bearer said. "Don't worry about a thing."

IV

Out in the darkness, next to the open window, Silbel whispered, "Did you hear that about his having money on deposit here? And about his brother owning the *Corinth*?"

"Get back from the window," Metinti ordered. "He'll see you. Come over here, behind this." They hid behind a woven reed mat that some housewife had hung out to dry.

"Metinti," Silbel said, clutching his companion's arm. "Did you hear? Do you know who owns the *Corinth*?"

"Yes, yes," Metinti said. "Everybody knows Demetrios the Magnificent owns the *Corinth*. This lout has to be joking. It's just idle bragging."

"But what if it isn't? What if he does find this Balu of Tyre and comes up with some money?"

"Well, what if it is true? What have you in mind?" But even as he said it, Metinti's face lifted into a smile clearly visible in the moonlight. "Are you thinking what I'm thinking?" His voice remained at a whisper, but it now had a trace of urgency in it.

Silbel nodded slowly, and his fingers tightened on the handle of his knife. "The girl. If he has the kind of money I think he has . . . Well, look how he dotes on her. She'd make for a fine ransom."

"Careful!" Metinti warned. "The guard's about to come out. You don't want him to see you." The two withdrew farther into the darkness and watched the bearer take up his station on the roof.

As Silbel turned to face Metinti, the moonlight caught his venal smile. "First we have to deal with that oaf he's leaving behind to guard her."

"And he doesn't look like much of a danger, does he?"

"No. The simplest thing in the world. But wait. How do we get in touch with the red-faced lout afterward, to present our demands?"

"*Hmmm.* Perhaps one of us could bring him a message?" Metinti suggested.

"And get beaten to a pulp? Look at his arms. Imagine those big hands on your neck."

"But if he knows in advance that if anything happens to the messenger, something will happen to the blind girl—"

"He'll have no choice but to go along," Silbel cut in.

"Let's do it," Metinti said. The words came out in an eager rush.

Halfway down the block, Iri felt a twinge of apprehension. He stumbled over his feet and had to put a hand on the wall of the building beside him to keep from falling.

For the merest beat of his heart, a picture of Keturah came into his mind, her dear, soft face contorted with fear. He imagined a harsh knocking on the door, and her timid answer, and then—

What if? . . . Had he closed the window? There was a bolt on the door, so no one could enter that way. But the door was a flimsy thing, not the usual thick, oaken barrier. And if the window had not been closed . . .

Iri cursed himself. *Nonsense. She'll be perfectly safe. That roughneck I left with her ought to be able to keep her from harm for the short time I'll be gone.*

He shook his head, clearing away the ghosts and fears, and once more began walking down the dark street. As he did, his right hand strayed to the sword belt at his side and loosened the sword in its sheath.

Keturah satisfied herself once more that the door was firmly bolted. Then she went to the sideboard for the basin of water the landlord had left and, tucking the washcloth under her arm, carried the basin to her chair. Her movements were more sure: She had almost memorized the little room by now.

She sat down and removed her sandals to wash her feet. Wanting to make herself fresh and beautiful for Iri, she carefully removed her jewelry. Since ornaments meant little to a blind woman, she would have worn none; but Iri liked them, so she wore the jewelry he had made for her out of love for him rather than personal vanity.

Now, as she removed the ring he had made for her left-hand thumb, it fell from her grasp. Where it landed, she could not say because at the moment it fell, there was a noise outside, and the sound of the ring hitting the floor was overpowered.

"Drat!" she said, then shrugged. Iri would find it for her later. She washed her hands and feet, then she put the rings and other jewelry back on.

She slipped her feet into her sandals and froze. What was that noise outside?

She turned her head, trying to pinpoint its location. It had sounded like something large and heavy falling onto the roof.

Suddenly she remembered the window she had left open a crack to get the cool evening breeze. She put out a hand to find the wall, then flattened herself against it. Quietly, she edged along the wall toward the window, one short step at a time, put out a hand, felt the open shutter, and pushed it. Something was in the way. She pushed harder.

"There, now, little one," a low voice said. "You don't want to do anything like that."

She backed against the wall, terrified. She could feel and hear the intruders as they came through the window. She thought there were two of them, but maybe more waited outside.

She wanted to scream; but she had hardly managed to take a deep breath before a rough hand clamped over her mouth and silenced her.

* * *

Iri was directed to a contact for Balu of Tyre in the second tavern he tried. The man had run errands for Balu several years before. Iri did not bother to ask why he no longer worked for the trader; in a rough location like this, virtually anybody he might talk to was suspect. "I'll make it worth your while," he said, "if you can take me to Balu."

"Now? At night?" the man asked, raising an eyebrow. "He'll set the dogs on you. No thanks, friend. Balu keeps mongrels that come up to your waist. I had one of them latch onto my wrist once. Look at the scar."

"He won't do that to me," Iri said confidently. "I'll protect you. I have to see him tonight, the sooner the better."

"You said something about making it worth my while."

"Name a price."

The man pondered. "The dogs make it dangerous. If I have to do something dangerous . . ."

Iri snorted, then pointed to a ring on his finger. "You can live six months on what you'll get for this from the pawnbrokers. Twice that if you sell it. I'll give it to you if you take me to Balu." He waited a beat. "If I have to waste time selling you on the idea, I'll find somebody else."

Iri knew his man. A hand clasped his arm. "Wait," he said. "I'll take you."

But as they moved toward the exit, the door opened and a boisterous group of men pushed and shoved their way into the tavern. Iri and his companion could make no headway against this tide of flesh.

"Damn!" Iri said. "These bastards smell like a pissing wall in a bad quarter of Thebes. Who are they?"

"Slave dealers," his companion replied. "Watch your step with them. They're a rough lot. It comes with the trade."

"Oh, they are, are they?" Iri growled, remembering the slave auction. "I'd been thinking of standing aside, but now they'll have to go through me."

He moved forward, shoving everyone out of his way with his elbows and shoulders. When men cursed him, he turned to show them his terrible face, a mad glare frozen on it. Most shrank back. Some resisted and he shoved one of them aside with such force that the fellow knocked over a chair and crashed to the floor. Another bulled up to Iri, chest to chest, and for his pains got a knee in the groin and another knee in the face. He fell to the floor, and Iri stepped over him. "Come on," he told his companion.

"You're crazy," the man said, and tried to pull away, but Iri's rock-hard hand closed around his neck and yanked him forward. "Hey! Stop that!" he protested.

Iri's answer was to shove the last obstruction aside and jerk his guide out the half-open door. But one of the slavers followed him out. "You! You with the face!"

Iri let a slow and malevolent smile pass over his ruddy visage. He turned slowly. "Face? Did you say something about my face?" He looked the man in the eyes. "Come out into the street, you slave-trading pig seducer!"

"Why, you ugly—"

Iri's hand reached out and clamped down hard on the slaver's nose. The man let out a howl of pain; Iri released his nose, only to plant a blow across it with his clenched fist. Blood gushed down his face. The trader staggered backward, his great hands covering his nose. Iri closed in and buried his other fist in the man's gut. The slaver lurched forward, and Iri grabbed him by the hair and ran him headfirst into a wall. With no protest he collapsed on his face and lay very still. Iri dusted off his hands.

"Come on," his companion urged in an awed but desperate voice. "That was the toughest man in the quarter you just took on. He has six brothers in that tavern. If they find out what you've done . . ."

V

After a block or so Iri's anger began to ebb, and he realized what he had done. *You fool! That slaver will be looking for you all over town. And you were going to keep quiet so none of these lowlifes would take any sudden interest in Keturah before you got out of here.*

He had been a coward that afternoon, preferring to see an innocent family sold into slavery, rather than draw attention to himself. And now he had raised a lot worse commotion and for infinitely worse reasons: because he could not control his pride and his terrible temper.

He pounded his fist into his palm, furious with himself. *You blundering fool! Aren't you ever going to learn to control yourself?*

"Now you've gone and done it," his guide was mumbling. "Now that they've seen me with you, I'll never be able to enter this quarter again!"

Iri snorted contemptuously. "Be quiet—unless you've got anything to say about where we're going."

"We're here," the man grunted. "This is it. Here on the right." No sooner had he said this than they could hear a deep, baleful baying of large dogs beyond the wall. "If he decides to let those monsters loose on us . . ."

"Oh, shut up. I'll cut one up and feed him to the others." Iri stepped up to the gate and knocked loudly with the butt of his sword. "Hail, the house! You there, Balu of Tyre, open up and let me in."

"Please," the guide begged as the dogs hurled themselves against the wall. "If they get out . . ."

"Just remember that if you run away you won't collect the ring I promised you." Iri pounded on the gate even harder. *"You there! Open up!"*

After a moment a door opened, and they could hear feet on the tiles, punctuated by the frenzied barking of the hounds. "Who's there?" a voice called. "Who's making all that racket?"

"I seek Balu of Tyre," Iri said in a strong voice full of confidence. "Tell him the brother of Demetrios the Magnificent is here."

"Brother?"

"Yes. Iri of Thebes!"

"Iri of Thebes! Well, why didn't you say so?" And Iri heard the harsh sound of the bolt being drawn on the other side.

After a few moments' terrified struggle, Keturah realized that fighting back was useless.

"Who are you? Where are you taking me?" she asked as they bound her hands.

"Gag her," one of the men ordered.

Keturah's mind raced. If she could not speak or cry out, what could she do? If she only could devise some way to leave a trail so that Iri could follow and rescue her. Then she remembered the lost ring, and it gave her an idea. She twisted her hands, trying to reach a ring on one hand with the other.

Rezon of Ashkelon picked up the little man and shook him. He was twice the size of the frightened little drunkard in his hands. "Damn your eyes!" he snarled. "You got a good look at the man who did this to my brother. Describe him!"

The little man looked from one to another of the fallen man's brothers towering over him. He did not want to get on their wrong side, but what would happen if the man with the red blotch on his face were to return and find out who had identified him? The red-faced man was as dangerous as any two of the brothers put together. "I—"

Rezon shook him until his teeth rattled. "Curse you! Out with it!"

"P-put me down and I'll tell you," he said.

The big man dropped him hard. "All right, tell me. And so help me, if your description doesn't match the one my brother gives when he wakes up . . ."

"No, no! I'll tell you." He omitted nothing: the horrible birthmark on Iri's face, his broad shoulders and bulging forearms, the mad light in his eyes as he spat out his challenge. "You couldn't miss him if you tried," he said, his voice trembling. "There can't be two people in the world who look like that."

"That's right," the big man agreed. "So when we find him, we'll know whether you're lying or not. And if you are . . ." His gesture was an eloquent one: wringing an imaginary neck like a chicken's.

"No! Please!"

"And we'll take you with us, looking for him. Just you point him out the moment you see him. We'll do the rest."

As Metinti clumsily carried her down the stairs, slung over his shoulder, Keturah managed to work one of her rings off and slide it down the last knuckle. Then, as he banged into the wall, she let the ornament fall. She immediately went to work trying to loosen another, but she held off dropping it until it became evident which way the men were going.

Silbel looked up and down the street. "This way. There's less activity down this alley."

"All right," Metinti agreed. "But maybe you can carry her for a bit. Who would imagine a little woman could be such a burden?"

Keturah had intentionally gone limp when he picked her up. He had barely been able to get her deadweight up to his shoulder, and now his knees buckled as he staggered down the street after Silbel.

She dropped the second ring, hoping it would land in a conspicuous place. Then as Metinti lumbered into the alley she managed to work one sandal off and drop it to the street, leaving a trail that Iri should have no trouble following, even by torchlight.

Balu, gray bearded and bent with age, waited patiently while Iri paid off his guide. "Stay out of that quarter," the armorer said. "Get out of town and find yourself another place to live. After six months they'll have forgotten your face."

He watched the frightened man scurry out the door, glancing uneasily at the huge dogs, which growled low in their throats as he passed. Then Iri turned to Balu. "What happened to this town?"

"The Sea Peoples," Balu answered. "What can one do? When the city was ruined by the wave, I was out to sea, thank the gods. Demetrios had given all of us enough warning. But the city was wrecked, and afterward the Sea

Peoples moved in. Now they outnumber us, and there isn't much a man of business can do here without dealing with them."

"I gather some of the old laws in the city are no longer enforced. There are slavers all over. That trade used to be very strictly regulated in the coast cities."

"That's true," Balu said sadly. "But now the city is full of slaves. In the next two days a thousand of them will be shipped out to destinations all around the Great Sea. It's a nasty custom, but the Sea Peoples don't seem to see much wrong with it."

Iri frowned. "I do. I'd forgotten how much I disliked it. All the more reason for us to leave. Do you mind if I bring my wife, Keturah, here until the ship docks tomorrow? I'd feel more secure if I knew she was safe."

"By all means," Balu agreed. "I'll send a couple of my men for her."

"No, I'll bring her myself. Maybe I'd better take one of your servants along. I tangled with a slaver on the way here, and someone said he had six brothers."

"I know who you mean. Rezon and his brothers are much feared around here. You'd better take two of my larger guards, who are trained to handle weapons."

"All right, but I'd better go now. I'm already later than I told Keturah I'd be. She'll be worrying."

"By all means. Just tell my men where you're going; they'll know the best route." He clapped his hands twice to summon the servants.

Rezon's little gang had become a mob. In the thieves' quarter it was well-known that ingratiating oneself with Rezon could help secure a much better position in life, and the best way to curry favor with bullies was to help them eliminate their enemies. Several of the thugs carried torches. They all rushed through the streets until they came to the central market.

"We'll split up here," Rezon said. "Ten each, right? One group to each quarter. Comb the town. Don't let the bastard get away."

"Wait!" cried the little man who was Rezon's only witness to the fight. "Look over there." He pointed to a man hurrying across the square. The light fell on his face clearly as he glanced their way. "That's the fellow who was with the man who beat your brother!"

"Get him!" Rezon shouted.

Iri's guide saw the large men coming toward him, and he took off, his heart pounding with fright. They caught him before he had gone a block.

VI

"Bring him here," Rezon ordered. "Let's see him."

They dragged the man to the middle of the square. "Look what he had in his hand," one of Rezon's brothers said. He tossed the jeweled ring to Rezon, who turned it over in his palm. "Where did a beggar like you get this?"

"Please," his captive begged. "It was a gift."

Rezon's big fist flashed in the torchlight and slammed the prisoner's head. "Don't give me that. You got this for helping the red-faced man. Helping him do what?" The other did not answer and got a vicious backhand cuff for his silence. "Answer me! Who is he?"

"H-he's the brother of Demetrios the Magnificent.

He's rich. It's true. He was just with Balu. If you let me go I'll show you how to find him."

"I'll teach you to lie to me, you sniveling bastard!" Rezon drew back his fist, ready to deliver a killing blow.

"No! I'm telling the truth. Where would I get such a ring if not from a rich man? A man who can in a moment lay his hands on more gold than any of us will see in a lifetime, just by asking Balu for it?"

Rezon stayed his hand. A thoughtful look played over his face in the torchlight. "You say he's left Balu's place now. Where is he heading?"

"H-his wife. She's blind. He left her with a servant to guard her. He mentioned where their lodgings are as we walked to Balu's house. Let me take you there."

Rezon looked around. "All right, boys, let's go." He reached out a huge hand and grabbed the informer by the neck. "But you—you'd better be telling the truth!"

"I am. Let's get this over with."

In the street Iri, trailing Balu's burly retainers and holding his torch high, saw something glittering against the cobbles. "Wait." He stopped, retrieved the object, and held it up to the light. He recognized it immediately: It was a toe ring he had made for Keturah, gold set with lapis lazuli inserts. "This is my wife's." He held the torch as high as he could and looked around. The area was not familiar. "Where are we?"

"It's the middle-class quarter," said the taller servant.

His face fell. "Come quickly! Something's happened to Keturah!"

He did not wait for an answer but set out double-time down the long street. "Wait, sir!" one of the servants

called after him. "That's the long way!" But Iri was not
listening.

In the alleyway behind them, a second clue lay unnoticed; a hand-tooled buffalo-leather sandal, the mate of the
one she had dropped back near their lodgings.

"Damn it!" Rezon snarled. "Nobody's here! You lying
little bastard!" He peered through the open door at the
empty rooms. "Wait! Look, boys. Would they just take off
without their baggage?"

"And look here!" one brother said, rushing into the
room. "A ring. Look at it under the light. Why, that's
worth six months' wages."

"There's something down here!" someone called up
from the stairs. "A ring. Rezon, look at this!"

Rezon scowled. "What's going on here? Blind or no,
the girl can't be stupid enough to abandon jewelry and
baggage."

A voice called out from the rooftop. "Hey! There's a
dead man out here. His brains are bashed out."

Dragging his prisoner along, Rezon went to investigate. "What's going on here?" he demanded.

The fellow gaped at the corpse. "I . . . I don't know."

Rezon swore. "Somebody got here before us," he
muttered. "But who?" He frowned. "This means the red-
faced man might not have gotten here from Balu's house
yet. Doesn't it?"

"It could. And somebody stole his wife," said one of
his brothers. "Why don't a few of us go looking for who-
ever snatched her, and the rest of us wait here?"

Rezon smiled. "Do that."

His brother hesitated. "What do we do if we find
her?"

Rezon shrugged. "Anything you please. My interest's in him. If there's any more jewelry like this on her, take it. Don't mess her up too bad, not if you have a mind to sell her tomorrow. There are traders in town looking for wenches." Rezon smiled again. "What are you waiting for? Go!"

Metinti and Silbel lumbered through the streets toward the docks, taking turns at carrying Keturah. Suddenly the door of a waterfront tavern opened and disgorged a group of Greek island slavers into the street. When they saw Metinti carrying a bound woman, they barred his way. "Just a minute!" said Hylax of Naxos, commander of the crew. "What have you here?"

Metinti stopped and stood wavering, exhausted. "Silbel! Do something!"

But Silbel had taken one look at Hylax's drunken, leering face and bolted—right into the arms of one of the Greek's confederates, who had emerged from a side door of the tavern.

"Come on, now," Hylax taunted. "Put her down and let's have a look at her. We've bought a dozen young bucks but no women in the sale today, and we've got to leave for the islands in the morning. We had a particular commission left unfilled for one of our best customers. Let's see what you've got."

Metinti lowered Keturah, half supporting her body against his. With trembling hands he pulled the cloth from her face. He sighed, surrounded, defeated, hoping to make them pay a bit for what they were going to take anyhow. "She's blind."

Hylax chuckled low. "The commission is for a bedmate, not a girl-of-all-work. What need would she have for eyes?

If she's pretty enough and can find her way from one end of the couch to another, who's to care? Remove the gag."

Metinti's hands shook as he withdrew the gag. Keturah tried to speak but could only cough. "Not bad at all," Hylax said. "She might just do. Our patron likes them dark complected. Tell you what, small-timer. I'll be generous and give you a gold coin for her."

"Please," Keturah managed to get out. "My husband will pay more than—"

But Metinti immediately plugged her mouth with a gag. She struggled and almost fell. "One gold coin!" he protested. "Why, the jewelry on her wrists and ankles, fingers and toes alone is worth that."

"I don't see any jewelry on her fingers and toes," Hylax said. "Although I agree that her bracelets and—"

In sudden panic Metinti looked her up and down. "The little bitch! I bet she's left a trail. Look, you'd better let us go. Her husband is a tough bastard, and—"

"So what?" Hylax said. "We were just about to go out to the ship, pull anchor, and row her outside the breakwater so we can sail early in the morning." His eyes narrowed. "Well, small-fry? What'll it be? Our price—or no price?"

"Your price is too low," Metinti said as he saw his whole night's work amounting to nothing. "If you could see your way clear—"

"Take her from him, boys," Hylax, tired of delays, said.

"No!" Metinti begged. "Please!"

But as two of the slavers pulled Keturah out of his hands, a third crept behind him and snagged a garrote around his neck and pulled it tight. He fell to his knees, clutching his throat, trying in vain to loosen the cord. With fading vision he saw one of Hylax's bullies throw the blind girl over his shoulder and move easily down the plank road toward the ship docked at the end of the wharf.

Iri pounded up the stairs, two at a time, his sword at the ready. "Keturah! Keturah!"

But the door was wide open. He looked around. The moon shone down on the inert body of the man he had left to guard her. *"No!"* he moaned, panicked and desperate. "Keturah! Answer me!" Even as he spoke, he knew it was hopeless. He turned round and round, staring into the darkness. "Keturah!"

Balu's two servants ran up behind him, but shadowy figures lunged from the darkness to batter them back down the narrow staircase. Iri watched as one turned heels over head and landed hard on the lowest step, his neck breaking with a loud crack.

Sword in hand, Iri lunged at the darkness, but a powerful blow to his temple drove him to one side. He turned to see the second blow coming, but too late. It caught him on the skull and knocked him cold.

Iri awoke with the sun shining in his eyes. Every bone and muscle ached, and there was a sharp stabbing sensation in his ankle. He tried to sit up, but the pain in his head made him cry out. He blinked, wiping his eyes.

Above him someone stood in his light. He could make out nothing but alternating blocks of darkness and blinding glare. He blinked rapidly, trying to focus. Suddenly the obstruction vanished, and he could see where he was.

He looked down and could also see he was naked, covered with bruises, scabs, and bloodstains.

90

He sat unsteadily atop a hardwood bench, its surface smoothed by the bare behinds of the gods alone knew how many of his predecessors.

His swollen ankle was enclosed in a small iron ring, attached to a chain that passed through the fetters on bare legs as far as he could see down the long row of benches. A large wooden oar lay within easy reach.

As he struggled to understand what had happened to him, a voice from above bellowed out in a harsh tone: "All right, you river rats! Hands on those oars! Line 'em up! And make it snappy if you don't want your worthless heads broken."

He was on a galley headed far away from his wife, the world he had known, everything he loved and cared for!

"Keturah!" he cried in anguish.

And then the whip fell on him for the first time.

CHAPTER FOUR

Paphos

I

On the great island that the Greeks called Cyprus but Israelites and Canaanites called Alashiya, Theon docked his cargo vessel, the *Issus*, at the port of Paphos. With his mate Sosilas he went ashore, leaving the rest of the crew aboard until customs could be dealt with.

The two strolled along the Ropewalk, the only straight street in town, and noted the indicators of hard times. Boats that should have been out on the water, bringing home precious cargoes or fish catches, sat moored in the harbor. Shops that should have been open and thriving were closed. Even the taverns were half-empty, their proprietors standing by the doors, hoping in vain to entice passersby inside.

"What a charnel house!" Sosilas exclaimed. "I've seen dead towns, but this is one of the worst. Everyone might as well be mummified. I'm almost afraid to check out the sluts. They'll probably all be a hundred and twenty years old and have beards a Thracian horse tamer would be proud of."

"I will take your low opinion of the local entertainment under advisement," Theon said with a wry smile. "As a matter of fact, I've been looking for someone to stay aboard the ship while the rest have leave. Now that I have a good candidate like you, I need look no farther."

Sosilas spluttered in indignation. "Wait a minute!"

"Only joking," Theon said. "Actually, I do have an errand for you. I want you to check into port for me. You know the ropes better than I do."

"Theon, listless as the town appears, I was looking forward to finding a whore and—"

"I'll buy our dinner and the first six drinks."

"How can you do this to me?"

"I could always order you."

"Theon, you never have had much interest in whores. While I . . . Damn it, we've been at sea for a week now."

"That's not long for an old salt like you. You're always bragging about the privation you seasoned sailors can endure."

"I must have been drunk when I said that. How long are you going to burden me with—"

"As long as it takes to get you to deal with the port officials. I want to find someone in the taverns. Frankly, it's a sticky business, and you're too well-known. If people see me with you, they'll stay away."

Sosilas made a wry face. "I see. My wretched reputation precedes me." He gave an exaggerated sigh. "I'll be paying for the rest of my life for half a dozen indiscretions committed in my wicked youth."

"Oh, it's not from your youth," Theon said sarcastically. "Nobody on Cyprus was alive then; it was too long ago. Let's see, how old are you now? Ninety-five? Ninety-six?"

Sosilas shot a disgusted glance at him. "Dinner plus the first six drinks, you said?"

"Make it seven. That's a luckier number. I'll have you carried back aboard afterward, since you can't hold your drinks."

"Look who's talking. All right, I'll do your cursed documentation for you, but one of these days you'll have to learn to clear a port by yourself. I can't hold your hand forever."

"And a good thing, too. People will start to talk." He grinned wickedly. "Meanwhile, go do the work for me, will you?"

When Sosilas had gone, Theon climbed a hill and from the top of a little rise looked down at the harbor. Despite the poverty of the town, there was no lack of ships. It was just that they had not been to sea in some time. No trade came in, no trade went out.

The goods he had on the *Issus* would sell for a tidy bundle, and that would stimulate the local economy. Not that it would affect it in the long term.

He studied the tall masts; they bore the ensigns of half the lands around the Great Sea. Surely he ought to be able to find what he was looking for: a man who could help him make contact with the Minotaur. He smiled. Or, for that matter, a man who would view his little boat as the sitting duck it was and would lead the Minotaur to him. He did not care whether he found the pirate chieftain or the pirate chieftain, smelling booty, found him. The main thing was to make contact.

He looked down at the little port and shrugged. *It's about time to go see what I can learn*. He had deliberately delayed the men's shore leave and tied up Sosilas with the clerical work required by customs. He wanted free time—alone—in port, to make himself vulnerable to any man who chose to strike up conversation.

Slowly he walked down the hill toward the sailor's quarter and the long line of semideserted inns and taverns.

At the tavern called the Sign of the Two Gulls, business had never been worse. The proprietor had sent everyone home but the cook and two bored-looking dancers who haunted the inn more like the whores they were than the entertainers they pretended to be. But even in this capacity there was no call for their services.

Now, as the afternoon wore on, a single man came in. He stood in the doorway for a moment, adjusting to the gloom. Finally he managed to identify two figures. "Manto! Labda!" he said, addressing the girls with mock courtesy. "Fancy meeting you here!"

The thin one called Labda turned to her voluptuous companion. "May the gods spare us, Manto," she said in a bored voice. "Nobody in port with two copper coins to jingle in his purse, and nobody to talk to except our friend All Mouth and No Money."

"Is that the way to greet an old friend?" the young man asked. Behind him the innkeeper lit the lamps one by one; the newcomer's curly hair and round, grinning face became evident. "Besides, how do you know I'm broke? For all you know I might have won a purse gaming."

"Please, Pandion, stop the dreaming," Labda said.

"Why are you here?" Manto asked, yawning. "Your credit's no good anymore. And if you're thinking you're going to sweet-talk either one of us into a free tickle, you might as well forget it. You're the sort of no-good that girls charge double anyhow and give half the time." She snorted. "And that's probably more time than you need."

Pandion pouted. "You wrong me. I'll have you know that the women of Poros spoke of me as 'Lord Half-the-Night' for my amorous feats."

"Labda," Manto said, "haven't you found that the bigger a man's mouth, the smaller his yardarm?"

"Yes," Labda agreed, "and they also say that the longer he talks, the shorter he takes."

Pandion of Poros grinned and sat down beside Manto. "Music to my ears," he said. "Forget the randy acts. I came to bask in the sound of your sweet voices and the lilting and lyrical poetry you speak. Ah, what paeans of praise! What—"

"See my boss glaring at you?" Manto said, crossing her plump arms over her substantial bosom. "If you're going to sit down, you'd better have some coin."

"I know," Pandion said with a grin. "But he'll soften when I tell him my news: There are three ships inside the breakwater heading for dock right now, and another—a little trader named the *Issus*—already docked, with a dozen thirsty men aboard."

The innkeeper looked skeptical. Then he went outside to see for himself and returned shaking his head. "I'll be damned. The harbinger of doom brings good news for a change. Girls, pour the freeloader a drink on the house."

"That's more like it," Pandion said. "And while Labda's going after the wine, Manto, you can come over here and give me a cuddle. How about it, my little dove?"

"Take a cold bath," Manto said.

II

Theon, too, had noted the new sails in the harbor. All three appeared to be cargo ships; but two rode low in the water, groaning with goods, while the other rode high. What was a cargo ship doing, coming into Paphos with no cargo to exchange? He intended to find out.

Indulging his curiosity, he headed toward the wharf. As he watched, he noticed another curious thing: The empty ship was dropping anchor out in the harbor. If she were to take on cargo, she would have to either lift anchor and be towed in or be loaded from a lighter.

Theon walked out onto the docks and tried to make out the name painted on the distant vessel's bow. After some squinting and guesswork he decided her name was the *Melos*.

To the right and left of him the other two ships were sailing in: the *Thasus* and the *Phoria*. The former came in to dock in the hands of a master pilot, at just the right speed; her deckhands jumped off and tied her up with masterly efficiency. The latter ship, filthy and poorly maintained, plowed into the dock. Feeling the planks vibrate under his feet, Theon shook his head in disbelief. The deckhands were blundering through their duties, like a bunch of half-drunken idiots who had never set foot on a ship before.

He studied the trade goods piled on the deck of the *Thasus*, however, and thought: *I've got a rival*. The *Thasus* seemed a worse sitting duck than his own *Issus* was. If the two were to set out to sea, the Minotaur would have a difficult choice.

The two whores had drifted away, and the innkeeper was wiping the tables on the other side of the dark room. Miraculously Pandion had come up with a coin or two, which he had spent on three more bowls of wine. Defying custom, he had not cut the wine with water, and his mind had worked its way from the jaunty mood in which he had entered the tavern to a dark unhappiness.

He toyed with his half-empty bowl, glowering into its depths. *Well, my friend, your quest has come to very little. You're no closer to your goal than you were six months ago. What are you going to do now?*

He cursed under his breath. What a damn-fool thing he had done, shooting his mouth off to all his relatives about how he would avenge his father's death. Everyone had told him that he was a callow, wet-behind-the-ears stripling! And had he anything to show for all that boasting? Nothing but empty gestures. Empty promises.

To be sure, he had made great progress at first. He had wormed his way into the organization with surprising ease and had almost been admitted to the very presence of his enemy. If that had worked, he would have had a chance to stick a knife into his father's killer. Even though that would have meant his own death, the eventuality had not frightened him.

Oh, yes, he had been brave enough. If only fate had not worked against him!

Across the room the innkeeper knocked something to the floor, and it fell with a loud crash. Pandion cursed at him under his breath. "Son of a bitch! Can't watch what he's doing. . . ."

You're getting drunk, he thought. *That's no good. You got drunk yesterday, and the day before that. Your money's running out. If you're going to win some money from those louts on the boats in the harbor, you'd better have your wits about you.*

He looked down at the bowl and considered draining it. But if he were going to get anything done tonight—he could not drink any more. He stood blinking, trying to organize his thoughts.

Fresh air, he thought. *That's the thing. Walk down by the water. Take a look at the boats that came in. See if any of the sailors look naïve but with newly earned coin in their purse, ready to lose it all in a friendly game of chance.*

He lurched out the door into the late afternoon.

The two whores spotted Theon immediately. "Look at him!" Manto breathed. "Am I dreaming, Labda? Is he as handsome as I think he is?"

"He's beautiful, built like a god," Labda verified. "And I smell money all over him. He must be in from one of the ships."

Manto nodded. "If I can't haul him into bed within an hour, I'll give up the trade and marry a drunken fisherman with bad breath. Every once in a while the gods steer something special into your hands. I'm going to enjoy going after this one."

"You're not thinking of giving him anything for free, are you?"

Manto looked at her, incredulous. "No! I'll just have the time of my life with this one—and *then* I'll drug him and lift his purse."

"You reassure me. You were beginning to talk like a schoolgirl. But what about me? Tell you what, let's take him on together. I haven't had a three-way romp in a long while. Come on. We'll split the take."

Manto shot a hard glance at her.

"All right, sixty-forty," Labda conceded. "You did see him first. We can use my extrasize bed. I've still got it, although the temptation to pawn it has been strong from time to time, with business as bad as it's been."

"Pawn your bed? Idiot! Where would you do it then?

Standing up somewhere, for a copper coin? Child, you're too innocent to be allowed out in the street by yourself. Come on, the two of us ought to be too tempting for him to refuse."

Arm in arm, they sauntered across Theon's path, their hips rolling seductively under the thin, clinging cloth of their long chitons. They walked past him, three steps ahead of him for half a block, letting him take in the sight of Labda's slim legs and Manto's ripe buttocks. Then Manto stopped and bent over, giving him an even better view. "Oh, dear! Labda, darling, I've a stone in my sandal."

Theon, close behind, could not stop in time and ran into Labda. "Pardon me. I'm sorry. Did I hurt you?"

Manto hiked her chiton halfway up her thigh to shake an invisible pebble from her sandal, showing off a dainty, slender foot with delicately rouged nails. "Ah!" she said, dragging her action out as long as possible before covering her leg again. As she rose, facing Theon, she let him have a generous glimpse of pink bosom, bare all the way down to the dark nipple.

"Are you all right?" Theon asked.

"Me?" Manto said, batting her long, dark eyelashes. "Why, thank you for asking, sir. *My* apologies. I have almost caused *you* to take a spill. Can you forgive me?"

"Forgive you? I'm the one to offer apologies. I must make amends. May I walk you ladies to your destination?"

Manto flashed her most dazzling smile. "How charming! But really, we were only headed for the nearest tavern. It's a warm day, and my friend and I were going to have a glass of wine on the upstairs terrace at the Sign of the Ram."

"Please," Labda said with studied impulsiveness, "won't you join us, sir? There's a nice grape arbor on the roof, and it's pleasantly cool—a delightful place to sit and watch the world go by on a warm afternoon. Perhaps you'll be our guest?"

"Oh, no," Theon said, playing the game with practiced ease. "By all means let me treat *you*. But first, let me introduce myself. Theon of Salamis, master of the good ship *Issus*." "Salamis" had been an improvisation; he had never been in the town in his life and hoped neither of the women hailed from there.

"A ship's captain!" Manto squealed. "A man of substance!"

Theon smiled. "A drink on the terrace would be a splendid idea. How thoughtful of you."

He offered an arm to each, and they strolled up the street toward the Sign of the Ram, looking not at all like the old friends that decorum required them to impersonate in the street in broad daylight.

Pandion, looking up by chance, saw them—the two whores and the tall, young sea captain—sitting together on the terrace of the Ram. He caught Labda's eye and offered an elaborate bow of congratulations. Labda turned up her nose at him.

He snickered. The girls were working fast today, that was obvious. The ships hadn't been in town an hour before— He looked out at the bay and saw new sails coming in. Six ships so far. No, seven. What a bonanza! And from everywhere—Crete, Sardo, Sicilia.

He would eat well tonight. With this many ships in port, if he could not find a good night's meal and the money to pay the back rent, he was a sluggard not worth worrying about.

What game would he play? The pigeon drop? The Iberian prisoner? Or perhaps no more than the game of peas and shells? A good operator, quick and alert, could take a man for six months' pay in a matter of minutes with the shells and the vanishing pea.

Whatever it was, he would make it quick. He flexed his hands, cracked his knuckles, and prepared for the night's work.

III

"Look, Manto," Labda said. "There goes Pandion. And he looks like he's had a bit more to drink than when we saw him last. I wonder where he got the money from?"

Manto made a shushing motion behind Theon's back and glared furiously at Labda. It was too late. Theon, sitting between them on the terrace, leaned forward and peered down at the street. "Is he a friend of yours?"

Again Manto tried to signal, but Labda paid no attention. "Not exactly a friend," she explained. "He's a ne'er-do-well that hangs around in the taverns looking for unwary sailors to swindle out of their sea pay and keeping an ear open for anything that might earn him a few coins. He'll never amount to anything."

"Look over there," Manto said. "Another ship's coming in. And here comes a sailor up the hill. He seems prosperous enough. I wonder where he hails from?"

"He is prosperous," Theon said with a laugh. "He's my first mate, Sosilas. He'll probably make more from this voyage than I will. I'll bet he's looking for me." He rose and waved his hand. "Sosilas! Up here!"

The mate looked up, waved, and entered the inn.

Moments later he joined them on the rooftop. "Well, you've made friends quickly. Good afternoon, ladies." He injected a touch of irony when he said the word *ladies*, but not enough to offer offense. "Theon, while you were up here diverting yourself with these little buttercups, I was earning us some money. I ran into a merchant from the *Phoria* at the customs office, and he wants to have a look at our cargo."

"Good. But why didn't you make the deal for the cargo then and have done with it?"

Sosilas sat with his back to the panoramic view. "That's what he says now, ladies. But if I'd sold so much as a pomegranate without consulting him, I'd have been skinned alive before dawn tomorrow. Be warned. He's a hard taskmaster."

"Never mind," Theon said good-naturedly. "The harbor's full of ships. We'll have no trouble unloading what we brought and perhaps be able to find a few goods to take on for other ports." He stood. "Sosilas, I've some business in town. Do you think you could possibly manage to entertain these ladies?"

Sosilas looked from one girl to the other. A smile spread slowly across his face. "I'll do my best." Manto glared at Theon for deserting her. "Have you paid up here?"

"No," Theon answered. He reached inside his garment and found two purses. He tossed the smaller to the mate. "Have fun," he said. "You, too, ladies." He saluted and took off.

"Now girls," said Sosilas, "how about some dinner? And we might start talking prices, eh?"

Manto was livid. She had been counting on a playful romp with a man ten years younger than she, tall and strong and handsome—and callow. Instead she would share the company of a rough-looking man of forty-five or so, weather-beaten, and, worst of all, obviously experienced in the ways of light-fingered whores.

Sosilas had a hand over the top of the cup he had taken from Theon. His smile was insinuating. "Come on, girls. How much? And what are your specialties?"

Theon hurried down the hill after Pandion. From the girls' description, Pandion had sounded like the sort of petty criminal whose tongue would loosen after a few drinks. With his familiarity with the port and sailors and the wrong side of the law, he might be a link to the Minotaur.

An idea was hatching in Theon's mind, one that would, with any luck, get him through the many layers of secrecy that surrounded the Minotaur's operation and allow him to break into the inner circle.

Time with Pandion was what Theon needed, a lot more than he needed the company of a couple of trollops who, he was sure, had serious designs on his purse.

But as he approached the little square where the main street and the Ropewalk converged, he looked around and could not find the curly-haired drifter.

Behind the tavern, in the tiny alleyway, Pandion looked both ways to make sure he was alone, then reached inside his chiton for the purse he had lifted from a sailor. He hefted it before opening it. The weight did not match the bulk.

He opened the purse and upended the contents into his hand: two copper coins and a handful of worthless pebbles—the kind a man might use in a slingshot—fell out. He cursed low and long, putting the stones back in the bag. Again he took measure of the purse's weight. He had pawned his knife the day before and was without a weapon. If one held the pouch by the string and swung it . . .

He put the purse away and rubbed the two nearly worthless coins together. A stake—that was what he needed. He could build even a small amount into something decent.

I need a drink, he thought. *A drink would help me think this out*. The coins would buy two drinks. Or he could gamble with them and, with luck, parlay the two coins into a larger sum.

The drinks won, and when they were gone, he wandered to a table where men were betting on cast bones. The objective was to bet on how many throwing sticks landed with the rough side up and the smooth side down for each toss. The drinks went to Pandion's head; on impulse, knowing the dangers but ignoring them, he bet money he did not have. He won, then bet that much again. And won again.

Before an hour had passed, he had won six thousand copper pieces and had finished a whole bottle of wine— and was still betting.

Theon found him sitting drunkenly at the table, behind piles of coins and surrounded by a sizable crowd.

"What's happening?" Theon asked an onlooker.

"Oh, this drifter came in, won a few times, then started playing double or nothing. When nobody was left to match him, he began covering all bets on the bones. Damn fool, I say. He's too drunk to keep track of what he's doing."

Theon's brows raised. He pushed his way through the

crowd to see Pandion sitting splay-legged, blinking down at throwing sticks from an old Egyptian senet game.

"Come on," Pandion mumbled. "Who's going to match me? I'm taking bets from anybody."

Theon hesitated to let this continue—yet how could he intervene? Even if Pandion managed to emerge a winner, his life would not be worth much the moment he strayed outdoors. Covering all bets was insane. Pandion had to be stopped if he, Theon, was going to have a conversation with him this side of the next world.

He took the bull by the horns. "Pandion!" he cried. "Imagine meeting you here!" He sat down next to Pandion and clapped him on the shoulder. "You drunken idiot! Don't you recognize your old friend Theon?"

Pandion blinked. "W-who are? . . ."

"Oh, come on, now." Theon faked an affectionate cuff at Pandion's chin and looked up at the circle of faces around the table. "Isn't that something? He knows me for five years when he's broke, but when he wins a potful of money we're strangers. But he doesn't mean it. Do you, Pandion?"

"D-don't know you from—"

"Well, I shouldn't wonder! You've probably drunk enough wine to float a cargo vessel loaded down with anvils."

"Take some." Pandion drunkenly shoved a pile of coins over at him. "Buy yourself some w-wine, too. Get drunk l-like me." He hiccuped loudly.

Theon looked around again. "Look, boys, he's too drunk to play now. I'd better get him home before he lands on his face."

"Leave him here," a rough voice demanded. A huge man wearing an eye patch glared down at Pandion. "If he can't hold his drink well enough to keep what he's won, what business is it of yours? Take off, mate!" When Theon did not move, the big man stepped closer, gesturing menacingly.

Theon stood and looked the tall man directly in the eyes. They were an exact match for height, although the ruffian weighed a third again as much. "My friend is my business. He's clearly not fit to continue. He'll be back in the taverns tomorrow to let you all try to win some of this back, never fear. But for now I think it's best that he doesn't try to tackle more than he can handle."

"He stays," the thug said. "Get out of the way."

Theon looked around and saw familiar faces. "Men of the *Issus*!" he cried out. "To me!"

His crewmen, eight against the ten behind the one-eyed man, surged forward. Just as they did, the ruffian swung on Theon. The young man ducked, laughed, and planted a fist in the big man's one good eye, causing a howl of pain.

The two crews converged. Someone charged Theon, head down, and rammed him in the belly, driving him back against the table. It toppled over, scattering the coins. Pandion howled in dismay as he dived drunkenly for the floor, tripping another of the one-eyed man's crewmen. Theon straightened up the man who had butted him with an uppercut, and the man's head snapped back. Suddenly all the tavern's patrons joined in, throwing punches right and left.

IV

Eventually the city guards came, and although they were outnumbered two to one by the rioters, they managed to establish authority and move the combatants into the street. "Get back to your ships for the night," the captain of the guard ordered. "All of you. If I see more than five people gathered together indoors or out on Alashiyan soil tonight, your ships will be fined a quarter of their cargoes."

His threat was greeted with a loud groan. Any crewman who allowed his factors to lose that much money through his own heedlessness would be forever blacklisted.

Theon's men surrounded him. "What shall we do, sir?" one deckhand asked.

"Go on back," Theon said. "I'll be along soon."

"But sir, somebody's likely to ambush you."

"I'll be careful. I have to go look for the fellow who won all the money. I'll see you back on the ship."

They left with some reluctance. Theon watched them go, then slipped back inside the inn. "Pandion!" he called. "Pandion, are you still here?" There was no answer. He stood in the middle of the room, looking around. "Now where could he be?" he muttered. "He wouldn't have left without all that—"

"All that money?" a voice asked.

Theon wheeled to see Pandion sitting in a corner, holding two small bags in his hands. Displeasure twisted his round face.

"Do you know how much they've left me? Less than half. I don't know how anybody managed to steal that much while a fight was going on, but they did. I got in first and scooped a bit into a corner. That's the only reason I have any left." He shook his head. "I was rich. Rich!"

"You're not doing too badly," Theon consoled him. "You've still got your skull in one piece. You wouldn't have had that if I hadn't interfered." He bent to offer a hand, and Pandion reluctantly allowed himself to be pulled to his feet.

"Which brings me," Pandion said, with an even more sour expression, "to what possessed you to step in like that? It was *stupid*! In half an hour you lost me more money than I've had in six months!"

"I saved your life, you fool."

"What business is my life of yours?"

"Someone pointed you out to me earlier, said you were a man who knew about this part of the world, and who knew which end was up."

"So?"

"I might have a way for a smart man to earn, easily and quickly, as much as you lost tonight."

"Oh, I see. You lost it for me, and now I'm expected to work to earn it back, eh? And you're doing me some sort of favor? Thanks. Thanks a lot."

"Quite a bit of money is involved. If things were to work out according to plan, each of us would make a bundle."

Pandion stared sourly at him. "We would, would we? And you'd be exercising the same sort of brains that just lost me half of the most money I've ever owned?" He spat. "Wonderful. Pardon me while I go somewhere else—anywhere you're not. Ow! My head's killing me! But," he said, grinning crookedly at Theon, "yours is going to kill you tomorrow. Do you have any idea what your face looks like?"

Theon stepped to a bronze mirror nailed to the wall. "Gods! My own wet nurse wouldn't recognize me."

"I wish they'd brained you. You deserved the worst they could do to you, you crazy bastard."

Theon turned to face him. "We're going to get thrown out of here the moment the innkeeper gets back. Is there anywhere we could talk?"

"Talk? I don't want to talk with the likes of you."

"Sure you do. You want your money back. And more."

Pandion glared at him. "And to get this phantom money I have to do what?"

"I can't talk about it here. It has to be somewhere private."

Pandion looked him in the eyes, skeptical. He said at last, "All right. Do you know the place called the Sign of the Two Gulls?"

"I was in there this afternoon. Briefly. It'd help if they'd clean the floor now and then."

"I need something to drink, and bad. My head is driving me crazy."

"Come along then. I don't feel well myself. Maybe I need a drink, too."

There was a back room at the Two Gulls furnished with two chairs and a table, and the innkeeper, looking warily at their beaten faces, brought a large bottle of strong libation and a pair of bowls, then left them alone.

"Now," Pandion said. "What's this precious proposition of yours? You're the captain of one of the boats in the harbor?"

"Yes, the *Issus*. But when I made captain I thought I'd be doing a lot better than I am now."

"You're young to be a captain."

"True. But I was also the youngest first mate the owners ever had. I'd hoped to earn enough to buy my own boat in a couple of years and be my own master. But by the time I get finished paying for licenses and bribing port officials, my first mate makes more than I do. I have all the responsibility but only a small share in the profit. Why should I take all the risk and be paid so badly? Tell me that."

Pandion shrugged. "I don't know. But go on."

"I've been mulling over an idea. But it'd require help. Are you familiar with the laws regarding salvage?"

"Roughly."

"Very well. The fleet I work for has been hit hard lately by the Minotaur. Do you know of him?"

Pandion offered an enigmatic smile.

Theon shot a hard look at him. "You *know* him."

"I'm not saying if I do or don't," Pandion retorted.

"All right. His pattern seems to be this: The attack is planned, and the Minotaur not only has galleys full of fighting men lying in wait for a ship whose itinerary he knows in advance, but also cargo vessels to carry off the booty."

Pandion rolled his eyes. "No pirate is that organized."

"This one is. The owners have analyzed the whole pattern of operation. He—" Theon stopped and stared at Pandion. "Are you sure you can't tell me whether you know him or not? Because—"

"Let's say I've, uh, met him. In this part of the world one eventually does. Not that he comes in blowing a horn. But if some big ox with a black beard comes into port in a boat with the wrong ensign flying . . ."

"What do you mean, 'wrong ensign'?"

"He'll arrive flying, say, the flag of Egypt. But if there's anybody in the whole world who looks less like an Egyptian than he does, I don't know who it could be. And of course none of the crew can speak a word of the Egyptian language."

"That would make a person suspicious, wouldn't it?"

"Anyhow, when he comes in, he isn't hard to meet. But why would you want to meet him?"

"If I could work out a deal with him . . ." Theon frowned. "The fact that he's so well organized . . ."

Theon poured wine for both of them. "What if I could steer him to my own vessel but make it look as if I'd wrecked the ship and it sank with the entire cargo? We'd split the take."

"Good luck. What happens when the owners investigate?"

"The boat would go to the bottom, somewhere deep, but only after the cargo had been transferred to one of the Minotaur's ships."

"Clever. And the crew?"

Theon put on a hard face. "Expendable."

"You're tougher than you look."

"I'm tired of taking the risk but not making the money. I want my own boat, and I'll do whatever it takes to get one."

"You wouldn't consider working for the Minotaur, would you?"

"Perhaps," Theon answered thoughtfully. "But only afterward. I want to come into the operation with my own money. I've learned that the hard way. I came into my present job broke, and I'm still broke. If I'd been able to buy into a decent share of the profits . . ."

"Pour me some more of that wine." Theon did so; Pandion drank. "I'm wondering where there's money for me in all this."

"If you can get me an introduction to the Minotaur and if he makes the deal with me—I'll make up the sum you lost when the fight broke out."

"That's not enough," Pandion said.

"And five hundred copper pieces."

"Well . . ."

But when Pandion looked up from his wine bowl, Theon knew he had his man.

*   *   *

The next morning, Pandion arose with a terrific headache, drank another bottle of wine to kill it, and walked to the water. At the docks he hired a skiff and rowed into the bay. The exercise was more than he had taken in six months; his back hurt and his hands were raw by the time he had pulled within hailing distance of the *Melos*.

"Ahoy the *Melos*!" he cried out. Instantly he was the target for half a dozen drawn bows. "Don't shoot! I have a message to deliver."

"We want no message from the dregs of the waterfront in a town like this," a bowman said.

"The message isn't for you. It's for the Minotaur."

The bowman's eyes flashed. "Watch your mouth! Who speaks of the Minotaur?"

"I do. Pandion of Poros."

"I know that name."

"Let me aboard," Pandion said wearily. "I was up all night drinking, and I feel like something puked up by a diseased squid. Trust me. You'll thank me for telling you."

The bowmen relaxed as their leader disappeared inside the cabin. When he came out, he waved at Pandion to come aboard.

CHAPTER FIVE

In the Arabah

I

Bending over the cool water of the well, Pepi caught a glimpse of his face; it was deeply tanned from the relentless sun. *For the first time in years I really look like a Nubian,* he thought. *When I go north to Selah, my friends won't recognize me.*

He drew back and looked at his bare arms, which were also burned dark brown. He wondered if posing as a Nubian—a representative of his distant kinsman King Het—had been such a good idea. Dressing after the Nubian fashion in this blazing heat was torture.

There was sense in the way the Bedouin dressed, covering their bodies against the punishing rays of the sun. Even the more moderate compromise that his friends the Israelites favored provided more protection than his present near nudity.

A man who had spent most of his life with the Israelites, Pepi had walked into danger by coming here. If anyone

114

were to connect him to the sons of Jacob, he would be killed. But his disguise had worked so far.

He stood and looked around, past the little fringe of scraggly palm trees, toward the rugged cliffs of Timna. *What a horrible place!*

But it was interesting. One of the most surprising discoveries was the primitive nature of copper smelting. The wretched slaves working under the brutal supervision of the hard-faced Egyptian soldiers of the Timna garrison still crushed the green malachite nodules by hand on granite mortars, reducing them to the consistency of gravel before heating them in crude bowl-shaped furnaces.

Then, in an oven that had been obsolete in the long-gone days of Kirta of Haran, they would work the ore raising the temperature with foot-operated bellows. The process produced a lot of slag and very little copper, and Pepi marveled that they could make enough to fill their outdated casting molds.

He had wondered why they deliberately ignored modern methods. But then, watching the brutal treatment of the slaves and the smoldering resentment they held for their overseers, he had begun to realize that the fault lay in the slave labor. Slaves did not produce the quality of work that freemen did—least of all in a blazing, bone-dry place like Timna. But it did not matter because they were slaves and there were so many of them.

He shrugged. If the Egyptians wanted to waste the rich Timna mines, it was no business of his. But he had abandoned the idea of buying their poorly mined copper ore.

The Timna garrison was still a formidable enemy—tough, disciplined, and brutal. The soldiers here were part of a keenly honed desert-fighting unit. It was a good thing Joshua had decided to go down to Ezion-geber to circumvent not only the fierce Edomites and their wild Ishmaelite brothers of Midian, but the Egyptians, as well.

Then he cast an envious glance at the rich cliffs towering high above. This was an almost ideal mining ground for malachite: The hills were soft, easily hewn sandstone, which bore incredible riches of the green ore. Even using such primitive means as a stone ax, a single man could mine enough ore in one day to yield eight pounds of smelted copper.

He forced his thoughts back to reality. The main thing was to get out of here and head north along the waterless, featureless wadi called the Arabah. Then, he would turn east and go through a hidden cleft in the hills to find the fabled secret city Selah, carved from the pink rocks of the Midianite hills. There he would meet Moses and the sons of Israel.

And what would he tell them? He would have to repeat what he had said before: *If you want me to arm you to take Canaan, take Bashan first. Get me the Succoth mines and the Jabbok malachite. And get me a source of tin.*

As Pepi returned to his bedroll and prepared to leave, he saw a caravan approaching from the north. He fed his animals, gathered his belongings, and watched the train of onagers come in, laden down with bundles. Finally, as one of the drivers approached the well to fill his goatskin bag, Pepi called out, "Friend, whose caravan is this and from where does it hail?"

The driver looked him up and down. "This is the caravan of Bata of Bast, stranger. Fresh in from Damascus and beyond, and from all trade centers en route. Bound for the Egyptian delta. I am Matanbaal of Arvad. And who might you be?"

Pepi considered honesty for a moment, then said, "Seti of Kerma, at your service, and a long way from home. Bata of Bast, he wouldn't be the son of the famous trader Sekhti?"

Matanbaal smiled. "I'm not accustomed to Nubians being men of the world. So you've heard of my master!"

"Who has not?" Pepi asked. "I serve King Het of Nubia. If I could meet your master and speak with him, some mutual advantages might well be explored. That is, if the noble Bata has any notions of opening up new routes of trade so far up the Nile."

"He might," Matanbaal said. "It's been many years since Bata turned down an opportunity to talk trade. Come to our tents at supper. We spread a good board as caravans go. Have you ever had Damascus dates? Lamb of Jezreel?"

"I have not, and welcome the opportunity to enjoy the hospitality of the noble Bata."

"Then be our guest. I insist, in the name of my master," Matanbaal said with a bow.

Although Bata, who was meeting with the commandant at Timna to discuss ore shipments, did not appear, his hospitality was indeed superb. Pepi ate like a king and was entertained by a man juggling flaming torches.

Finally Matanbaal came to him and said, "My master would like to see you in his tent, if you please." Pepi let himself be led to a tent of good cut and expensive materials.

"The noble Bata," Matanbaal said, bowing. "My master, may I present Seti of Kerma, representative of—"

Bata laughed. "Never mind. Unless I miss my guess, I'm at last meeting Pepi, master arms maker to the one-time prince Moses of Egypt. Am I correct?"

Pepi glanced back at the doorway, where Matanbaal was exiting. "I don't know how you penetrated my disguise, but the Egyptians take me for this Seti fellow. If they were to find out I'd lied—"

"Rest easy, my friend, and sit down. Wine!" Bata ordered, clapping his hands. Instantly a servant brought a goatskin bag and placed it between the two men as Pepi sat cross-legged on the carpet. "My abode is yours! And my silence as well. Did you think I wouldn't know you? A man as tall as you out here near the mines, and as new to this much direct sunshine?"

"I—I'm amazed," Pepi marveled.

"A trader makes it his business to know everything. My father and I have been friends of Prince Moses's for more than twenty years. You might even say Moses is a kinsman—our wives are sisters. I was staying with Jethro the day Moses came down from Mount Horeb telling us he had spoken directly with the God of his fathers for the first time."

"We are well met!" Pepi said. "You'd blush to hear how well Moses speaks of you."

"He is too kind. May I ask what you are doing here, in the territory of your enemy?"

Pepi explained. "Now I'm going north. Is there anything you can tell me about Sihon and Bashan?"

"Ah, so that's the way the wind blows. I knew I should have made a stop at Selah this trip, if only to see my relatives. You're going to meet Moses there?"

"Yes, and Joshua and the army. You'll have guessed our mission by now, observant as you are."

"A good trader has to have an ear open, or he can never survive. Yes, I can guess Moses's strategy. And he's doing the right thing. For all the Bashanites' fearful reputation, they're the soft underbelly of Canaan; Amalek is the scaly backbone. Of course Joshua will have his hands full with Bashan. But on the basis of what I heard about his retaliation upon the men of Arad, I'd say he's got a good chance of being in Hebron by the end of the year."

"What happened at Arad?"

"The Amalekites and the Canaanites alike will be talking of *that* for a while." He shook his head. "It appears our Joshua has enough of the savage about him to succeed, after all. There *isn't* any Arad anymore, my friend. Joshua and his men wiped it out. He burned the cities and killed every man, woman, and child—to give notice to Amalek and Canaan that this will happen to them, too, if they resist him."

Pepi's heart sank. Women and children killed. The cities burned. The demon of violence was loose again in Joshua, and he was feeding it.

II

In the morning after Pepi loaded the pack animals he went to thank Bata. "Pepi the armorer," Bata said with a smile. "Have you any other arts at your command, like other members of your family?"

"No, I'm strictly an armsman. You want to talk to Iri, my uncle. He's going back to working on jewelry full time now that I've become the official armorer for Moses and Joshua."

"Iri making jewelry? This is good news indeed. I am tempted to halt the caravan and go with you to Selah to visit him. If I could secure the exclusive rights to his work—"

Pepi held up his hands. "You're a little late, I'm afraid. Iri left us. He married recently, and his wife's with child. They're going to live with Demetrios, on his mysterious island."

Bata's face fell. "Demetrios. Always one step ahead of me! But what can I expect? They're brothers." He waved the thought away with a fatalistic hand. "With the world as it is, I'm sure Iri wants a safe environment in which to raise a child."

"I wish I could find a secure, quiet, *peaceful* homeland," Pepi said with longing.

Bata's eyes narrowed. "You're not happy, are you? I couldn't help noticing your disapproval last night, when I talked of Arad. Of course I share your sentiments—as a trader I never know who's going to be in charge in six months or whether my contracts will be honored. But to find a distaste for fighting in a man whose livelihood is the making of weapons—"

"My view of weapons is that one has them to warn off other nations from attacking. And it's not specifically the fighting I deplore but your account of Joshua's putting the women and children of Arad to death. This was the first full-scale battle his young army had undertaken. It will set the pattern. If the Israelites earn the reputation of being vicious killers of women, children, and the elderly—"

"It is a harsh world," Bata said. "But Arad swore to destroy Israel and had tortured and killed the prisoners they'd taken. If Joshua had let them get by with that . . ." He held his palms skyward. "If Israel does win that vicious reputation, it will be as effective as a weapon. Other nations will certainly not be quick to challenge them."

"Bata, Joshua and I have been friends since we were children. We've shared all the hard times of his people. For fifteen years we hardly spent a day apart. I thought I knew him."

"Didn't you realize that he was being groomed to lead his people's army?"

"Well, yes, but—"

"And you had no idea that when the war for Canaan began, it would be a war to the death?"

"I knew," Pepi said miserably. "Moses was very clear about that. But Moses is a man of peace. As a youth he lay down his sword forever and vowed never again to strike a blow in anger."

"A noble sentiment. But when Israel lashes out at an enemy that has threatened its destruction, whose word does it follow?"

"Why . . . Moses's. And by extension the word of Yahweh."

"And you do not honor Yahweh? You do not believe in Him?"

"No. Do you?"

"Not at first. I was a businessman who cared only for trade goods and gold coin. But I became a son-in-law of Jethro, a prophet and priest of Moses's people. As a holy man, Jethro would not permit me, an unbeliever, to marry his daughter. So I spoke with Jethro many times and soon became one of his people."

"I thought you had married into his family to strengthen relations with a trading partner."

Bata smiled. "Yahweh works in enigmatic ways. My faith in Him is complete and sincere. If the word of Yahweh commanded Joshua's army to put Arad to the sword, then it was a righteous act."

"Even the killing of women and children?"

"One either believes in the word of Yahweh completely, or one does not believe in Him at all." Bata reached out and put a fatherly hand on his shoulder. "Be patient with your friends. They may know something that you do not. And is it possible that you fear the thing in Joshua because it may also exist within you?"

Pepi fought to stifle his quick hot flash of anger. At last he replied, "I will think about what you have said."

Pepi set out northward and on the second afternoon found the cleft that led to the secret path to Selah. He walked his animals carefully up the hill and threaded his way through the long passage, calling out the password Moses had given him to the sentinels guarding the narrows of the gorge. Finally he stood in Selah, the delicately beautiful rose-red ancestral home of the tribe of Jethro, where the inhabitants made their homes in cool and spacious caves.

To Pepi's amazement, the Israelites had settled in. He found Moses in a cave next to the one that had been Jethro's home. Blinking at the poor light, he called out "Moses?" at the cave's mouth.

"Over here, dear friend," the old man answered. "Come sit with me. I'll send one of the young people for wine."

Pepi joined him, sitting cross-legged on a rug. "I thought I would find everyone ready to move northward," he said.

"Pepi," Moses said sadly, "you haven't heard. Aaron is dead."

Pepi was stunned. "I always thought Aaron would outlive all of us."

"I believed the same," Moses said. "But as we neared the border of Edom, God spoke to me. 'Aaron will not live to enter the land that I have given to you,' He said. 'Within a day he will be gathered to his fathers.' "

"Did you tell Aaron?"

"No, but he knew. As Yahweh had commanded, I took him and his son up Mount Horeb, and I asked Aaron to wear the full robes of priesthood." Moses smiled. "He was happy, Pepi. He was at peace with himself and with God. We did as God had commanded by taking the robes of the priesthood off Aaron's back and putting them on Eleazar's, confirming the young man as leader of the faith. Then Aaron died."

"Has he been buried?"

"Pepi, that's the beautiful part. One moment he was lying there, peaceful and serene. The next moment he was nowhere to be seen. I believe that God took Aaron to His bosom."

"I'm relieved that his end was painless and that he had you at his side," Pepi said.

"We have one more week of our month of mourning and prayer," Moses said. "But Joshua wants to act now." He sighed. "The anger and violence are still upon him. The raid on Arad only gave him a taste for it."

Pepi's words came in a rush. "I know we have to learn to kill if we're going to fight our way into Canaan, but—"

"But somehow you think it can be done without our turning into barbarians."

"Yes. At Timna I ran into Bata of Bast, the trader—"

"He's a kinsman, you know, and a believer."

"So he said. But Moses, I'm not a member of your tribe. I'm not a believer in Yahweh, for all that I can see what your own belief in Him has done for you."

"I had hoped to see you accept the faith."

"I doubt that will happen. I wish I could believe; it would make a lot of things easier. But as the Bedouin say, that may be a well I cannot drink from."

"Do not dismiss the possibility, my young friend. I myself began as a pagan."

"I'm not dismissing anything. I'm just stating things as they are at this moment. Bata told me that the army killed women and children, the old and the sick at Arad. I'm concerned. Is this the kind of thing we—"

"Be patient. Trust. You fear for your friend. I understand. You fear he is becoming someone you don't know and won't respect."

"Am I right?" Pepi demanded. "Is he turning into a stranger? Have I gone all this way thinking I knew him, only to find that—"

"Pepi. Patience, patience. Not every question can be answered in the same breath that spoke it. Trust Joshua." He looked Pepi in the eyes and spoke in a voice that rang with sincerity. "Trust me. Trust, if only for a little while, the God in Whom you cannot bring yourself to believe."

Pepi bit his lip. He could not look at Moses. "I'll try," he murmured.

CHAPTER SIX

On the Great Sea

I

Above the low-pitched voices of the rowers and the *keleustes* who cried the stroke to them, the shrill feminine wail of the flute played by the *trieraules* sang a song from Tarraco. It was a song of pain and longing, and to shut out its poignance the men sang their own monotonous tune, pitched deliberately at odds with both the flute and the boatswain's low, rhythmic growl.

"*Op!*" sang the *keleustes* on the stroke. "*O-op!*" he sang on the recovery and next stroke.

"*Rhup-pa-pai!*" sang the rowers, trying to drown out the voice of the *keleustes*.

The flute keened, and never once in the long and punishing day did they manage to drown its doleful lament.

And the stroke went on, endlessly, tirelessly, as if it were not men rowing the galley—men who could grow weary, who could die of this pitiless labor—but powerful gods with no need to rest.

125

* * *

Ten days into his life term on the oars, Iri decided that if those first days did not kill him, he could not be killed. If his heart had not broken altogether, it would endure.

How much better to have been defeated and killed. Now he was constantly aware that somewhere, beyond the reach of his two strong but impotent arms, his beloved wife was enduring humiliation and unknown horrors.

He had thought himself so strong, able to protect her from all harm. Instead he had failed her. He had let her be taken from him, delivered to some unimaginable fate. And then, instead of searching the world for her, he found himself chained to the guts of a fighting galley, condemned to pull the oar until he died and was thrown overboard to the sharks.

It was all his fault. He was being punished by the gods for his failure to help the family he had seen stripped naked and sold on the slavers' platform. The oar was his sentence. The gods were evenhanded, after all. He had done wrong, so here he sat, naked, chained, a beast of burden among other beasts of burden.

As he pulled the oar and added his own raucous, hoarse voice to the discordant chorus, he realized that it would have been easier to bear his fate if undeserved—the innocent victim who suffers the illogical judgment of unjust gods. But he *had* deserved this, and now there was not a moment's passing that he did not curse himself for his cowardice and his weakness.

"Op!" said the boatswain. *"Op!"*

"Rhup-pa-pai!" sang the slaves beside him.

And the flute wailed.

* * *

Every so often the flute would stop playing, the boatswain would cease his toneless singing, and the cry "Up
oars!" would sound. Then the ship would drift to allow the
rowers to rest, and Iri, desperate for any diversion, began
to break a long-held rule of the ship: He began to ask the
men beside him who they were.

It took days to learn all. Some men were less dis-
turbed by anonymity than they would be by suddenly
becoming names again. But one by one he wore them
down.

Behind him was Agenor of Tyre, a short, frail-looking
man who somehow managed to match his mates stroke for
stroke despite the bad lungs that never allowed him to put
on weight. Iri worried about him, uncertain that Agenor
would live out the year.

At his side, on the starboard oar, was Zimrida of
Sidon, a man who looked obese, with his huge belly and
thick neck, but who was the strongest man on the galley;
the rolls of fat concealed a frame of iron. Zimrida liked a
good laugh despite the rules against merriment, and he
was not above courting the lash for the sake of a joke. Iri,
a strong man himself, enjoyed watching the gusto with
which Zimrida attacked the oar, and he began to model
his own stroke on Zimrida's. "The oar," the Sidonian said,
"will feed you strength through the wood if you let it, if
you stop fighting it and ride with it."

Directly ahead of Iri was Abishemu of Byblos, a man
who, like Iri, had been snatched from his family and sold
into slavery. In three years he had not heard of his wife
and children and assumed they were dead or suffering a
fate perhaps worse than his own. He advised Iri on how to
avoid letting the dark thoughts control him. Sometimes
the advice helped; sometimes it did not.

These were virtually the only people in Iri's world for

the first ten days on the galley, other than the boatswain, Labrax, and the two brutal *toixarchoi*, or oar masters, whose job it was to enforce discipline. The one on Zimrida's side, Mikaya of Canaan, never bothered Iri, but he harbored a fierce hatred of Zimrida.

Iri's nemesis was the port-side oar master, Rasap of Ebla. Rasap, a man who gloried in insulting Iri for his ugliness, was well named: Rasap meant "snake" in the dialect of the Syrian city. He had managed to break virtually every man on the port side of the ship and harbored a particular malice for any inhabitant of Iri's bench. Perhaps there had been a rower, many years before, who had incurred his wrath; perhaps it was some other reason that drove him to goad Iri so mercilessly. Iri never learned.

Now, taking a breather, the Son of the Lion leaned on his oar and looked over at his starboard oarmate. "Zimrida, my hands won't toughen. What do I do about the blisters?"

"Dip them in saltwater every chance you get," he advised. "Use the bilge water at your feet. It'll hurt at first, but eventually they'll toughen." He looked at Iri's compact, big-chested body. "You're no sissy. You might even outrow me, one of these days, when the oar starts helping you instead of hindering you. How did you get those arms?"

"I was a blacksmith," Iri explained. "I ought to have tougher hands than this, but I trained apprentices to do the donkeywork. You can lose calluses damned fast."

"That you can. Not that I ever had many calluses. I was rich, and I was always strong without having to work."

"What happened?" Iri asked.

"Sidon lost a war. The Sea Peoples came in, and my father fought them. They killed him—cut off his head right in front of my eyes."

"I'm sorry," Iri said.

"Don't be. I killed twelve of the bastards before they got to me. But we lost land that had been in my family since before Abraham came to Canaan."

"Abraham!" Iri said. "There's a name to conjure with. I know quite a number of his descendants, including Moses of Egypt."

"Never heard of him. I've been on the boats since I was sixteen. What goes on in the world doesn't trickle down to the likes of rowers."

Iri sighed. "Then I may never know what has become of my loved ones." In a flat, lifeless voice he described what had happened to him, afraid to allow any display of emotion for fear that he would break down completely. "I try not to think of her. I—" He swallowed hard. "Look at me. Who'd love me but a blind girl? And," he said, swallowing again, "it was my own fault."

"There now, my friend, you can't look at it that way. Work up some anger and take it out on the oar. Tell yourself you're going to strangle that damned oar to death, pull its head off. And on days when that doesn't help, work it out on the oar master."

"But he's got a whip, and I don't."

"That's all right. Tell yourself he's a damned weakling who needs the advantage. Remind yourself you're a tough son of a bitch who can take anything he throws at you."

Iri nodded, feeling a small seed of strength begin to take root within him. "But what if I don't turn out to be tough, after all?"

"Why shouldn't you be? You're a strong fellow. They can't hurt you. They can kill you, maybe, but what would they get out of that? They'd only have to buy another rower, and that costs money. If you—"

"You, fat man," shouted Mikaya, the starboard oar master. "Fatso! Shut up down there."

Zimrida winked at Iri before looking up. "Don't worry," he called. "We're not gossiping about your mother anymore. Everybody knows about her already. Half the slaves have had her themselves."

"Shut up, you bastard!"

"—and those were the desperate ones, the ones who couldn't do any better—" The lash licked out and caught him on the shoulder, drawing blood. Zimrida laughed and did not flinch. "—than a one-copper slut with calluses on her back and her nose half-eaten through with the pox."

The lash hit him in the face. He blinked. There was a thin line of red across his forehead. Blood dripped down slowly from the line.

"And the ones who've had her aren't bragging!" he bellowed. "They're complaining about not being able to afford something better. Like a young sheep, perhaps, or an old man."

Now the whipping began in earnest. Through it all Zimrida grinned doggedly at Iri and did not flinch.

II

Several times Iri was on the verge of intervening; but each time he felt Abishemu's hand on his shoulder. "Don't," the slave from Byblos whispered. "You can't do anything."

Finally the oar master, satisfied that Zimrida could not survive much more, put down the whip and disappeared only to return to drench the whipped man with a bucketful of saltwater. Zimrida's body twitched, then lay still.

"Is he dead?" Iri asked.

Agenor looked and after a moment shook his head. "No. This has happened before. It will take more than that to kill him. I don't know why he provokes them."

"Can't anyone talk him out of it?"

"No," Abishemu answered. "We've tried. The whip scars on his back are so many and so close together that they look like the wrinkles on the face of a ninety-year-old crone. One of these days, they *will* kill him."

Iri twisted around. "But—"

"I think he wants to die. Perhaps I will, also, when I've been on the ships as long as he has or when I give up on the hope of ever seeing my family again. You and I have something to live for; Zimrida has no one. I would caution you against modeling yourself after him in anything other than the way he pulls an oar when he's working hard and well."

Iri frowned and nodded. As he looked over at the stricken giant, Rasap's knife-edged voice cut into his thoughts. "You down there, wake up, you scum! Down oars! And you with the boiled face, don't let me catch you yammering again, or you'll get what the fat one got! You hear me, you ugly son of a bitch?"

Iri looked up but said nothing. His lips were set in a thin line; only his eyes held any emotion, and he narrowed them to slits. His hands grasped the oar, and he waited for the signal to begin the stroke once more.

That night they dropped anchor in a sheltered cove off an unnamed island. The guards threw down baskets of moldy bread and hard cheese, and Iri ate listlessly. Beside him Zimrida lay unconscious in deep shadow. From time to time Iri heard him groan. Once he called out to the poor man, but there was no answer.

Finally the moon rose, and a ray of light fell on the fat man's face. Painfully, slowly, Zimrida sat up. "I've done my job too well," he said in a hoarse, rasping voice. "This one is beginning to learn how to use his whip." He grinned, then winced as a cut reopened on his lip. He tried to bend over, but the effort hurt too much. "My friend," he said in a strained voice, "could you do me a favor?"

"What?" Iri asked. "Do you want some food? I kept some cheese for you."

Zimrida moaned. "Rat cheese! I've no appetite. But could you reach the bucket down and haul me up some bilge? I want to wash this blood off my face. I can't seem to see very well."

Iri lowered the bucket. "Careful," he said, handing the half-full bucket across on its chain. "The saltwater will be painful."

Zimrida moved back into shadow. "They ought to give me the finest wines to drink and fresh spring lamb to eat," he said. "A week with me, and I'd have their oar masters trained in the whip better than six months' practice on straw dummies would have done." As the water burned its way into a fresh wound he let out an agonized grunt. "Still, I raised his ire, didn't I?"

"That you did," Iri agreed, peering into the darkness. "But if I were you, I'd go easy with Mikaya. There may be a grain of truth in what you said about his mother. I suspect that's why it enrages him."

"That's why I do it," Zimrida replied from the gloom. "I—*Ahhhhhhhh!*"

"What happened?"

"Damnation! That hurt." He stopped. "I must have

gotten something in my eye. I still can't see out of it. I thought I'd washed it out." There was a tense moment of silence and then a low moan.

"What's the matter?" Iri asked. "Come into the light and let me see. Maybe it's something that requires another pair of hands."

But as the giant moved into the patch of moonlight and turned toward Iri, the armorer drew in his breath sharply.

Zimrida's left eyeball was gone. His face was a mass of red pulp around a dark hole.

In the morning they were surrounded by a thick fog and lay at anchor. The crew and the *epibatae* stripped and dove joyously into the chill water of the cove, to swim and splash about and then emerge to dive again. The grizzled *kybernates*, or master of the ship, stayed below studying his charts.

Meanwhile, the *proireus*, or mate, wandered down to the oar wells. "The rowers stink to high heaven," he told Mikaya. "Get them up on deck and wash them down."

"But, sir," Mikaya protested, "we never know when we're going to need to—"

"Nobody's going to attack in fog this thick," the mate said. "Get them up on deck. I want to see what we've got on the benches these days. Yesterday, when the flute player called for battle speed, we lagged a bit."

As the slaves were released from their chains and came blinking up to the deck, naked and unhealthy looking, the mate studied them carefully. "There's one missing. Has anyone died?"

"Uh, no, sir. One of them's indisposed."

"Get him up here!"

Mikaya went below and unlocked the special fetters he had put on Zimrida. "You talk about what happened yesterday," he threatened, "and I'll take your other eye out."

Zimrida glared at him. "I can't hear you, my little flower. Your effeminate voice is too soft. Step a bit closer and put your sweet little lips to my ear, and let me grab you by the neck and ram an oar up your—"

"Oar master!" a voice called from above. "What are you doing down there? Bring him up!"

"Don't try any tricks," Mikaya said with a snarl.

Zimrida shot him a nasty grin and climbed the ladder slowly, as Mikaya followed, cursing. When the fat man emerged the mate glared at him. "What happened to this man? How did he lose the eye?"

"He defied my authority, sir."

"He was chained to the keel, you idiot. How much harm could he do? Can't you learn to control the rowers without half killing them?"

"Yes, sir, but—"

"A good oar master figures out how to get the best work out of his men without hurting them so badly they can't pull an oar. Yesterday when I wanted battle speed was this the reason why you oar masters couldn't give it to me?" He nodded toward Zimrida.

"I suppose so, sir, unless he was malingering."

"Malingering! If any man malingers on his oar it's the fault of the *toixarchoi*." He turned to Zimrida. "And you're not to row for a day and a night."

He turned to Mikaya. "You leave him alone until he's back on the oar. If I ever again hear of your beating a rower so badly he can't work, I'll see that you get a whipping yourself. Who's this man?" he asked, staring at Iri.

"The, uh, the one with the face is an ugly devil—but a good rower. He's got the right heft around the shoulders and upper body, and a good pair of arms."

"You, come over here," the mate ordered.

Iri had been standing in line, waiting to be splashed with sea water. He came over and stood before the mate, trying to keep his expression neutral. "Take the day off and help your benchmate."

"Yes," Iri said.

"You didn't call me 'sir,' " the mate said.

"I'm not your subordinate. I'm the ship's slave. You get no honor being praised by a slave, or saluted by one, either, I'd say."

"A cool one."

Iri nodded. "Can I go?"

The mate grinned and shook his head. "All right. Go on below."

"I'm in your debt," Iri said to Zimrida later. "We won't be chained to the keel."

"So they took you off your oar to balance me, eh? Well, be my guest," Zimrida said sourly.

They were interrupted by a cry from above. "Ships ho!"

"Battle stations!" the mate ordered.

Iri and Zimrida exchanged looks. "You don't suppose—" Iri began.

Zimrida smiled. His face, with its swelling and bruises, was as ugly as Iri's. "Wait." He slipped up to the oar well and peered around the bulwark that shielded the oarsmen. "Friend," he said, "do you believe in miracles? It's the Minotaur bearing down on us! The Minotaur himself! And we're about to get rammed. Hang on to someth—"

The port side of the ship was struck with tremendous force, and the hull broke open. Water rushed in. The rowers, chained to the keel of a doomed ship, began screaming. "Get topside—quick!" Zimrida shouted.

The ship was already listing mightily to port. Iri emerged on deck just in time to see the heavily armed crewmen from the two ships with black sails swarm aboard. With raised swords they began hacking away at the defenders. A huge man, broad of chest and shoulder and as hairy as a bear, stood aboard one of the enemy ships watching. Black-bearded and square-faced, he remained still and expressionless as his men took the galley with practiced ease.

For a brief moment Iri thought about diving over the side, but he was immediately surrounded by men with drawn swords. "Come with us," one of them ordered. "We can use a strong rower like you."

Iri shrugged. One rower's bench did not differ from another.

But it did not work out that way at all.

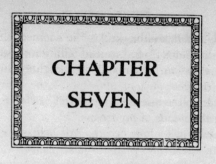

CHAPTER SEVEN

East of Edom

I

Caleb, riding a Moabite horse, came up from the rear of the long column. "They're ready," he reported. "The rear guard will prevent anyone from falling behind."

Joshua nodded curtly. "Good. Give the order to move out." His face was hard and his eyes mere slits as he turned to Pepi. "May I have your permission to order the army of Israel to move northward?"

Pepi frowned. "Why must you be sarcastic? You can go anywhere you want to, as long as you've cleared it with Moses."

"I have," Joshua said. "But I didn't want any dissent from the pacifists among us. I have enough trouble with backbiters."

Pepi felt a cold hand grab at his heart. "In the name of the gods, man, your own people were doing the back-biting in Selah. I supported you. And I'm not a pacifist."

"But you think that a conquest can be managed with

toy swords and that after you kill the adult snakes, you can spare the little ones," Joshua said with a sneer.

"There has to be a middle ground between pacifism and barbarism."

"Keep that nonsense to yourself. I don't want you poisoning the minds of my troops."

Pepi expelled a long breath. "All right. Our argument is a private one. Now, what are your plans?"

"We're going to avoid the Edomite people for now, although I intend eventually to come back and clean them out, along with the Midianites. From Selah we strike east—"

"Not to pick up the King's Highway!"

"No, we're heading farther east, to the Way of the Wilderness of Edom. Once we've crossed the brook of Zered into Moab, we'll pick up the King's Highway."

"Sounds good. I'm glad Moses talked you out of a confrontation with Edom at this stage."

Joshua watched as the army began to move slowly. "I'd rather have had it out with them once and for all, but it's no good arguing with the old man. He doesn't understand the ways of warfare."

Pepi was incredulous. "But he conquered Nubia."

"That was long ago," Joshua said arrogantly. "And in a totally different country. There were no forests in Nubia. None of this cursed underbrush to cut through. It has to be done my way, not the way Moses in his dotage thinks he'd have done it all those years ago." He snorted. "At least I don't have to fight Apedemek."

Pepi's hand went to the sword at his belt. "I can't help my parentage," he said in a quiet voice. For a moment the two men locked eyes.

Then Joshua looked away. "I'm sorry."

Pepi relaxed slightly. "Apedemek was a mean bastard and a formidable adversary."

"I wonder how well I'd have done against him," Joshua said. "The Apedemek you and I saw in our childhood was a man who had lost much of his strength. But what your father was like in his prime? . . ." He grinned disarmingly, almost his old self again. "Do I take it I have your leave not to like him?"

"You do," Pepi said with a nod. "Once I saw him in action, I didn't like him myself."

The track through the Edomite wilderness was so rough that no caravans passed over it except those whose home nations were actively engaged in hostilities against the fierce Edomite horsemen. The Israelites maintained a single column through the highlands and picked up the road as it wound along the foothills of the long ridge called Mount Seir. They were within Edomite territory, but the Edomite patrols seldom ventured this far east.

It was a sparsely settled area given over to grazing and to farming, and the farmers had erected crude stone fences to wall out marauding sheep.

The region had only two seasons: one of gradual dying and one of gradual rebirth. The winter was traditionally mild, with chill nights when it was more likely to rain than to snow. Now, with the beginning of winter, rain clouds were gathering on the horizon, watched eagerly by the Israelites who had not lived in land washed by rain since emigrating to Egypt generations before.

As Moses, too old and ill to march, rode slowly on a patient and surefooted onager, he looked at the sky and wondered if he would live through another winter. He had always felt that Aaron would survive him, and now that Aaron was gone, he did not expect to live many more months. The brothers' lives had been so closely linked, surely their deaths would be, too.

I love this land, he thought. *How sad it will be to die without ever seeing the Land of Abraham, without ever reaching down and touching the soil made holy by Jacob.*

Closing his eyes, he prayed. *Let me enter the land beyond Jordan. And if this is too much, Lord, let me see another spring before I die. Let me at least look across the river and see the land of my fathers!*

II

On the third day they encamped in the valley of the brook of Zered and looked out over the stream to Moab. Caleb posted pickets and kept the army on alert. Just before dark, emissaries from King Balak of Moab crossed the river under a flag of truce and asked for an audience with "the leader of the Israelites."

Caleb arrived as the men were delivering their message, and his men turned to him for orders. "Call Joshua," he decided.

"Joshua, sir?"

Caleb reconsidered. "Call Joshua *and* Moses." A guard hurried away as Caleb turned to the two emissaries. "Which of you is the messenger?"

"I am," said the taller. "Mesha of Nahaliel."

"And is your message friendly or unfriendly?" His eyes narrowed. "Moab and Edom derive as we do from the sons of Shem, but Edom seems to have forgotten the ties that bind us. How is it with Balak and his people?"

"I am a man not given to many words," Mesha said. "Let me say it before your leader, who approaches now.

Would this be Moses, the great leader who has laid down his sword forever?"

Caleb chuckled. "Not likely, my friend. This is Joshua. He will lay down his sword when the breath leaves him forever and not a moment before. Joshua, is Moses coming?"

"No, he's resting. Who's this?" he asked, nodding at the foreigners.

Mesha bowed. "Mesha of Nahaliel, on orders from King Balak of Moab."

"Speak your message," Joshua said. "And make it friendly because we will pass over your land on our way to confront Og of Bashan, whether you are friendly or no."

Mesha's brow rose, but his voice remained calm. "My king Balak bade me welcome the sons of Israel, our brothers of the ancient tribe of Shem. The sons of Esau, Jacob's brother and the grandson of Abraham the Prophet, open their hearts to their brothers and wish them safe journey along the King's Highway from Zered to the Arnon where the land of the Amorites—may their damnable names be thrice accursed—begins, and where Sihon the Usurper lays questionable claim to stolen land."

Joshua nodded. "Balak has as little reason as we do to love usurpers. Sihon holds land of yours, then?"

"Sadly. But we are outnumbered by Sihon's warriors more than two to one. Sihon fought against us and captured and burned the city of Ar. Those he did not kill he enslaved, be they women or children or the very old. This happened in the time of Zippor, the father of my king Balak. My own kin were taken slaves. Thus do the Moabites owe Sihon an ill turn."

"So it would be a favor to Balak and to his people if the Israelites fought the war the Moabites would like to fight."

"You would find Balak grateful. What is an advantage to you would also be an advantage to us."

Caleb pulled at Joshua's sleeve.

Joshua turned to Mesha. "Would you excuse us?" he asked, letting Caleb draw him aside. "What is it?"

"Don't you remember what Moses said about our passing through the Amorite country?"

"Of course. To ask politely and give Sihon every chance to allow us through peacefully." He grinned wickedly. "But I'm going to provoke Sihon. By the time I've done insulting him, his troops will be massing on the Moabite borders ready to fall on us like wolves on the fold."

"But Moses will be angry!"

"And by the time he finds out about it, Caleb, the deed will be done. I not only want a clear and uncontested road through the Amorite-held lands, I also want another fight before we face Og and the Bashanites. Our troops could use the experience."

"But how will Moses treat your disobedience!"

Joshua's eyes were hard. "There's only one thing I'm sure of: God wants us to win back the Promised Land. I have opposed and disobeyed Moses before. Has he ever laid the curse of Yahweh on me, as he did on the complainers who ran into the field of poisonous vipers? Has he ever told me that I would not live to enter Canaan? No. In that fact alone you hear the inescapable and unmistakable voice of Yahweh Himself. He wants us to win—by whatever means."

Caleb reluctantly nodded.

When Joshua spoke again to the Moabites, he said, "Very well. You will sup with us tonight. Allow us to celebrate with you the agreement and newfound friendship between your leader and ours. Our camp is yours."

"It is with deepest regret I cannot accept your kind offer," Mesha said. "But I am under strict orders to convey your decision to my king with all possible speed."

"So be it. Convey to him our sincerest good wishes. Tell him we will smite his enemies. And express our gratitude for his hospitality."

"That will please him greatly," Mesha said. "And shall I tell him that the stolen lands taken from his father will be restored to us?"

"Tell him whatever he wants most to hear."

Watching the messengers leave, Joshua felt pleased with the new developments: One battle before Bashan would be advantageous. A clash with Sihon would sharpen the troops. Two battles would be superfluous. Besides, Moab was hardly worth fighting for—the real prize was the territory that lay along the Jordan to the north. When these lands had been conquered, then he could strike across the river, hitting the Canaanites in the soft underbelly. Once the cities on the west bank of the Jordan— Jericho, Bethel, Shechem—had been conquered and subdued, the rest would be easy. If invincible Jericho, the capital and most heavily fortified city, were to fall to the Israelites, the rest of the Amorite Canaan would quickly follow.

Word of the Israelite threat had spread. What else could explain the groveling of a proud man like Balak through his emissary Mesha? No king, no matter how small his domain, wanted a foreign army passing unchallenged through his lands.

Of course, Balak was using him, just as he was using Balak. There was no friendship between the two. The king would attack him in a moment if he showed any sign of weakness. And if the Israelites were defeated by Sihon and driven back in disgrace, they would no longer find themselves among sympathetic friends.

"Call a messenger," Joshua told Caleb. "I want to send a message to Sihon."

"And not one we will tell Moses about?" Caleb asked with a grin.

"No bowing and scraping for us, my friend. We will send a message so insulting, the king will attack us within an hour of our arrival on the far side of the Arnon."

The moon was still high when Mesha reined in his horse before the city gate of Heshbon and called the password to the guards on the walls. The king was readying himself for bed when Mesha was let into the royal apartment. "Well? You got through to Moses?"

"No. Joshua. He seems to be running everything—not only the army. The old fellow wasn't even up to seeing me."

"All the better. One less leader to contend with. But what did you think of Joshua?"

"A formidable opponent, Sire. If he weren't so strong, I'd suggest that we fight them. Their numbers aren't as great as we had thought; none of the soldiers are over twenty-five. I imagine the older warriors will be used as an occupying force when Joshua conquers new lands." He shot the king a significant glance. "Midian, for instance. And Edom. He has a grudge against both; they wouldn't let him pass through their territory."

"He'll have his hands full with those Ishmaelites." Balak sneered. "And when he's busy elsewhere, we can recapture territory from his occupation force."

"Remember, Sire, his army is small but tough. They annihilated Arad. And they've got a master arms maker who knows how to make iron."

Balak looked up, alarmed.

"A Child of the Lion, Sire."

"What's his name? I hope it isn't Iri of Thebes."

"No, Iri's gone. But the young fellow he left behind is brilliant. His name is Pepi of Kerma."

"Kerma! He's a long way from home."

Mesha paused. "Rumor has it he's the son of Apedemek."

Balak's eyes widened. "A sorcerer like his father?"

"Not that I know, but if he gets his hands on the copper deposits of the Jabbok . . ."

"If Israel captures all the land to the north, has free access to the Damascus trade, and gets its hands on iron ore . . ."

"Terrible, Sire. A Child of the Lion loose in a land with access to iron. The consequences are too terrible to contemplate!"

III

The men Joshua had sent to spy on Sihon and Bashan returned just as the emissary to Sihon was preparing to leave. At that moment Joshua saw Pepi heading toward him. "Caleb," Joshua said, "get rid of Pepi if you can."

Pleased, Caleb went to head off Pepi. He forced himself to greet the armorer cheerfully. "Pepi! What brings you here?"

Pepi shot him a sharp glance. "Business. Last time I heard, I was armorer to the army." He stared across the camp fire. "Is that Joshua?"

"Yes, but—"

"And aren't those the spies we sent north? I'd better talk with them."

"Later," Caleb said. "Now I want to bring you up-to-date. We got a friendly message from the king of Moab."

"I heard that we're being allowed to pass through Moab. Is there more information?"

"Well . . . no. But the emissary did say that Balak of Moab has a grudge against Sihon. Sihon killed Balak's father, and two Moabite cities were destroyed by the Amorites just before Balak came to power."

"So it would be to Balak's advantage if we put Sihon's cities to the sword and cut off his enemy's head?"

"Uh . . . yes. Anyhow, he's allowing us to cross through his country on the King's Highway. Not that he'd be able to offer any serious resistance," he said with a smirk.

"So Balak believes that we're going to fight a war with Sihon and avenge his father?"

"It couldn't have worked out better," Caleb said.

Pepi glared at him. "It was *my* understanding that we were to avoid war with Sihon. Joshua assured Moses that no offense was to be offered Sihon, that the only people we wanted to fight were the Bashanites, who were *his* enemies. *You* were there, Caleb. Wasn't that the order?"

"Well, yes, but—"

"The message for Sihon was to ask permission to pass through his lands. We would agree to travel the King's Highway and stay out of his fields and vineyards. We were to carry our own water and not even use his wells. Surely Joshua won't dare disobey Moses and send a different message."

"Pepi, you've never had to bother yourself with protocol and politics. Sometimes you have to phrase things in one way in order to make them sound like something else."

Disgusted, Pepi made a move to pass Caleb, but his way was immediately blocked.

"Pepi, if you'll just wait a few minutes for Joshua—"

"Please get out of my way, Caleb."

Caleb turned around. The emissary to Sihon was gone. "If you insist, but I don't know why I let myself get talked into getting in the middle of these things."

Pepi stalked toward Joshua. Caleb moved closer to listen. "Are you giving Balak the impression that we are going to fight his battles for him?" Pepi demanded.

"I told the messenger to let Balak think whatever he wanted to think, so long as he allows us free passage," Joshua answered. "Why?"

"I think Moses ought to know what's going on."

Joshua's expression was one of offended innocence. "Moses? Why? What business is this of yours, anyway? For a man who isn't even of our people—"

Pepi stepped back, incredulous. "How dare you?"

Joshua backed off. "I didn't mean that. I know you're a loyal friend of our people."

"I've shared every privation, every danger."

"Every one except the danger of battle," Joshua shot back. "If you're going to take that high-and-mighty tone with me, at least be accurate."

"Armorers aren't here to fight!" Pepi shouted. "A cardinal rule in my family is, we don't take sides in battle. But I've been the personal armorer of one side in an ongoing war. And what are the thanks I get?"

Joshua's eyes glittered with fury. "Come off it. Seth took sides against Nubia, and then against Kamose. Teti became a warrior-maiden and led an army—not as an armorer but as a fighter."

Pepi clamped his lips shut. "That wasn't what I came here to talk about. You promised Moses that we wouldn't fight anyone on the way to Bashan. So why did you tell Balak of Moab that you were going to fight Sihon?"

"What makes you think I said anything like that?"

"You know that was what you told him. I know we

can't avoid fighting Og of Bashan—he's sworn to kill you. And if we're to control the copper mines near Succoth, we'll have to win them from Bashan. I also know that you can't find a base from which to attack Jericho across the river unless you can secure Bashan."

"You know a lot for a mere armorer—a noncombatant!"

"Why, for two coppers I'd show you once and for all. . . . If I were to arm Bashan, you'd suddenly find that the mere noncombatant is a lot more valuable than you'd thought."

"So you're turning traitor!"

"No, I'm considering my options. And they aren't limited to working for people who not only don't pay me, but don't appreciate me, either."

Joshua's face was set in a mask of suppressed rage. "If it were anybody in the world but you talking to me that way—"

Pepi's fists were balled; his forearms were as hard as carved oak. "What? Would you strike me dead? Cut off my head? I promise you'd find that more difficult than you'd bargained for."

"Take care!" Joshua said with a snarl. "You go too far."

Pepi held up his arm. "Look at that. The time you've spent fighting, I've spent making arms. And in all the lands we've passed through since we left Egypt, only Iri was my master for strength." His forearm looked like another man's thigh. He towered over everyone. "Put a sword in that hand, and I defy any man in the world to beat it down, be he Og the Giant in Bashan or anyone else." His eyes were slits. "Including you, despite your blustering." He spat the words out. "I can counter your every move. There never was a time when you could get the advantage over me. And it hasn't come yet."

Joshua, breathing hard from his mouth, stared at him. An assistant armorer who had come to speak to Pepi stood watching in horror. Finally he stepped forward. "You don't mean these words! Please. Calm down before something awful happens."

Joshua took a deep breath and turned to look at the man. "You're right. Pepi, I apologize."

Pepi let out his breath, then forced a smile. "I do, too. We'll talk in the morning, after we're rested."

"Good enough." The men embraced stiffly and parted. Without another word, Pepi walked off, the tension still showing in every muscle of his enormous body.

Joshua turned to Caleb. "We could have come to blows, something I don't want. He's a good man, and we need him. But he does infuriate me sometimes."

"Are you going to talk it out with him in the morning?"

"No," Joshua said flatly. "We march at dawn. The message has gone to Sihon in which I make light of his manhood and his mental powers. If he doesn't attack us before we've crossed the Arnon, he's not the man I think he is." His jaw firmed. "Curse it, we've come to fight. Don't worry about Moses or Pepi. To them it'll look like an unprovoked and treacherous attack by Sihon. We'll counterattack and wipe them out down to the last man— and to the last woman and child. We have a nation to win back by the sword."

CHAPTER EIGHT

On the Great Sea

I

Slowly, following the familiar trade routes, Theon and the crew of the *Issus* worked their way along the coast, heading north, then west, until they reached Kas, in Arzawa.

Here, for the first time, they heard news of the pirates. The Minotaur had struck at a convoy off Halicarnassus and taken the entire fleet. Later, two of the vessels had been found adrift; a third had gone aground on an islet near Rhodes. There had been no sign of the crew.

Now, under sail off the Arzawan coast, Theon's vessel lost the wind. Becalmed for a night and a day, the ship lay at anchor. The *Issus* was a poor ship to move by the oars, and it was deliberately undercrewed. Theon settled down to wait—for wind or for company, he did not know.

As the watch changed he joined his mate, Sosilas, on deck. "Anything happening?"

"Not the faintest hint of a breeze," the mate said.

"Why can't this happen when we're in port, with a fat purse in our pockets and all those taverns and whorehouses?"

"Poseidon obviously has it in for you," Theon replied. "Actually, someone as lazy as you ought to look forward to the opportunity of nothing to do but order the men to swab the decks. It's a sluggard's paradise."

"I'll put them to work, all right. Idle hands lead to fistfights and other mischief. There's a spare sail to mend. If they finish that, I'll set them to painting. Don't worry, I'll get our month's pay out of them."

Theon smiled and looked toward the horizon. "I have a feeling this time. We're in Rhodian waters. All the Minotaur's action lately has been off the northern coast of Rhodes. And that nest of islands to the west would be a wonderful hideout."

"We're also getting close to the old Home, which was due west of Rhodes," Sosilas said with a shake of his head. "Home was a beautiful place. I'd always counted on settling there when I got too old for the sea. Hard to believe it was destroyed."

"Was it as beautiful as the new Home?"

"I'm not sure. I'm perfectly happy with the new Home, but the old place . . . well, I had a certain affection for it over the years. There'll never be another place like—"

His words were cut off by the cry of the lookout: "Ship ahoy!"

Theon and Sosilas exchanged glances. "But the only kind of ship that can move without any wind would be—"

"A galley," Sosilas replied. "It could be one of the war galleys policing the coast, to catch the Minotaur. On the other hand . . ."

"Look how fast he's coming at us."

"Damn fool," Sosilas said. "We're too close to the

coast for that. There are underwater promontories along here waiting to catch any unwary ship. Easy to get your bottom stove in." Then, with a whistle he said, "Look at those furled sails. Well, Theon, you've got what you came for." He grinned like a fox. "I hope things turn out the way you planned." Turning toward the stern, he bellowed, "All hands on deck. Break out the longboats. Prepare to abandon ship."

Theon squinted at the sails in the distance. They were black. The sails of the Minotaur's fleet.

"Half speed," ordered One-Arm, captain of the pirate vessel *Gades*.

Sciton, his mate, turned his head and barked out the words to the crew. Then he studied their quarry. "They're abandoning ship. Shall I have our men go after them? Or we can use the longboats for target practice."

"No," said One-Arm, frowning.

"You're going to let them go?"

"Doesn't matter. Let 'em tell people what mean bastards we are."

Sciton's brows went up, then he shrugged. "If that's the way you want it. We haven't any galleys in need of new oarsmen at the moment, anyhow."

Sciton had learned not to argue with One-Arm. After the first exchange he would curse you. If you persisted, up would come that handless arm of his, the one with the razor-sharp bronze dagger attached where the wrist used to be. Then . . .

Boarders swarmed over the rails of the *Issus* and secured her. "Sciton! Look here," one of them called out.

"There must have been a mutiny. They've left this poor bastard tied to the mast."

Taking a running start, the mate leaped from one deck to the other and confronted the prisoner. Sciton stood before him. "Big fellow, aren't you?" he said to the man roped to the mast and gagged. "But not big enough to put down a mutiny." The prisoner shook his head angrily and mumbled unintelligibly through the gag.

Sciton yanked the rag free. "Now you can give us your funeral oration. What did you do to get your crew to abandon you?" With his knife blade he tipped Theon's chin back. "Speak up, my lad, and we might let you live the day out before we make bait of you."

"None of your damned business," Theon growled. "If you're going to kill me, do it."

"Ain't we the feisty one?" Sciton said, playfully running the dagger down the front of Theon's bare chest. "Don't mouth off at me, my lad. I'd just as soon cut your guts out and throw 'em to the fish while you watch."

"Wait, Sciton!" one of the men said. "Look what he's got at his waist."

Sciton stepped back. "An iron sword! Cut him loose. I want a look at that."

The pirates sliced through Theon's bonds, and his body fell to the deck. His legs had gone to sleep. Sosilas had obeyed his instructions and tied the knots extremely tight. As one of the men yanked the sword out of its scabbard and handed it to the mate, Theon climbed to his hands and knees.

"Where did a harbor rat like you get this? Speak up, you scum."

Theon got unsteadily to his feet, weaving on weak legs. "I made it."

Sciton spat on the deck at his feet. "Don't lie to me, you bastard!"

"I'm not lying. I'm an arms maker, and a good one."

"I'm tired of your boasts," Sciton said. "Here, boys. Hamstring him and toss him to the fish."

Two stout pirates grabbed Theon and dragged him to the rail. One pulled a knife and was about to follow orders.

"Stop!" A voice rang out, harsh and full of authority.

Sciton turned. The guards stood motionless, holding Theon.

One-Arm stood before them. With his good hand he rubbed the stubble on his chin. He stepped closer until his eyes met Theon's. "You say you make weapons?"

Defiantly, Theon stood his ground. "Yes. Better than the ones your men are using."

One-Arm's bad arm came up, and the dagger strapped to the stump gleamed in the dim light. "Better than this?"

Theon studied the blade. "That's good hack-journeyman work. But I do better."

For a long time One-Arm stared at him. "Turn him around," he finally ordered. Without warning One-Arm sliced through Theon's loincloth. The cloth fell to the ground, leaving Theon naked.

"Well, now," One-Arm said. "Look at that, will you? You've seen that mark before, I'll wager. The paw print of the lion, right there on the lower back. A damned Child of the Lion." He turned to Sciton with a sneer. "And you were going to make bait of him, eh? Do you have any idea what a Child of the Lion would bring on the slave market, you idiot?"

As Sciton fumbled for words One-Arm turned back to his captive. "You say you made the iron sword, eh?" He grabbed the sword from the hand of the man still holding Theon and held it up with his good hand. "Not bad. I used to have one of these. Can you make more like this?"

"With the right equipment. And the right ores."

"Good," One-Arm said. "Sciton, take charge of this man. Don't let him out of your sight. If he goes overboard, you go overboard, too—with your throat cut."

II

Their sails furled, the mysterious transfer ships began to appear. They were little more than cargo lighters, half the size of the *Issus*. They anchored alongside the round ship, and the pirate crews proceeded to unload her.

As they worked, Sciton called out to Theon. "You, over here. Where would be the best place for you to repair our weapons?"

Theon looked around. The only available platform was situated just before the master cabin. "There. You're going to have to build me a forge. With brick and mortar." He smiled. "Unless you want me to build a fire on the deck and burn a hole in the middle of the ship."

Sciton scowled. "Smart-mouthed bastard, aren't you? Well, you've picked your spot. I hope you like it, because you're not leaving it." He hailed a passing seaman. "Come here. Fix this one a collar. And run a chain from it to a cleat in front of One-Arm's cabin."

The sailor looked Theon up and down. "Is this One-Arm's new watchdog?" He sneered.

"Just do as you're told," Sciton said. "Give him two body lengths of play on the chain."

"Make it three," Theon said. "You have to move around to keep the fire going. And I need an assistant to pump the bellows."

Sciton frowned. "I'll see if there's a spare rower." As the sailor closed a metal collar around his neck Theon folded his arms over his big chest. "At least you understand what an armorer needs. You could have insisted that I work the bellows with one foot while I work the metal with both hands. You might tell One-Arm that I won't be able to work iron on shipboard, even if he finds me the ore. That requires a much hotter forge."

"Never fear," Sciton said. "One-Arm thinks you're going to make an iron knife for his missing hand. He doesn't know how heavy the stuff is. Lugging that around awhile, he'll wish you'd made it of wood."

Theon grinned. "I'll make it even heavier, then he'll need to take on a boy slave to help him carry it."

Sciton grinned. "You've a ready tongue, I'll say that. Maybe you will come in handy around here. I was for throwing you to the sharks."

"I know. I'd probably have done the same if I were you." Theon watched the crew transferring the last of the *Issus*'s cargo to the lighters. "I'd even played with the idea of joining you boys. The owners weren't paying me nearly enough. I wanted a boat of my own."

Sciton stared back at him. "And how were you going to achieve that?"

"Make a deal to lose ships to you for a share of the profits."

"Hah!" Sciton said with a bellow. "And here you are instead, a prisoner nailed to the deck, without a share of anything."

Theon winced as the sailor pulled at the chain, yanking him a step forward. "Suit yourself. I could have steered several boats to you before anyone caught me."

"Having an inside man with one of the big trading companies might have come in handy," Sciton conceded.

"Then you'll suggest it to One-Arm?"

Sciton's reply was a derisive laugh. "Not a chance. You're his pet tinker. Once he's got an idea, you couldn't pry it out with—"

"With an iron sword?" Theon asked. "Am I stuck here forever? Is it never possible to move up?"

Sciton thought for a moment. "Well, there was a fellow on one of the Minotaur's ships, a slave on an oar. When we were attacked and the enemy tried to board, this fellow fought the bastards with his oar. He held them up long enough to allow us to bring up more men, and we repelled 'em. Afterward the Minotaur heard how the *keleustes* had run. 'Take off the chain. Let 'em change places,' he said." Sciton chuckled. "Now the man who used to be an oarsman is a mate. So you never can tell."

"The Minotaur, what's he like?"

Sciton eyed him warily. "You're a cool one. We own you body and soul, yet you stand there talking as if you were in the agora in Pylos, discussing trade figures."

"And you answer me as if you were a highly knowledgable banker. I'm not the only crazy one here."

Sciton let out a hearty laugh. "You're right! We're both mad!" Then he shook his head and smiled. "Look, don't make any trouble and do your work well, and life won't be too hard. You could wind up with that chain off your neck someday." He turned, his burly shoulders rolling with the gentle pitch of the deck.

That night they set fire to the *Issus*. The pirates, fortified by a great amphora of wine from Theon's ship, threw a feast, which grew rowdier as the evening wore on. Theon sank back to the end of his tether and watched.

At midnight a great hulking bear of a man called

Scarface—named for a terrible knife wound that left white, ragged tissue from the lower left corner of his right eye to the curve of his jaw—lumbered over to him, carrying a cup of wine. "Look what we have here, One-Arm's little pet."

Someone came up behind him. "Easy, now," he warned. "One-Arm isn't on deck, but he's right behind that door and he won't like hearing you talk that way about his new boyfriend."

Theon's eyes flashed, and he looked from one man to the other.

"Curse One-Arm," Scarface growled. "Let him listen. If he's going to be picking up beardless boys every time we take a ship, he'd better expect some guff. You hear that, One-Arm?" he bellowed over the roar of the burning ship and the revelry on deck.

Behind him the pirates looked at each other apprehensively.

"One-Arm!" he shouted at the still-closed door. "If he objects, let him fight me. And as for his pretty boy, if One-Arm can't take care of his own conquests, he'd better expect other people to. Hey, pretty boy, come here and give me a kiss." He mimed a loud, wet kiss.

Theon glared at him. "Are you talking to me?"

The pirate grinned, showing broken teeth. "Yes, Dark Eyes, I'm talking to you. Let's have a little party. You're mine, sweet stuff. Come here and sit on my lap."

Theon's voice was a powerful baritone when he chose to use it, and it could be heard from one end of the galley to the other, telling Scarface to sit on his own lap and suggesting various other anatomical impossibilities, all obscene.

Angry, the scar-faced man tossed his wine bowl over his shoulder. "One kind of fun is as good as another, and I haven't had any fun today. If you won't come to me, I'll have to come to you. But you won't like it when I do." He slowly moved toward Theon. "Where I come from, slaves do what they're told. Otherwise we tend to give them a lesson in obedience."

Slowly Theon stood, brushing off his bare bottom and turning. "See the circle the chain makes? All that space is mine. Anybody who enters it is fair game."

The scar-faced man grinned. "The little pretty boy has spirit. I like that." He approached the circle.

Around him the men made room. On the fringe of the circle, clearly visible by the light of the fire, Theon could see Sciton, standing, watching. It was obvious that the mate was not going to intervene. Theon had to defend himself.

"Pretty boy yourself," he said calmly. "Not that I can imagine anyone wanting to couple with you. How did you get that scar? Scratching your behind with a dung fork?"

The scar-faced man roared. "Now you're really going to get it!" He moved forward. The spectators' eyes went to the broad back of the scar-faced man, then to the broad shoulders and powerful forearms of the new slave. Theon could hear them laying odds.

"Are you coming inside the circle," he demanded, "or do I have to ask someone out there to throw you in so I can reach you?"

With a roar of anger the scar-faced man charged.

III

Theon—legs bent slightly, hands loose, a small smile on his face—awaited his opponent. Just as Scarface reached him, he stepped to one side, feinted a short punch to the pirate's chin, and whipped the same fist downward in a powerful blow that landed in the pit of the big man's gut.

Scarface slammed into the wall of One-Arm's cabin with a heavy thud and bent double, clutching his stomach. Theon positioned himself and straightened Scarface up with a looping punch from waist level. It caught him in the mouth and drove him back against the bulkhead again.

Theon could hear the odds changing rapidly. His eyes narrowed. "You back there, if I had something to wager, I'd match anyone in the house. I'd give three to one."

Scarface shook his head groggily. With a growl he lowered his head and made for Theon, only to be met with a punch in the mouth and another, with the other hand, on the temple. He staggered and nearly fell.

Theon stepped back to give him room to recover. "Now if I had any money, this is where I'd clean up. I'd let him hit me twice, and I'd feign being hurt." He grinned. "And then as you raised the odds—"

He did not finish the sentence. Scarface recovered, balled his big fists, and struck. His first punch caught Theon below the eye and drove him back almost to the length of his chain. His second came around from the sided and landed on Theon's cheek. Theon staggered, almost dropping.

Scarface did not stop. His fists continued to rain blows on Theon, but the armorer blocked them. Behind Theon shouting grew louder, bets changed, and odds rose.

Scarface bore in. Theon was near the end of his tether, and the pirate was trying to drive him back so the chain would pull him up short. If he could do that, the bettors realized, there would be no hope for Theon.

Scarface feinted, then swung. The blow could have taken Theon's head off, but at the last second Theon ducked and came up with a powerful, smashing uppercut, which caught the pirate in the groin. Scarface fell to the ground clutching his privates and gasping.

"Now," Theon announced calmly, "having worked the odds up with these nasty tricks and gotten the lot of you betting against me, I'd start putting you out of business. Scarface will get up now and come at me in a desperate rush. But my punch to his groin took the wind out of his sails, so his next blow won't have much force. If I had some money to bet, I'd win enough to buy my own boat."

A gallery of puzzled faces stared back at him.

"But you can all keep the money I was going to steal from you by these ruses," he continued. "Not only have I no money to bet, I don't have any big bruisers to collect my winnings. Alas! I'm a good businessman, but a man cannot be successful without the initial capital. I need a manager and a consortium to back me in these games of strength and skill. We could all get rich, the ports are full of fools who can't hold on to their money and—"

At that moment, Scarface charged again. And as he did, it became apparent that Theon had been watching him out of the corner of one eye. Midword he turned. Scarface ran into a fist the size of a dressed hare. The pirate stopped dead; his eyes rolled up; he crumpled heavily onto the deck.

Theon bowed, and after a moment's stunned silence, the cheers rang out.

Theon was sitting cross-legged, watching the men drag his unconscious opponent away, when Sciton came up to him. For a long moment Sciton stared down at him, saying nothing, and they regarded each other with quiet amusement. Then Sciton spoke. "Where by the gods did you learn to fight like that?"

"How do you think I won a command at my age?" Theon asked, casually examining one bruised knuckle.

"You don't look that strong."

"I told you. I've been trained as a weapon maker, and I used to double my earnings arm wrestling in the taverns."

"And that sarcastic monologue—how do you have the presence of mind to chatter while under pressure?"

Theon shrugged. "I was trying to get the audience's attention. The bettors were drunk, and they might not have paid attention to me. Had they been sober, I'd have looked naïve and stupid to drive the odds incredibly high." He smiled. "It takes more than one man for this kind of scheme: You need a fighter, a hustling odds maker, and a couple of strong men to enforce collection." He inclined his head toward the inert Scarface. "A couple of bruisers who look as tough as he does would come in very handy."

"You'd consider offering him a piece of the action for his services?"

"Why not? If he were collecting, people would think twice before welshing on their bets."

Sciton shook his head in wonderment. "You're shrewd. How'd a smart fellow like you get on the short end of a mutiny?"

"I trusted my mate, Sosilas, and where did it get me? They planned to steal the cargo and leave me tied to the mast. There I'd have been when the inspectors came on board. I'd have been blacklisted by every fleet on the Great Sea, assuming I did not die of thirst." He sighed. "That's what I get for trusting anyone."

Sciton grinned. "You do need a manager. You'd make a lot of money for your master."

Theon looked at him steadily. "No, I wouldn't, my

friend. I won't fight for a master. Nobody can force me to fight. I'd die first."

Sciton looked thoughtful. "So you'd cooperate only as a partner, eh?"

"Exactly. I'm a performer at heart. You can't buy a good show cheaply. But in my case, you get the best. I had you fooled. You actually believed he had me there for a moment. But I slipped every punch and made it look as though I hadn't. Single-handedly I rearranged the economic structure of this vessel. Can you see me doing the same thing with my partners working a large crowd, convincing everyone what a pushover I'll be?"

Sciton raised his eyebrows, intrigued. "Go on."

"Because nobody's gotten through to scar my face or break my nose, I don't look tough. Think of how much money that could make for my partners and me." He smiled. "My partners. *Not* my masters."

Sciton whistled. "You've got it all figured out."

"Not completely," Theon admitted. "I haven't figured out how to get out of this collar, how to stop being a slave, or whom to trust."

"I don't know about those first two points just yet," Sciton said. "But as for the third . . ."

"Yes?"

"Don't trust anybody."

Theon grinned. "*You're* a sarcastic son of a bitch, aren't you?"

"You might say that."

"When can I get this collar off?"

"Maybe when we run into ships from our fleet you can have it taken off temporarily. And then at the autumnal equinox, when all the ships gather to compare notes and plan the year. There's feasting and women—"

"Ah?"

"Drinking and athletic competitions—"

"And gambling, perhaps?"

"You read my mind. If I can keep the news of what happened tonight quiet—"

"If this is going to be a case of the mate exploiting the slave . . ."

"What if I open an account for you and record your earnings as my partner until you're freed? Of course, One-Arm put you in that collar, and you're going to get out of it permanently if and when he decides to take you out of it."

Theon considered it for a moment. "All right. By the way, how much did you make off me tonight?"

Sciton scowled. "I didn't. I lost. A month's pay, curse you."

Only when Theon's soft snoring could be heard over the gentle lapping of the waves did the door to the cabin behind him slowly open. A burly figure appeared. One lamp lit his broad face. He smiled, chuckled softly, and disappeared into the cabin again.

IV

Theon was awakened at dawn by the shrill wail of the *trieraules*'s flute, rousing the rowers. The morning tune was fast and lively, and it quickly woke everyone. Theon sat up and stretched the kinks out of his muscles. It had been a chilly night to sleep naked, and he had gotten little sleep.

Someone had left a bucket of water within reach, and not caring if it was intended for One-Arm, Theon performed his perfunctory ablutions.

Then he turned to watch the activity around him. Sciton was in a foul humor, barking orders and cursing. It was painfully obvious that he was suffering from the night's drinking. Theon leaned back against the cabin, arms crossed nonchalantly over his big chest, and watched. When at last there came a break in the almost uninterrupted noise, he asked, "Is anyone going to feed me today, partner?"

Sciton ignored him. "You," he bellowed at a crewman. "Get moving. I want taut lines all around."

"Well, then," Theon called out, "if I'm not going to eat or drink and if there's no work for me to do, I'll sit here and regale all of you with witty observations about your shortcomings as men and pirates. That mainsail's worn, for instance. Surely you've got a spare down below?"

"Shut up," Sciton said with a snort. "You, up aloft, keep a sharp eye out. Leadsman, give us soundings." He bellowed even louder. "We're in shallow water."

"Of course," Theon said calmly, "it isn't a slave's place to criticize or offer advice, but if I were in charge, I'd move this tub out to sea, unless you want to haul up on a reef."

"Quiet," Sciton said. But he called out to the steersman, "Three degrees aport there!"

"That's better," Theon said. "By the way, what did you say this worm-eaten slop bucket was called?"

"The *Gades*." Sciton's voice throbbed with annoyance.

"I can't do any work until you give me tools. Hammers? Crowbars? Charcoal?"

"That'll have to wait," Sciton growled over his shoulder. "We've never had a tinker aboard."

"You mean you didn't check the hold of the *Issus*

before you set her afire? There was a whole shipment of metalworking equipment, and you sent it all to the bottom."

"How did I know?" Sciton demanded. "Be quiet, for the love of the gods. The skipper will be up any moment now."

Theon's voice rose into a falsetto soprano. "Don't tell me you didn't mean it last night when you told me you loved me and I was your little buttercup!"

Sciton hurled a string of oaths at him. "Keep your mouth shut, will you?"

Theon's voice dropped an octave. "Tell me where we're headed today."

"A rendezvous with another ship of the fleet, to exchange information." Sciton turned around to look at him. "You're an inquisitive son of a bitch."

"Of course I am. If you want to shut me up, give me work. Idle hands, you know."

Sciton snorted, then grinned. "You've got spirit. I might get to liking you one of these days, if I haven't killed you by then." He shook his head. "Now let me get back to work. I'll have food sent to you. And if the boys can find any tools, I'll have those brought up, too."

As the *keleustes* called for a faster beat, the galley moved smartly around the great Phrygian headland, then northward into the Aegean. Theon watched with interest, making mental notes, calculating the probable speed of the galley, taking the measure of the distances covered, and trying to reconcile them with his memory of the map of the region.

To his disgust he found that he could not remember the names of all the islands, but he had a sense of where they were. He was sure he could find this place again.

He watched from the lee rail as they moved into a nearly circular bay. A second galley, black-sailed like the *Gades*, stood at anchor in the bay. The *Gades* approached the other boat, and at a given signal the rowers shipped oars and let the boats drift together. When they were close enough they were secured with anchors fore and aft and grappling irons.

The captain of the new boat—it was called the *Philea*—hailed the *Gades* in a loud voice. The cabin door behind him opened and One-Arm, ignoring Theon, came on deck.

The one-armed man greeted the newcomer formally. "Boreas," he said. "I trust you've had a good trip."

Boreas, a squat, powerful-looking man with a full gray beard, did not move to embrace him. "We've done well enough. With the aid of the *Hephaistos* we took a small convoy this morning."

"So the Minotaur is in these waters now?"

"Yes, and he said he might see us again if we're here in the morning. He had another rendezvous nearby."

"The sooner the better," One-Arm said. "We captured a ship of Demetrios's last night. That's her captain chained to the deck."

"That overgrown puppy?" Boreas asked. "Don't tell me it's so hard to find new help."

"This one isn't as green as he looks. Besides, look at that mark on his back."

Boreas came closer. "I'll be damned. Is that the real thing?"

"Appears to be. And he's sharp enough. Tell me, do you have any tinker's tools aboard?"

"Need some tinkering done?"

"Some repairs. I could also use some brick to build him a forge. Not necessarily an oven for smelting."

"I'll see what's in the hold. Meanwhile, you haven't offered me wine yet."

"I'm growing forgetful in my old age. Mate, wine!"

Theon watched with interest. Apparently One-Arm was not going to tell the new captain that the tinker claimed to work iron. And while the crew of the two ships were fraternizing, Sciton deftly steered the men of the *Philea* away from him. He obviously had no intention of letting anyone know about the fighter who looked like a scholar.

Good enough, Theon decided. This meant he had found a place aboard the *Gades*. With both the captain and the mate protecting him from indiscriminate contact with strangers—albeit for quite different reasons—he could maintain his anonymity. He had been dreading the moment when someone might recognize him.

In fact, he had been surprised that One-Arm had connected the *Issus* with Demetrios. There had been no identifying markings on the vessel, and Theon had taken pains to blur her provenance by registering her in the wrong home port. These pirates were more sophisticated than he had guessed.

He looked toward the mouth of the lagoon. An afternoon fog was rising, one that would mask off the mouth of the bay within the hour. Apparently they would stay here tonight. He wondered if Sciton had plans to swindle the men from the other ship.

As he turned back toward the main deck, a face leapt out of the crowd of sailors. The man wore the loincloth of a common sailor, plus the obligatory dagger at his waist. But the face was not one he would forget soon. Pandion. What was he doing here?

V

Obviously Pandion would have preferred to pretend they had not recognized each other. But both men knew it was too late. Pandion winced and hesitated before walking across the deck toward Theon.

"Well, I see your circumstances have changed," he said. "Are they treating you well?"

Theon caught the odd tone, but not understanding it, simply replied, "As well as anyone ever treats a slave. You don't seem surprised to find me in this state. Does news travel so fast, then, in the Minotaur's fleet?"

Pandion's face flushed. "Then you don't know?"

"Know what?"

"I—I'm sorry. I did it in a moment of weakness—I sold you out. But I'll do what I can to get you released."

"I don't know what you're talking about." Theon shook his head. "You were going to see if you could get a message through to the Minotaur's people for me."

Suddenly a look of understanding passed over Theon's face.

"Yes," Pandion said in a miserable tone. "I'll make it up to you. You see, I needed something very badly."

Theon's eyed flashed with anger. "What? Money? I could have lent you money."

"No, not money. I needed to get back into the Minotaur's fleet. It's a long story."

Theon shrugged. "I have all the time in the world."

"No, it will have to wait. I can't talk here. But my apologies. I betrayed you."

"You had nothing to do with this. There was a mutiny. My men took off just as the *Gades* came into view.

But it could have been worse. One-Arm could have tossed me to the sharks."

Pandion frowned. "Why didn't he?"

"I pointed out ways in which I could be useful to him."

"Such as?"

"I was trained as a metalworker. I make weapons. I can do general tinker work."

"Well, I'll be damned."

"Quite probably you will, you scoundrel." The words were filled with good humor, and Pandion looked up, surprised to see Theon grinning at him. "Did I hear something about a festival coming up? A gathering of the fleet?" Theon asked.

"Next month. At the equinox. But it's all very secret. If the Minotaur's enemies were to find out where and when the festival is going to occur, they'd wipe us out to the last man."

"I'm in a poor position for selling anyone out," Theon said, pointing to his collar. "But isn't the time of the equinox common knowledge?"

"Yes, but the location of the gathering is known only to the captains. Ships come in one at a time. It's usually on a well-traveled route, so the traffic doesn't attract attention. We exchange the black sails and run up fake flags."

"Any rumors as to where this year's conclave will take place?"

"There are. But only rumors. And I'd better not pass on anything."

"You're being cagey."

"I have to be. Look, I have to get back to my ship, but I'll see you at the conclave."

As Pandion left him Theon saluted.

*   *   *

What secret reasons did the man have for "selling him out"?

He thought about the conclave Pandion had spoken about. If only he could smuggle a message to Demetrios, the Minotaur's operation could be destroyed. He cursed under his breath at the missed opportunity.

Looking up, he saw Sciton coming toward him, trailed by several crewmen carrying tongs, hammers, and an anvil. "Ah, partner! You've found some tools from the *Issus!*"

Sciton shook his head. "The equipment went down with the ship. I had to trade the *Philea* an amphora of your good wine. They had bricks, too. We'll build you a forge tomorrow, so you can start making repairs."

"And where do I smelt iron?"

"I talked to One-Arm. If you've minded your manners he'll set you free at the rendezvous. He says there's an old forge there."

Theon's eyes brightened. "A forge. That narrows down the list! Maybe I can guess where the secret meeting is taking place."

"You'll never guess, not in a million years. Now where do you want this stuff?"

"Anywhere within reach," Theon answered. "And if you can bring me the supplies to make mortar, I'll build the forge tomorrow. Thanks, partner."

"Curse you!" Sciton muttered under his breath. "Don't call me 'partner.' You'll tip everyone off. I intend to take those dolts from the *Philea* for a bundle tonight."

"I haven't tipped them off. Those were our own crewmen."

"But they can't keep a secret. And what were you doing talking to that fellow from the other ship? I didn't like his looks."

"We ran into each other in Paphos, got drunk together, and got into a fight in a tavern. Because of us the city guards closed the town." He snorted. "I don't know what his other attributes are, but he's no fighter and he's no drinker."

"Just stay away from him."

"How can I? I'm nailed to the deck. If he comes here, I can't avoid him. What have you got against him?"

"There's something about that face. . . . I know he's trouble."

"I'll remember. But you'll have to keep him away yourself."

Theon turned away and stared out to sea. The fog was thick, but as he watched, a dim light began to glimmer through the mist. Gradually a huge, bulky shape appeared.

"Gods!" Theon said. "What is it? I've never seen anything like that in my life."

Sciton's voice was hushed. "Gods indeed! It's the *Hephaistos*! What's she doing here?"

Theon stared out at the vessel. Her oars were shipped, pointing skyward.

Her oars. There were too many of them.

Suddenly Theon realized that he was seeing the legendary flagship of the Minotaur's fleet, the ship that could overtake the fastest galley on the Great Sea, the ship no one could catch. There were two ranks of oars on the great galley, not one. He gasped. Someone had finally invented a working bireme—a galley with upper and lower banks of oarsmen and twice the speed and power.

At the bow of the ship stood a hulking and burly man with a black beard. Master of all he surveyed, he could be none other than the Minotaur.

And then Theon's eyes focused on the *Philea*. Pandion stood at the rail staring intently at the Minotaur. On his face was a look of extreme hatred.

VI

The fog was growing thicker. The *Hephaistos* ground slowly to a halt, pulling heavily on the fore and aft anchors. Theon's eyes were riveted to the Minotaur, standing tall and proud and apart, his bearded face unreadable, his massive arms crossed over his broad chest: a mysterious figure . . . mysterious and immensely powerful physically. And, Theon decided, noble. A noble pirate? Bloodthirsty, yes, but somehow elevated above his fellows. It was a contradiction in terms, but it seemed to fit the leader who now stood watching his crew as they maneuvered his ship toward the two smaller galleys.

The *Hephaistos*! Theon thought. Its secret was revealed. Who could have devised the brilliant ship's plan, and how had the Minotaur come by it?

For more than a century shipwrights had been grappling with the problem of how to increase the speed and power of a galley without making it unmaneuverable.

With a single rank of oars, there was a limit as to how much power one might produce. And that limit had already been reached by the Greek *penteconter*—a ship of fifty oars, twenty-five to a side. For more oars, one had to make a longer boat. But it was impossible to increase the beam, because then the craft would become too heavy.

Theon was sure that the problem was insoluble as long as the shipwrights limited themselves to a single rank of oars. His father, Seth, and he had tried, but until now no one had solved the problems a bireme would pose.

There was the further dilemma of what to do with the seating of the rowers and the positioning of their oars.

Obviously the oarsmen had to have a clear stroke and recovery. If the two ranks were not far enough apart, "catching crabs"—being unable to get one's oar out of the water in time to keep up with the other ranks—would result. A rower would end up with smashed knuckles, broken ribs, and other injuries, in addition to breaking the rhythm.

By the gods! Theon thought. *How I'd love to get a glimpse of her belowdecks!* He stared at the *Hephaistos*, sitting becalmed with both ranks of oars shipped. *I'll bet they use two ranks only at times of extreme need. That's why nobody has spread the word about her yet. People may have seen this big hulk and thought her an odd sight, but they would seldom see her under full power.*

He looked at the upper rank of rowers, their heads just visible above a screen that only half protected them from the arrows of enemy archers. *When I steal this design, I'll alter it to protect the rowers better.*

He looked back at the silent figure of the Minotaur who, as he watched, turned slowly to face him. The dark eyes, under beetling brows, bored into his. The great long-fingered hands gripped the rail. The Minotaur leaned forward, staring at the shivering slave chained naked on the deck of the *Gades*. Theon blinked and tried to look away. But the big man held him, held him with his eyes.

The contact was broken when the dark leader looked away. Suddenly Theon was cold, deadly cold. His teeth chattered, and he hugged himself, but he could not stop his shivering.

Sciton found him chilled and miserable. For a moment he looked down at the slave, then shook his head and disappeared. When he returned, his arms were full.

"Here," he said. "A chlamys for the day, a sheepskin for the night. I'll probably be in trouble for doing this— One-Arm didn't want you hiding a chisel in your clothing and then braining him as he walked by."

Theon put the chlamys on, then wrapped himself in the sheepskin. "You're unusually liberal with One-Arm's property today."

"I can't let my money-maker get sick."

"Your what? Did I hear the word 'partner'?"

"All right, curse it, partner. The men of the Minotaur's ship are flush and cocky. They claim to have a champion of their own, and they're willing to bet everything they have. If we can cover all their bets, our fortunes are made." He grinned. "You'll be able to *buy* your way off that chain, my friend."

Theon looked interested. "Do you know anything about their champion?"

"Nothing. They're not going to let us see him until the bets are down."

Theon frowned. "I'm not sure I like that."

"This is for big stakes. Freedom. A boat of your own! Look, partner, I'm betting everything I've got; so is the crew. If we leave here losers, I'll have to take that chlamys back to cover my bare behind."

"And if I lose, I suppose the crew will cut my throat or roast me over an open fire."

"No," Sciton assured him. "I understand your concern. I can guarantee you that the crew of the *Gades* will leave you alone if you lose."

"Wait a minute," Theon said. "You're not looking me in the eyes. What are you keeping from me?"

"Nothing you need to know. I've been assured it will be an evenly matched fight. No hidden weapons. No unfair rules."

Theon stared at him. With difficulty Sciton met his gaze at last but blinked several times. "And if I win I'm a free man—and rich."

"That's a promise. This is a great opportunity for you. You can lick anyone I've ever seen fight. You don't have to worry."

Theon looked around. A delegation from the *Hephaistos* was approaching, flanked by several of the *Gades*'s officers and One-Arm himself. At their head was the Minotaur.

"What's he doing here?" Theon asked Sciton.

"He's the guarantor of the bet. The men don't actually have the funds; they're on deposit with him. And he's betting on the fight himself."

The newcomers stopped before them. "This is the man, then?" the Minotaur asked in a rich, booming bass.

The pirate chieftain looked even bigger up close. He projected a sense of dignity mixed with an aura of unpredictability and danger.

One-Arm nodded. "Last night he beat our strongest man."

"You," the Minotaur said, staring down at Theon. "What do they call you?"

"Theon," he answered as he glanced past the rail at the imposing bulk of the *Hephaistos*. To his surprise, a woman, young and beautiful, stood on the deck. She was dressed modestly, but the gold ornaments on her hands and feet glinted in the lantern light. Under the intensity of her gaze, Theon was suddenly painfully aware of his near nudity; the chlamys covered only his shoulders and chest.

"The bets are made," the Minotaur announced in a deep, resonant voice. "I understand that if this young man defeats our champion, he goes free."

"Yes," Sciton said, "and shares handsomely in our profits."

"And if he loses?"

Sciton answered reluctantly. "We lose all our possessions."

The Minotaur smiled. "You haven't told him yet?"

Sciton shook his head, avoiding Theon's gaze.

"Then I'll tell him. Theon: if you are defeated . . ."

"Yes?"

"You yourself will be one of the possessions they will lose." The voice was silky. "That is the wager."

Theon gulped.

The Minotaur looked around him. "Are we ready? May the fight begin?"

There was a roar of approval from both sides.

One-Arm stepped forward. "Fine. But where is your champion?"

The big man smiled. "Think: On whose shoulders would we place the burden of defending all we have won in this most recent voyage? Whom could we trust to represent us, with such important stakes in the balance?" He gave a mock bow. "I am the champion."

VII

A gasp arose from the crowds on the decks of the ships. Theon saw that the rails of the *Hephaistos* were lined with eager spectators. He wondered where the beautiful girl had gone.

But he forced his attention to more immediate concerns and turned to Sciton. "Why didn't you make the conditions clear?"

"I wanted to tell you, but—"

"Some partner you are," he muttered under his breath. "Whose life is on the line here? I have to take the chances, while you—"

"Enough!" the Minotaur commanded. "Are we going to stand here all night long quibbling over minor matters?"

Theon shot a look of annoyance at him. "It may be minor to you, sir, but to me—"

"Let the fight begin!" someone in the crowd shouted.

The Minotaur removed his himation; he would wrestle in his chiton. His body was powerful with heavy, rock-hard arms and thick thighs.

Theon cast his own chlamys aside. "Someone spoke earlier of a fair fight. Can it be when one opponent is chained to the deck?"

The Minotaur's eyes narrowed. "Release him. We will fight as equals."

Sciton and One-Arm moved forward together to unlock the chain, but they left the collar around Theon's neck. Sciton tossed the chain aside. "All right, Theon," he whispered. "We're counting on you."

Theon stepped back and surveyed his massive opponent. Weighing the advantages and disadvantages, he wondered if he had any chance at all. He studied the Minotaur's thick neck, broad shoulders, and bulging forearms. How many men, he wondered, had stood before the master of the pirate fleet, as he now stood, waiting to see if they could match his strength and skills? And how many had gone down to defeat? And even to death?

He glanced at the *Hephaistos*. The girl now sat atop the aft cabin—the Minotaur's, no doubt—with a shawl over her shoulders. The fog made her look like a wraith, insubstantial and impossibly beautiful. Her face was turned toward him, and her eyes dwelt on his tall body.

Who are you? he thought with a shiver.

"Let the contest begin," the Minotaur ordered.

Theon stared at the dark, emotionless eyes. "Yes. Let it begin."

As Theon moved, danced, maneuvered, and feinted, he realized that the psychological tricks he generally used in a fight—exploiting his opponent's overconfidence, getting the other man to undervalue him—were useless against the Minotaur.

He feinted and delivered what should have been a crushing blow to the Minotaur's jaw, but the punch had no effect. The chieftain merely shook his head, smiled, and bore in. His first jab—a glancing blow to the rib cage—knocked the breath out of Theon.

He staggered, wincing from the sharp pain in his chest. *He's broken my rib.* He danced back, almost to the rail, to catch his breath. But, like lightning, the Minotaur moved in on him.

The big man grabbed him by the arm and twisted. Never had Theon experienced such brutal force as his arm was forced slowly downward.

He fell to his knees under the pressure. The pain was exquisite.

"Give in," the Minotaur commanded. His voice was firm but gentle. "Give in, or I'll break it."

"Never," Theon said through clenched teeth.

The Minotaur smiled down at him. "If you give in now, you'll do so with a body that's whole. You can do nothing with a ruined arm. You can't make weapons, you can't fight for money."

Theon looked up at him through blurred eyes. The pain in his chest and arm was beyond endurance. "D-do what you must."

The Minotaur's free hand came down on his neck, pressing firmly.

*   *   *

Theon awoke on a rolling deck. Through the boards he felt the rhythmic motion and could hear the familiar music of the oarsmen and their hortators. He put a hand to his neck—wincing at the sudden pain in his chest—and felt the collar and chain.

He sat up and looked around.

He was on a larger ship than the *Gades*. The cabin was barely visible in the fog, but he could make out a rich pattern of carving above the door, a bird's-eye view of a maze. The Labyrinth, the emblem of the Minotaur, whom all men sought, but no man could find.

He stood and yanked the chain. It was just long enough to allow him to walk in a tight circle but not reach the rail. He clutched his chest as pain from his broken rib shot through his body.

You lost! He toyed with you as if you were a child, and you lost. As he balled his fists impotently and cursed his own weakness and folly, he saw the shuttered window of the Minotaur's cabin push slowly open.

The girl looked out at him, her face half-covered by a sheer veil that hinted at the lovely features beneath it.

The eyes were exquisite, large and melting, hypnotic, and darkly unreadable. Gold gleamed on her fingers and her neck. Although she wore a slave's collar like Theon's, hers was of gold.

Beneath her sheer veil he could see ripe lips open. But she did not smile. Her eyes were full of awe and sadness.

"W-who are you?" he asked hoarsely.

The shutters closed immediately and did not open again.

*   *   *

In the oar well of the *Philea,* Zimrida and Iri once again pulled oars. The fog had lifted, and they faced clear sailing as they passed through the harbor mouth and into the open sea.

"Well, my friend!" Zimrida said. "How are you doing this morning? No bad dreams about absent people, I hope?"

"No worse than before," Iri said. "But someone with my looks learns early in life to keep his feelings under control."

Zimrida bent forward to begin the long stroke again. "I suppose so. You're no mama's boy, that's for sure. And a good thing, too, if you hope to stay alive." As he pulled, the muscles of his shoulders bulged.

"Why was our layover so short?" Iri asked.

"Seems there was to have been a fight. Our crew wagered on the wrong man and that means we're back to work, spotting a cargo vessel ripe for the taking. Did you see that other galley?" Zimrida asked. "What a monster!"

"Yes, a bireme. I wish I'd gotten a closer look at her."

His words at last drew the attention of the *keleustes,* and the lash cracked over their heads. "Shut up down there!" he bellowed. "Pull, damn you. Pull."

CHAPTER NINE

East of the Jordan

I

When the army of Israel crossed the River Arnon into the kingdom of Sihon, the Amorites were waiting to ambush them. But Joshua was no fool. A token force, banners flying, drums beating, marched along the King's Highway. To the right and left two mighty detachments of troops traveled unobserved through the countryside.

Sihon fell upon the Israelites at Jahaz, and within an hour realized his mistake. In a pincer maneuver the hidden troops hit the Amorites, doing terrible damage. Sihon tried to retreat, but in so doing, he stretched his lines thin and found his main striking force cut off, surrounded by the Israelites, and totally demoralized.

The day was won. Pepi, watching the battle with Moses from the hilltop, asked, "Why doesn't he call for surrender?"

"Do you mean Sihon?" Moses asked, blinking down at the scene with eyes grown dim.

"He's a brave man. He's resolved to fight to the death."

"No, I mean Joshua. Why isn't Joshua arranging for surrender?"

Moses sighed. "In his place I might do so. But Joshua has his own ideas, and God has put the management of our military campaign in Joshua's hands. I believe it would be unwise for me to offer advice."

"Unwise? You're the spiritual leader, your people's conscience."

"The Lord who is God of all, Yahweh, is their conscience, as He is mine," Moses replied, but there was little tranquillity in his tone. "His ways are strange, and I confess I seldom understand them these days. But as I learned many years ago, it is not my function to question but to obey."

Pepi snorted. "Well, I'm still a stranger among you, as Joshua has been at pains to remind me recently, and I feel justified about questioning a decision by Joshua—or anyone else—when it goes against my conscience."

Moses looked at him mildly. "It is not important whether or not you are one of His people. I believe His hand is upon you, and has been ever since you were a small boy."

Pepi looked down at the slaughter below and winced. "Joshua should beware: If my conscience tells me that my standards are being flouted by the men I have armed . . ." He stopped. His affection for Moses overrode the urge to speak his mind. "Look, down there. The Sihonites are begging for mercy. But Joshua is going to kill them all."

Moses averted his eyes from the battlefield.

"Moses," Pepi said earnestly, "when you pass on, not only the military control will be in Joshua's hands, but the moral, ethical, and spiritual control, as well."

"Ah, my young friend, this is not quite true," Moses said. "Spiritual control of our people will remain in the hands of Yahweh Himself. And as for ethical and moral questions, these are provided for by the Law."

"But administered by whom? By a bloodthirsty, unmerciful—"

"By a system of judges, one to each tribe. I am in the process of appointing these learned men. Yahweh will speak through them."

"And from whom will these judges be drawn?" Pepi asked.

"From among the elders of the tribes."

"All of whom have been told by Yahweh that they, like you, will not be allowed to enter the Promised Land because they have sinned and are being punished."

"All men are sinners," Moses pointed out. He sighed deeply, his eyes still averted from the scene of carnage below. "I can only trust the will of Yahweh to guide my selection."

Pepi refused to provoke the old man, who had been a second father to him. He shook his head and watched as the last defenders fell. The victory was complete. A horseman separated himself from the Israelite force and came riding up the hill toward them. "Here comes a messenger from Joshua, probably delivering a scolding for my not fighting."

"Remind me to speak to Joshua about that," Moses said in his cracked old man's voice. "It isn't your function. Every man has his place in this campaign, and nobody should feel that he has not done his best."

Pepi knew Moses would forget but did not press the matter. "It's all right. Don't worry about it."

The rider threaded his way through the rocks. "Greetings to Moses from Joshua," he said with a salute. "The victory is ours, we are going to press on. There is enough daylight left to take Heshbon today and to send units to pacify the smaller towns."

"You're going to take Heshbon?" Pepi said. "Why?"

The rider's eyes narrowed. "I was not sent here to debate tactics with foreigners."

"Foreigners?" Pepi said, bristling. "You half-grown whelp, I was defending your people before you were born."

"Yes, defending them from the sidelines," the messenger said with a sneer.

"Why, you—" Pepi said, his hand reaching for his sword. "Would you like to back up your accusations?"

"I don't fight cowards," the messenger said, turning to Moses. "My message is delivered. I will rejoin the army."

"Wait just a moment, young man," Moses began. "There's no call at all to be disrespectful—"

But the messenger had already turned his horse and cantered off.

Pepi cursed until finally Moses put a hand on his forearm. "People act rashly in the heat of battle."

"That was no battler," Pepi said. "That was a messenger. If anyone's watched the fight from the sidelines . . ." He spat. "He wouldn't dare speak to me like that if he hadn't heard Joshua do likewise. This is a symptom of a larger ill, Moses. My authority—even my right to be here—is constantly under question."

"Remember that you began the quarrel when you criticized Joshua's deportment in battle."

"Are you turning against me, too?" Pepi asked sadly. "Then my days here are surely numbered."

"No," Moses said quickly. "You'll always be welcome here, as long as I have voice to speak."

Pepi clenched his fist. "He used to put up with me because I had your protection, but now he sends striplings to insult me, even in your presence."

"He intends to take Heshbon peaceably. At least that was what he told me last night. He plans to press on all the way to the Jabbok, where the land of Bashan begins. The Jabbok, that was where Jacob, our forefather, entered Israel after his long exile in Haran."

"And it's where the copper mines are," Pepi said. "I need to look at them, if they're to become a resource for us."

"They're on the far bank, inside Bashan, as I remember," Moses said. "Maybe something good can come from all this, after all. It's just that—"

"I know. The violence. I sometimes ask myself, 'Is it all necessary?'"

"And what is your answer?"

Pepi did not reply.

II

Joshua looked down at the figure sprawled at his feet. "He doesn't look like the man who boasted that he was going to scatter our bones over the valley, does he?"

Caleb raised one eyebrow. "You mean this is—was— Sihon? Who killed him?"

"I did," Joshua said, kicking at the mangled remains of a man's body. "You don't think I would have left a job like that to a subordinate, do you?" He spat at the dead man's feet. "I'll say this, he could fight. People who'd seen him in action or suffered at his hands told me that he was tough and resourceful. They were right. But he wasn't smart. Imagine allowing yourself to be tricked like that."

Caleb chuckled. "Now on to Heshbon! Do you think we'll meet much resistance?"

"Not until we get to the Jabbok. Sihon was a fool. But I don't think you could say the same about Og of Bashan, for all I've heard about him."

"But do you think there's any chance that once the news of today's victory gets about, Og will march out and attack us this side of the Jabbok?"

Joshua shot an appreciative smile at him. "Now you're thinking like a soldier," he said. "I've given some thought to that, and now that we're in command of Sihon's domain, or will be by this time tomorrow, there's no reason to continue marching down the middle of the King's Highway in broad daylight."

"So you're going east!"

"No, but that's what I want Og to suspect."

"So he will. But where will we be?"

"From Heshbon there is a road running due west. We'll be on that."

"But won't he see us and move to head us off?"

Joshua smiled. "We'll settle in as if we were going to stay the night, just outside Heshbon. Then instead of bedding down we'll strike out in the moonlight and come into Bashan very near the Jordan, on the road they call the Path of the Plain." He chuckled. "We'll be so close to the river we'll be able to see into Canaan. They tell me you can almost see Jericho from that road."

"But what if he outsmarts us and falls on us in force by the river?"

"Then we'll fight him—which is what we came to do anyway. But we'll do it in country we'll know by then as

187

well as he does. The land's flatter there. Nobody will have the advantage. I don't even care if he has more men. This little scrap with Sihon whetted my appetite. I'm spoiling for an all-out pitched battle, with someone worth fighting."

"You'll get that," Caleb said. He looked up the hill. "Here comes that messenger you sent to Moses."

The young man dismounted and saluted them. "I carried the word, sir," he announced proudly. "The armorer was there, too."

"What did he have to say?" Joshua asked.

"He complained about killing all the prisoners, and he didn't like the idea of putting Heshbon to the sword."

Joshua's eyes narrowed. "Indeed, and what did you say?"

"I did what any red-blooded man would have done," the messenger said. "I told the cowardly slacker off."

Joshua's eyes flashed. Neither the man nor Caleb saw the blow coming. His hand swung out and connected with the messenger's face, knocking him to the ground. Joshua's fists were balled, and the rage was upon him. "Don't you ever let me hear you being disrespectful to Pepi again, do you hear?"

The young man held one hand to his face. "B-but, sir, I thought you said—"

"What I can say and what a nonentity like you can say are two different things," Joshua said in a voice filled with anger. "Get up. Get up before I run you through."

The messenger scrambled to his feet. "I—I don't understand. I heard you tell Caleb—"

"Get going while you still can," Joshua said. "This time your punishment was light. It won't be again. And if I hear any gossip about this I'll know who it came from. Then you'll wish you had never been born." He grabbed the young man's cloak. "You didn't insult him for being a foreigner, did you? Because I've said if I catch any man talking that way, he will be whipped until he can't stand."

"Uh . . . no, sir. Of course not, sir."

It was obvious that the boy was lying. Joshua thrust him away, a look of disgust on his face. "You've had three escapes today. You've escaped from the wrath of Sihon. You've escaped from Pepi, who could kill you with one hand and juggle oranges with the other and not raise a sweat." His voice took on a frightening edge. "And you've escaped my own wrath. But you won't again. Report to the Third Troop for discipline. Tell them you're docked your next two months' pay. And if you don't, you'll provide entertainment for the whole army, while you last."

The messenger could barely stand. "Y-yes, sir. May I go now, sir?"

Joshua snarled at him, and he disappeared. Joshua turned to Caleb. "I won't tolerate that from anybody. That includes you. Make sure everyone understands they're to leave Pepi alone. Blood means a lot in this world, but it isn't everything, and Pepi has served us faithfully for a long time. He gets on my own nerves now and then, but whatever argument I may have with him personally is my own concern and isn't to be gossiped about."

Caleb gulped. "I'll make sure everyone has been informed."

But as he turned, he saw Pepi, mounted on an Edomite horse, making his way slowly down the hill, alone. *There's trouble coming*, he thought. *Better to be as far away as possible when it happens*.

Once on the battlefield Pepi did not dismount but rode slowly through the valley, staring down at the scene of destruction. Bodies of the enemy lay everywhere. They had died in a number of ways, all of them violent, but where Sihon and his courtiers had made their last stand, most of the soldiers had died with their throats cut. So rare a way for a man to die in battle was this, that it caught Pepi's eye.

The realization came upon him suddenly: *They've been put out of their misery systematically!* Joshua had decided to take no prisoners, so someone had come through the field slitting the throats of all survivors.

It was a flagrant breach of civilized behavior. Red-hot rage flashed through Pepi. He dismounted and stooped to inspect first one corpse, then others. All of them had been killed by a single cut across the neck with a razor-sharp knife—one made by Pepi's hand, no doubt!

He breathed deeply and smelled the raw stink of death. *They've been left here unburied, meat for the crows and the vultures. Dead meat to stink and decay, to remind all passersby of the might of Joshua and the fate of those who dare oppose him.*

Suddenly Pepi became aware of a presence behind him. He turned to face Joshua. His temper rose like sour bile in his throat. "Many of these men could have been saved, yet you had them put to death. Why?"

Joshua did not answer.

"Damn you!" Pepi said. "Answer me. These weren't dumb animals. They were men. With families. Wives and children and elders to provide for. Who will provide for them now, Joshua? Answer me that."

Joshua's lips moved, and he seemed about to speak. Pepi waited, but no words came. Joshua's eyes were hard and fixed.

Suddenly Pepi knew. "The others," he said in a strangled voice. "The families. The wives, the children, the old people—you don't intend to let any of them live either, do you? What matter whether the breadwinner is still alive or not if there aren't going to be any dependents for them to support, isn't that it? Damn you! Answer me! Isn't that your wretched plan?"

Joshua's eyes were cold and unreadable. It was as if he had resolved to be accountable only to Yahweh Himself.

III

Pepi stayed in camp with Moses until the army had taken Heshbon and disposed of the unfortunate city as Joshua wished. He wanted no part of it, wanted, in fact, to know no more of it than he absolutely had to. But in the morning, as he and Moses and the older Israelites waited at Jahaz, a runner arrived from the forward positions. Pepi ran out to meet him.

"How went the battle?" Pepi asked. His ironic emphasis on the word "battle" went unnoticed, although everyone knew that Heshbon had largely been left undefended.

"Greetings from Joshua, " the runner said with distant politeness. "He says to tell you that there's been a change in plans. They're not striking westward after all."

"What's the matter?"

"There's no sign of a defense along the King's Highway. Our scouts went past the Jabbok without encountering any sign of the Bashanite army."

Pepi's eyes narrowed. "Where did they finally find Og's troops?"

"They never did. They rode as far as Mahanaim before turning back. All they know is that rumor has the Bashanite army encamped near Ashtaroth."

"So far?" Pepi said. "That's strange. What explanation does Joshua have?"

Pepi noted the runner's politeness. Perhaps it was due to Joshua's orders, out of respect for their long friendship, however strained it might be now.

"Joshua is aware that we're being drawn in," the runner assured him. "He knows that Og wants to lure us deep into his own territory and then cut off our supply lines."

"Then why—?"

"He doesn't care. It's a calculated risk. The only element of surprise we retain is how fast we can move into Bashan. He is planning a forced march, and we will be across the Jabbok by nightfall. We expect to encounter the enemy for the first time on the third day."

"So soon? Well, so be it. Does he have orders for me?"

"He says you are not needed in this fight. The army captured enough weapons from the Sihonites. He wishes you well and sends his respects to Moses."

"Thank you. You can go back now. Tell Joshua not to lose."

He even managed to smile when he said this, and the young runner smiled back as he saluted. "Yes, sir!"

Pepi watched him go. *It's a trap. But if that's the case, why am I not worried? Perhaps because I have a deep respect for Joshua's military judgment.* But then the realization came to him: *I'm not needed here now. And if the road is clear all the way to Jabbok, is this not a good time to break away and visit Succoth?*

If he rode west along the Path of the Plain, he could

make it to the river in half a day. Then he could head northward along the Jordan. If he were going to establish a smelting operation at Succoth, he would have to know how the mines were situated. He could not have enemy attacks disrupting his forges as they produced arms for the conquest of Canaan. He would have to decide how to fortify the area, and this was an excellent opportunity. It remained only to tell Moses.

Moses was on his way to meet with the tribal elders, who were vying for the privilege of occupying lands Joshua had conquered. He stopped first to speak to Pepi and said of the elders with a small smile, "If only they knew of what little worth the land they are fighting over really is. But how can they not notice? The good land is all beyond the Jordan. But people sometimes wind up getting what they think they want and then being sorry."

"True," Pepi said. "And there's something I want right now. I'm not sure whether I'll be sorry for it or not." He quickly delivered the runner's message and outlined his own plans.

"How I envy you," Moses said with a sigh. "I wish I could go, but I would only slow you down. How I had looked forward to riding along the river, able to look across and see the Promised Land with my own eyes!"

Pepi put a hand on the old man's shoulder. "It's cruel of me to mention it. But I have no idea whether Og has a detachment of troops stationed where the Jabbok flows into the Jordan, and there I'd be, trying to protect the spiritual leader of Israel. They'd take you and hold you for ransom. Then Joshua would have to give in."

"I'm afraid you don't know Joshua as well as you think you do," Moses said. "And if he faltered I would order him not to give in. The conquest of Canaan is too important to hinge on the fate of one old man."

Pepi smiled and gently squeezed the old man's shoulder. "How happy I am to know you," he said in a voice full of genuine affection "You've made an enormous difference in my life. Because of you, I know what a kind, loving, yet manly father is like. What am I? A bastard with a man like Apedemek for a father. Now I'll be able to teach my children what being a man means, when I finally get around to having a family."

Moses smiled. "We've been waiting for you to settle down," he said. "You know that when you do, you'll break the heart of every maiden in Israel."

Pepi smiled sheepishly. "Look what happened to Iri. At his age, with his disadvantages, yet the last time I saw him he was as deliriously happy as a child with a new toy."

Moses studied him. "You have my blessing. Go and investigate your mines. Most likely you will notice things that the rest of us would miss. Feast your eyes on the land beyond the river and tell me about it. You will be my eyes. Remember my pain at knowing I will never set foot on that land, and give me solace."

"I will. I'll do my best," Pepi said, as the men embraced.

As Pepi rode westward, he realized how thrilled Moses would have been with the trip. West of Heshbon the road ran directly to the Jordan, and from the ford one could almost see Jericho on the heights. And he could clearly see the city of Gilgal.

On both sides of the Jordan the land looked alike. To the north of the Salt Sea was the immense plain of the Jordan, with the dark green ribbon of the river jungle winding through its length, the purple mountains of Gilead to his left, and the furrowed gray and yellow ridges of the northern wilderness to his right.

The picture people had drawn for him of the River Jordan bore little resemblance to reality. Along the water's edge lay a semitropical jungle, so dense it hid the river. This swampland was home to lions, bears, and other large predators, as well as poisonous insects and reptiles.

The path that led down to the ford was overgrown. Pepi dismounted, hobbled his horse, and walked down to the river. It looked cold and yellow. He knew that the current was treacherous, and the bottom was dotted with patches of quicksand. The water was dank and foul with ooze and slime. The shores were mud banks littered by driftwood and uprooted trees.

He watched the curious, unpredictable zigzag pattern of the current, a current strong enough to drag a man into the middle of the fast-rushing channel. No wonder the Canaanites did not bother to post guards along the far shore or man fortresses in the valley near Gilgal.

Moses had expressed concern that when the tribes had been settled on the two banks of the river that threaded its way through the Land of Promise, the river itself might come between them, alienating one from another and making the land of Israel impossible to govern. Pepi realized that Moses's concern was valid; it was obvious that there was little communication between the Amorites of this side and their fiercer cousins within Canaan.

Somewhere on his journey he had left the land once ruled by Sihon and entered Bashan. There were no border guards, and the road bore no markers to distinguish one land from the other. Perhaps in the days before Sihon's death the border had shifted back and forth, as Sihon and Og contested ownership, although the land was hardly worth fighting over. The few springs said to flow from the rocks on the shores of the Jordan emerged on the far bank, and the Jordan lay too far down in the rift to make any form of irrigation workable on the Sihonite side of the valley.

Pepi recognized a rock formation that had been described to him: He was approaching Succoth. He was eager to inspect the mines. Word had it that they had not been worked for many years, since the coming of the Sea Peoples. The locals, displaced by the newcomers, had abandoned them and would not work except as slaves, but the Bashanites had not found it worth their while to enforce labor.

He rode on, and still there was no sign of a Bashanite military presence. At the top of a rise he stopped and looked out across the valley at Succoth. This was holy ground to the Israelites; their ancestor Jacob had received Yahweh's promise not far from here. And it was important to the Children of the Lion, who had worked ore from the Jabbok for many years.

Today it was in Bashanite hands. But who would control it a month from now?

IV

The token guard at Heshbon had offered resistance. Young and rash and rebellious, the small force had hurled stones down from the high walls of the city and, once the walls were scaled and the gate opened, had fought to the last man. Now Joshua's men, having disposed of the last of them, lined up the civilians in the public square and sent a messenger to ask him what to do with them.

Joshua heard the messenger out. "What do we usually do with the residue of a battle?" he asked. But as he looked out over the little crowd huddled miserably in the marketplace, he remembered the look in Pepi's eyes. Here were women with infants at their breasts, half-grown boys and girls, and the very old.

He let out an explosive breath. "Damn it. Turn them out. Turn them out into the countryside. Our people will occupy the city."

"You're not going to kill them?" Caleb asked.

"Kill them? No, no." He pounded his fist on the table. "No, wait. Leave them here. There aren't very many of them, are there? And with the young men dead, there won't be anyone to help with the harvest."

"You could make slaves of them," Caleb said. "Under the law, that's permissible. You'd have to offer them their freedom at the end of seven years, but at least you'd have the seven years of service out of them. That might pay us back for the losses we suffered in the field, few as they were."

"It's a possibility," Joshua said, biting at his lip. "But . . . no. Let them stay in the city. Leave our guards to watch them until the settlers arrive. Moses is relocating the tribe of Reuben in this country. And they can have it, as far as I'm concerned."

"You're just letting the prisoners go?"

"Yes," Joshua said impatiently. "How many times do I have to tell you something?"

"I'll give the order," Caleb said with a shrug. "But, are you sure this is what you want to do? Pepi has ridden to Succoth. He isn't here to nag you."

"Damn your eyes! I'm not doing this for Pepi. I'm doing it because I want to."

Caleb stepped back. "Whatever you say. Now, do we march on Bashan immediately?"

"Yes," Joshua said. "A piddling fight like this one isn't enough exercise for the day. Tell me: Have there been any new reports in from the north?"

Caleb nodded. "Only to confirm what we already know. They're probably lying in wait for us somewhere up beyond the Yarmuk."

"That's a long way for us to march into Bashan without encountering any opposition," Joshua said. "I doubt we'll have to wait until we reach the Yarmuk before we run into them. They'll hit us long before then. But as for whether they have anyone ready to hit us from the rear and encircle us, no. I've had riders covering all regions up to Mahanaim. There won't be any surprises until then. But they could hit us there. Incidentally, intelligence reports say they have the edge on us in numbers."

"Ah. And what kind of fighters are they?" Caleb asked.

"It's a wonder they didn't lay claim to the whole of Sihon's domain," Joshua answered. "They'd have made short work of him. The only explanation I have is that they didn't want the land."

"Or didn't want to waste men, guarding the captured territory instead of raiding the North. I understand they've even challenged some of the territories claimed formerly by Damascus."

"They're ambitious enough," Joshua agreed. "And Damascus would be a far greater prize than anything down south in this godforsaken pit."

"Godforsaken?" Caleb asked. "Is that the proper description for the Promised Land, where the tribe of Reuben will soon reign?"

"Reuben? No, these northern territories will go to Gad and Manasseh, if we can win them for them. And don't forget, the Promised Land lies across the river, not here. *That's* the real land of Jacob. Not this dried-out, inhospitable country." Joshua chuckled. "The Reubenite elders think they've scored a victory, landing the first territory conquered. They'll change their minds when they find out they've been cut off from the heart of Canaan by a virtually uncrossable river."

"Uncrossable? But I thought—"

"Oh, we'll cross it, Caleb. When the time comes, nothing in the world is going to keep this army and me from taking every last league of the land promised to Jacob. Have no fear of that. But Reuben? The elders? They'll be stuck over here. They've been a thorn in Moses's side for years. When we're in Canaan they won't be able to bother us every other day with complaints and grandiose claims."

"You said 'nothing' would keep you from taking Canaan. Does that include qualms over how you have to go about taking it?"

"Curse you, Caleb. I told you no. Can't you hear?"

"I thought . . . Of course, as long as Pepi continues to remain among us . . ."

"Well, keep those thoughts to yourself! Do you hear?"

In the hills above Heshbon, Pepi inspected the disused mines. At some time in the far past the area had been worked; there were signs that men had hacked into the soft, malachite-bearing sandstone. Pepi knew that others, standing by as the cutters dug into the hills, would smash the malachite pieces into smaller chunks for easier transporting, and a third group of laborers would haul the ore to a central location where it could be finely ground for smelting.

There were even signs of a primitive smelting furnace, one of a kind that had been old when Belsunu had worked at arms making in Canaan. This one had originated in Egypt and still used the foot-powered bellows that he had heard about from Iri. He even found ring-shaped pieces of slag abandoned by the smelters many decades before.

The hills were rich enough, he decided. Once the area had been pacified and Joshua's administrators established, he would set up an efficient operation, one that could provide for an army much larger than the present sleek, stripped-down one. Eventually a great fighting force could be assembled here, one that could not only take the land but keep it.

Finished with his inspection, he mounted and began to ride out of the little valley where the mines lay. Curious, he decided to look at the land on the far side of the river. He turned the horse and urged it up a goat path.

From the top the broad valley of the Jordan stretched all the way to the mountains. If Joshua were to ford the river near here—and the Jordan, just north of the place where the Wadi Jabbok joined it, did have a solid bottom—he would have clear sailing almost all the way to Jericho.

He was about to turn and trek down the mountain when he happened to look into a canyon parallel to the one in which the mines lay.

It was full of soldiers!

He blinked with disbelief, dismounted, hobbled his horse, and crept along the hilltop, crouching down, trying not to present a silhouette against the midday sky. Finally, he crawled to the edge and looked down.

He blinked again. *Why, this is an army the size of Sihon's whole force! And they're flying the banners of Bashan!*

Their plan was obvious. This force, and perhaps another, were positioned for a sneak attack on Joshua. If Joshua were to push farther into Bashan now, these men would be able to cut him off, severing his supply lines and encircling him.

I've got to do something and quickly! But what? If I take the normal route I'll pass the mouth of the canyon where the troops are hiding. They'll see me and give pursuit, and Joshua will walk into a trap.

He had to find a roundabout route. But how? Where?

He looked up the narrow center of the wadi. The terrain grew rougher as the level of the dry streambed rose. He could not go that way.

What about a trail across the ridge?

No. If the trail petered out he would lose valuable time. He had to go back along the route he had used before, take his chances riding through the farmland to the east, and hope that no farmer would see him and tip off the army.

He went back to his horse, undid the hobble, and led the animal down the hillside. At the bottom he mounted and headed back toward Succoth.

When he was out of earshot of any pickets he nudged the horse into a canter, then into a full gallop. He skirted Succoth proper, using the high road, and headed back to the fork that led eastward through the hills.

The road meandered, steering a course between one farm and the next. Pepi cursed at its slowness and finally decided to go as the crow flies, cutting across farmland.

A league from the road he came to a tidy, well-kept farm with spreading orchards and a beautifully tended, carefully watered garden surrounding a snug little house. He rode through the garden, threading his way among ornamental plantings.

But as he did he was greeted by a string of what could only be curses in some strange foreign tongue, and a rock whizzed past his head.

He looked around, startled. "What the—" he began just as another rock came hurtling past, missing his head by a handspan. He turned to face his attacker. He had never seen anything like her in his life.

She was almost as tall as he, long-legged and broad-shouldered, full-bosomed and with wide, womanly hips. Her face bore the golden tan of a light-skinned person living in southern country, and her hair was the color of gold.

"I can always go back," he said, ducking another rock. "I'm sorry about your garden. I meant no harm. I'll pay for the damage."

His apology brought on another long string of the unintelligible but unmistakable curses as she looked about for something else to throw. He stared openmouthed, too thunderstruck to defend himself. She was dressed much as a male worker might be while working the land: A tunic of leather covered her trim but formidable body to midthigh. She was quite simply the most beautiful thing he had ever seen.

He started to dismount, but this time what she threw at him was a rock the size of his fist. He ducked just in time, and the rock smashed against her house. "I'm going!" he cried. "Just let me get out of here!"

She paused, another rock clutched in her large but lovely hand. She looked him up and down, as if she'd never seen anyone his size before. Men like himself—dark-complected, bearing the heavy tan of the desert—tended to be smaller around here. "You are not from Bashan," she said in a heavily accented voice.

"No," he said. "I come from Nubia. But where do

you come from? I've never seen hair like that before. Golden hair and blue eyes. And you're almost as tall as I am. And . . . you're beautiful!"

"Bah!" she said. "Stay back! Get off my land! If you come one step closer I'll kill you!"

He held up both his hands to show they were empty. "I'm going. Just let me back out of here, and I'll never bother you again!"

He thought he had gotten through to her, but as he turned, out of the corner of his eye he caught the motion of her arm. He turned back to her and caught the stone in the middle of the forehead. There was a blinding pain and then darkness.

V

As soon as the stone left her hand she regretted it. Now she looked at him sprawled at her feet, his eyes closed, blood flowing from the gash on his forehead. "Tirzah, you fool!" she said to herself. "What have you done? You've killed him, you stupid woman!"

She knelt beside him, bent over very low, her face close to his. *Let him still be alive,* she prayed to the gods of her mother's family. *Don't let me be a murderer. Please.*

To her relief, he was still breathing, and she sat back on her heels. "Now what am I going to do?" she wondered aloud. "When he awakes he will be terribly angry. He may even try to harm me." She looked down at the sword at his belt and after a moment's hesitation reached down and removed it. *Perhaps if I hide it . . .*

But as she sat with the sword held across her thighs, she studied him for the first time. He had said he was not a Bashanite, and surely this was true. Bashanites were fair, perhaps not as fair as her mother's people had been, but certainly a lot fairer than these Canaanites they had come to settle among.

On the other hand, only Bashanites, of all the people one met hereabouts, ever grew to anything like her own size, much less the towering height of this dark man.

She looked at his fallen body. He was well muscled, and his arm, when she touched it, was firm and strong even in repose. She inspected the open, relaxed hands and saw with approval the heavy calluses of a working man. Looking closer, she saw the tiny scars from a hundred forge fires and knew him for a smith.

The face she could not read at all: It showed traces of parts of the world about which she knew nothing. But the features were handsome and rugged while retaining a certain delicacy and vulnerability. He had not seemed a violent man when he had spoken. Perhaps when he awoke he would spare her and give her no more than a beating for having wounded him.

The blood was beginning to clot on his forehead; he was going to have a terrible headache. She went back to the house to dip a cloth in a bucket of water. When she returned his eyelids were fluttering.

She bent over him and began to bathe his forehead gently and wipe the dust from his face.

Suddenly he opened his eyes and looked at her.

She shrank back with a little cry. "Please! Don't hurt me! I didn't mean it!"

He tried to sit up and discovered his pain. "What happened?" he asked, letting his head sink back.

But before she could speak he blinked and seemed to

remember. "You . . . you threw something at me, didn't you?"

She tried to move back, but his hand gripped hers. The grip was a smith's, powerful and impossible to break. "Please!" she said.

To her surprise he let go of her hand. "I mean you no harm," he said. "I just didn't want you to run away."

"I . . . hurt you. I didn't mean to. Please forgive me." He stared at her face, but she could not read the emotion in his dark eyes. "Please," she said again, "I was only going to wash your wound. I'm afraid I hit you very hard. I wanted to call the stone back."

"I'm sure you did," he said. "I was trespassing. I shouldn't have been." He winced as the pain shot through him. "I've got to get out of here."

She put a hand on his arm. "You can't travel now. You were badly hurt. You could collapse a league down the road."

He patted her hand, and she withdrew it. "Thank you for your concern, but I was on my way to . . . to do something very important. How long have I been unconscious?"

"Not long," she said. "Please, stay. I'm sorry. But you frightened me, coming out of nowhere. The Bashanites did that once. And they killed my husband. I thought they were coming back to—"

"Then you're not a Bashanite? But of course you couldn't be, with that hair and that coloring. What's your name?"

"Tirzah," she said. Seeing the look of puzzlement on his face, she said, "I know, it is a Canaanite name. My father was a Canaanite, and my mother's people came here with the Sea Peoples, from a land far, far beyond Cimmeria, a cold land where everyone has light skin as I do."

He smiled and winced again as he moved his head. "I was going to ask if everyone there was as beautiful as you, but of course that couldn't be true." For a moment she had the feeling he might stay. A longing lit his eyes. But then he pulled away. "How I would like to stay and talk. But some friends of mine are in terrible danger, and if I don't get to them in time to warn them . . ."

"I understand," she said. She stood up and held her hand down to him. He took it, and she pulled him to his feet. She felt a thrill in looking up into his eyes. She had towered over even her well-built Canaanite husband. "You're sure you couldn't wait? I could get you something to eat."

"No, thank you. If I could just have water for myself and my horse . . ."

Pepi stared after her with wonderment as she disappeared into the house. He had never dreamed that such a creature existed and yet here she was: tall and powerful, yet graceful and utterly feminine. And she'd said her husband was dead.

Whoa, he thought. *Don't get ahead of yourself. The first thing you've got to do is get to Joshua and warn him before the enemy attacks. Then, perhaps after that's done with . . .*

But that last look had fixed her in his mind forever. She was the most lovely woman he had ever seen—perfectly proportioned in every detail, strong and athletic and light on her feet. She moved like some great cat: a leopard or cheetah, perhaps, and with the same harmonious feline rhythm.

Gods! he thought. *I'd better stop thinking like this, or I'll never be able to tear myself away from here.*

He forced himself to remember that he had to warn Joshua and that unless he could be warned in time, the army of Israel could be wiped out entirely.

He wondered how long he had been unconscious. He had no idea what she considered "not long." A few minutes? An hour?

Now temptation entered his mind and sowed its evil seeds: *What if you just stayed here? What if you got to know this beautiful young widow? What if you took up her invitation to eat with her? Who would be the wiser, after all? Couldn't Joshua take care of himself?*

After all, look at how Joshua—and some of the others, emboldened by Joshua's contempt—had been treating him lately. He had been offered nothing but disrespect by the younger men who had joined the army recently and had not been around for his twenty years of faithful service to the army of Israel. What did they know of him? To their eyes he was only an able-bodied man who would not fight.

But his service had been honorable. There was no doubt about that among the older soldiers, the ones who had been retired by Joshua. They had been there when Iri and he had armed the penniless Israelites, using their own credit to buy ore and making every sword needed for the first battles in the desert. He had served his entire apprenticeship under fire, with enemies attacking from all sides.

His backside still bore scars from working the bellows as Iri pounded the glowing bronze, and cinders and hot coals popped right and left, landing on his unprotected ten-year-old body. He had howled, but he had held his ground, and the work had gone on. Iri had taught him his trade under fire and on the run as the Israelites threaded their way in one valley and out the other, staying a step ahead of Amasis's marauding Egyptian patrols, and he had continued to practice it as the arrows fell out of the sky around him.

And this was the thanks he got from all those years of selfless service. And for no pay at all when a Child of the Lion, particularly one trained at the sure hand of Iri of Thebes, could have earned a staggering sum in the outside world.

And what kind of life would he have led? Why, he would have been happily married by now, with tall, handsome young sons and daughters, children to gladden his heart as he grew older. He would have been a rich man who lived in a fine house and had dozens of servants scurrying about doing his bidding, and an elegant wife to love him and care for him.

He sighed as he saw Tirzah returning. Who would ever have imagined that a woman could be that large and yet so perfect? His heart stirred at the creamy perfection of her skin, sunburned as it was from the unrelenting Canaanite sun, and the deep blue of her eyes, and the straight and proud nose. No matter how long he lived he would never meet another beauty like Tirzah.

He accepted a cup from her and drank the cool spring water. Then he took the bucket and poured it into a trough for his horse to drink. "Thank you." He looked her in the eyes and smiled. "My name is Pepi of Kerma. I come from about as far away from here as you do, only in the opposite direction. Kerma is in Nubia, a land many days' journey up the great River Nile."

She looked at him with puzzlement. "Pardon me," she said with that lovely little accent. "These place names mean nothing to me. Where is the Nile?"

He laughed, and she blushed, closing up like a night-blooming flower. "I wasn't making fun of you," he said. "You don't have to know where the Nile is. I'll tell you all about it sometime. But now I must go save my friends. Honor demands it."

"Yes," she said. "Honor I understand. If you're sure it's safe, with your wound . . ."

"It's all right," he said. "Do you think I might come back this way and see you?"

"Of course," she said with a small smile, as if he'd asked a silly question. "I'll be here."

He squeezed her hands for a moment, then released them with a grateful smile and escaped while he still could.

But many leagues along the road north he found he still could not get the sight of her out of his mind.

"Tirzah," he whispered to himself.

VI

Slowly, Og of Bashan began to spring the trap. From the west, where the right-hand units now rode against the Israelites, and from the east, where another large force had lain in wait behind the hills beyond Gerasa, the two pincers began to close. To the north the main force under Og marched from their main base near Edrei toward a head-on collision with Joshua's army.

Og, at the head of his column, called back to demand a stepped-up pace. "Move, you laggards! Do you want me to have to fight these foreign swine all by myself?"

It had been a carefully planned campaign, and he had put it together with a chariot maker's precision. First he had gotten to Joshua's spies in the north and bought them out. That had been expensive but worthwhile. From the moment of Joshua's entry into Edom, he had been receiving false information from his forward scouts.

Now it would pay off handsomely. When the word got around that his army had outsmarted, outcampaigned, and outfought the army that had slaughtered the Sihonites, Og's own prestige would be increased a hundredfold.

For now, though, the objective was to crush the would-be usurpers from the south, who had made their ridiculous claim to the land his Sea Peoples had conquered a generation before. And to this end he had devoted the most feverish and ingenious planning. Joshua would fall victim to his onslaught.

Og smiled, then turned to bellow impatiently at his troops: "Damn you! Move. Where do you think you're going? To a funeral?"

A league from Tirzah's farm, Pepi came across the first sign that the army he had spied upon in the hills above Succoth was already on the march and ahead of him. Dirt of the high road had been stirred up by the soldiers' hasty passage; dung from their horses lay on the road; broken belts and harnesses and abandoned sandals were tossed by the roadside.

Impatiently, he nudged his horse forward, but when he caught something out of the corner of his eye, he slowed his horse for a better look. On the nearby hilltop was the silhouette of a mounted man, seated upon a gray Moabite horse and looking down to the east. Pepi squinted, and saw to his amazement that the figure wore the robes of an Israelite soldier.

Suspicion flashed through his mind, and he suddenly turned his horse toward the hill and set off at a gallop.

The sound of his hoofbeats startled the figure on the hill, and he turned and began to ride away, but the track up which Pepi was riding was narrow, and the man was forced to await Pepi's arrival.

"Did you see them, sir?" he demanded.

"The Bashanite soldiers?" Pepi asked. "I did." He looked down at the scene below, where the Bashanites moved slowly and inexorably toward the ridge beyond. "I gather Joshua's army is on the far side of the ridge."

"Yes, sir. He'll be just opposite that hill over there, sir, if I've got the thing right."

Pepi scowled and without warning grabbed the Israelite's robe with one powerful hand. "And you *have* got the thing right, haven't you, you traitorous son of a bitch? Answer me, damn you!"

"Sir, I must protest that I haven't the smallest idea what you—"

"Don't give me that, or so help me, I'll cut your head off right here and now. You sold us out, didn't you? You were the scout up here, and you sent back false information from Bashan. You led Joshua into this trap."

"Sir, I had nothing to do with—"

Pepi shook the man's body. "Stop that!" he screamed. "If you confess I may give you a chance to redeem yourself by dying in battle. But if you persist in these damned lies, so help me, I'll kill you right here and now. I'll cut your guts out and leave you for the birds. May that God of yours strike me dead on the spot if I don't."

The spy gulped and tried to avoid Pepi's eyes but found he could not. "Sir . . . please."

"You conveniently ignored this whole army over here when Joshua told you to let him know where the Bashanites were. There's probably another army just like it to the east, ready to fall on Joshua as he passes through the valley. Right? Answer me, curse you!"

Once more the spy tried to dissemble, but Pepi's sword was under his chin, pricking the skin. "Pray to Yahweh, my friend. Pray to Him that your terrible sin is forgiven. Because you're about to meet Him face to face and answer for what you've done."

"Sir, let me explain. Please!"

"Do!" Pepi said without letting up on the pressure of the blade against his neck.

"Sir, Og told me that my people were all going to die anyway. He said that when his men won, I'd be the only one of us left alive. He said I'd have a place in the new kingdom and would be a member of the court when he conquered Damascus and Ebla."

"And for these false promises you'd sell out your friends, your neighbors, your kin? I ought to kill you right here and now, you slimy, cowardly . . ."

Pepi stopped. "But while we talk the army is advancing on Joshua! It's too late to warn anyone, but if we were to charge their column from the rear, creating a diversion, we might buy Joshua time to regroup." His eyes narrowed. "There is another column coming up from the other side, right?"

The spy nodded. "Then Og will hit Joshua from the front?" Again the spy nodded. "You've bought yourself an hour of life," Pepi said. "They're going over the ridge now, and you and I are going to come up behind them and attack them from the rear." As Pepi spoke, the point of his sword dug into the spy's neck. "And if you think you're going to use this opportunity to get away . . ." He smiled, released the man's robe, and reached behind him for his long Nubian bow and the quiver of arrows. "You've seen me shoot in the competitions," he said. "You know I can hit a bird on the wing. If I see the smallest move toward defection, you'll die as quickly as if you'd stuck your head in a lion's mouth, and your name will be blackened forever. Do you understand me?"

"Yes, sir."

"But if you join me and fight, perhaps when the battle's over and you lie dead, I won't tell anyone what you did. You'll get a decent burial and spare your family the embarrassment of having spawned a traitor as black as any that ever walked on this earth."

The spy gulped in fear. "Sir . . . yes. I'll do it. And I'll fight hard. Maybe we can do something after all."

"You'd better. And if I catch you slacking off I'll kill you on the spot, slowly, and I'll see that your body is desecrated and your reputation ruined."

"Sir, trust me. I want to repent for my sin."

"Spare me the hypocrisy. Lead the way. And remember, I'll have an arrow trained on your back."

In the valley the unit from the east had already attacked when the western force appeared over the top of the hill. Joshua's men barely had time to form a ragged line and break out the bows before the second unit swarmed across the ridge and down the hill.

"Hollow circle!" Joshua cried. "On the double!"

The Israelites maneuvered into position. The archers stood at the ready, awaiting the call to fire. "Wait until they're within range," Joshua ordered. "Don't waste arrows!"

To the east the Bashanites came within range. The Israelite archers let fly a volley of arrows. A dozen enemy soldiers fell, but a hundred more pressed on. They attacked Joshua's front line and the fighting began. To the west the Bashanite army came within range, and the Israelite bowmen turned to fire off a volley of shafts at them.

The eastern troops took advantage of the opportunity and broke through the line. Sword in hand, Joshua rushed them, hewing the limbs off three men and running another man through. Grasping his bronze sword in both hands, he swung right and left, cut one throat and almost beheaded another Bashanite.

But as he cut through the enemy army, Joshua heard the cry of one of his men: "Look at the highway! Here comes the main force."

VII

With a great echoing battle cry the right wing of the Bashanite force fell on the Israelites. As they did, Og's chariots separated themselves from the main force and barreled down the King's Highway.

Under attack from two sides, Joshua's men, formed in a hollow circle, engaged their attackers on the left flank and managed to drive them back. But on the western side, the Bashanites broke through almost immediately. Joshua and Caleb, rallying their men, went on the offensive, hacking to bits the few soldiers who had penetrated the Israelite lines.

As they closed the gaps in the line, Joshua once more looked down the road at the chariots careening toward him. For the first time he was worried. At the head of the mounted attack was a giant who could be none other than Og.

Joshua cursed under his breath, following it up immediately with a hurried prayer to Yahweh, asking him to deliver His people. But even as he prayed, the Israelite line was once more breached. Fighting like two men, Joshua parried a lance thrust from a towering Bashanite and ran the man through, pulling his sword free in time to beat off a furious attack by a hulking swordsman.

Glancing down the road he saw that the chariots were almost upon him. To the right and left, his soldiers were fighting for their lives. How could they stop the horsemen?

But as the chariots closed in, Joshua saw one of the charioteers, a man next in line to the giant Og, suddenly clutch his neck, drop the reins, and fall heavily to the ground, an arrow sticking out of his throat. The chariot next in line ran right over the body, and the driverless chariot crashed into Og's! The axle tore into the spokes of Og's right wheel, and the wheel shattered and spun off. Og flew through the air, landed on the ground, and rolled.

Out of the corner of his eye, Joshua saw a sword poised above him. He wheeled around and stabbed the man in the face, grabbing the sword out of his dying hand. A weapon in each hand, he lit into two Bashanites. With his left hand he parried a thrust, and then delivered a crushing blow to one man's head with the pommel of his sword; with his right hand he battered back a vicious attack and skewered his opponent through the guts.

A hasty look at the chariots showed that more than half were driverless. And as he watched, two more men fell from their chariots. One lurched forward, an arrow through his kidney, and fell under his own wheels.

Looking westward, Joshua was stunned to see Pepi and one of his own men, seated on horseback, calmly firing into the Bashanite ranks.

A wolfish smile came over Joshua's face. Looking back he saw that his men had closed the breach in his lines and were counterattacking with power and ferocity. He turned to the north, dashed through his own lines, and made for the fallen charioteers. Og, tall and powerful-looking but groggy, was clambering back onto the high perch of a driverless chariot.

"Og!" Joshua called in a ringing voice. "Og of Bashan! Come back and fight. I am Joshua, son of Nun, leader of the army of Israel. Step down from the chariot and meet me man to man."

Og glared down at him and whipped the horses forward, straight at Joshua.

Joshua, laughing aloud, stepped back and, as the chariot went by, hacked at the horse's legs. The animal staggered and fell. The chariot tipped, but just as it rolled over, Og jumped clear. Sword in hand, he snarled at Joshua.

Before either man could move, an arrow swished past Og's face, missing him by no more than a handspan.

Joshua grinned, let out a bellow of scornful laughter, and charged.

The big man recovered immediately and met his enemy's attack head-on. Joshua found Og was as strong as he looked and amazingly quick. He parried Joshua's first lunge and caught the Israelite's arm with a glancing blow that drew blood. Joshua gave ground—one step only—and counterattacked with a series of feints and stabs that came within a hairbreadth of killing Og. Only with great difficulty did Og parry these lunges, giving up ground one grudging step at a time.

At that moment the Bashanite archers began to return the arrows of Pepi and the Israelite. Arrows fell around Og and Joshua. Joshua ducked, narrowly missing being hit. And Og, eyes narrowed, his face full of rage, stalked him.

Far behind Og, the rest of his army marched closer.

Watching them, Joshua was caught off guard, and Og suddenly lumbered forward, slashing his left forearm.

Ineffectually Joshua parried, spun away, gave ground. Og, a hate-filled sneer on his face, pressed him hard, holding his sword in both hands and hacking away at Joshua's weapon as he attempted to parry. Joshua gave ground, trying to get a second wind, but feeling himself steadily losing strength.

Suddenly Og staggered as if struck from the rear. From his chest protruded the bloody tip of an Israelite arrow—with one of the distinctive arrowheads only Pepi could fashion. The giant's eyes glazed over. He fell to his knees and slowly pitched forward.

Then Joshua saw Pepi standing ten paces behind the fallen man, his bow still in his hand. Blood gushed from a gash on his forehead. As Joshua watched, Pepi slowly spun around and dropped to the ground.

Before Joshua could rush to Pepi's side a new contingent of Bashanites swarmed toward him, hacking and stabbing. The thought of his fallen friend—whom he had abused and mistreated and lied to in the service of this war, who had saved his life and perhaps the battle—filled his heart with hot rage and gave him new strength. His Bashanite opponents suddenly found themselves fighting a man who seemed to be three men or perhaps even more, a man whom no sword's point could pierce, a man whose arm never tired, a man who fought like an angry god instead of a man.

For many months afterward deeds done by Joshua that day would be talked about among the Israelites. There would be other heroes too, high and low in rank, experienced warriors and novices, the strong and the weak. But in the long nights of tale telling by the campfire it would be Joshua that men remembered. He had fought like a man possessed, like a man who did not know fatigue nor the meaning of fear.

When at last the prisoners were disarmed and herded into a group, Joshua allowed himself to trudge, weary at last, to where Pepi had fallen. Suddenly the weight of the ages lay on his broad shoulders as he knelt beside the body of his friend. "Pepi, I knew you'd come around," he said to the inert body. "I knew you wouldn't desert us when the time came, that all that talk against the war was meaningless. You were a fighter, the best I ever saw. And look what you've done, you reluctant warrior, you won the battle for us. You saved my life and those of a hundred other men at least, you and that other fellow with you."

He let out a deep breath and looked around. The "other fellow" lay nearby, his quiver empty, his throat cut. He had fought valiantly to the end. *He's a hero,* Joshua thought. *They're both heroes. But recognition comes too late to do them any good.*

Now, through his overwhelming fatigue, the rage against the people who had done this thing, who had killed Pepi and ambushed his army, came back. He got to his feet and looked around at the bodies covering the ground, some Bashanite, some Israelite.

The price was too high. He threw back his head and bellowed, "Caleb, Caleb, come here!"

Caleb walked tiredly toward him, wiping the sweat from his brow. He was bleeding from half a dozen small wounds. "That's Pepi, isn't it?" Caleb said. "Too bad. He did himself proud today. We'll miss him."

"Somebody is going to pay for this," Joshua said with clenched teeth. "A *lot* of people are going to pay for this."

"Speak and I obey. What sort of price did you have in

218

mind? Suppose we put those prisoners to the sword for starters?"

Joshua nodded assent. "But it isn't enough. The whole damned nation of Bashan is going to pay. One life for another, Pepi's for Og's, isn't nearly enough. Fifty lives for each of our men lost today isn't enough. I want everyone in this accursed nation of foreign scum to pay."

Caleb nodded wearily. "But in what coin?"

"Their land. Their possessions. Their freedom. From this moment everything in Bashan belongs to Israel. Including every man, woman, and child in the land, and every pet and every beast of burden and every head of livestock. Every house and every barn and every square cubit of land. I want the inhabitants of Bashan to know once and forever what usurpation feels like from the other side. They stole the land and everything on it from Sihon. Now we steal it from them and make slaves of them. Send a messenger back to Moses to bring the tribes in here— Gad *and* Manasseh. I'm going to divide it between them."

Caleb nodded and turned to leave when he happened to glance down at Pepi. He stopped and looked more closely. "Joshua, he's alive. I saw his eyelids flutter."

Joshua dropped to his knees and bent over Pepi's face, where he felt the faint stirring of his breath. "Thanks be to Yahweh! Quick, send for the physicians. I want him cared for day and night, treated like the hero he is. Quickly, why are you standing there?"

CHAPTER TEN

On Board the *Hephaistos*

I

The men of the *Hephaistos* had been as good as their word. They not only had won a fortune on the outcome of the fight but had won virtually everything the crewmen of the *Gades* owned. Thus, before the end of Theon's first day on deck, they were able to bring to him all of the equipment the *Gades* had assembled to build a forge for him. With a shrug he had thrown off his chlamys and gone to work to build himself a forge that would do for tinkerwork, if not for serious arms making.

The crew had work for him almost immediately. The *Hephaistos* had captured a shipment of arms a month before, and some weapons were in need of fixing; Theon, glad for the chance to relieve his boredom, went to work, whistling and singing songs he had learned in his childhood from Seth and Demetrios.

But after a time the work got to be vexing, restricted as he was by the short chain around his neck. Finally, making no attempt to hide what he was doing, he forged new links and simply lengthened the chain himself. At day's end the Minotaur strode past him, looked down at the newly forged chain, and smiled.

As he worked, Theon was conscious of the power of the ship under his feet. He could perceive it as the ship, propelled by two banks of oars, surged forward, and he could see the waves rushing by and feel the spray as the ship mounted a wave and came crashing down on the far side.

This vessel was a new and important invention. If someone were to capture the *Hephaistos*—or merely smuggle out a set of plans—this new design could revolutionize life upon the Great Sea. A new fleet of such ships could change the balance of power among the seafaring nations for centuries to come.

Was this why the Minotaur took such pains to hide his great ship? If one of the nations whose merchant navies had been so victimized by pirate vessels like the *Hephaistos* were to produce a fleet of biremes, pirate ships would be put out of business within a year, and the Minotaur would be brought to port in chains for a public execution.

There was a certain logic in almost everything the Minotaur did, although the pattern was not always immediately evident. If the *Hephaistos* was seen clearly by the crew of the victim ship, so that they could, if freed, report on her in the seaports around the Great Sea, they were taken prisoner and exchanged with other pirate ships as oarsmen. The biggest and strongest among them always wound up manning an oar aboard the *Hephaistos* because the oars of the bireme were longer and heavier than those of a normal galley. Keeping to the stroke required enormous stamina and power that few ordinary oarsmen could command.

Only when they had not clearly seen the *Hephaistos* were crewmen of captured ships set adrift and allowed to find their way to shore. There, their vague, amazing stories of the magical speed of the vessel that had overtaken them would spread fear and apprehension among sailors and shipowners.

Every night before going to sleep in the sheepskin on the deck, Theon looked up at the stars, trying to compute his position, using the reckoning system taught him by his father, Seth. At times like these, as at times during his workday, he was aware that someone was watching him. But when he looked around he could see no one.

Still he remained alert to any information he could pick up. One day the Minotaur met with his first mate, Prodicus, within earshot of Theon as he was repairing the handle of a sword.

He heard Prodicus say, "The rendezvous is coming up shortly. I thought we might confer about it."

"There are ships where a certain rebelliousness has taken hold," the Minotaur said. "I wouldn't be surprised to see some trying to break away from our fleet if I don't take drastic action."

"A ship can't be run by taking votes, and I was going to ask you to forsake your customary leniency in one or two of these cases. You know which ships I have in mind."

"I do, and we are of one mind in this. Perhaps the fleet has seen a bit too much of this fabled leniency of mine"—there was a sharply ironic tone to the Minotaur's voice—"and could stand to see my other, more severe side. Thus we kill two birds with one stone."

"Fine. I'll see you're backed up. Now the second order of business is the plan for the big raid. We'll discuss it on the second day of the rendezvous. I've asked a number of our captains to report on Demetrios's shipping patterns."

At the mention of Demetrios, Theon pricked up his ears. So this was what they had in mind! He listened as the two men discussed a planned raid on one of the Great Sea ports—try as he might, he could not make out the location—when the biggest vessels of Demetrios's fleet would be in port. If this raid could be managed successfully, it would seriously damage Demetrios's enterprise.

Theon leaned forward, trying to hear more as the two men, their backs to him, spoke; but the *keleustes* chose that moment to increase speed, and between his chanting, the *trieraules's* flute playing, and the toneless, off-pitch singing of the rowers, he could hear no more.

From time to time the men of the crew brought tinkerage work to him: broken tools, broken buckles, bent cleats. But one day, as the rowers took a break and the *Hephaistos* drifted with the tide, the *trieraules* came to him.

"Tinker," he said, "it's my flute. You may have noticed the tone was gone, and there's a tendency to shriek." He looked down at the wooden instrument in his hand. "Do you think you can fix it?"

Theon took the instrument from the man and looked it over. "Look," he said. "The fipple's loose. No wonder you've been having trouble." He took up his hammer and tapped it gently into place. "That ought to do it."

He set the flute to his lips and struck up a tune, jolly and spirited: a quick dance in triple time that a sailor from Sicilia had taught him. His fingers flew on the stops; his head moved rhythmically in time with the cheerful dance. As he played, the Minotaur, startled, turned and looked at him. Men atop the yard looked down, grinning, and on deck two sailors had linked arms and were dancing in time to the music. Abruptly he brought the song to an end. "There," he said. "Sounds all right to me. If it happens again just—"

But the *trieraules* stood dumbfounded. "Gods!" he said. "Even the man that taught me the flute couldn't equal your skill."

Theon shrugged. "The knack for music runs in my family. My father used to sing to me when I was a child. Did you hear the 'Song of the Cranes,' from the Valley of Two Rivers? But it really ought to have a kithara accompanying it."

The Minotaur's voice was not loud, but it carried and had a ring of authority. "Nuhara!" he said. "Bring the lyre!"

Almost immediately the door to the Minotaur's cabin opened, and the girl Theon had seen before emerged carrying a battered kithara. Looking shyly into Theon's eyes, she handed him the instrument in her tiny hands and withdrew to the cabin.

Theon tuned the kithara. "I'll have to teach you the flute's tune first. Do you pick up tunes quickly?" he asked the *trieraules*.

The man nodded eagerly, and Theon put the flute to his lips and played the same tune through twice, then he handed the flute to the other man. The tune came forth, haltingly at first, then with more confidence. As he played, Theon added chords on the kithara. Smiling, he looked around. More than one head was nodding in time with the tune, and—wonder of wonders—the Minotaur had begun a half-comic, half-serious little dance.

He speeded up the pace, and as he did, the Minotaur's heavy body—he was surprisingly light on his feet for such a massive man—moved into the next part of the dance with practiced ease. The Minotaur was like a man transported. He knew all the steps and moved from one phase of the dance to the next with perfect ease. From the half-open door of the cabin, Theon could hear finger cymbals clanging, and he saw Nuhara come out on the deck and start dancing. He half turned to look at her. She twirled and pirouetted on little bare feet, her bangles jingling. How he hated to bring the song to an end.

The crew applauded, and Theon made a mock bow and handed the kithara back to the girl. To his disappointment she immediately disappeared into the cabin.

Watching Theon, the *trieraules* leaned close and whispered, "Don't let the Bull notice you paying too much attention to her. She's his, not to be touched, or lusted after."

Theon nodded and looked across the broad deck to where the Minotaur stood, arms crossed over his huge chest, staring at him. His expression was unreadable, and his dark eyes conveyed no more emotion than the eyes of a basilisk, but he held the look for a long time before turning away.

II

From that day on any barriers between Theon and the men of the *Hephaistos* came down. No one hesitated to drop by and bring Theon work or, once his vast fund of general knowledge was recognized and appreciated, ask him questions. Once a day, the *trieraules*, Tromes, came for a lesson in flute playing.

Theon kept expecting to see Nuhara, but on orders

from the Bull, she kept to the cabin during the day. Theon understood why: It could be disruptive to have a young and nubile girl around on a galley like the *Hephaistos*.

One of the enigmas about the Bull was that he had seemed to know the song Theon played on the kithara. The song was an ancient one, written centuries before by Shulgi of Ur, and Theon had learned it from Seth, who told him that most of Shulgi's songs had passed forever from common knowledge. They survived, if at all, only in families like his own with a strong sense of history and continuity.

Who, then, was the Bull? No one seemed to know. Rumors said that he was a bastard son of the last emperor of Crete, but Theon dismissed this as speculation fed by the old folktales of Knossos, which had Minos fathering a son with the head of a bull and the body of a man and hiding him within the fabled Labyrinth of Crete.

There was something regal about the pirate chief, however, and the more Theon watched him, the more impressive the man seemed. He had the rare knack of enforcing obedience by the power of his presence. The one time Theon saw an ordinary seaman challenge the Minotaur his punishment was handled with utmost fairness. The Bull himself attended to the whipping with a detached authority and no pleasure.

Nor did these rare qualities mark the limits of the Minotaur's talents. Theon eagerly anticipated seeing him in action at the rendezvous. Would some other, barbaric side of his character appear when dealing with men of savage and violent ways?

One day, after giving Tromes his flute lesson, Theon asked the *trieraules* if he had an extra flute. "The old songs seem to come back to me when I have my fingers on an instrument, but not before."

Tromes brightened. "Wait a moment," he said, and went away, returning with a serviceable-looking instrument carved from plain wood. "Although this doesn't look like much, it's well made. But I'm glad you have another trade; otherwise you'd have had my job by now."

"Don't worry, I'd make a poor hortator," Theon said.

"I won't. Arms makers are harder to come by than flute players. They're not likely to take you off a job like that to replace the likes of me. And as you say, I'm used to it. I can keep it up all day long without tiring." He smiled, and got up. "See if you can remember some fast songs that will make the rowers respond when we really need to move."

The day before the scheduled rendezvous, problems arose. Several seafaring nations had launched small, fast fleets of armed galleys aimed at counteracting the pirate threat. In the Aegean, off Melos, two of these—sleek Theban vessels armed with huge metal battering rams—intercepted the *Hephaistos* just as she was closing in on a tubby trader from Corinth and managed to bottle her up in a narrow bay.

One of the galleys blocked the *Hephaistos*'s exit to the sea; the other came toward her at full speed, broadside. As the Theban ship bore down on the *Hephaistos* the Minotaur watched. Realizing what was happening he bellowed, "Portside row oarsmen! Up oars!" The rowers obeyed with disciplined precision as their chains were unlocked and drawn free by a crewman. "Now, up and out."

The speeding galley came closer; its bow was pointed directly at the Bull. He stood his ground. "Brace yourselves!" he ordered. The galley rammed the *Hephaistos* broadside.

Theon, knocked to the deck, rolled until he hit the cabin. The timbers of the *Hephaistos* shook but held; however, the collision opened a gash in her hull.

"She's breached!" someone yelled.

The Minotaur, a sword in his hand, cried out, "All hands on deck. Prepare to repel boarders."

The second galley now came about and swung around, hemming them in from the starboard side. Sailors tossed grappling hooks over the side, and the enemy swarmed aboard the *Hephaistos*.

But then the Minotaur's force struck back. From atop the yard two bowmen let fly burning arrows aimed at the enemy sails. The arrows struck home. The furled sails soon caught fire and blazed in the light breezes.

As the first of the enemy clambered over the side, the Minotaur himself met them, killing one man instantly with a powerful thrust of his dagger. As the second man came at him, he stabbed him in the eye and dropped him into the sea.

Within seconds the deck of the bireme seethed with invaders. Thanking the gods that he had lengthened his chain, Theon kicked one boarder back into the sea with his bare foot. He reached down for his smith's hammer—it was secured to the deck by a chain as long as his own— and smashed the face of another invader. As the man fell, Theon grabbed the sword out of his hand.

The bloody fighting continued without letup. Theon, attacked from the side, gave ground to find himself pulled up short by his chain. He parried a hacking blow before shoving his attacker back by sheer brute strength. Just then a new attacker came at him from behind. Theon dispatched him with his hammer, hurling it at him so that the chain wrapped around the man's neck, strangling him.

The first attacker regained his strength and came at him again. Theon caught the blade of his knife with a twisting motion of his sword and disarmed him. He watched as the knife flipped high into the air, over the rail and into the sea.

Out of the corner of his eye Theon saw two men opening the door of the cabin. There was a shrill scream from within.

Theon charged the cabin, only to be pulled up short by the chain around his neck. He stumbled and fell. In the blink of an eye the partner of the man in the cabin rushed at him.

With his sword Theon hacked at his attacker's legs. The man let out a scream of pain and staggered backward. As he did Theon lunged.

Once more the chain pulled him up short, but his sword reached and penetrated the man in the chest. As he fell, Theon turned in time to see the other man come out of the cabin, holding Nuhara. His big arm pinned her arms to her naked body as she kicked and screamed and tried to bite her captor.

Giving a snarl, Theon charged.

To save his life the man had to release Nuhara, who dived to the deck and rolled out of Theon's way.

Theon ripped the chlamys off his shoulders to free his arms and, naked, bore in, hammering his enemy with strokes of incredible power. He seemed to feel a new and unfamiliar power flowing into his arms as he attacked, driving the stranger back to the rail and beating the sword out of his hands before feinting one way and then hacking the other. His sword cut clean through the enemy's neck; the severed head went flying through the air to land on the deck.

Theon turned to see Nuhara as naked as he himself,

staring at him. Her eyes were large and round with fear and disbelief.

"Get inside, woman. Bar the door and don't open it until I tell you to!"

Without question she obeyed, and Theon turned back to the fight. Amidships the Minotaur, one huge hand busy throttling an enemy attacker, stared at the armorer for a moment.

Then the fight continued. Everyone understood that it was to be to the death. The attackers knew too much and could not be allowed to live. Theon, held to the deck by his chain, watched as the men of the *Hephaistos* finished off both of the enemy crews one by one.

When it was all done, they rowed away and let the two burning galleys sink. Then, one by one, they tossed the corpses of the attackers to the sharks. Only when the decks were at last clean did the Minotaur once again turn to Theon with his dark, unscrutable eyes. Replacing the bloody sword in its scabbard, he walked slowly toward him.

As the Minotaur reached his huge hands out toward Theon's neck, the young man braced himself, realizing their enormous, inhuman strength.

Then, in one single, powerful movement, the Minotaur ripped the slave collar apart.

"From now on you work free of chains," he said in his strange, toneless voice. "And you fight free of them, too."

III

Free of his chain, Theon moved around the ship to inspect the damage. The timbers had buckled just above the waterline, and while the *Hephaistos* was safe in calmer waters, the moment even a slight squall struck her or the ship reached her full speed, the rowers in the lower seats would be awash.

He climbed down to examine the damage from inside; then he lowered himself to the waterline to examine the exterior damage. Prodicus, who had gradually come to realize and appreciate Theon's knowledge of ships, leaned over the edge and called down to him: "How bad is it?"

Hand over hand Theon hauled himself back up the rope. "It's a good thing the rendezvous is set for tomorrow," he said. "But I hope the site isn't far away."

He pulled himself up on deck to find Prodicus staring at him, sharp-eyed. "Why do you want to know?" Prodicus asked.

"Well," Theon said, dusting his hands off, "if you've any travel on the open sea I hope it isn't far. The first sign of heavy seas, and I doubt she'll hold. The shorter the journey the better. What she needs is to be careened and repaired."

Prodicus thought the matter over before replying cautiously. "It isn't far. We'll dock this evening around sundown."

"That's at normal speed or less?"

"Yes."

"All right. But keep the speed down and try to avoid any sudden maneuvers. The ship's repairable—it won't even take long, once she's lying on her side on the beach—but I won't promise the same if you give her rough usage between here and port."

"We'll limp into port as slowly as we can afford to. Do I take it you've a background in ship repair as well?" Prodicus asked with a voice brimming with skepticism.

"I was raised in a seaport. I used to help out in the

shipyards. That's where I got the crazy idea of going to sea."

Prodicus smiled sardonically. "But you can supervise the repairs?"

"Most likely. The underlying structure wasn't badly damaged. You just have to shore up the broken spots. And, of course, you have to balance the added weight with the same weight on the starboard side."

"More weight," Prodicus said. "I'm not happy about that."

"I'm afraid you're stuck with it, unless you want to have me redesign the whole ship. And that'd use up fifty men for six months."

"The Bull would sooner build a new boat."

Now it was Theon's turn to narrow his eyes and look sharply at the mate. "Build a new one? Pray tell: Who is competent to build another one of these? Because if there's a shipyard on the Great Sea that's equipped for the likes of this monster, I don't know about it."

Prodicus met his gaze steadily. "You're a cagey one, aren't you?"

Theon shrugged. "If I'm going to be with your ship for a while, I'm eventually going to learn most of your secrets anyhow. You might as well stop keeping me in the dark if I'm going to be of use to you."

"Fair enough—but only up to a point. As for your first question—where we're going—you'll learn the answer by nightfall. As for this other, well, you'll find that out in due time, I suppose."

The *Hephaistos* slowly limped out to sea and sailed due south. Theon, taking note of her course, wondered where they were headed. There was nothing to the south but Crete and beyond that, Africa. Either destination was too far for the damaged ship to reach, particularly by nightfall.

The wind rose; the sea became choppy. Prodicus ordered the hortator to cut the stroke, and he sent men down to bail out the rowers' bays. To Theon he said, "We may not make it by nightfall, after all."

"We can't spend the night out here in deep waters like this," Theon said, putting down his work. "Do you want her shipping water in the middle of the night? And what if a squall comes up?"

"Then we're in trouble. But perhaps we can reach the island, although we won't be able to enter the bay. We'll find a sheltered cove, anchor there, and hope for the best."

Theon, who had been looking forward to getting a glimpse of this mysterious place, was disappointed, but he sighed, shrugged, and went back to work. As the sun beat down, the wind blew softly, and the hammer sang. The *trieraules* played a song of Ur that Theon had taught him. Aft, in the cabin, Theon could hear a familiar, deep voice singing softly along with it.

The journey south took longer than Prodicus had predicted, and when at last they dropped anchor within sight of the island, Theon, peering into the darkness, got no more than a vague image of towering, jagged hills.

After dinner he lay on the deck, staring up at the sky and trying to estimate their exact position by the stars. But drifting clouds passed across the skies, and after a time, he let himself drift off into sleep.

He awoke a few hours later, shivering in the light fog, and he sat up. Standing against the rail, a man's warm chlamys thrown over her shoulders, was Nuhara. She watched him with large dark eyes that gleamed in the moonlight.

He blinked. Looking at her, he threw off the sheepskin and stood up. Only then did he become aware of his own nakedness. He pulled the sheepskin up around him and looked her in the eyes.

She did not say anything as she stood looking at him.

"How late is it?" he finally asked.

"Very late," she said in a soft voice, one that bore a trace of an accent he could not identify. "Everyone is in bed. I could not sleep."

"I . . . I gather we're at the rendezvous."

"Yes," she said. "You saved my life today."

He fidgeted. "Won't the Minotaur be angry if he wakes up and finds you gone?"

"I do as I wish."

Suddenly Theon could feel the Bull's monstrous hands at his throat, choking, squeezing. "You'd better go back below. If he comes out on deck now and—"

"I hear you singing now and then. You have a beautiful voice. I could listen to you sing all night. Will you sing for me sometime?"

He glanced once more at the closed door. He shook his head. "Not here."

She smiled and moved toward him. He backed into the rail, but she pressed her body against his, pushing aside the sheepskin and the shawl that covered so that their bare bodies touched. "Tomorrow, at the conclave. Meet me on the meadow above the harbor. There is a small grove of half-grown trees. I will be there."

"I don't even know if I'll be allowed to go ashore," Theon said, pushing her back gently but firmly.

"You will be allowed. He will make you give your

word not to escape but to return to the camp by sundown. Give him your word and then come to me."

"If he finds out about it . . ."

"You fear him? I do not fear him."

"I can't figure him out," Theon said. "People tend to fear what they can't understand. There is something very mysterious about him."

She slipped inside his arms again and pressed herself to him. He could feel her warm belly and her soft breasts touching his nakedness. She reached up and pulled his face down and kissed him. His heart pounded. His head swam.

Then she pulled away and at last did as he had told her to; she ran on silent bare feet to the cabin door, opened it, and disappeared.

He awoke to bright sunshine, remembered, and wondered if it had all been a dream. He felt the slow, steady pull of the oars beneath him, sat up, rubbed his eyes, and looked around.

The *Hephaistos* was entering the harbor of the strangest island he had ever seen. Above him and on all sides was evidence of great devastation. Mountains had been blasted to bits. The sad remains of what had once been a city were now covered with solidified lava through which scorched roofs emerged. But away from the main lava flows, life had begun to return little by little to the island. There were plants and bushes, small trees, and even stunted forests.

Then he understood and threw back his head and laughed. No wonder they had chosen this island. No wonder no one ever came here and caught them.

The island had been destroyed in his father's day.

Smoke and ash had blotted out the sun for three days. Burning ashes had been spewed into the air for hundreds of leagues around, setting fire to distant cities, destroying entire civilizations.

The island was the one Demetrios had called "Home" for many years—and then abandoned just before it was destroyed.

IV

Aboard the *Philea*, already at anchor in the harbor of the island, the morning began with Parakos, *keleustes* of the ship, drenching the sleeping rowers with ice-cold water from the bay. "Get up, you lazy bastards!" he bellowed in the ugly nasal voice they all knew so well. "There's work to do!"

Iri wiped his eyes off with his hands, for the ten-thousandth time stifling a hot reply. He counted to twenty, slowly, breathing deeply, and finally his clenched fists relaxed and his fingernails stopped biting into his palms. He turned to Zimrida, who had suddenly tried to stand erect—only to be pulled down by the chain he wore. "Easy," Iri said.

Another bucket of cold water came crashing down. Zimrida's fists were clenched; his great shoulders shook with rage. He started to bellow an obscenity at the hortator, but Iri reached over and put a hand on his arm.

"We're in port," Iri said. "We could get a day on land to stretch our legs. Don't foul that up. If I don't get a chance to stand up and walk around, my legs will drop off."

Zimrida looked up toward the *keleustes*. "Someday I'll kill him. If just once I could get my hands on that scrawny neck of his—"

"Bide your time," Iri said. "Don't start a fight with him when you're chained to the bench and he's free. Look, if they kill you, who will I have to talk with? I'd go crazy."

Slowly Zimrida managed to smile. "You're right. What good will it do if I can't even reach him to hit him?" He looked over at Iri. "Thanks, friend, I'll hold my temper. But when the time comes, stay out of my way. Or he'll kill you, too, and then you'll never see that little wife of yours again." The moment the words left his lips he regretted them. "I'm sorry. I spoke before I thought."

Iri pushed his comforting hand away. "It's all right. I find that if I try to concentrate entirely on the oar . . ."

"I understand," Zimrida said, and was about to say more when Parakos bellowed something obscenely abusive at one of the rear-rank rowers. The whip lashed out.

"Talk back to me, will you, you son of a dog!" Parakos asked in that nasty accent of his. They could see him curl the whip behind his back and suddenly lash out again at the cowering rower. Six more powerful, punishing blows fell.

"He's got the handle of the whip curled around his wrist," Zimrida said. "If I were to grab one end of it and yank hard, he'd be right down here in the middle of us, and I'd—"

"Quiet," Iri said. "He might hear you."

Zimrida's great fists balled. He breathed deeply before he got his temper under control. Then he looked back at the aft banks of rowers. "Gods! Look at the poor son of a bitch, the weak one from Ilios. He can't take that sort of punishment. Now he won't be able to row for a week."

237

Iri bent so his words would not carry. "The chap in front of me told me that this isn't the way a galley in the Bull's fleet is supposed to run. Our captain would be in trouble if word ever got out."

"You mean this Bull fellow doesn't approve of using the whip?"

"No, it's supposed to be the last resort. This fellow says the Bull thinks his captains ought to be able to maintain discipline without violence."

"He's right. If they treated me better they'd get a good pull at the oar out of me all the time, not just when I damned well felt like it." Zimrida was scowling.

"The other fellow said that there's trouble brewing between our captain, Boreas, and the Bull, and that it could come to a head while we're here in port."

"Boreas, eh? So that's the bastard's name. And he's behind this pig Parakos and his heavy hand with the lash?"

"Yes, but there's a quarrel between him and the Bull going way back. And it wasn't helped the other day when the Bull won that bet and took Boreas for everything he owned."

"He took Parakos, too," Zimrida said with a low, appreciative chuckle. "The more I hear about this Bull fellow the more I like him."

"Perhaps," Iri said sourly. "Although any way you look at it, it's his shackles on your leg and mine, no matter who's wielding the whip."

The big man dismissed the distinction with a wave of his hamlike fist. "That was quite a run we made in here last night, wasn't it? We sure as hell showed 'em how to row, didn't we, partner? Let me tell you, you're the first man I've ever had on a bench beside me who could match me stroke for stroke. They make real men in the smithing trade."

"I'm all right when it comes to muscle," Iri said. "It's my intelligence that I worry about sometimes. If I hadn't been so careless, Keturah might be—"

"It's no use fighting a war all over again. What's done is done."

Iri's fists were clenched. "Zimrida, she's blind and pregnant. She's totally helpless. Who knows what sort of swine they may have sold her to by now, or what kind of treatment she's getting at their hands."

"Don't think about it. Here, I'll arm wrestle you. You beat me yesterday. I'm not going to let that happen again."

As Pandion stood at the rail of the *Philea*, looking up at the broken cliffs above him, the *Hephaistos* came limping into port. He turned to Eumenes, the first mate. "Look what's happened to the *Hephaistos*."

Eumenes turned and said with a whistle, "Gods! I wonder how that came about. Imagine a ship that could catch up to her in the first place, much less ram her."

"Anybody can be outmaneuvered," Boreas, the captain, said in a sour voice. "Even the great Minotaur himself." He smiled, but not pleasantly. "I'm going to have fun asking him all about it."

"Careful," Eumenes advised. "You know what happened the last time you started ribbing him."

"He can go to Hades," he said. "He cost me a fortune a few days ago. Believe me, if it takes until the end of my life, I'll find some way to pay him back!"

Pandion turned back to the rail. "I can understand the Bull's being touchy. If there's another bireme on the water, I'd want to know about it. And I'd think you would, too."

"Now that's an interesting idea," Boreas said. "What

if His Highness weren't the only man in the world in command of a two-ranker? What if he were just another damned sea captain, and not a man who could draw his authority from the fact that he commanded a ship faster than anybody else's?"

Eumenes's eyebrows lifted. "Oh, I don't know. You've got to give the Bull his due. I've seen worse leaders. I've *served* under a few. There was that son of a bitch from Tarraco when I was a kid."

"The Bull!" Boreas said with a snarl. "That's all I hear about around here! His superior strength. His superior wisdom. His superior ship. You'd think he were some kind of god, come down from the heights to show us mere mortals a thing or two." He stalked away.

Eumenes and Pandion exchanged glances. "Touchy, isn't he?" Eumenes said. "I have a feeling that it would be a good idea to keep him away from the Bull."

An idea suddenly blazed in Pandion's mind. "What if I were to accompany him every time he went near the Bull, to keep him out of trouble?"

"No," Eumenes said. "He needs someone of enough rank to argue with him. I'd better do it myself. But thanks for the suggestion."

Pandion cursed silently. There had to be some way to do it. "That's quite a bash the *Hephaistos* took. He'll have to repair it here. There's no way he can go out to sea with her in that condition."

"Have to careen her and shore her up there, and go to work with hot pitch. Then they might as well scrape her and look to her boatworms while they're at it."

"Isn't that dangerous? Won't she be vulnerable while all that's going on? If someone were to blunder in here and find her on her side, on dry land . . ."

"That's the chance he'll have to take. Hell, *every-*

240

thing's dangerous for people like us. If the same somebody were to sail in here right now—a punitive fleet, for example, loaded with armed men . . ."

Pandion studied the gash in the galley's side. "He's going to have to add weight, shoring up those cracked timbers. That means he's going to have to add rowers."

"They're already under full complement," Eumenes said.

"Or he's going to have to get better rowers." An idea suddenly struck him, and he turned to Eumenes. "Are you as broke as I am?"

"Am I? I'm going to have to borrow money to bet with. Who would have thought the Bull himself would wrestle that tall kid? I thought we had a sure thing."

"I did, too. I'd even seen him fight. But who can stand up to a monster like the Bull? Whatever our august captain may say about him, he's got an arm of iron. Anyhow, I'm cleaned out, too. I wonder if we can promote something."

"Such as?"

"You're in charge of the rowers. And those two we took on a while back would be just the thing to offer the Bull when he starts looking around for new men to carry a heavy oar, wouldn't they?"

"The red-faced one and the one-eyed fellow? Why, yes, now that you come down to it. What are you saying, now?"

"Then let's offer 'em to him. We're two men over capacity now. Boreas would never miss 'em. And we might get a generous reward."

Eumenes stared at him for a moment, before his face broke into a slow smile.

V

At high tide the men of the *Hephaistos* carefully guided the big galley into shallow water and anchored her. When the tide went out the boat would remain on shore, beached and lying on her side, with the great wound in her hull exposed.

Working together Theon and Prodicus directed the crew when, as the tide receded, they manned ropes to pull her gently onto her side. Then she was secured with long ropes to the rocks nearby. As he worked, he looked up and saw the Minotaur staring down at him impassively.

The first day of the rendezvous, as the ships were straggling in, was traditionally given over to revelry and drunken feasting. Only after the crews had gotten this out of their systems would the captains attempt to discuss business and make plans. Theon had heard that a big event was coming up and hoped he could learn all the details.

Not wanting to feast and drink and having promised to be back in camp by nightfall, Theon found himself free. He roamed through the sad, lava-choked ruins of the town where Demetrios had lived and worked, trying to relate it to the stories he had been told in his youth by the men who had lived here.

He purposely avoided the meadow above the harbor, where Nuhara had asked him to meet her. There was always the chance that they had been overheard talking the night before, and he had no idea what the Minotaur would do if he were to catch him with the girl.

He tried to sort out his own feelings about her. Admittedly, he was strongly attracted to Nuhara. Who would not be? But what would be the Minotaur's reaction if he discovered the tryst? Was he afraid, as Nuhara had said?

More to the point was the reason he was here in the first place: to spy on the Minotaur, to learn more about this operation and discover where his soft spots lay, so Demetrios could destroy the pirates. And if he got himself killed . . .

He wondered how much he could tell Nuhara. Not much, he guessed; not at this point, anyhow. He would have to remain a man of mystery until he knew her better.

So he let his mind run as, almost unconsciously, his steps drew him ever upward, up the hill toward the waiting grove of half-grown trees, where he knew he would find her.

At noon, to Iri's amazement, Parakos came to the edge of the deep pit in which the rowers sat and called to him. "You with the red face, get the one-eyed fellow and come up on deck."

"On deck?" he asked. "But we're still chained. How can we?"

Parakos disappeared, and Iri could hear him talking to someone on deck: "Get him for yourself, but watch out for that nest of vipers. With nothing to lose, they'd readily strangle you."

"There wouldn't be any reason to do that, now, would there?" an unfamiliar voice chimed in. "I'm coming down to offer them their freedom—for an hour or so, anyway. Give me the keys; I'll unlock them myself."

Iri looked over at Zimrida. Two pairs of brows went up. "Too bad Parakos isn't coming down to see us," the one-eyed man said. "What a nice welcome I'd have given him."

"Shhhh," Iri whispered. "Wait and see what happens. When I hear the word 'freedom,' it arouses intense interest." He nudged the big man. "Keep your hands to yourself when this new fellow comes down. No tricks. I want to see what the deck looks like. I haven't seen it since the day they chained me down here."

As he spoke the new man came down the rope ladder. He was strongly built, young, with a round face and curly hair. As he unlocked the manacles on Iri's and Zimrida's ankles, he said, "All right, on deck, both of you, if you please."

Iri grinned at Zimrida. " 'If you please?' " he echoed, a comically quizzical look on his red face. "What language is that? I'm sure I've never heard the phrase before. Whatever could it mean?"

This drew a grin from the curly-headed stranger. "Up you go, boys. We're going to take a little trip."

Standing behind them as they mounted the rope ladder, he glimpsed the red blotch on Iri's back, just above his buttocks. He was surprised but managed not to let it show.

Up the hill a delightful breeze was blowing, the sun was warm, and the air was balmy. Theon, barefoot, avoided the lava flow and kept to the dirt path as he threaded his way along the track to the meadow.

At the top there was a bare spot where ash had miraculously not fallen, and seedlings had taken root here. But it was a dwarf forest that looked intended for children. It was an enchanted place, this little spot of green in the middle of the devastation.

He turned and looked back and down at the scene below. The water of the bay was the deepest blue he had ever seen, and the arms of land encircled it like the claws of a giant crab. Some of the original island was gone forever, blown away or sunken under the Great Sea. What remained was a fragment of the largest part of Home.

Even as he stood here he could feel a minor tremor under his bare soles, a signal that the wrath of Poseidon the Earth Shaker was not yet abated, that the mountain still had power deep within its bowels.

Suddenly he became aware of a presence nearby, and he turned. Nuhara stood before him. She wore a brief chiton that hid little of her slim body. Her trim legs and little feet were bare. Her hair was braided, and her skin was a delicious golden color.

"I knew you'd come," she said, taking his hand. "Come, I want to show you something."

The touch of her hand was suddenly exciting. He let himself be led along a path through the dwarf forest. Where the trees ended, Nuhara and Theon found themselves on the edge of a great cleft. Below lay a pool of incredible blue water.

"A private place even they don't know about," she said. "You can't see this cove from the sea, and it's too small for a boat to explore. Nobody's ever been here before, I'll wager. It probably didn't exist before the great earthquake when the rock split and the sea seeped in." She stopped for a second and looked down. Then impulsively she turned and hugged him. "I'm so glad you came. Ever since I first saw you I've wanted to be alone with you."

Theon did not reply, but when he looked down into her dark eyes and saw such unbridled joy, he found himself smiling, too. Suddenly she reached up and kissed him.

It was not like before, a playful kiss given quickly before she danced away. This time she drew him down, and he could feel the pounding of her heart next to his, and as her body pressed his he was very aware of his own nudity under the chlamys. She put her hands on his cheeks and kissed his mouth, and his nose and his eyes and his chin.

When he tried to pull her closer she laughed and raced surefootedly down the path.

Startled, he followed. But she was quickly out of sight, moving swiftly down the narrow path. He hugged the hillside, always mindful of the sheer drop.

Suddenly he came upon her. She was standing on the lip of the cliff above the deep pool.

She grinned mischievously at him and reached up and pulled the chiton over her head, revealing a lithe body, slim and graceful, with pert breasts and a tight little bottom.

"Join me!" she called.

Without hesitation she stepped to the edge and dived off the cliff into the chasm, arching gracefully, until her golden body parted the waters.

He gasped and rushed to the edge of the cliff. To his relief she surfaced and swam around, her delicate face framed by the blue waters. Her light laughter rose up to him. "Come in," she called. "It's wonderful!"

He firmed his jaw, threw off his chlamys, and dove into the heart-stopping void.

He came up gasping and flailing. The fall had taken his breath away. She swam to him and led him to a flat piece of granite that had broken free during the long-ago quake. It lay half submerged in the water. He pulled himself up, and then helped her up. "I don't know how I talked myself into doing that," he said.

"Poor darling," she said, then stopped his mouth with a kiss, sweet and playful. They were alone; their clothing was far away upon the hillside. They had nothing to do, nowhere to be. And they were alone. With the sun shining on her slim body, Nuhara was the most bewitchingly beautiful woman Theon had ever seen.

He reached his powerful arms around her and drew her body to his. Now it was his turn to play the aggressor, and she abandoned herself totally. The afternoon became one long erotic game, in and out of the water. He took her lovingly, passionately, and joyfully. Until this day he had no idea of the extent of his own hunger.

VI

Pandion stood at the edge of the crowd, watching the show. One of the boats had brought an entire Rhodian brothel to the conclave. Their number included acrobats and contortionists and dancers as well as prostitutes. The dancers had brought their own musicians, and the afternoon's festivities had begun with mummery and would end with lecherous, drunken revels.

Pandion's eyes, however, kept returning to the great black-bearded figure of the Minotaur, who was listening halfheartedly to Eumenes's proposition about the two rowers. The Minotaur always seemed to be surrounded by large numbers of his people. So far it had been impossible to catch him alone. Pandion, an ordinary seaman on a ship, whose captain was a known enemy of the Bull's, would have a hard time getting access to the Minotaur under any circumstances.

The ruse involving the two rowers was the only scheme he had been able to come up with so far. If he did not take action during this conclave he might never have another opportunity.

His earlier attempt had been a failure. He had shipped out on one of the smaller vessels of the Bull's fleet, hoping to get close enough to the pirate chief to kill him, but his ship was attacked, sunk, and sent to the bottom of the Aegean.

A strong swimmer, he had made it to shore, but it had taken him two years to maneuver himself back into a position to make contact with the Bull's agents and be hired on again. And the only way he was able to do it was by betraying Theon.

That action had cost him some pangs of conscience. Was assassinating an evil man worth the cost if you were obliged to betray friends and do evil deeds of your own?

Staring at the large crowd surrounding the Minotaur—a crowd composed of armed men who thought nothing of killing—he knew as surely as he stood there that he would never escape. He would have to settle for killing the Bull, and then dying at the hands of the men who guarded him night and day.

Pandion let the idea sink in. It sent cold chills up and down his spine; but as he thought about it and braced himself for the task, he realized that it had always been part of the plan; he had never had any illusions about being able to escape. He had just refused to face up to the truth.

Now it was time to face it. He straightened his back. His eyes narrowed, and he studied his enemy. The Minotaur would be a hard man to kill. The stroke had to be just right. What a wasteful and ignominious fate if he were to fail to kill his enemy yet lose his own life.

Pandion had been the son of a prosperous Poros trader, and he had stood to inherit the family's business. While his father plied the seas, Pandion was sent to be apprenticed in the arts of business and trade with a friend. But one day his father, en route home to meet Pandion and receive him formally into the business, had run into the Minotaur's fleet. There had been no witnesses to tie the Bull himself to the actual stroke that had killed Pandion's father. But he had gone from port to port searching for men who had been on that voyage. Finally he found a man who said he had seen the Bull strike the skipper's head off before massacring his crew.

From that day Pandion had been thirsty for revenge. Now the fateful day had come. He had to strike during their short stay on the island. And the stroke had to be perfect. He had to kill the Minotaur, or his father would forever remain unavenged.

Theon lay on his back in the sun, watching Nuhara rise out of the water. Her body glistened. He could not get enough of her. Smiling, she climbed up onto the rock and sat down beside him. Resting his hand on her naked thigh, he kissed her once more. "The sun's getting low," he said. "We'd better go back."

She looked crestfallen. "Do we have to?"

"I gave my word to be back by nightfall and not try to escape."

"I've been thinking all afternoon about that. Dear Theon, I'd hoped . . ."

"Yes?"

"I don't want to go back. Why would I want to go back to a man like the Bull? Can't we just run away? It would be so easy. You know how to sail a boat. And there's a fishing boat beached on the far side of the island. I found it last time I was here."

His hand toyed with her delicious little breast. He watched the nipple react to his gentle stroking. How could he bear to say no? He watched her hopeful expression begin to fade. Finally he said, "But I gave my word."

"You gave your word of honor to a pirate. What would a pirate know of honor? What would he care?"

"If my word didn't mean anything to him he wouldn't have bothered to ask," Theon said. "Besides, one doesn't honor a pledge for someone else's sake. One honors it for one's own sake."

Nuhara turned up her small nose. "Men!" she said. "You get a chance to run away with me but won't take it. And I thought you'd begun to care for me."

He pulled her forward until she lay on his chest. His hands came around her back and cradled her round buttocks. "I care enormously about you. That's why I don't want you to have anything to do with a treacherous pig who won't honor his word." He smiled and kissed her playfully on the end of her uptilted nose. "We'll have other chances. We'll make other chances. And maybe the day will come when we can do what you wish in safety and without sacrificing honor."

"Pooh! How are you going to do that? You're never free from him. You spend the entire day right under his nose."

"True," he said. "But I gain more freedom every day."

She pouted and drew back from him. Her small breasts dangled in his face, and he chuckled and reached up to kiss them. "Ah, Nuhara, how you've pleased me today. But I wonder who you are. How did you come here? Are your parents dead?" He saw the hurt in her eyes and did not press his question. "Your accent is Cretan, or I miss my guess. Where did you come from? Knossos? Mallia? Were you a slave there?"

"I was free," she said. "My mother was a bull dancer. The best in Knossos. She was thought to be the most beautiful girl who ever danced with the bulls. At the festivals she would go out, wearing no more than a tiny loincloth, and vault over the heads of the bulls as thousands watched."

He smiled. "She didn't like to wear clothing any more than you do. Well, if you and I ever get free, you'll come to live with me in my big house, and you won't ever have to wear anything. As a matter of fact, I won't let you wear anything. I'll have the servants keep your entire wardrobe under lock and key, and forbid them ever to give you anything to wear."

"You cruel beast!"

"Except jewels. Pearls. Rubies. Emeralds. And gold everywhere a woman can put gold on her body."

"I love this daydream. Tell me more. But . . ." Her face clouded over now. "It could never happen, could it? We'd wind up living a quiet life in a little house."

Theon threw caution to the winds. "You'd be surprised. I'm rich. Rich enough to buy and sell whole cities. I have a house you could comfortably fit the *Hephaistos* inside. It has fields and forests and lakes, and hundreds of servants to tend the farms and orchards."

"You're teasing me."

He chuckled and kissed her again. "I'm not. I wouldn't tease you about a thing like that."

"But you're a slave."

"I am now. But I'm told that even that can change. If I perform valuable service, the Bull can manumit me any time he wants." Theon grimaced. "And here I am, sneaking away to make love to his—"

"Don't worry, he's too busy to notice," she said hastily. "And we'll go back by different routes." She sat up. "But please don't tease me. Rich. With a house and lands."

"It's true. Someday, if we're lucky, you'll see it all."

"Then why don't we go there right now?" she asked eagerly. "Don't tell me. I know. You're cruel to make fun of me like that."

"I'd never make fun of you," he said. "You have to believe that. But keep the picture in your mind—I certainly will—of walking naked around my house, wearing gold and jewels and nothing else."

"In your house the size of the palace at Knossos. Sure. And with dozens of servants."

"It's not quite that big," he said. "But it's more beautiful. It was designed by the man who rebuilt Babylon."

"Now you're absurd. Can't you ever talk sense?"

He sighed long and hard. "All right, don't believe me. But let's get back before we get into trouble. If we wait much longer we won't be able to find our clothes in the dark or make our way up the cliff without falling off."

VII

They parted with a kiss just above the great lava flow, and Nuhara came down the eastern slope while Theon took the western. As he made his way down the hillside he could see a roaring campfire. The flames leapt high and danced about in the breeze.

Many of the pirates were already drunk, and not a few of them were asleep under the trees. Others were gathered in small circles playing games of chance, and in one Theon recognized a familiar face. The man hastily got up.

"Here's my former partner, looking more prosperous than he did last time I saw him," Sciton said. "How are you, Theon?"

"Better than I was," Theon answered. "You'll note I'm out of the collar these days. Still a slave, but treated more or less like a member of the crew." He told of the fight with the two galleys and of the new use the Minotaur was making of his skills as a repairman. "It's a rare opportunity to work on a bireme. It's a fascinating design. I'd never have worked out the seating of the rowers in a million years."

"And why didn't you tell us about these other skills of yours?"

"You didn't ask me. The only thing you seemed to be interested in was my skill as a fighter."

"Which," Sciton said ruefully, "cost me dearly." He sighed. "It's my own fault, and the same is true of all those on the *Gades* and the *Philea* who lost everything betting on you. We got too greedy. There's no way in the world I'd ever again wager on a fight when I didn't know the opponent, no matter how good my own man was."

"Betting on anything but your own skills is a fool's game," Theon said. "And sometimes even then . . ."

"So you'll not be doing any fighting here during the rendezvous?"

"You forget, I'm nobody's partner here. I'm a chattel, whom people tell what to do. And nobody's told me to fight. I'm lying low, staying away from the Bull as much as possible. The less he sees of me while we're here, the better." *How true this is!* he thought. But he said nothing. He just wondered where Nuhara was and hoped she had gone back to the ship safely.

"Come on down to the fire," Sciton said. "At least the wine doesn't cost anything. I just got cleaned out again, playing the game of peas and shells."

"You didn't bet good money on that!" Theon said, shocked. "You're mad, you know, to wager on such a game."

"Tell me about it," Sciton said. "I deserve it."

After several cups of strong wine Sciton's wounds seemed to be healing. He grabbed one of the whores and started dancing with her, singing along with the musicians. Theon spotted Tromes, the *trieraules*, among the musicians and took the flute from him; Tromes manned the big drum, and the two struck up a lively dance that everybody joined in. The party was just beginning.

Pandion brought up the two rowers. He coughed loudly and finally caught the Minotaur's eye. "Sir," he said, "here are the two I was telling you about. They're the best we've taken on in the past year. This one-eyed monster has a terrible temper, but he pulls a good oar."

"Come into the light, you two," the Minotaur said. "Now turn around. Let me have a look at you." Pandion had found a tattered chlamys for each, protection against the chill of the evening. "Ah, yes," he said, looking Zimrida over. "A bad temper, eh? And I see he's suffered for it. How did you lose that eye, my friend? A fight?"

"The man doesn't live who could best me in a fair fight," Zimrida said. "Not even you, for all the rumors I hear. No, this came from the lash two ships ago. Some cowardly son of a bitch who couldn't have faced me if I didn't have a chain on my leg. You know the type."

"Indeed I do," the Minotaur said. "Well, if I take you from this gentleman, my friend, you'll have to curb that temper. If you do, I can promise you better treatment. The *Hephaistos* is a big ship, and it requires men with strong arms and the dispositions of water buffaloes."

"Which have tempers of their own," Zimrida said stubbornly.

"That they do," the Minotaur said. "On the other hand, a man can learn patience." Their eyes locked for a moment, and the Minotaur almost smiled as he turned to Iri.

"You seem to be quite another kettle of fish, my friend. I don't see any sign of the lash on your body. That means either you're more phlegmatic or you're new to the rowers' benches."

"There's a third possibility," Iri said. "I might be as angry as Zimrida at the injustice of slavery, but I know how to control myself."

Iri's comment drew interest from the Minotaur. "Turn around, will you?" He looked at Iri's compact but power-fully muscled body the same way a horse trader might look at a particularly fine stallion. "You are new to the boats, aren't you?"

"I was pressed into service involuntarily by a kidnap-per in Ashkelon," Iri said, looking him steadily in the eye. "My pregnant wife was sold into slavery as well." He spat the words out. "She's blind. And totally helpless without me. May the gods protect her, because I'm no longer there to do so."

The Minotaur looked at him intently. "A harsh story," he said. "You've the body of a man who's spent his life doing heavy work. Are those a smith's scars on your forearms?"

"I've spent thirty-five years at a forge."

"You're older than you look. Perhaps it's hard to tell with the birthmark. That is a birthmark, then? That and the one on your back?"

Iri only nodded. If anyone happened to know the legends of the Children of the Lion, that was all right with him; but he was not going to offer information.

"Very well," the black-bearded man said. "I think we'll be able to make a deal. Pandion?"

During the long conversation between the two slaves and their prospective buyer no one looked at Pandion. But now, in the flickering light of the distant fire, he lunged out of the darkness. The firelight glinted on the slim Egyptian dagger in his hand. The Minotaur instinctively held up one hand to defend himself, and the thrust that had been aimed at his heart caught him in the forearm.

Iri acted without thinking. Unchained and free, he rushed forward, bowling Zimrida over. Then he stumbled to one knee but managed to grab Pandion's arm just as he was readying another attack. The enormous pressure on Pandion's wrist numbed his hand and the knife dropped to the ground.

With his other hand, Iri grabbed Pandion by the back of the neck, then twisted his knife arm behind his back. Everyone else was too stunned to move. They stood openmouthed, watching.

The Minotaur calmly looked down at his bleeding arm and nodded to Prodicus. "Get someone who knows doctoring. There's a man aboard the *Corinth*, I think. And does anyone have a wineskin handy? I need to wash this off."

Someone brought a clean rag and bound his arm up. Only then did the Minotaur look at Iri and Pandion.

Iri stood relaxed and did not even seem to be breathing hard. "Here he is," he said, nodding at the immobilized Pandion. "He's at your disposal. Sorry I couldn't catch him sooner."

The Minotaur grabbed Pandion by the hair and pulled him up. "You tried to kill me," he said. "Why?"

Pandion's mouth was set in a rigid line. The Minotaur nodded at Iri, and Iri twisted the arm harder. "N-no!" Pandion said in a tight voice. "I won't tell you!"

The Minotaur's eyes locked with Iri's once more, and he nodded again. Iri twisted until Pandion groaned. "You can b-break the arm if you want to," he said in a strangled voice. "But you'll never get it out of me."

The Minotaur's voice was almost gentle. "I'm sorry, I'd like to have known." But with a slight shrug of his shoulders he dismissed the thought. "What shall I do with him?"

"He seems fit enough," Iri suggested. "I understand you need strong men to row that heavy boat of yours; you could do worse than to throw him down in the rowers' bay."

"And if I have him killed I may never find out why he wanted to kill me."

The Minotaur looked Iri in the eyes. "Very well, you've called the turn. He lives and sits beside you pulling an oar."

Iri's heart sank. For a moment, he had nursed the hope that, having saved the Minotaur's life, he would be freed. But now he and Zimrida were destined for the oars again, this time on a ship whose oars were a forearm's length longer, a ship that had a reputation for destroying rowers faster than any other.

CHAPTER ELEVEN

Bashan

I

There came at last a day when Pepi awoke, looked around, and seemed to know who he was. "Where am I?" he asked. "What am I doing here?"

The girl watching him was a daughter of the tribe of Manasseh, and she had fed him and washed him and looked after him ever since his injury. Now, seeing him conscious, she let out a little shriek and ran from the room.

Pepi turned and swung his feet to the ground. His head ached dully, and there was a terrible taste in his mouth. He started to rise when he felt a pain shooting through his head. Cursing, he sat back down hard, just as the girl returned with an older man.

"What are you doing up?" the man asked. "It's too early for that. You'll hurt yourself. Just lie back down."

Pepi glowered at him. "I recognize you. Your name is Helek. You're head of one of the subtribes of Manasseh."

The old man exchanged glances with the girl. "Praise be to God!" he said. "He's himself again!" He knelt before Pepi. "What's your name?"

"Pepi of Kerma," the armorer said. "Why? Is there some doubt? I've only lived among you twenty years and more."

Helek turned to the girl. "Have someone bring Moses here. He'll be so pleased."

Once more Pepi tried to get up, but the stabbing pain stopped him. "What's happened to me?" He reached up to his throbbing temples.

Helek put a cautionary hand on Pepi's knee. "Easy, my young friend. We weren't sure you were going to come back from where you've been."

"What do you mean?" Pepi asked.

"For a month you had no idea who you were or what you were doing here."

"*A month?*" Pepi asked incredulously. "You mean I've been out of my mind, unaware? Gods!" Pepi tried to push himself up. "But what happened. . . ."

"You received an injury in the great battle in which Joshua defeated Og of Bashan."

"No, no I remember now. I was hit in the head with a rock before the battle." He stared around him. He was in a house, large, well furnished, and nicely kept. "I don't recognize this place."

"It was given to me when Moses assigned Bashan to the tribe of Manasseh," Helek said. "I live in it with my family. The daughter of one of my cousins was looking after you."

"But what's happened since . . . since I left?"

"It's been a sad time," the old man said. "The plague, many people died. It was the will of Yahweh, a judgment of God against our wickedness. Our young men had been sinful, lying with the women of the heathen. Even while we were holding a council to determine what to do about the plague, one young snip of the tribe of Simeon flaunted his Midianite mistress before us.

"And Aaron's grandson, Phinehas, son of Eleazar, arose in righteous wrath and took a spear to both of them. Skewered whore and whoremaster alike with one blow. And because of that, Yahweh has spared the rest of us. But many died before this. So shall perish all who fraternize with the enemy and lie with Midianite sluts."

"Are you quite sure," Pepi asked, "that was caused by—"

"Our blood is not to be mixed with that of the heathen, the ungodly, the uncircumcised."

To which number I myself belong, Pepi thought wryly. And one day someone is going to use that argument to do something unpleasant to me, as well. How self-righteous these people can be. "And Moses and Joshua are of the same mind in this?"

"Moses issued the order. Joshua probably agrees. I cannot say for sure because Joshua took the army to Midian. He intends to wipe out the armies of Midian to the last man."

Pepi's eyes widened. "Midian! But Midian is very strong. There are half a dozen kingdoms. If they were to combine forces, Joshua and your army wouldn't stand a chance."

"Their army does not have Yahweh at its head. Joshua is very confident."

Pepi clenched his fist. "The fool! The crazy fool! He's going to go charging in there and get slaughtered."

"Easy," the old man said. "You're going to get yourself too excited."

Pepi sighed and let his shoulders slump once more.

"Besides," the old man continued, "you'd be too late to do anything now. They'll have already fought their first engagement. And no one can do anything with Joshua once he makes up his mind. Not to mention that the girl Phinehas killed was the daughter of a Midianite prince. She was Cozbi, the daughter of Zur."

"I see. So killing her amounted to an act of war." Pepi shook his head. "I hope Joshua knows what he is doing, taking on the whole of Midian."

"Moses spoke with him. Joshua believed that the princelings of Midian would never be able to fight under a single leader."

Pepi's expression began to lighten. "He's right. He might stand some chance after all."

Pepi finally got to his feet. "This is a nice house," he said. "And it must look like a palace after living in a tent for twenty years."

"And in hovels for a long time before that," the old man said. "Yes, we of Manasseh are very fortunate to have been given Bashan. And I'm pleased with this house. The more so as it came with enough slaves to take care of it."

Pepi stared at him in surprise. "Slaves? Since when has Israel had slaves?"

"They have to be released at the end of seven years, unless, of course, they have fallen into debt and have to extend their servitude to pay it off. It's an old custom. I keep forgetting that you are not originally of us. Do they have no such customs in Kerma?"

"Yes, we have slaves in Kerma, although some of us think it a barbaric custom. But I had had the impression that your religion forbade the owning of slaves." He didn't bother to hide his distaste. "And how did you come by these slaves? From the lands you seized?"

"Yes," the old man replied. "And then there are the former owners."

"You mean you grabbed their lands and possessions and then enslaved them?"

"It is the custom in the northern lands."

Pepi frowned. He did not want to offend his host. As soon as he got dressed . . .

A picture suddenly flashed in his mind: a beautiful, tall woman with blue eyes and blond hair.

"Tirzah!" he said.

"Did you say something?" the old man asked.

Pepi turned back to him. "You say that the losers' property was seized? And then they were given over to the new owners as slaves?"

"Why, yes."

"All of them? Not just those who fought?"

"Certainly. They are all heathens, unbelievers, members of an enemy nation."

"What about the people not of the Bashanite race? People living here but not Bashanites? Would their property have been seized, too? Would they become slaves also?"

"That would be the logical procedure, yes."

"Get me my clothes, would you?" Pepi requested. "I've got to get out of here."

"But you're still ill. And Moses will want to see you."

"I'll be sorry to have missed him. But I have urgent business. I only hope I'm not too late."

"But your head . . ."

"I can't stay here. Not when—"

"Not when what? Surely you've no business that's more important than your health."

"You probably wouldn't find it important," Pepi said. "Consider it a matter of honor; that's one thing your people and mine have in common, even if the actual honor isn't the same."

"If Moses finds out that I've let you get away like this, when you're still ill—"

"I'll take the responsibility. Now could you have someone get my clothes and saddle my horse?"

II

The elders of the tribe had gathered in a meadow to hear Moses speak. Now the old leader had spoken, and the meeting was breaking up. A girl tried to wriggle through a clear space, only to have her arm grabbed by one of the elders.

"This isn't any place for you, little one."

She struggled, trying to get loose. "I've got to get to Moses. I have a mes—"

"Come along. It can wait. This isn't women's business, you know."

The girl's mouth opened as if she were about to say something, but she closed it again and counted to ten before speaking. "I understand, but I have an urgent message for Moses. Besides, your meeting's over."

He patted her arm patronizingly.

Suddenly she spun out of his grasp. She circled the crowd, standing on tiptoe to look over people's heads, trying to see Moses. Finally she found an olive tree and pulled herself up.

She saw him, still standing in the midst of a large crowd. Just behind him, there were fewer people. She jumped down and ran until she found the hole.

But as she got near Moses, one of the Levites who

always gathered closely around him, asserting their status as the official priestly caste of the Israelites, grabbed her arms. "Where do you think you're going? Women aren't allowed here."

"Let go. You're hurting me!"

"Whose child are you? I'll see you're disciplined for talking back to a priest of the—"

"I have to see Moses! I have a message."

"What message? Give it to me, and we'll see whether it's worth delivering. Moses can't be bothered by just anyone."

But just then she saw the crowd part, and the familiar face of Moses appeared. "Moses!" she cried. "I have a message from—"

"Shut up, girl!" her captor hissed. He drew back his free hand as if to hit her.

"Wait!" Moses said. "I recognize this child. Let her speak to me."

"But this isn't proper. If we start letting females—"

"Yahweh alone decides what is proper," Moses said. "It is His law that I have been compiling for you in recent months. If you, as a member of the priesthood, are charged with the responsibility of administering it, I would suggest that you study it. One of the things it says is that Yahweh created women as well as men and loves them, too."

The Levite released her, and she approached Moses. "Nobody would let me through. But you told me to let you know the moment Pepi awoke."

"Pepi? He's conscious? Take me to him immediately!"

The Levite closed in. "But, Moses, we were going to discuss the boundaries of the territories to be occupied by the tribes. There are some heated disputes over this already, and they need to be adjudicated."

Moses turned on him and stared him to silence. "Adjudicate?" he asked, a slight edge to his voice. "What is there to adjudicate about judgments handed down by Yahweh? These are not negotiable. They spring directly from His own words, as delivered to me on the mountain."

"Yes, I know, but there is great controversy."

"Which is a polite term for disobedience. Let us not mince words. Are you going to defy the will of God and bring down more punishments upon us?"

The elder bristled. "Sir!" he said indignantly. "One does not speak so to a priest of God!"

Moses stared at him, and his jaw line firmed. "I would not do so if indeed I *were* speaking to a member of the priesthood. But you are no longer one. Let all who stand here be witness to the fact. It was Yahweh who made you a priest, and He has just unmade you. You are hereby stripped of all your priestly functions."

"B-but—"

"Let this," Moses said, swiveling around and facing each of the watching elders in turn, "be witness to the will of God as He has given it to me. None of us stands above his brother. We have no dignity, no stature, except that which Yahweh gives to us.

"We are not a people chosen by God because we deserved to be singled out for special treatment; quite the opposite. Indeed, we are not God's chosen race because of our own excellence, but by the strange and mysterious will of Yahweh we have been picked to bear witness to His greatness and mercy.

"We cannot oppress others because of our arrogant sense of superiority. Who is superior, God alone will judge."

The Levite shrank back, pale and silent. Moses glared at him until he turned and slipped away. Then he spoke to the girl. "Is Pepi all right?"

"Yes, sir," the girl said. "And Helek thought you would want to speak to him."

One of the elders stepped forward. "Moses," he said. "Your voice will be needed in council."

"Soon you will have to get along without me," Moses said. "You might as well begin getting used to it now. I will trust you to be as aware of the Law in my absence as you would be if I were present."

Everyone nodded.

"Then you do not need me. I will go to see our friend Pepi, who is at last restored to us."

He turned on one heel and, leaning on the girl's arm, slowly walked away. The years lay heavy on him, but his steps were decisive.

Although he was dressed and his sword belt was buckled around his waist, Pepi still felt groggy. Every quick movement sent pains stabbing through his head. He settled the belt in place and reached for the basin of water Helek had brought him. As he bent to wash, a piece of shiny metal on the wall caught his attention. He studied his reflection.

The face that looked back at him was haggard and drawn; the eyes were haunted. It was the face of a lost man.

And that was his problem. Where did he belong now? The rift between him and his oldest friend, Joshua, was growing. Soon Joshua, as leader of Israel, would have the power of life and death over him as well as all other heathens and foreigners among them. And he, Pepi, would have to make his choice: swallow his conscience or be driven out of the newly conquered lands that were slowly taking shape as the new land of Israel.

What would he do? Let friendship rule, keep his mouth shut, and do what he, as a hired hand, was paid to do? Or would he tell Joshua what he thought of the barbarous behavior of the Israelites? Then, after twenty years' faithful service to the Israelite cause, he would surely be driven out to live among the other heathen.

He heard a noise and turned—too quickly. He winced and cursed as the pain went through his head. He clamped his hands to his head as he staggered outside.

"Bring the horse here, will you?" he said to Helek. He stood on the porch of Helek's new—stolen—home, watching the old man lead his mount from the stables.

"Are you sure you're doing the right thing?" the old man asked. "Moses will be sorry to have missed you and angry at me for letting you go off like this, when you're still sick."

"Give him my best and tell him I take full responsibility for my actions. You're not to blame."

As he threw his leg over the horse, the pain returned. Cursing under his breath, he leapt into the saddle. The exertion made him dizzy, but after a few seconds he nudged his horse into a trot and then a gallop.

He had to find Tirzah!

III

Helek was waiting for Moses. "I'm sorry," he said. "But he's gone."

"Gone? You mean you let a sick man wander off? Have you taken leave of your senses?"

"I'm sorry, but talking about restraining Pepi and actually doing so are two different things. He is a most resolute young man."

Moses's shoulders slumped. "I so wanted to speak with him one more time. Well, if God had wished me to speak with the lad, I would have done so."

Helek took Moses's arm. "Come inside. You must be tired. Sit down, and I'll have one of the slaves bring you some refreshment."

"No," Moses said. "While I still have strength, there is something I must do. I must go on a little journey. I won't be long."

"I'll send a couple of the slaves with you," Helek said.

"Your girl has done me service today, despite the arrogance of my men. She's earned the right to accompany me." He turned to her. "Are you willing, my dear?"

"Oh, sir," she said. "If you'd only be so kind as to let me."

With a smile Moses turned to Helek. "There you are; I have a helper, and I need no other. Now if you would please bring me a donkey? This young lady will lead the animal for me and make sure I don't stray off the path."

"Certainly," Helek said. "But what path? The elders will be very angry with me if I let you go off somewhere without knowing where you've gone."

"I'm going to climb Mount Nebo. God has told me that my days among you are few. He has also promised me that if I cannot enter the Land of Promise, I will be allowed to see it. And where better than from the top of the mountain?"

"At your age? I can't let you."

"You cannot stop me. If you tried, God Himself would stay your hand."

*   *   *

From time to time, as Pepi rode, the scenery around him would blur, his head would swim, and it would be all he could do to remain in the saddle. But as he skirted the long ridge and headed eastward toward the Jordan he reminded himself of the importance of his errand.

As he rode he passed farm after farm, now occupied by newly prosperous Israelites, while the former owners were slaving in the fields as chattels. Whenever his path brought him close to their houses the usurpers watched him, but he would avert his eyes, embarrassed to be on the side of the victors.

How could Joshua have given such an unjust order? Stealing the land of honest, hardworking people was wrong! But Joshua was becoming more single-minded, and the idea of justice—particularly when it applied to foreigners outside the Covenant—did not concern him.

But if Tirzah had had her property stolen by these arrogant tribespeople of Manasseh, surely he could take the matter to Moses and expect fairness. Moses would certainly see the injustice in Joshua's treatment and make amends. As he looked around he recognized the neatly plowed fields, the well-pruned orchards, the carefully tended paths. It was Tirzah's property.

As her house came into view he reined in his horse beside three others. Their riders stood in Tirzah's garden. He recognized none of them, but the robes they wore were those of Israelites. He dismounted and approached.

One of them turned and said, "You're off the main road. This is private property."

"Private property, indeed," Pepi said. "Who are you?"

But the man who had spoken to him was not the one who answered. Instead, a gray-bearded man turned and studied him. "Why, it's Pepi the armorer. You're off the main road, young man. If you're heading for the river

269

you're going the wrong way. If you retrace your steps and then turn left at the road—"

"I don't know you," Pepi said, irritated at the possessive attitude of these strangers. "What happened to the woman who owns this farm?"

The bearded man's eyes narrowed. "This farm was given to me," he said. "I am Shallum, of the tribe of Manasseh. These are my sons. What gives you the right to question us in this tone of voice on our own property?"

"Your property? I intend to bring this matter before Moses. And I doubt that he'll defend your right to steal from the true owner of this land, even if the young men of Israel *have* conquered Bashan for you."

"You can't talk to my father like that!" one young man said.

"Where's the young woman?" Pepi asked. "The one with the golden hair? Have you thrown her off the property?"

"She is a servant working off her indenture," Shallum said haughtily. "Although I don't know what the affairs of a Bashanite slut have to do with the likes of you."

"Take warning. You're trying my patience. My head hurts, and if you continue giving me a bad time, I won't be answerable for the consequences. The woman—where is she?"

"None of your business," said Shallum's older son. "Now get off our land."

Pepi ignored him. "Shallum, where is she? Bring her to me right now."

"I've had about enough of this," the younger son grated, drawing his sword.

Pepi stood very still and looked at him. "The army is away in Midian," he said. "All the young men of Israel who aren't cowards or slackers are fighting with it. Why

270

are you here, impersonating real men but stealing from unprotected women?" The sneer in his voice was reflected on his face.

The young man looked down at Pepi's empty hands—he had yet to reach for the huge sword at his belt—and drew the wrong conclusions. "You talk very big for a man unwilling to defend himself."

"Son, wait," Shallum said. "This is the hero of the battle of Bashan you're talking to, after all. If I were you . . ."

For the first time a wariness appeared in the young man's eyes, but not in his words. "Are you suggesting we let this braggart drive us off our land?"

"No," Shallum said. "Just go and get the girl."

Pepi's head was killing him, and there were spots in his vision, but he refused to show any sign of weakness. "This braggart still intends to drive you off land you stole."

Shallum abandoned his caution. "And why should Moses take the word of a foreigner, a nonbeliever, over one of his own people?"

"Because Moses is an honorable man. Because he knows that law of yours insists on justice."

"Nonsense," Shallum said. "The law governs the faithful, not the unbelieving rabble. Besides, Joshua gave us the land. You talk to Moses, but Moses won't be around long. And when Joshua becomes leader of Israel, you'll find that he looks at things from our point of view, not yours."

"I guess we'll have to settle the matter once and for all before Moses steps down, won't we?" Pepi said. Then, turning to the elder son, he added, "Don't the sons of Manasseh believe in obeying their fathers? Shallum told you to get the woman. Now go get her."

IV

Pepi led his horse to the trough. Taking another look at the still-unused sword at the armorer's side, Shallum whispered to his elder son, "Get the girl."

"But, Father—"

"Do as I say. We may have to give ground . . . at first. He does have the ear of Moses, and if we bring something before the old man for adjudication and we lose . . . "

"But if we delay bringing it before the magistrate until Joshua has returned and the old man has died . . . " the young man said with a smile.

The younger son snorted. "So meanwhile we let this foreigner grab our property and hand it over to the heathen bitch. If you'd just let me take him on right here and now—"

"He'd chop you to pieces," his father said. "He has the reputation of being second only to Joshua in his skill with the sword. And he does not even fear Joshua."

"And Joshua," his elder son said, "fears only Moses. Your idea is a good one, Father. I will go find the woman."

The younger son spluttered. "B-but—"

"We are agreed," his father said decisively. "A strategic retreat. After Moses has passed on, we will regain this land and more. I know the magistrate well. He owes me favors. Without Moses to countermand his decisions, he will restore to us everything due us. And perhaps there will even be a stiff fine against the foreigner. I know he's rich. He and Iri were said to be related to Demetrios, the richest man in the world. If there's a levy on his property, a punitive one for bringing false litigation—"

"And for defrauding one of the chosen, perhaps?" his older son suggested with a smile. "He's not popular, and if in the meantime we plant rumors about his being too familiar with the golden-haired foreign woman . . ."

"Splendid," Shallum approved. "Go and get the woman."

Moses dismounted with great care, leaning heavily on the girl. Finally when he had both feet on the ground he looked around and located the path up the mountain. "Thank you, my dear," he said. "Now if you would only be so kind as to mind the animal here while I make my way to the top."

"But, sir," the girl said. "The path is uneven and rough, and if you were to fall—"

"It's all right, my child. I have been negotiating more difficult paths all my life, and I promise to be careful. I have Aaron's staff to lean on." He smiled. "This gnarled old piece of wood has wrought many miracles by the will of Almighty God in the past, and perhaps it has one more in it." He paused. "As a matter of fact, I'm sure of it. God has promised me that before I died I would see into Canaan, and now is the time."

"Well, sir . . . if you're sure that's what you want. The elders would punish me if they thought I let you come to any harm."

"Be assured that Helek will bear witness that this was my idea and that I was quite adamant." He patted her affectionately on the arm. "Don't worry, my dear. God will spare me until I'm safely back down the hill. I have His promise."

She smiled timidly and took the reins of the ass from him. He turned and very slowly made his way up Mount Nebo.

From the top, he could look down on the plain below. The green patch of vegetation that hid the Jordan from view wound its way through the rolling land below. To his left was the Salt Sea and beyond it the hills of Jericho. Somewhere far beyond was the Great Sea.

A land of milk and honey? Actually it looked arid and forbidding. But a land looked as the people who loved it wished it to look. Moses knew his people would make a garden of the land if only their combative neighbors would allow them enough time to transform it.

O Israel! he thought, suddenly saddened. *It won't be your neighbors who get in the way of your plans for this land. It will be your own wrongheaded and willful behavior.*

Yahweh had forewarned him, that day only weeks before, after he had officially named Joshua as his heir. Appearing in a pillar of cloud God had told him: *You are soon to lie with your fathers. And the people will go astray, after the alien gods in their midst, in the land they are about to enter. They will forsake Me and break the covenant I made with them. Then My anger will flare up against them, and I will abandon them and hide My countenance from them. They shall be ready prey, and many evils and troubles shall befall them.*

And of course Moses knew it was so. The Israelites had always been wayward and rebellious, and it had been all he and Aaron could do to keep them under control during the years of trekking through the desert, with hostile tribes and Egyptian patrols hunting them down like wild animals.

It would be Joshua's problem from now on. His own burdens would be laid down. He would be sleeping in the bosom of Abraham and knowing at last full communion with the God of All. At God's command he had, for many years, been burdened with earthly matters. Now the burden would fall to the others; they would make their own mistakes and celebrate their own triumphs. His part was done.

He smiled, letting his eyes sweep over the land one more time, and turned to head slowly down the hill. At the bottom he saw the girl, her large brown eyes watching him.

"Please, sir," she said. "Don't be sad."

"I'm not," he said. "I feel very much at peace. I don't know how many years it's been since I felt this much at peace."

But even as he said it she saw him begin to fade. The light left his eyes, and his knees buckled. She rushed to his side, but she was not strong enough to keep him from falling. And when she knelt over him and felt for his pulse, she knew that it was too late. His race was run. And on his old face was a look of peace and innocence. For all his great age, his face was that of a sleeping child.

"Here she is," Shallum's son said, pushing Tirzah forward. She wore a plain robe, the kind the Israelites gave servants, but it was two handspans too short for her body and her long, bare legs stuck out. The sleeves fell halfway down her arms. Pepi, seeing the half-angry, half-confused look on her face, thought she was the most beautiful of women.

"I'll thank you to take your hands off her," Pepi said. "She's a free woman, not to be manhandled." The young man released her and stepped back. "And you can go, all of you. Gather up only what you brought with you when you came to Bashan and get out."

The younger son started to speak, but Shallum quickly put a restraining hand on his arm. "This is not the last you'll hear of us," Shallum said.

"It is a matter of complete indifference to me whether I ever hear of you again," Pepi said. "But if the young lady ever hears of you again, you will reckon with me. You could lose everything you claim to own."

"And how could we do that?" the younger son demanded.

"I could take it from you by force," Pepi said. "With or without your law. With or without the approval of Moses. And what I might then take from you could include your lives."

The young man's hand dropped to his belt, but once again his father restrained him. "We'll discuss this later."

The three of them backed into the road and scurried away to where their horses were tethered.

For the first time Tirzah spoke. "I . . . I don't understand. I thought you were one of them."

"I'm not. As they've reminded me many times. Never mind that I've traveled with them all my life. Suddenly these things don't matter." He put one hand to his head and grimaced. "My head is ready to burst."

For the first time Tirzah noticed the scar across his forehead. "You're hurt!" she cried, then stopped. "Is that what I did to you? And here you've helped me."

"It's all right. I've just been ill, very ill, and perhaps I may have gotten out of bed earlier than I ought to. Perhaps I could sit down somewhere."

"Let me help you. Lean on me."

"Suddenly I'm dizzy," Pepi said. "And I can't catch my breath. It's ridiculous a strong—"

But he did not finish the sentence. He fell to his knees, and it was all Tirzah could do to maneuver his deadweight into the house. There he lay like a dead man, barely breathing.

*   *   *

Shallum and his sons crossed the ridge into the valley where the great battle had taken place and met a rider bound for the Jordan.

"I have good news and bad," the rider told them. "The good news is that of the great victory in Midian. Joshua has put the Midianites to the sword. He has taken great booty. Midian as a separate nation is no more."

"You said there was bad news as well," Shallum said. "What was it?"

"Moses is dead."

The messenger waited for signs of shock. Instead there were smiles of triumph.

V

Pepi sat up and stared around. Where was he? Desperately he searched his memory; but then golden-haired Tirzah appeared, and he remembered.

"You mustn't exert yourself. Lie back and let me bring a wet cloth for your head," she said.

He waved the suggestion away and swung his feet to the floor. "It's all right. I just overestimated my stamina. It was a long ride and . . ."

Her hand, large, strong, beautifully shaped, and tanned, fell on his shoulder, sending tremors through his body. "Lie down. I don't want you having another attack."

He looked up. Her smile was warm and genuine, and her pale blue eyes were bewitching. "I did act stupid, didn't I?" he said. "Imagine challenging those men. What if I'd had an attack right then?"

"I thought you were wonderful, brave, and caring. But aren't you going to get into trouble? Those people have conquered the land, and Shallum is obviously a man of standing."

"So am I," he said, cradling his head, hoping to stop the dull ache. "Even though I'm not of their race. And Shallum would be ill advised to stand in my way. I don't get along well with Joshua now, but I can't imagine Moses letting such an injustice be done to me or to anyone I befriended."

"But how is this?" she asked, sitting next to his bed and looking at him intently. "I thought they were people with little regard for anyone not of their blood and had plans to conquer and enslave all of Canaan."

"They may not be quite that bad," Pepi said. "Moses is a good man; he's been like a father to me since I was a boy. He would not knowingly let anything unfair happen."

"Then how were they allowed to seize my house and lands and make a slave of me? I'm not even a Bashanite."

He patted her hand and felt the shock waves through his body. "I intend to find out. Meanwhile no one is going to bother you."

"How kind of you," she said. "Coming back to help me."

He waved her words away. "I won't tolerate injustice. Particularly when it comes from a people who are sworn to follow a law that condemns injustice. If the Israelites forget, I'm going to remind them about their law."

Tirzah looked at him for a moment without speaking.

"When you left I found a strange thought running through my mind, and I almost gave in to it. I told you that you could visit, but I wanted to say more. I wanted to say that if you had no woman, you should come to me."

He stared up at her, startled. Her great blue eyes

were warm and open, and for a moment he thought he could see straight into her soul. He opened his mouth but could not speak.

"But then I thought about myself," she continued. "I am this great oversize cow of a woman, half again as big as all the local men. Everyone likes small women, and I would only be making a fool of myself speaking so to you."

His voice was soft and full of wonderment. "How you can have lived this long and not had fifty, a hundred men tell you that you were the most beautiful woman in the world, I cannot imagine." He took her hand in his and felt the thrill. "You are exactly the right size for a man like me. I would not have you any different. I . . . I have no woman. Traveling with the Israelites, there was little chance. I have known few women and never one such as you."

There were tears in her eyes. "You are kind," she whispered.

"No. I always tell the absolute truth. It gets me in trouble, but I do it."

"Tell me more about yourself," Tirzah said. "I want to know everything about you. I think that perhaps, whether I knew it or not, I have been looking for someone like you all my life. And if I am right and I have found that person at last, I want no secrets between us."

Now it was Pepi who was crying. He had not cried since he was a child and, until this moment, had not known he was capable of tears. As her big, beautiful hand stroked his cheek he found desire stirring in him, a desire that eclipsed any he had known before. He felt like a stallion, a bull, a wild animal.

He pulled her face to his and kissed her. Weeping uncontrollably, he covered her golden face with kisses. Suddenly her tanned goddess's body stood naked before him, and he was taking her.

*　　*　　*

Hanniel, son of Ephod, had been named by Moses as magistrate over the tribe of Manasseh and all the lands assigned to the tribe. He listened patiently to Shallum.

"Well?" asked Shallum's hotheaded younger son. "Are you going to do something about it? We can't have nonbelievers taking property away from our people, can we?"

"My son is impetuous," Shallum apologized. "This is a fault, as is speaking tactlessly to men of substance and dignity. For these I apologize profusely; I shall discipline him. His positive qualities include a simple and straightforward nature, incapable of dissembling. For these I value him. He does say what is in all our minds."

Hanniel smiled wryly. "You put the matter to me most delicately, and in truth you would appear to have been dealt with unfairly. Unfortunately, I can do nothing for you for many days."

"How many days?" Shallum asked.

"Thirty," Hanniel replied. "It is the period of mourning for Moses. During that time no legal action can be taken. I'm sorry if this inconveniences you."

"Inconvenience? We have no home."

"But in the meantime . . ."

Shallum understood the venal light in the magistrate's eyes. "Yes?"

"I could for a consideration, you understand . . ."

"That of course can be arranged," Shallum agreed.

Hanniel nodded. "In the meantime I can be studying the reasoning behind your complaint and checking it against the codified law."

"So that when the thirty days are up, there will be no lengthy delays?"

"Precisely."

"I quite understand," Shallum said, "that no reasonable person would ask a magistrate, whose time is valuable, to do such work without compensation."

"You have a certain way with words, if I may be permitted a personal remark," Hanniel said with a sly grin.

Shallum leaned forward and whispered in Hanniel's ear. "Now," he said, stepping back, "is that sufficient?"

"It is a fair figure, neither too high nor too low. If you will have the scribe write up your grievances, I will begin considering them."

The passion had arisen in him three times, and Pepi had satisfied it as many times. On Tirzah's lovely face was a complacent look. She yawned behind her hand and smiled at him. "You are every bit the man you look." She leaned over and kissed him, and laid her golden head on his brown chest. "How happy I am."

"And I." His hand smoothed her golden hair. "You've heard the story of my life; do you still think well of me?"

"How can I not?" she asked. "What side have you shown me so far other than that of a gallant and righteous man. How could I not love you?"

"Love?" he said. "You speak of love?" He sighed. "So that's what it is that I feel. I was wondering what to call it. How glad I am to hear that it has a name."

She raised herself on her elbows to look at him. "The moment I saw your strong blacksmith's arms, I wanted to feel them around me."

He pulled her close to his heart. "I love you," he said with a sigh. "I am not used to those words. I know only the friendship and fatherly love I received from Moses and Iri."

"I'm glad there was someone to befriend you," she

said. "But now you have me. You need no other love. If another woman looked at you I'd kill her."

He smiled. He was deliriously happy. He was in love.

VI

Shallum's family had depleted Tirzah's garden, and she had to go to market in the closest town. When she returned she found Pepi repairing her front door. "How wonderful," she said. "I've needed a man who can fix things."

"You'll have one from now on. Come, let me unload the donkey."

"Wait a moment," she said. "I'm afraid I bring bad news. I heard in the market that Moses is dead. I'm sorry. I know how much you loved him."

Pepi's smile faded. His eyes filled with tears. "I'll miss him. He was a good, wise friend." Suddenly his expression became wary. "With Moses here no one could speak against me. Now, with Joshua at the helm . . ."

"But I thought you and Joshua were childhood friends."

"We were. But things have grown sour between us in recent years. And I may be partly to blame. He's a soldier, and I'm a man of peace. I'm afraid I've been trying to act as his conscience."

Tirzah shook her head. "In the village they speak of you as the hero of the battle of Bashan. And they take their cue from Joshua, except . . ."

"Except what?"

"At the market, the Israelite women talked about the

heathen slut who's leading the foreign armorer astray."
She sighed. "As if I were a sorceress who had seduced you
through magic."

Pepi smiled. "You did. There is a magic about you,
you know. At least it works on me."

"Hardly anyone spoke to me. One woman refused to
sell me anything. And she made the sign of the evil eye at
me."

"Fools," he said contemptuously. "Idiots."

She took a string bag of fruit off the donkey, then led
the animal into the stable. "Moses is gone now, and if the
behavior of the Israelites depended on his wisdom and
compassion, I'd say people like myself are in great trouble."

Pepi shook his head. "No, they wouldn't dare fool
with you, not once it is known you're under my protection. At least I don't think they would. If anyone harms
you or tries to take your property—"

"But you said the law was largely what Moses said it
was. And that it was he who would protect us. Now who
will protect us?"

Pepi frowned for a moment. "I don't know the new
magistrate here. Perhaps I should go see him. When did
Moses die?"

"Four days ago, I think."

"Good. That gives us . . . twenty-six days."

She smiled, her eyes full of love. "I'm sure that we
won't run out of things to occupy us."

"We won't," he said fervently. "But I was thinking
about something else."

"Yes?"

"You know Canaan, don't you?"

"Yes. My husband had relatives there. We used to
visit, but when he died I lost contact with them."

"That doesn't matter. Do you think it would be safe
for me to go there?"

She thought for a moment. "I don't know why not. You don't look like an Israelite. If anything you look like a dark-complected Bashanite."

"I was thinking I'd like to go over to Joppa and perhaps stop by Jericho on the way. I want to look around and see if I can find any sources of tin among the traders. I was going to check out Damascus, but Joppa's closer."

"Then you want to leave me so soon?"

"No, I was going to take you with me. I want to be able to discuss with you everything that happens."

"What a nice thing to say."

Pepi smiled. "I mean it. I don't ever want to sleep alone again. Or, for that matter, with anyone else but you. Come with me. We'll take a trip to the seacoast and have an adventure. I'll hire someone to look after your property and your animals while we're gone."

"One of my own old servants is still living on the farm. He can do it."

"Splendid. We'll go see the city, and we can find my uncle's agent and inquire about him."

"Uncle? You mean Iri?"

"No, although we can inquire about him, too. I mean Demetrios the Magnificent. He's also my uncle. The richest man in the world. The man whose merchant fleet is larger than that of Crete and perhaps even Egypt."

"How exciting! Will we meet him?"

"Not now. He's getting on and seldom, if ever, leaves his private island. But perhaps some day we can visit him."

"Oh, Pepi, let's go. At least as far as Joppa."

"All right," Pepi said, his mind made up. "We'll leave as soon as possible." Every day he felt stronger; his headaches were gone, and he was ready for adventure.

*   *   *

In the days before Moses's death, the Gadites and the tribe of Reuben had split the kingdom of Sihon of the Amorites, and had then begun one by one to occupy the conquered lands. Some of the cities Joshua's men had captured were reoccupied; others were left in ruins and used only by wandering herdsmen. As the Israelites settled in, the land and the names of some cities were changed. The Gadites rebuilt Dibon, Ataroth, Aroer, Atroth-shophan, Jazer, Jogbehah, Beth-nimrah, and Beth-haran; the Reubenites occupied and renamed Elealeh, Kiriathaim, Nebo, Baal-meon, and Sibmah but kept the name of ancient Heshbon because it had been known to Abraham and Isaac and Jacob.

Manasseh alone was allowed to expand its territory. The subtribe of Machir, son of Manasseh, had gone to Gilead and captured it after a brief resistance; the subtribe of Jair, son of Manasseh, had conquered a cluster of towns and renamed them after their patriarch himself; and the subtribe of Nobah had done the same with old Kenath. There was no resistance, and the women, young boys, and old men of the Sihonites and Bashanites were easily conquered by the slackers and noncombatants of Israel. Yet there was a feeling of self-satisfaction among the conquerors, who treated the vanquished with reprehensible arrogance.

This did not long survive the triumphant return of Joshua's army. These young men were real soldiers, and as they watched the arrogant new overlords oppressing the newly conquered, they wondered why they had risked their lives for such as these.

Joshua sent Caleb on a tour of these outlying areas. And when he returned, Joshua listened to his recitation silently, with no emotion.

"What do you think, sir?" Caleb asked. "Should we

give the land back to the Sihonites and Bashanites and kick our distant cousins out into the desert to die? This is not what I fought the enemy for. When we put Bashan to the sword, I believed we were conquering land for upright and God-fearing people—not self-righteous hypocrites."

Joshua frowned. "You're talking about our people. And what is wrong with dispossessing heathens whose sons and husbands fought against us and lost? Even though, mind you, they ambushed us and we were outnumbered."

"But they fought bravely and now their widows and children are being treated like dirt by those who were too lazy or too cowardly to fight."

"Why are you taking the side of this rabble of unbelievers?" Joshua asked.

"Sir, I study the law just like the next man. Remember that it says 'Cursed be he who subverts the rights of the stranger, the fatherless, and the widow.'? And 'Cursed be he who will not uphold the terms of this teaching and observe them.'?"

Joshua was becoming irritable. "Can't all these supposed wrongs be redressed by the judges appointed by Moses?"

"Sir, the foreigners don't know about judges. All they know is that they've lost everything they owned and are now slaves. They see themselves as having no rights at all."

"Well, have someone explain their rights to them at the next gathering."

"But that won't be until after the period of mourning is over. By then I doubt any of them will believe us. They don't seem to realize the law applies to them, or to our dealings with them." He paused. "Unfortunately many of our own people—and even some of the magistrates—share this perception."

"Bah!" Joshua said. "Tell me about this later. Frankly, I'm getting tired of all this weeping and gnashing of teeth over the lost 'rights' of the heathen."

"But, sir, the law clearly states—"

"Whatever happened to Pepi?" Joshua asked. "I expected to find him waiting for me when we came marching home, ready to scold me for not treating the Midianites better." He chuckled humorlessly. "If he'd actually seen what happened, he'd *really* be indignant. Not that I'm sorry. They killed too many of our men. They had to pay."

"About Pepi, sir, I have heard rumors. . . ."

"What kind of rumors?"

"It would appear that he's taken up with some Bashanite whore and driven a family of Manassehites off the land assigned to them and given it to the woman."

Joshua's eyes widened. "Pepi, bedding some Bashanite slut? I can hardly believe it. How reliable was your source?"

"Very. There's been a formal complaint by the family Pepi drove off the land. They said he threatened their lives."

"Pepi the pacifist?"

"And some of the villagers say the woman is a witch."

"Have you talked to the magistrate?"

"Yes. He thinks the family is right."

"The matter can't be acted upon now. But keep me informed."

VII

Shallum greeted his sons at the door of the house Hanniel had allocated to him. "Come in," he said. "You're just in time. Hanniel will be here soon. We now have a friend."

His elder son nodded approvingly at the house. "I can see that. According to the villagers this house belonged to a half brother of Og of Bashan. How did you manage to acquire it?"

"Your father did not get where he is," Shallum said, "by being a trusting, credulous fool, or a simpleton who knows nothing of the way business is done in this part of the world."

His younger son grinned. "So you've got the whole thing fixed. Congratulations. I knew I'd gotten my acquisitive streak and my devious turn of mind from somewhere."

"When Hanniel is here, we will treat him like visiting royalty. And when the blond witch's property becomes ours legally, we will keep this house as well. Perhaps I will give the Bashanite slut's farm to the two of you."

"Sounds good to me," the younger son said. "Meanwhile I've been busy, spreading rumors. The Bashanite is now known as a witch, a prostitute, and a blaspheming follower of the great goddess."

"Good," Shallum said, turning to his other son. "And what news have *you* for me?"

The young man beamed. "Not that I like to brag, but I think that my news may even surpass yours, not that I had anything to do with it." He paused, allowing his words to sink in. "Pepi and the Bashanite have crossed over into Canaan."

Shallum's mouth hung open; his eyes were wide with surprise. "What did you say?"

"They crossed the Jordan yesterday. Riding the woman's horses, and leading two pack asses. As if," he added, "they were going for a long time."

"But this is splendid," the younger son said. "We can reoccupy the land."

"No," his father said. "I know Pepi's reputation as a swordsman. And he also knows the law. He'll certainly be back before the mourning period for Moses is up, and unless we have a signed order from Hanniel—"

"But how are we going to get anything like that?" his son asked. "Hanniel is forbidden by the law to take any legal action now."

The older son nodded his understanding. "When Pepi drove us away you went to Hanniel; after the mourning period, he ruled in our favor. This, of course, made the ruling valid. If the armed representatives of Hanniel are on the property when Pepi and the woman return . . ." He smiled nastily.

"Meanwhile," the younger son continued, "there is certain advantage to be gained from the fact that Pepi and the woman—whose loyalty is suspect in the first place—have crossed into enemy territory. What if I were to spread the rumor that they were spies, in the pay of Canaan?"

Shallum nodded. "Do it immediately."

They spent the night in Jericho, where Pepi made copious notes on the city's fortifications, and they reached Joppa and the sea at noon on the second day.

Tirzah was delighted. "Oh, Pepi, smell the air. I've been dreaming about this for years. How I'd love to be able to live within the sight and smell of the sea."

After stabling the animals and unloading their gear at an inn, they walked the streets of the ancient town. The sea was indeed beautiful, and Pepi, who had spent very little of his life near the water, suddenly wondered what it would be like to do as Iri had done and find his way to Demetrios's island and settle down with the woman he loved.

"We could live by the sea if you liked," he said. "Goodness knows there's little enough to hold me to life inland these days. Let's think about it."

Tirzah squeezed his hand happily. As they passed through the open-air market she paused to look at this stall and that. She bought a head covering made of cloth from Greece and admired a pair of Egyptian-style sandals.

"Just remember that I didn't have much money to bring along and may not be able to buy you anything expensive just now," Pepi said as she stopped at the jeweler's stall. "But if we found something you couldn't do without, I could find Demetrios's agent and draw on my funds."

"So you've funds on deposit?" she asked. "Do you mean I've found myself a wealthy man after all?"

"Well, I'm reasonably well-off, I think. Demetrios administers the family funds. I have no idea what I'm worth, but it must be considerable. Demetrios's agent would know and would advance me funds, I'm sure."

"I'll try to be frugal, for now," she said with a giggle, "but I can't guarantee anything." She bent over the flats full of gleaming gold jewelry. "Oh, look, isn't this beautiful."

She pointed to a lovely gold anklet and a matching pair of bracelets. Pepi examined the pieces.

"I've seen these before," he said, turning to the proprietor of the stall. "Excuse me, sir. Whose work is this?"

"This is a rare find indeed," the vendor said. "The maker of these pieces had been out of the business for twenty years or more. He was a great master of the craft. And these are the first new pieces of his that have turned up for many years. They were, oddly enough, found on a slave being prepared for auction."

"What 'master of the craft'?" Pepi demanded.

"Why, Iri of Thebes, of course. Any jewelry dealer

around the Great Sea would recognize this work. If you like it, sir, you'd better grab it. It won't last long."

"Iri? That's my uncle. How did you say you came by this?"

"Why, traders brought in a new group of slaves today. They took these from one of them. A pity, in a way. Without the gold they'll have a hard time finding a buyer. Who'd want a blind woman?"

"Today?" Pepi asked.

"Why, yes. She'd be one of the lot that's going on the block right about now. Why? If you're curious you could probably catch the last of it."

"Where?" Pepi said, his voice tense.

"Down by the docks. This woman seemed to be some sort of desert tribal, if you could judge by her coloring and the robes she was wearing."

"Excuse me," Pepi said. He grabbed Tirzah's wrist and pulled her along after him. "Quick. There isn't a moment to lose. I have a feeling something horrible has happened."

They rushed headlong toward the docks, colliding with other passersby, blundering into goat wagons. At the end of one long avenue a slow-moving oxcart blocked their progress. Pepi cursed while the cart moved ponderously along. "Oh, gods, Tirzah," he said, checking his purse. "I don't have enough money to do any good."

"But Pepi, why do you need money?"

"Don't you understand? That slave might be Iri's wife."

"You said you could get money from Demetrios's man here."

"But I don't even know his name. It would probably take all afternoon to find him. And what happened to Iri? How could a strong man like him let her become a slave?"

The ox cart moved jerkily past, and Pepi grabbed Tirzah's arm, and they dashed through the opening. As they sprinted down the street, Pepi was surprised at how easily Tirzah's long legs kept up with his own loping stride. When finally the street ended they could see a crowd gathered in the square before a long platform. They stopped, stood on tiptoe, and scanned the sad faces of the people on the platform.

VIII

Tirzah looked at the slaves and then at Pepi. His face was contorted with anger. "Pepi," she said. "The one fourth from the left. The pregnant one. Is that she?"

He nodded. "Look at her. Look at all of them. Do they have to do that? Do they have to destroy the last vestige of their dignity?"

She turned to the girl, standing naked on the platform while the auctioneer took bids on a tall, strapping Nubian. The great bulge in her belly made the girl— Keturah? Was that the name—look all the more vulnerable. She was not many weeks away from delivering. Tirzah's heart went out to her. She carried herself, even in these disgraceful circumstances, with a quiet sense of her own worth and was obviously doing her best not to let herself be destroyed. "The poor thing. Pepi, can't we do something?"

Pepi's mouth was clamped in a thin, angry line. "Not without challenging that whole squad of guardsmen over there. I could get us all killed or hauled up on the slave block." He hefted his purse again. "Let's see, there are three slaves before her." He looked at Tirzah. "Can women bid for slaves here?"

"I—I think so," she said. "As representatives of men, at least. Although when the sale is actually formalized, a male is required to make his mark on the contract."

He tossed her the purse. "I'm going to try to find Demetrios's man. Usually his agents are powerful and can intervene in any civil problem. If not, I can at least get enough money from him to come back here and outbid anyone for her."

He squeezed Tirzah's hand. "In the meantime, bid for her. Delay things any way you can until I get back and outbid everyone or stop the whole proceeding. I'll be as quick as I can. And Tirzah . . ."

"Yes?"

"Speak to her if you can. Tell her not to give up hope. Tell her we are trying to help her."

As unobtrusively as her height permitted, Tirzah worked her way through the crowd, toward the slave block. When she finally pushed her way into the front row where she could reach out and touch the boards, she waited for a lull in the bidding and then whispered, "Keturah, is that you?"

At first, the girl did not seem to hear, or perhaps she could not connect the strange voice with anyone she knew. Then Tirzah reached up and touched the girl's bare foot. "Keturah!" she said again. "It's a friend. Don't be afraid."

A sighted person would have turned toward Tirzah, but Keturah only cocked her head to hear better. "Who's there?" she asked softly.

"You don't know me," Tirzah said. "I'm Pepi of Kerma's

woman. My name is Tirzah. Pepi has gone to find some money to outbid these people for you."

"Pepi!" Suddenly, through the desolate look on her face, a thin smile broke. "Dear Pepi, how good of him! But where is my Iri? He never came back. Have you heard from him? Is he safe?"

"I don't know. We just got here. Pepi's gone to see if he can find Demetrios's representative."

"That's just what Iri was going to do. He never came back. And then I was kidnapped and transferred to several different ships before I was brought here."

Tirzah glanced anxiously at the slave dealer. He was calling for another slave. Now there were two ahead of Keturah. "I'm supposed to stay here and delay the bidding until Pepi returns."

"No, you can't. You can't do anything to anger the dealer. If anyone gets in his way they'll get taken away by the guards. He's a vicious, evil man. Last night he raped one of the other girls."

Tirzah shuddered as she forced herself to study the dealer. He was an ugly specimen. One of his ears was missing, and his face bore the scars of knife fights. His expression was one of brute stupidity. "Don't worry, Keturah," Tirzah said, trying to ignore his forearms, which were as big as Pepi's. "We'll protect you. We won't let him touch you."

"Please! He's a brutal man. Don't do anything that will make him angry at you."

Tirzah bit her lip and looked up. A squad of guards, fearfully armed, stood at the far end of the platform.

"Sold," the dealer announced. "Sold to the gentleman from Arvad for fifty shekels." He handed the slave over to her new master and turned toward Keturah. "Give me that next one. Quickly."

*   *   *

The trade representative's name was Geshem of Joppa, and he had recently inherited his position from his father but had spent most of his youth working as a moneylender in Sidon. He looked at Pepi, at his plain desert-dweller dress, and his heavy forearms and thick calluses. "I'm sorry," he said. "You must understand the need for caution. You, whom I don't know at all, expect me to believe that you are Demetrios's nephew and that I should stop a slave auction taking place under respectable auspices—"

"For the gods' sake there's no time to waste! You'll be sorry if you don't help me. Does Demetrios's business mean anything to you? Will you survive in trade without it?"

"Are you threatening me? I'll have to ask you to leave."

"Damn it!" Pepi said, hiking up his robe to reveal the birthmark on his back. "Under the robe I'm as light-colored as you are. I've just spent twenty years in the sun. And do you perhaps recognize this birthmark? Every male member of the clan, regardless of where he was born, bears this mark."

"Well . . ." The man was beginning to waver, but caution still ruled him. "I've heard rumors, but any man can bear a mark like that. If you only had something else to show—a seal ring of Demetrios's, for instance."

"And any man can steal a ring." Seeing the stubborn look on the man's face, Pepi changed direction. "Look, this is Iri's wife I'm trying to save. Can you imagine how angry he'll be if he finds out you allowed her to be sold into slavery?"

Geshem shrugged off his words. "Iri isn't here. He's still off in the desert among the barbarians."

"What?" Pepi erupted. "Iri isn't there! No one in

Demetrios's organization has heard from him?" Pepi's patience was at an end. He grabbed Geshem's cloak and pulled him so close that their two faces almost met. "If there's even the smallest hint of resistance from you, so help me, I'll break your neck. Apparently you haven't met many Children of the Lion and don't know much about us. Well, let me tell you: We have a number of traits in common, and one of them is that we're all very strong. We also have very little patience with idiots. So if you value your neck, do as I say."

Geshem's feet dangled off the ground. "Put me down. I'll get the m-money."

But when they arrived at the square they found Tirzah, weeping uncontrollably and wringing her hands. The sale was over, and the slaves were nowhere to be seen.

"Oh, Pepi!" she sobbed. "I did my best. I did. I held the sale up as long as I could, but then they insisted, and I didn't have enough money. One more coin, just one, and maybe I could have bought her. But I didn't have it, and the men who were bidding against me knew it. They made fun of me. Keturah, the poor thing, was hauled away naked. I tried to give her my robe, but they laughed and threw it in the dirt."

"Where did they take her?"

"To the boat," she said, tears streaming. "Maybe if we run we could catch them."

Pepi glared at Geshem, who averted his eyes. "Come along. You, too, Geshem. You're about to find out whether you still have a job."

As they dashed out onto the pier the last of the merchant ships was heading out to sea, sails billowing.

"See there by the starboard rail?" Tirzah shouted. "That's Keturah! And someone's given her a blanket. They're loading the slaves into the hold." She rushed to the end of the pier and cried out: "Keturah, don't give up hope. We'll find you! Can you hear me, Keturah!"

But the wind blew her words away, and Tirzah buried her face in her hands.

Pepi stared Geshem in the eye. The agent tried to look away, but Pepi grabbed his chin and forced him to look after the departing vessel. "Tell me everything you know about that ship."

Geshem's voice was tight and constricted, his face fearful. "She's the *Massilia*," he said. "I read her manifest today."

"Where's she bound?" Pepi asked, his voice shaking with anger.

Geshem swallowed and spoke in a voice that was suddenly weak. "Every port of the Great Sea," he said. "Every place between here and Tarraco. You'll never find her now."

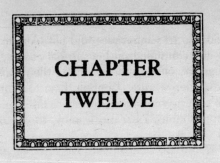

CHAPTER TWELVE

On the Great Sea

I

Iri manned the oars of the *Hephaistos* with a newfound anger and bitterness. Despite his vow not to give in to wishful thinking, he had expected some change in his status after saving the Minotaur's life. Instead, he had been thrown back into the rowers' bays and given a larger and heavier oar to pull.

It was a painful lesson, and as he hauled the long pole he sometimes asked himself if he had been right in saving the pirate's life. One side of his mind said that the pirate, an evil man, should have been allowed to die. But the other side told him that his instinct had not played him false, that somehow there would emerge an opportunity to turn the action to his advantage. After all, as the other rowers were quick to admit, there were many masters worse than the Minotaur. At least the black-bearded man was scrupulously fair, and a slave who minded his business and did as he was told would likely get in no trouble.

Zimrida, to Iri's annoyance, did not seem to acknowledge this and continued on his suicidal course, insulting the oar masters, cursing them, calling their mothers and sisters pox-ridden whores, taunting them to fight him.

From time to time Iri would try to intervene, but he was no longer Zimrida's seatmate, able to whisper words of caution to him.

The oar master had noticed that Iri's powerful arm could turn a weak oar into a strong one, so Iri was used to shore up weak spots in the galley. At first Iri had held out hope that they would leave him free of the chain, the better to move him about.

But this hope, too, had been dashed. Instead of allowing him more freedom the oar masters, surrounded by burly guards armed to the teeth, had come down into the pit and affixed to his right ankle a second manacle.

One after the other the days of incessant brutal labor passed. On hot days the sun would beat down on the heads and backs of the upper rank of rowers and leave them drenched with sweat, while the foggy nights would find them equally unprotected against the damp chill of the mists of the capricious and uncaring Great Sea.

For many days as he was moved from bench to bench, Iri never found himself seated near Pandion. Then in the chill of one morning he found himself sitting on an inner bench on the port side, with Pandion as his starboard opposite number.

The oar masters tried out various strokes, testing the balance before finally ordering a halt. Iri looked over at Pandion and caught his eye. "Do you hate me for stopping you from killing our beloved captain?"

Pandion looked him up and down. "No," he said resignedly. "You did what you thought was right. I suppose you had notions of earning your freedom. And it was a sensible enough hope. The Minotaur's given men their freedom for much less." He shrugged. "It was I who bungled the job. I can't blame you or anyone else for my failure."

"Well, then," Iri said, "let's be comrades, or if not that, at least not enemies." He crossed his legs and leaned back. "Why did you do it, anyway?"

"It's none of your—" Pandion began. Then he stopped, his shoulders slumped. "My father's dead because of him. I swore to avenge my father, whom I loved very much. But now I've failed not once but twice, and perhaps I'll never get another chance."

"Perhaps not," Iri said. "Certainly not in your present position. But we all have something that we can't help thinking about. The best solution is to concentrate on the rowing."

"You sound like a man who follows his own advice." Pandion studied Iri's massive arms. "You pull a good oar. What are you trying to forget?"

Iri tensed for a moment and then relaxed. Painfully and barely able to hold his emotions in check, he spoke about Keturah. Afterward he breathed deeply, expanding his enormous chest. "I blame myself for losing her, and I would think about her every waking moment if I did not have the oar to distract me."

"You've a heavy burden to bear, my friend," Pandion said. "I won't make it worse for you in the future."

"That's the spirit. Now, I've been watching you. You're going about this rowing business the wrong way. You're wasting effort and fighting the oar instead of letting it feed strength to you. I can help you if you like."

"Anything else you have to say will find me a willing and grateful listener," Pandion said with unaffected humility.

*　　*　　*

But if Pandion listened when Iri spoke, Zimrida did not. The one-eyed man seemed determined to lose, at best, his other eye, at worst, his life. Day and night he tormented the oar master, an Assyrian named Shadunu. Whenever Shadunu was on duty he could count on receiving nothing but abuse from the pit. At first the ingenuity of Zimrida's insults was admirable; but as the days went by even this palled, and the men on the oars beside him began to fear for his life.

Once, just once, the oar masters assigned Iri to the bench next to his old friend's, and Iri tried to talk sense to him. But Zimrida had passed the point of reason and would not listen.

"You're getting soft, Red Face," Zimrida said. "Things are too easy aboard this tub. You're forgetting what you ought most to remember: Those bastards on the top deck are keeping you from your woman."

"Easy, now," Iri said.

This was touchy territory, as Zimrida well knew, but he plowed on nevertheless. "Easy; just because you're growing complacent and forgetting that little blind wife of yours, don't expect everyone else in the pit to suffer your loss of memory. I'm going to hate these sons of bitches as long as I have breath."

"Look, Zimrida, I'm only trying to keep you from—"

"Do me a favor," the one-eyed man hissed. "Mind your own business."

As always, the rowers remained unaware of what was happening on deck. Nothing drifted down to them except the shout of the *keleustes* and the flute playing of the *trieraules*. But one day, as they rested, a new flutist took over. Iri, who had a musical ear, recognized the change almost immediately, not only because of the different tunes he played but because of the compelling lilt.

Iri was sitting next to a huge African when the playing changed. "That's going to be a lot easier to row to, don't you think?" he asked.

The black man smiled, displaying a gold tooth. It was the only thing of value he still owned, and the only reason he still had it was that no man had had the temerity to take it from him. He had bitten one man's hand to the bone already. "It's still forced labor," he said, "and repugnant to me." They spoke in Achaean, the common language of the sea, and the man's speech was uncommonly precise and almost totally lacking in accent. "But I'll agree with you for the sake of the conversation. This player has a flair."

"We haven't talked before," Iri said. "Who are you? You're Nubian, aren't you?"

His seatmate shook his head. "People use the word imprecisely. They call me a Nubian, but I come from the Mountains of Fire, many thousands of leagues south of Nubia."

Iri looked at him again in surprise. "Have you ever heard of a man called Akhilleus?"

"That name awakens no memories," the black man replied. "Should it?"

"He went under another name among your people. 'Akhilleus' was the name our people gave him. He was a very great man. It seems to me that the men of my family, who knew and loved him, said that he came from your part of the world and was a great man among your people as well. The name, what was it? I think that some of your people called him 'Akillu.' "

Now it was the black man's turn for surprise. "*Mtebi!* You speak of the great Mtebi, king of kings!"

"That's the name," Iri said. "He was the first man ever to unify all the tribes of your nation. But when he had once won a crown among you, he refused it and came back north to become—"

"—greatest of the Nubian kings. Yes, he was an ancestor of mine. For the sake of Mtebi many of our young men came north and took positions with the Nubian army. We worshipped him as if he were a god. This is how I came north, although it was my own folly that lost me my freedom. I will not blame that on Mtebi."

Iri's eyes blazed with excitement. "His destiny was tightly entangled with those of many of my ancestors, too! Did you know that he became the richest man in the world? That he founded the great fortune now administered by my brother, Demetrios the Magnificent? That if it were to be known that you were a slave on a galley on the Great Sea, Demetrios would move mountains to find you and free you?"

"I am gratified to learn of this," the black man said. "Nevertheless, here we are, you the brother of the great Demetrios and I the descendant of his benefactor, and yet we are nothing more than slaves pulling oars on a boat captained by one of his deadliest enemies. It is a very great irony."

Throughout their conversation, Zimrida had kept up his abusive harangue. Finally Shadunu could take it no more. "Shut up down there," he yelled. "If I hear another word, so help me I'll make someone regret it."

Zimrida belched loudly. "All around me, nothing but words," he said. "All threats and never a stroke. Surely any ordinary coward, with the usual cravenness in his yellow system, would—"

And then, without warning, came the lash.

303

II

Theon had been playing an Ionian dance to the rhythm of the *keleustes*'s toneless song. Now, as Shadunu stood over the oar pit and vengefully lashed at an unseen rower below, the sight unnerved Theon so much that he lost the beat and let the tune degenerate into a dirge. Again and again the whip lashed down into the invisible ranks of the rowers; Theon winced, wondering why the man below did not cry out. "Prodicus," he cried out to the mate, "stop him! He's going to kill that man!"

Prodicus shrugged. "It's just that crazy one-eyed wretch again. He's been begging for it."

Reluctantly Theon picked up his flute. But the tune that he played was not the Ionian song. Instead it was a Chaldean march that had been old when Belsunu had trained in distant Ur. For a moment he did not understand why the song suddenly sprang into his head. Then he remembered the words: It was a song written during a slaves' revolt in the Valley of the Euphrates two centuries before.

As always, Zimrida displayed donkeylike endurance, refusing to acknowledge the pain from the whipping. But Iri watched silently, inwardly seething, for as long as he could, then he cried out, "Stop that! You'll kill him!" Clearly out of control, Shadunu bellowed, "Tend to your own business, or so help me, you'll get more of the same yourself."

Iri and the black man beside him exchanged glances.

The lash cracked over their heads, so close that it would take only the smallest misdirection for it to land on them. "Don't do it," Iri's seatmate advised. "Leave well enough alone. Zimrida wants to die. Unlike you, he has no one to live for."

Iri started to stand up. "I watched this happen once before, when they cut up his eye. I'm not going to watch it again." He stood up and hollered, "*Shadunu, stop it! Stop it right now!*"

In answer, the lash changed course, cracking down on Iri's shoulders.

But Iri had been expecting it, and when the lash licked out at him he grasped the leather thong with one rock-hard hand, yanking hard on it and wrapping it around his wrist. Then he pulled down with all his might and felt the oar master tumble over the edge of the pit.

The oar master landed in his lap, knocking the breath out of them both. Shadunu recovered first and, nearly hysterical with fear, tried to claw his way up the rope ladder and out of the pit.

But Iri grabbed the back of his neck and pulled him down. "I told you to leave him alone. One or two lashes, perhaps, to maintain order, but you were trying to kill him."

Shadunu held up one forearm over his face. "Don't kill me," he pleaded. "I was only doing my duty!"

His words were lost as Zimrida reached out for the oar master's throat, throttling him with a huge hand. "Now, the tables are turned, are they? Well, say your prayers, because I'm going to send you to your fathers."

"No!" Iri said. "Don't kill him!" And, as strong as Zimrida's grip was, the one-eyed man felt even stronger fingers prying his hand off the oar master's neck.

"Get away from me, Red Face!" Zimrida said. "Since

when do you save the lives of rotten bastards who'd whip a helpless man to death?"

"Kill him, and they'll kill you," Iri said, pinning the oar master's arms back. "I don't want you dead."

Suddenly the crewmen swarmed down the rope ladders, pulled Shadunu to safety, and roughly hauled both Iri and Zimrida up onto the deck.

The Minotaur had not emerged from his sanctum in several days, and Theon had not seen Nuhara since his return to the *Hephaistos*. Now, however, as the crew hauled the men out of the rower's pit, Theon heard a noise behind him and whirled to see the black-haired captain standing in the open doorway.

"Prodicus!" the pirate chieftain called in an unmistakable voice of command. "What's going on here? Why are the oars stilled? What are those rowers doing on deck?"

"A disturbance, sir," Prodicus said, and he explained the situation.

The Minotaur scowled. "Bring them here!" he ordered in a voice that was only a step below a full-throated roar.

Theon was leaning against the wall of the cabin, watching, when he heard a soft voice behind him. "Theon!"

He started to whirl only to feel a soft hand over his mouth. "Don't turn around or make a fuss," Nuhara whispered as her small hand stole under his chlamys to caress him.

"I'm not supposed to be on deck," she said, "but I've missed you so much. Be awake here tonight, and I'll come to you. He keeps tight control over me, and it's been worse ever since we were ashore."

"Does he suspect?"

"I don't know, but he watches me day and night."

"How dangerous is it for us to meet tonight?" he asked. "I don't want you to get into any trouble."

Her hand ran up and down his back and caressed his bare buttocks seductively. "You can't go through life worrying about getting into trouble."

His hand stole around his back under the chlamys and touched hers. She guided it to her bare breasts. "Easy," he said, detaching his hand. "Or I won't be able to hide my reactions. Go back inside now. I'll see you tonight."

She touched him softly again and slipped back through the door.

"Turn him around," the Minotaur said tonelessly. The crewman to either side of Zimrida slowly spun him around. Angry red welts covered his upper body, his neck, and his shoulders. There were even welts on his face, one dangerously close to his remaining eye. "So this is the loudmouth who provoked the trouble?"

"Yes, sir," Prodicus said. "And the red-faced one is the one who pulled Shadunu down."

The Minotaur faced the two of them. "You lost that eye through the whip, didn't you?"

Zimrida nodded in a surly manner.

"If you continue haranguing the oar masters you're going to lose more than your other eye. You understand that, don't you?"

The light in Zimrida's good eye signaled comprehension.

"Very well. You seem to have had your whipping for today, though. Rather more than I'd have ordered just for mere insubordination. No further punishment."

Some of the crew gasped, looking on. Shadunu frowned and seemed on the verge of protesting.

"And you, you with the red face, I understand your wanting to rescue your friend and I haven't forgotten that you saved my life, but I can't have my oar masters pulled down into the pit. Five lashes."

Iri's brow rose. He had expected ten lashes at the very least.

"And you, Shadunu," the Minotaur said. "What have you to say for yourself?"

"Sir," the oar master said. "Five lashes are too few for this one. And to let the other one off with—"

"Ten lashes," the Minotaur declared.

Shadunu stared. "But I thought you said . . ." he began. Then it dawned on him what the captain had meant. "Ten lashes? For me? But I've got to maintain discipline. How do you expect me to—"

"I expect nothing of you except obedience. You are hereby demoted to ordinary seaman, and your next brush with the ship's authority will earn you a lashing you'll never forget."

Iri turned once to look back at the Minotaur as he was being led away. Five lashes—this kind of punishment he hardly feared at all. It was harsh but fair. Who would have expected fairness from a pirate. He let himself be led to the capstan, and when the whipping came he bore it in silence. When it was over and they had doused him down with saltwater—then he almost cried out against the pain—he prepared to return to the pit.

Instead a crewman cut both manacles off Iri's legs. "Captain's orders," he explained. "Too much bother, taking you on and off the chain all the time." He winked at

Iri. "Shadunu—no damn good. Somebody should have done it a long time ago."

Iri stared at him as he walked away. It had been a day of surprises—not the least of which was the strange tune the new *trieraules* had been playing. A tune of Ur, hardly known outside the Valley of the Euphrates these many years later by anyone but the Children of the Lion. Who was the player and what was he doing here?

Theon returned to his forge, shaken and strangely moved. He had never seen anything like this at all before. Ordinarily, summary justice at sea was administered with a heavy hand, to inspire fear. But this had been justice, pure and simple.

For whom? This was the greatest shock of all. The face could have been mistaken for someone else's. To be sure more than one man had a disfiguring facial birthmark. But then the naked rower had turned his back, and there was the red birthmark of the Children of the Lion, as distinct as Theon's own.

Only one man in the world would have both of these marks, as well as smith's scars from a thousand sparks blown up by the forge fire, *and* a smith's powerful forearms and broad shoulders.

Iri of Thebes. What was he doing here, slave labor on a pirate galley?

III

Once more Iri took his seat next to the black giant. As they settled into the familiar long-distance stroke, the black man leaned over and said, "What happened? Why did they take your manacles off?"

"I don't know," Iri said. "But apparently the Minotaur has his own rules. Shadunu got twice as many lashes as I did, laid on more heavily, too. He won't be able to work for a week. But no new whipping for Zimrida. They're both recovering now."

"With a guard to watch them, I hope," the black man said with a smile. "Otherwise Zimrida will soon have a murder charge to answer to."

"They're both chained up and will lie there calling each other names, I suppose."

The black man gave a deep and hearty laugh. "In an hour's time you realize you've changed your life. This despite being a slave on a rower's bench, a man who doesn't even own the plank his bare bottom sits on." He let the big laugh boom out again. "Well done, friend." He stopped suddenly. "Pardon me, but I don't know your name."

"Iri of Thebes," he said. "For a long time I didn't bother with names down here. But now I'm beginning to feel like a human being again."

"Me too, thanks to you," the black man said. "I am Okware, a king's third son. And you're a Son of the Lion, aren't you?"

"How did you know that?" Iri asked, almost missing a stroke in his surprise.

"All men in the lands where Mtebi roamed know of the Sons of the Lion," Okware said. "I think we shall have much to talk about as the days go by. And I shall count the day lost when they move you to another bench."

Prodicus joined the Minotaur on the bridge. "You wanted to see me now, Captain?" he asked.

Seeing them, Theon edged forward. "Yes, we have to discuss the raid. We've passed along the necessary information about the time and place. Now you and I need to talk strategy."

"Yes, sir. The current plan, as I remember it, is for the fleet to gather outside the harbor at Poros when we know the harbor will be full of Demetrios's cargo vessels. Then we blockade the harbor and lay siege to his fleet."

Theon's heart was in his throat as he pretended to replace the handle of a knife. The Minotaur smiled. "And with better than half the ships loaded down to the gunwales, it will be a rich harvest."

"Your informant is reliable?"

"He hasn't let us down so far. Agis is one of Demetrios's most trusted advisers. The information will prove correct, and if there are any changes, he'll get word to us in time."

Theon almost dropped his hammer. So Agis was the traitor who had been selling Demetrios out to the Minotaur. But how could a spy have penetrated undetected so deeply into Demetrios's domain?

He could not believe his ears, but he had to. The attacks on Demetrios's ships in the last few months had been too deadly to be coincidental.

He chewed at his lip. Something had to be done immediately. Demetrios had to be warned. Someone had to get a message to him or with one blow Demetrios's fleet would be destroyed.

But how? He could not do it. If he left the ship now he would be abandoning Nuhara to whatever uncertain fate lay ahead for her as a pirate's slave.

He frowned. The more he thought about the situation, the more Iri of Thebes—if indeed he was right, and the red-faced man was his kinsman—came irresistibly to his mind.

But how to find an occasion to speak with him, without exposing himself as a spy.

At sundown they anchored in the lee of a dry, uninhabited island. As Prodicus and the Minotaur discussed the upcoming raid, Theon sat back, ate his small meal, and then pretended to repair Tromes's sword. As he sharpened it he listened and made mental notes.

Later that evening Tromes came to him to inspect the repairs, and the two sat down with their flutes and exchanged songs, each man teaching the other. Soon the sailors began to drift toward the music, and Theon struck up a lively tune from Samos. The sailors began dancing. Someone broke out a wineskin, and the simple diversion became a full-scale party.

This soon led to drunkenness and fighting and eventually to Prodicus's cursing and ordering them back to quarters. Theon shrugged, put away his flute, and lay down on the deck.

After he had slept for he knew not how long, he felt a small, warm body crawl under the blanket and nestle next to him.

"Nuhara," he whispered. He opened his eyes. The moon lay behind a cloud; the night was dark. "You came. But isn't it dangerous?"

"He's sound asleep," she said. "And everyone else, including Prodicus, will be too drunk to investigate. Hold me. I'm cold. I slipped out without anything on."

"Yes, you did, didn't you?" He chuckled. His hands roamed over the small soft-strong body next to him. "You feel wonderful."

"Oh," she murmured. "Keep doing that. Right there. Yes."

The time passed and finally she kissed him and slipped away into the darkness. He could hear the door to the cabin close softly behind her.

For a long time he lay awake thinking, trying to sort out his thoughts, in particular his feelings toward the Minotaur. The two were sworn enemies, even if the Minotaur might not realize it. Theon had volunteered to infiltrate the pirates' fleet and bring back information that would allow Demetrios to wipe it from the sea. And, having seen the devastation the pirates wreaked, he had no doubt that it was necessary to destroy the Minotaur.

Then why did he suddenly feel guilty about spying on the Bull? Why was he suddenly seeing the black-bearded man with more tolerant eyes?

He cursed his ambivalence and reached under the cover for his chlamys.

A slice of moon slipped out from behind the cloud. He threw off his blanket and stood up. As he looked down the long, narrow deck of the great bireme a thought came to him. It was a dangerous and rash idea that could land him in terrible trouble if it failed.

He tiptoed down the deck and peeped over the edge of the rowers' pit.

As he did, the moon came out from behind the cloud, and a single ray penetrated the pit, illuminating the bent backs of the sleeping rowers and falling upon the upturned face of the man with the birthmark, who was looking up at him with steady eyes and an unreadable expression.

Taking a deep breath, Theon whispered, "Iri! Iri of Thebes?"

"Yes," said the man. "But who are you?"

Theon started to speak and then saw, in the light of the moon, the man's bare ankles. "Come on deck. There's no one here."

The red-faced man silently climbed the rope ladder. "You didn't answer me," he said. "Who are you? Because if you betray me, so help me, I'll—" His huge hand reached out and grasped Theon's neck and then relaxed, but not before letting him realize the strength of his hand.

"It's all right," Theon said, touching his neck nervously. "I'm Theon. The son of Seth of Thebes."

"The son of Seth!" Iri said. "I'm so glad to know you! How is Demetrios? These people capture one of his ships every two days, by my own reckoning."

"It was Demetrios who agreed to let me spy on the pirates. That's why I came to you. We have to get the word to Demetrios. The Minotaur intends to stage the most devastating raid ever directed against a cargo fleet. I've also learned who the Minotaur's spy is inside Demetrios's command."

"Tell me more," Iri said. Tension emanated from his enormous body. "Tell me everything."

Theon told as much of it as it made sense to tell. "If we can warn Demetrios, there's a chance he can stop it." He paused. "Of course, his ships can't just avoid the harbor where the raid's scheduled to take place. Then the spy would simply pass the word along and the pirates would stay away, too. And they won't have a chance of catching the Minotaur and bringing him to justice."

"I see." Iri nodded eagerly. "And the only way is to warn Demetrios and let him take action."

"Yes, he'll have to play along until the last possible moment, then imprison the spy and set sail with his warships."

"That's assuming you can get the message to him in the first place. And how do you propose to do that? Are you going to go over the side?"

"No, I can't, I gave the Minotaur my word that I wouldn't escape. I want you to."

"You gave your . . ." Iri was dumbfounded. "Wait just a minute. Lift up that chlamys and turn around. Yes, there's the birthmark. And with that sense of honor, I suppose you're who you say you are. Seth would have thought just that way."

"I forgot. You knew him, didn't you?"

"And loved him very much, as we all did." Iri took a deep breath. "All right, I'll carry the message for you. Tell me where we are. Remember, I'm no experienced sailor."

"If you can get to the far side of the island, perhaps you can find a fishing boat anchored offshore and catch a ride. I realize the odds against this are enormous."

"I'll take the chance. Now tell me exactly how to find Demetrios and what you want me to say to him."

Theon did so. Afterward, Iri gripped Theon's hand, then embraced him before silently slipping over the side.

In the cabin doorway Nuhara watched Iri's escape. She closed the door just as Theon returned to his spot on the deck.

From inside the cabin a deep bass voice asked, "What's happening out there?"

"The red-faced one went over the side after Theon talked with him. Now go back to sleep. Everything's going according to plan."

IV

Iri scraped his knees on the rocks and fought the pounding until he was exhausted. Finally he lay gasping for breath, wet and cold, on a patch of dark sand. A little after dawn, he rose and looked out to sea. He could not believe his eyes. The *Hephaistos* was gone!

Still incredulous, he climbed to the rugged top of a hill and looked out over the Great Sea. Shading his eyes against the thin morning light, he spotted a dark speck far out across the water. He waited quite a long time. It did not get closer.

"Amazing," he said, shaking his head. "It shouldn't have been that easy." How could they not have missed him and sent out a search party?

No need to question good fortune, he decided, setting out along the spine of the hill. An hour later he found himself standing atop the highest promontory on the small island.

To his surprise, hidden on this side of the island was a much better harbor. And anchored in its blue waters were three small fishing boats and a cargo ship.

Suddenly he understood. The need for secrecy had made the Minotaur deliberately avoid the safe anchorage. And, for the same reason, they had taken to the high sea as soon as possible.

Iri grinned, waved his arms, and yelled for joy, knowing that no one could hear him or see him. It did not matter. There was no sign of activity so he knew none of the ships would pull anchor and take to sea before he could make his way down to the harbor.

He chuckled to himself and set out down the rocky hillside. He would seek out Demetrios. In a sea full of his ships there should be no problem finding him. He would pass Theon's information along and help in whatever way he could to rid the Great Sea of the Minotaur's fleet.

And then he would go in search of Keturah. With the full resources of Demetrios's wealth and influence, he could not fail to find her and their child. And then no power in the world could keep them apart.

*　　*　　*

As usual the business of getting under way was handled by Prodicus, and the Minotaur did not appear for an hour or two.

Theon set to work in the thin sunlight, throwing off his chlamys as the sun and the work warmed him. He had three swords and daggers to repair and used the humble tinkerwork to calm his nerves.

Remarkably, nobody seemed to notice Iri's absence. The only explanation Theon could think of was that the other rowers were covering for him. Perhaps the new oar master did not know the men and would not notice Iri's absence on his own.

Theon pounded away on the sword before him, hoping against hope that this meant Iri had safely escaped and would make his way to Demetrios in time.

As he worked he sang: love songs from Egypt, which he had learned from Demetrios, and story songs, including fragments from the great Gilgamesh epic and the "Tale of Two Brothers" and the "Song of Sinuhe." Singing, he could feel his tension lessen and the power flow into his forearms.

Suddenly he heard a noise behind him. Startled, he turned to face the Minotaur.

"That song you were singing," the black-bearded man said. "Do you know any more of it?"

"Quite a bit," Theon said. "A man on one of the boats I served on knew it and used to sing it to me."

"I have not heard that song in many years. It had some meaning for me once."

Theon watched him as he walked past, seeking out Prodicus. The song was one of Canaan. Did this perhaps mean that the Minotaur was originally from there? Or that he had a Canaanite mother perhaps?

When he finished the song, Theon did not start another but kept his eyes on the Minotaur's broad back and listened intently as captain and mate discussed the raid. The more he heard, the more fervently Theon hoped Iri would warn Demetrios in time. If the attack were not stopped, Demetrios would be ruined.

He was about to resume his hammering when he heard the Minotaur's words: ". . . if this works, our fortunes are made. Demetrios will fall into our trap, and we will have not only his fleet, but him as well."

The two men walked off. Theon sat on his heels, the now-cold sword in his left hand and the hammer in his right, wondering what they had meant. Trap? What trap? Surely everyone knew Demetrios never traveled on his own ships; it was far too dangerous.

Theon blinked. What if the whole thing was a trap? Agis had obviously told the Minotaur that Theon was a spy. What if he had been fed the false information to draw Demetrios into this trap? What if Iri had been deliberately allowed to escape? His heart almost stopped as the possibility struck home. Prodicus turned toward him. "Armorer," he bellowed, "get back to work!"

That night Theon dozed, expecting a visit from Nuhara, but she did not come. Finally he slipped off to sleep.

It seemed only moments had passed before he felt someone shaking him roughly. He opened his eyes to find himself surrounded by the angry faces of men carrying torches.

"Get up, you son of a bitch," someone cried.

Rough hands hauled him to his feet. "He's the one!" someone called from the rear. "He's the one who helped the red-faced one escape!"

"Bring the captain," came another voice. "He'll know what to do."

Just then the door opened behind Theon, and he felt the Minotaur's presence.

"What's going on here?" the pirate chief demanded.

"The red-faced rower, sir. He escaped over the side. This man was seen helping him."

The Minotaur glared at Theon from under beetling brows. "Is this true?" he asked in a voice that was as cold as the Great Sea.

Theon stared up at him. No answer he could give would make things better for him, so he did not reply at all.

"Why?" the Minotaur asked.

Again there was no answer.

The Minotaur sighed. "Five lashes, and chain him to the deck."

Chained again. This meant that when the big battle came, if the *Hephaistos* were to go to the bottom, he would go with it.

V

Iri hailed the fishing vessel from the beach, waving his arms wildly and crying out until someone motioned to him to come aboard. He dove in and swam out into the harbor, trying to forget the pain as the saltwater bathed the raw wounds on his back. The fishermen had to drag him into the boat, exhausted and numb.

Sitting on the port rail with a blanket over his shoulders and a cup of dark, resinated wine in his hand, he finally was able to answer their questions.

"How did you wind up dumped bare-ass naked on an island without food and water, anyhow?" the boat's owner wanted to know. "You can tell us. We won't tell the authorities. This island's a smuggler's haven anyhow. The only reason for coming here is to trade stolen goods."

Iri took another sip of wine and studied him. "I took passage for Cos," he said, "but the ship started having trouble, and somebody decided that I was bad luck. It's this damned face of mine. People think it's a bad omen, that I'm cursed, so they go to work making it come true by getting rid of me."

"So you were marooned by a lot of superstitious sons of bitches. How long have you been without water or food?"

"They left me enough to last the week. The food ran out a week ago, but I'd been stretching the water. I ran out of that yesterday. You came along just in time."

"Someone would have come along. This is a popular spot for people who aren't satisfied with what they can make pulling fish out of the sea. I'm surprised you had to spend two weeks here."

"I must have been on the wrong side of the island," Iri said. "If you can get me to Cos, I can get the money there to pay you handsomely for my passage."

"Not necessary, but we could use a spare hand to help with the nets. We lost a man a week ago, and it's all we can do to haul up a half-filled net. If you can work—and you're built like a man used to heavy labor—I can get you to Astypalaea. That's as close as we ordinarily come to Cos."

"It has to be Cos," Iri said. "I have an urgent mission there. I've lost two weeks already, and I may be too late.

If you can get me there I'll not only work for you, I'll pay you well."

"How much?"

Iri looked him in the eyes. It was time to tell the truth. "I'll give you the price of your boat, but you can keep the boat."

The fisherman looked at him skeptically. "I don't want to call you a liar, but . . ."

"But you don't believe that I'm worth that kind of money? I'm an armorer. We make good money, and that blotch on my backside ought to tell you I'm a Child of the Lion. My brother is the richest man in the world."

"Demetrios is your brother?"

"The same. Look, who else would have a paw-print birthmark on his back *and* have forearms like these? And see these scars? Nobody but a smith bears burn scars like these."

The fisherman nodded. "I'll accept that you're who you say you are."

"How much?"

The fisherman named a high figure.

Iri did not blink. "Done. Here's my hand. Get me to Cos quickly, and the money is yours."

The fisherman paused. "I say you have a deal."

According to Theon's information, Cos was the nearest island with a major port. Iri had no idea where Home was located, but in Cos Demetrios's agent would find him a ship. He stood by the rail and let out a great sigh of relief. At last he was on his way.

A vision of Keturah's face filled his mind. He could feel her body against his and hear the sound of her sweet voice. Suddenly, after so many weeks of stoic silence, he found himself weeping.

And then, almost as soon as they had begun, his tears were replaced by anger, a seething, burning anger. Someone would pay for this.

Theon now worked on a chain only long enough to allow him to stand up and to take three short steps in any direction. It was not only confining but humiliating.

Before, the crew had come to him with requests; now they came with orders. Even Tromes avoided him and sat with his back to Theon as he played the tunes Theon had taught him.

As the afternoon wore on, the Minotaur came out of his cabin. "Armorer," he said, "you claim you can work iron?"

Startled, Theon looked up. "I can, with the right equipment."

"Make the equipment. Ask Prodicus for whatever you need. I want an iron sword as soon as possible."

Theon stared at him. "For the big raid you're planning?" he asked. "The one on Demetrios's ships in Poros?"

The Minotaur stared back at him. "So you've been keeping your ears open? And I suppose you fed the information to the red-faced one before he went over the side?"

Theon almost blurted out a yes but thought better of it at the last second. There was a chance that the Minotaur still did not know his identity or that he was a spy for Demetrios. "I have no idea what information he learned during his time as a rower."

"You could have escaped over the side with him, yet you did not. Why?"

Theon bit his lip. "I'd given my word that I wouldn't run away."

The Minotaur looked at him thoughtfully. "Honor means something to me, too," he said. "But aboard our ships the only thing that keeps a man from breaking his word is the sure knowledge that if he's caught he could wind up food for the sharks."

"I see," Theon said, pushing. "Then you've given up the ideals of your youth."

"Why? Is that the way you look at me?"

"To be frank," Theon said, "I haven't figured you out yet."

"And I suspect you have a more complicated history than you've admitted to."

"I would say much the same of you," Theon replied. "I can't imagine, for instance, how you became leader of this fleet. Aboard the other boats I could easily imagine how a man might become captain of the vessel. He would fight for it."

"You know I can fight."

"But such a man would have to kill his opponent."

"So he would, most likely. But go on."

"How many fighting ships do you command now?"

"About thirty galleys at any given time," the Minotaur said. "Plus the lighters and loaders. And the ships belonging to our spies."

"Thirty?"

"More or less. We've lost some in the past year. Others, old ships, too slow and tubby to maneuver in a fight, we've gotten rid of."

"And how many men did you have to kill to get where you are?"

The Minotaur looked at him for a long while before speaking. "I killed nobody. Only later on, when I had to put down a revolt. Do you know how I became leader of the fleet?" There was a small smile on the Minotaur's mouth. "I was asked to."

This answer was so unexpected, and surprising, Theon sat up, gaping.

"The old leader was killed in a battle with war galleys from Corinth. When he died, the fleet simply could not function without a strong and knowledgeable power at the top."

"But without bloodshed? Without fighting? And why you of all people?"

The Minotaur shrugged. "Because I wasn't afraid of anyone. And I can get along with anybody I want to get along with. It's that simple. I knew all the captains well. I had whored and drunk with them and fought alongside them. I knew their strengths and weaknesses. I knew which ones I could intimidate if necessary and which ones I had to flatter. And since I don't care what anyone thinks of me, I'm free to do whatever is necessary to maintain order."

"And it works," Theon said, fighting down a growing admiration for the pirate captain.

"Up until now. But if I'd suffered from pride or a need to dominate, I might have been dead by now. Yet I am still here. But no man knows what the future will bring."

VI

Iri stood at the starboard rail, watching the rocky outline of an island come up over the horizon. He turned and bellowed at the boat's owner, "Is that Cos?" But the winds blew his words away and Iri had to walk over to where the owner stood adjusting the sails.

"How long until we dock?" Iri yelled against the wind.

The fisherman shrugged. "Not long. That's Cos on the horizon. It's easy to tell you're not a man born and bred to the sea. Boats and the weather teach a man patience." He clapped Iri on the arm in a friendly fashion. "Don't worry."

Iri nodded gravely and walked back to the rail. If all ran according to plan, he ought to be able to get to Demetrios in time.

But he had lost so much time in the search for Keturah. How could he possibly pick up so cold a trail?

For the thousandth time he found himself imagining what life must be like for her, blind and dependent, alone and friendless, amid hostile and abusive strangers.

And, he reminded himself bitterly, wondering where he, her protector, had gone. He cursed under his breath once more, allowing his broad shoulders to bear the blame. He made the costly mistakes and poor, blind, helpless Keturah had to pay.

And his child, his first child. How bitter this was.

He who had wished all his life for love and never found it until she had come along; he who had hoped for a son someday to pass his fortune along to; he who had lived for so many years with such terrible loneliness—he had gotten it all only to throw it carelessly away.

He watched the island of Cos take shape: long, narrow, craggy. How long had it been since he was enslaved? He was not sure. Months. At first he had tried to keep count; but then the guilt and frustration had threatened to drive him mad. Then he concentrated on learning what the oar had to teach him and becoming the best rower on any vessel.

At night he had not been able to keep the nagging

thoughts out of his mind, however, and even in dreams his mind accused him: *Fool! Accursed fool! How can you ever make amends?*

After they had docked, the fishermen gave his three crewmen leave, and he and Iri went ashore together. The captain of the port told them how to find Demetrios's agent. "He has a place at the end of the Ropewalk. It has a green roof. You can't miss it."

They walked out into the bright Aegean sunshine and headed down the long, straight street where the rope makers backed slowly along the street, braiding their hemp. "It won't be long now," Iri assured him. "You'll have your money, and you can go with my gratitude and blessing."

"I'm still not sure whether or not to believe this," the fisherman confessed. "This will be more money than I've ever made in a month. No, make it a year."

"You've earned it and more," Iri said.

At the house with the green roof, Iri gave the special knock Demetrios had taught him. A face appeared at the window. The owner blinked and hesitated for a moment as he studied Iri's distinctive face and the rough fishermen's clothing he and his companion wore. Then he opened the door. "You can only be one man in the world. Iri of Thebes. How can I serve you?"

"First, let me draw on my accounts. This man here did me a great service, and I owe him money." He named the sum, and the agent, Ios, nodded and disappeared into a back room.

The fisherman was bug-eyed with amazement. "You mean that's all it takes?"

"My face isn't easy to fake."

When Ios returned, Iri turned over the handful of

coins. "My friend, here's your money. And my thanks." The two embraced like old friends, and the fisherman left, disbelief written on his face.

Iri turned to Ios. "I have a very important message for Demetrios. It concerns our pirate friend the Minotaur and some plans he has for our fleet. I've already lost too much time. Is there a ship of his fleet in port now?"

The agent shook his head. "But one is due to dock at sunset, if nothing has gone wrong."

"Good," Iri said. "And can you give me an idea how long I've been gone?"

"Nearly three months," Ios said. "I could work out the exact day if you like."

Iri stared openmouthed. "You . . . you know what happened to me?"

"No, sir. Only that you disappeared."

"And Keturah, do you have her? Is she safe?"

Sadly Ios shook his head. "I'm sorry. No one seems to know."

Iri grabbed his robe. "Do you know anything at all?"

Ios looked down at the huge hands, and Iri, embarrassed, released him, muttering apologies.

"Well, sir, for quite a long time all we knew was that you had left Moses's people but had not arrived at Home. Only last week something did turn up. Pepi, your nephew, was in Joppa. He saw your wife there being auctioned at a slave market. He rushed to Demetrios's man Geshem to get the money to buy her and keep her from falling into strange hands."

"A . . . a slave market?" Iri asked, his face twisted in anguish. "What happened?"

"I . . . I don't know how to say it. But Geshem refused to believe Pepi. He hesitated until your wife had been sold. When Pepi reached the docks all he saw was her ship sailing away."

"What ship? Did he get her name? Her port of registration?"

"The ship's the *Massilia*. She was bound for various ports all around the Great Sea, but nobody seems to know her proper itinerary, so we haven't found her yet. We will eventually find her, though. Messengers have been sent out to every port, instructing our representatives to board the *Massilia* the moment she docks. If your wife is still aboard they will find her." He looked Iri in the eyes.

"I see. She could have already been unloaded. But this is, at least, good news. As of last week she was still alive. And well, I hope?"

"Apparently, sir. Pepi's woman spoke to her and told her not to give up hope."

"Pepi has a woman? The more good fortune to him! What did she say about Keturah?"

"That she seemed to be well but frightened. She asked after you, of course, but at the time Pepi knew nothing at all of what had happened to you."

"Last week in Joppa," Iri repeated.

"Yes, sir. Meanwhile, there's something you could do. Go down to the docks and talk to some of the men in port. Perhaps one of them has seen the *Massilia* or at least heard rumors."

"Splendid idea, Ios. You're a good man, and I'll pass the word along to Demetrios when I see him. But what happened to this Geshem? So help me, if I get my hands on him . . ."

"Unfortunately, sir, he seems to have met with an accident in Joppa. Most unfortunate." Ios's eyes were cold. "The Children of the Lion take care of their own."

"You mean Pepi—"

"No, sir. Another of Demetrios's people. Geshem was suspected of embezzlement and taking bribes. We had a man there keeping an eye on him."

"Say no more. I'm going to take your advice now and go to the docks. I'll be back before dark. Make sure you hold the ship in port until I can board her."

"Yes, sir. I will. The *Barcino* will not leave without you. I promise you that."

As Iri emerged onto the street it was evident that something was happening. The streets were full of people heading in the direction of the harbor. He jumped up onto the well next to Ios's house and, craning his neck, looked out to sea.

Well beyond the docks, inside the seawall but in the deep water, was a sad sight: a ship, her sail a blackened shred attached to a charred pole, was limping into port. A fire blazed aft, and the crew were battling to keep it from spreading farther. Men on the docks were screaming at them, telling them to stay out of the dock area and not endanger the other ships.

"What ship is she?" a voice asked. "And where's she from?"

Iri blinked, trying to bring her name in focus. "I can't make it out. Get up here and tell me. Maybe you can recognize her."

The man studied the ship for a long time. "She was only here a few months ago. I wonder what happened?"

"Who is she?" Iri asked.

But somehow he knew what the man would say. The sense of foreboding was strong.

"The *Massilia*," the man answered.

VII

Ignoring the rickety timbers, Iri dashed out to the end of the dock. He could see the remaining crew feverishly passing buckets of water aft and tossing them on the blaze; but it was a losing battle. Even as he watched the flames grew higher.

He looked around desperately and finally grabbed up a length of rope. He ripped a thick length of railing off the dock, tied the rope around one end, and with massive muscles bulging, heaved it out, as far as he could, into the harbor.

He grabbed the other end of the rope just before it dropped into the water. "It's no use! She's dead in the water!" he bellowed at the men on the ship. "Get off while you can! Grab the railing, and I'll pull you to shore!"

The first time they did not hear him. He repeated the message, then noticed one crewman gesturing to another. Finally the exhausted men all dropped their buckets and rushed to the rail.

"Is there no one else on board?" Iri bellowed out.

One man shook his head and they all began diving over the side and swimming toward the floating timber. When they were all grasping it firmly, Iri began backing away, pulling at the rope. From behind him he could hear the murmurs of astonishment over his strength. Finally several men joined in and helped pull. After much cursing and fumbling, they hauled the survivors up onto the dock.

One of them looked up at Iri and winced at his ugly face but said, "Thanks, friend. We didn't have a chance." They turned and looked out at the doomed boat. "She's got a load of pitch in the hold. She's going to blow at any minute."

"What happened to you?" Iri asked. "And where's the rest of the crew?"

"We were attacked by pirates a few hours out of Cos," the man said, sitting down wearily on the dock. "Gods! but I'm tired. We've been fighting that fire ever since—"

"Pirates?" Iri asked anxiously. "Ships of the Minotaur?"

"You'd think there were no other pirates on the sea, the way people carry on about that fellow! No, Atticans. At least, that's what I think they were."

"No," someone said. "From Lemnos or Thasos or Achaea or someplace like that, up north. You could tell from their accents."

"You're crazy. No Lemnite ever talked like that. Whatever they were, they were a bunch of damned barbarians. Pigs! Damned filthy brutes!"

Iri nodded, forcing himself to be patient. "But the rest? The captain? The mate? And what about any others on board? Women? Slaves, maybe?"

"They killed the officers and took all the slaves they wanted. Although some of them didn't look as if you could get any work out of them, or a decent price, for that matter."

"W-what did they do with those?" Iri asked anxiously, his voice strained.

"Seems to me they killed a few and threw some overboard. The rest they took. Then they set the boat on fire and cut her adrift, daring us to get her into port. Dirty bastards."

"There was a blind woman, a slave on board. Did you see what happened to her?" Iri asked, his patience worn thin.

The man turned to his fellow crewmen. "Blind woman?" he asked. "Do you remember any blind woman?"

"Not offhand," said another. "Of course, I wouldn't have had any truck with slaves." He spat out into the water. "Look at her. She's going to blow any minute now. Maybe we'd better get on land. When she goes she'll throw timbers all over the place." He looked back at Iri. "Sorry, friend. I couldn't say."

"It's very important to me," he said, scanning the sooty faces of the survivors. "I'll pay for information."

"Friend, you've already paid for it, saving our lives. If we had any more information, we'd give it gladly. A lot was going on. I had a knife at my throat. I was sure that son of a bitch was going to slice me open. I'm still not sure why he didn't."

"But did they take any of the woman slaves with them? I'm trying to find—"

"Sorry, I didn't notice."

"Wait," one of the survivors said. "You're forgetting the pregnant one. They said she'd bring a good price in the marketplace."

"A pregnant one?" Iri demanded. "A dark woman, dark like a Bedouin?"

"That's the one. I saw him load her on board. Her and that big Nubian one, and the twins."

Iri stared at him in amazement. Keturah was alive! But the trail was dead. Achaeans? Lemnites? Nobody knew where the pirates were from or where they were going. How could he possibly find her?

Once more the pirate vessels convened in the harbor of the island that had once been Demetrios's Home. The captains gathered aboard the *Hephaistos*. The crews were allowed a half day ashore. Theon worked on the iron-smelting forge on deck for much of the morning; then, with so many strangers underfoot, he abandoned the effort and sat in the warm sun to watch the pirate chiefs confer and to try to overhear some of what they were saying.

Gradually he became aware of a quiet scratching behind him. Unobtrusively, he turned. The door to the Minotaur's cabin was open a crack. He maneuvered to the end of the cabin and sat with his back propped up against the wall of the cabin as if he were resting. He spoke softly, taking care not to move his lips. "What do you want?"

"I have to talk to you," Nuhara said.

"Can you come tonight?" he asked.

"It'll be too late then," she said. "We're not going to anchor here overnight. I need to talk to you before we leave the island."

"Can you talk now? Nobody's watching."

In answer her small, warm hand stole from behind the door and touched his back. "Oh, Theon, I can't take this life anymore. I thought I could last it out, but then I met you. I want my freedom. And I want you to come with me."

"Wait," he said. "There may be a possibility sometime soon."

"I can't wait that long. Theon, let's escape. I can get you out of the chain."

"I gave my word."

"Break it. He's only a pirate."

"And I've explained why I can't."

"But Theon, I need you. I can't get away from him without your help. And if I got away and you didn't, it would be no good."

"If we can get you to some safe place, I can get free later. There's a chance that during the big raid—" He stopped, knowing he'd said too much already.

"I know you're planning something. He knows, too. He knows that's why you helped the red-faced slave escape. Theon, if you can get free during the raid, I'll be waiting for you. I'll wait for you in Poros, or anywhere you want me to."

"Nuhara, it's too dangerous."

"No, Theon!" Her voice rose in intensity but not in

volume. "What's dangerous is staying here, wanting you and not being able to do anything about it. One of these days I'll get caught. I'll do something that will betray us. I'll get desperate."

"I know. If I were ever to relax my own vigilance for so much as a moment—"

"That's why you have to help me escape. Today, Theon. Help me. Please, darling."

Theon sighed. "It has to be today?"

"It's the only chance I'll have before the raid. I know where there's a boat hidden on the island. It's in a cove not far from the one we went to that day."

He thought a moment. "I won't go, but you can escape. If you could get to Poros, Demetrios has a representative there, and he could warn Demetrios."

Theon stopped dead. He had said too much. What a fool he was to mention Demetrios. He had betrayed himself and his whole plan.

"Yes, Theon?" she said, her voice ripe with innocence. "Go on. Who is Demetrios and what has he to do with all of this?"

Theon held his breath. He swallowed and finally spoke. "Nuhara. I . . . can I trust you with a secret that you must absolutely not betray on pain of death?"

She pressed his hand. "Theon, if you can't trust me, whom can you trust? Please, darling, tell me what to do. Find my way to Poros, and look up this man Demetrios's friend, then what?"

"He'll do the rest. I only hope you can get there in time. Can you navigate as far as Poros?"

"I was a sailor's daughter."

"Fine. Now here's what you have to tell them. . . ."

* * *

She went ashore. Theon stayed behind, chained to the deck, struggling to overhear any talk about the raid amidst the din.

In the early evening, the Minotaur headed back to the cabin. As he passed Theon, he stopped. "I know all about you and your red-faced friend and Demetrios."

Theon's heart sank, but he fought to keep all emotion from his face. "Who's Demetrios?"

"Don't be ingenuous," the Minotaur said. "He's your cousin, and you're here to spy for him. Iri of Thebes was to have been your messenger, informing him about the trap we've set for him in Poros."

Theon could not conceal his shock. He started to say something, but his throat was too dry for speech. "W-where did you get this nonsense from, anyhow?" he finally croaked.

"Why, from Nuhara, of course," the Minotaur said. "She tells me everything. You have a lot to learn, my friend. Particularly about women."

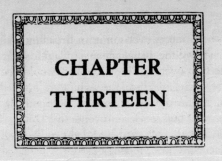

CHAPTER THIRTEEN

Canaan

I

With time left before the end of the official period of mourning for Moses, Pepi and Tirzah lingered in Canaan, traveling to one city, then another, and always surreptitiously taking notes on their defenses.

They spent several days in ancient Shechem, inspecting the still-intact fortifications left behind by the Shepherd Kings when Kamose and his army had driven them out of Canaan.

"Shechem was always a tough nut to crack," Pepi explained. "And the Shepherds had to mount a major siege before the city fell. Those walls couldn't—and still can't—be breached. The Hai had to starve the inhabitants into submission. Only when people began to die of hunger did the city fathers finally open the gates to the conquerors.

"See that long sloping outer wall? It's characteristic of the Hai. They built that into every city they destroyed all the way from Carchemish to the delta of Egypt. They built their capital, Avaris, that way."

336

"And no one is ever going to breach a wall like that. At least not by the usual means," Tirzah said. "You certainly can't go over it. The defenders would see you coming and pour hot oil down on you."

"You're a fast learner. So what do you do when the city has a wall that can't be breached?"

She smiled and squeezed his hand. "Nobody ever asked me man-type questions before. Let me see: I think I'd try to place a spy inside to subvert the city. Someone who'd talk people into opening the gates and letting the besiegers in. Someone who'd convince everyone that if they ended the battle the conquerors would treat them fairly."

Pepi raised an eyebrow. "Splendid," he said. "Now if only I could talk Joshua into listening to you. But he likes to fight too much. When his blood is up he won't listen to reason. Once he's killed all the soldiers then he goes after the civilians."

"It sounds as though he isn't always in control of himself."

"He isn't. Joshua's not a bad man at heart. It's just that the qualities that make him such a splendid soldier keep him from being a good peacetime administrator. And I trust even less the people he'll appoint to administer newly conquered territory. The only thing that has kept the conquered tribes from rising against us so far is the even-handed justice Moses dispensed."

"Pepi," she said. "You and Joshua were the closest of friends once."

"He was the first friend I ever had. Mother wasn't up to raising me. Now I realize that during those first years of my life she was a little crazy with anger, hatred, and a thirst for revenge against my father, who had raped her."

With a sigh Pepi began the story of his childhood. His

mother, Neftis, and her brother Iri had inherited their parents' sizable estate. Demetrios, their older brother, had already left to administer the greatest shipping fortune in the world, so Iri—ugly, lonely, strong, and sensitive—had taken it upon himself to care for his older sister but had not known how to handle her headstrong nature.

Inexperienced, unaware of life's dangers, she had been easy prey for Apedemek. He had corrupted her for the sheer joy of it, demanding she submit to him sexually and convincing her that the degradation he made her endure was essential to her being.

Despairing and convinced of her own worthlessness, she had tried to kill him. She failed and retreated into madness.

It fell to Seth and his wife to raise Pepi. Convinced of his own worthlessness and the fatal taint of Apedemek's blood, Pepi began to wonder if Apedemek's way—proud and locked into a ruthless search for power—might not be preferable to the path of goodness followed by Seth.

Then came the great confrontation when Apedemek's power had once and for all been tested. Only it had not been Seth who faced him, it had been Moses. And it was Moses's God who had destroyed Apedemek right before Pepi's eyes.

Shortly thereafter Apedemek committed suicide, and Moses took the boy in hand. Pepi had been raised with Joshua. The old man had taken the two of them in tow and taught them the ways of war. Joshua had become the soldier; Pepi had become the armorer, apprenticing himself to his uncle Iri and following the tradition of the Children of the Lion.

Gradually a rift grew between the two young men. An armorer only made weapons; he did not fight. But

Joshua, increasingly bloodthirsty, could not understand this.

Pepi sighed from the bottom of his heart. "Neither of us wished for this. Both of us, I think, would have preferred to remain the friends we had been as boys.

"It is all going to come to a head soon," he confirmed. "And the break will be bitter. It won't help that both of us realize it was nothing more than a misunderstanding between two friends who have had to set their feet on different paths."

"I can't accept that," Tirzah said. "People can work things out." She searched his face for signs that he believed her. "Don't let this misunderstanding spoil a valuable friendship. Don't give up on Joshua, please."

II

They stopped at an inn in Bethel, and while Tirzah rested in their room until the heat broke, Pepi wandered through the city.

As he walked the streets of the old town, making mental maps, he wondered why he was doing this. Did he still believe that there could be a reconciliation with Joshua and that he would be able to continue living peacefully with the Israelites once they had crossed the Jordan?

Perhaps Tirzah was right and his friendship with Joshua was so important that they would both try to heal the breach. Now the best course might be to continue spying on the Canaanites' defenses. Then, when he returned to Bashan to settle Tirzah's affairs, he could present the information as a peace offering to Joshua.

This resolved, he stopped at an outdoor tavern, where he sat beneath a grape arbor with a cup of wine and enjoyed the breeze. Soon traders approached the table next to his. "Hizki!" one said. "When did you arrive in town? I thought you were away in Midian."

The two men embraced, then sat down. "Midian? No one goes to Midian these days. There's a war going on. Hadn't you heard?"

"But I would have thought that was over by now. The Israelites won, didn't they?"

"Yes, they burned the cities and laid waste the whole countryside. And everyone who survived the slaughter was enslaved."

"Slaughter? You mean they killed civilians?"

"Oh, yes. Joshua just let the troops loose on the general population. Let me tell you, it was horrible. I still don't think the area's safe. I won't let any of my caravans travel the King's Highway now—not until I've seen some sign that the barbarism of these wretched invaders has abated."

Pepi narrowed his eyes, listening. "Next thing you know, they're going to come charging right across the river and challenge us. We'll be unprepared, at the mercy of those foreign savages. You know that they've sworn to invade us?"

"Yes, and to take the whole of Canaan. They say the land was given to them by some god nobody's ever heard of."

"Yes, a hundred years ago? I say possession is more important." He sighed. "The king of Bethel agrees with me, but he thinks that he can wait until the last minute to arm the city and muster an army."

"The more fool he. And you, Tilon? What are you going to do?"

340

"I'm taking everything I own out of Bethel."

"A wise move," Hizki said. "But what am I to do? I make my living off caravans."

"Hmmm. Is there any way to bribe the Israelites? To ingratiate oneself with Joshua, perhaps, and promise him special treatment if only he'll let your business alone?"

Hizki shook his head. "From all I hear he's as incorruptible as he is savage, but . . ."

"Yes? Tell me!"

"It would appear that some appointments have been made in the conquered lands. And some of these magistrates are not above listening to an offer of a bribe now and then."

"Do you have any names?"

"The first one that comes to mind is Hanniel, the magistrate for Bashan. He's busy making deals now, before the period of mourning for Moses runs out."

The two men drained their cups and prepared to leave. "Good luck to you. I've no confidence at all in our ability to stand up to these desert barbarians. Now take Shechem: They think those tall Shepherd walls will protect them, but Kamose breached them, and Joshua can, too."

The other man shook his head sadly. "I wish someone in Jericho would look at things realistically. The city officials won't even recognize that there is a danger. The ordinary people are frightened half to death. They know that Jericho will be the first place Joshua hits when he crosses the river. And they know all about his army."

"If Joshua is the type they say he is, he'll take the land and be very rough on the present inhabitants."

Pepi kept his eyes fixed on the cup in front of him, making every effort to look like a man whose mind was a thousand leagues away. Well, this had been a fruitful bit

341

of eavesdropping. Spying was not just a matter of drawing sketches of a city's physical defenses. There was a human side to it, and it would help for Joshua to know that there was a split between the common people of Jericho, who were deathly afraid of him, and the city fathers, who, hidden behind their thick walls, did not take him seriously. Perhaps it would be a good idea to go into Jericho and look around, talk with people.

But why am I spying on these people, with whom I have no quarrel, and gathering information for people who no longer even think of me as an ally? Most likely Joshua will tell me to mind my own business and leave the soldiering to people with the stomach for it.

Gall rose in his throat, and his resentment began to build. Why should he risk his own life for people who would only prove ungrateful in the end? And why should he risk Tirzah's as well after the way they had treated her?

He raised his wine cup. *You're making too much of nothing. This trouble between you and Joshua will blow over. You've spent too many years among these people; they won't turn you out because you're not of their blood.*

But, as reassuring as the thought was, part of him refused to believe it. The only thing that had held him to his long-standing unwritten contract with the Israelites had been his love of, and devotion to, Moses. And now that Moses was gone . . .

III

By the time he returned to the inn and Tirzah, however, Pepi had calmed his nerves and shifted, at least for now, the angry streak of resentment that had risen in his heart.

Tirzah embraced him at the door. "The heat's broken," she said. "Why don't we go out to the market? I'd love to do some shopping."

"No, Tirzah," he said irritably. "I—I'm sorry. I don't feel up to that sort of thing just now."

She took his hand in both of hers and looked at him. "Tell me about it. Perhaps I can help."

But he turned away and faced the wall. "Damn! I'd thought I'd gotten this behind me."

"It's about you and Joshua, isn't it?"

He let out a deep breath. "I have this awful feeling that it's all coming to an end, that it's over between Moses's people and me, and there isn't a thing I can do about it."

"Sit down." Her hand, soft and strong, caressed his neck.

He told her everything that had gone through his head as he had listened to the two Canaanites. She heard him out in silence, rubbing his neck gently. "Try to relax," she said. "It's going to be all right."

"That's just it, in my heart I know it isn't. Joshua's whole plan depends upon rallying the Israelites not just against Canaanites, but against everyone else in the entire region who isn't of their blood and faith. There won't be a place for us."

"Then we'll go somewhere else. I'll be happy wherever you are. Let's go out now and look Bethel over. It looks like a nice town. Maybe we could settle here. Or Jericho. I don't care. Any place where you can be at peace with yourself."

"I don't want to live here. He'll soon be swarming over this place with his army, laying it to waste, killing

343

and enslaving everyone. It's going to be worse than in Bashan because this is the real Canaan, the Promised Land."

"You've spoken several times about this Home, the island where your uncle Demetrios lives. We could go there, far away from Joshua. You'd be happy, Pepi." She bent down, kissed the top of his head, and hugged him to her soft bosom. "I'd make sure you were."

He turned and looked up at her. "But what would they need another armorer for? And I haven't any other training. I'd just be underfoot."

"You wouldn't need to work. You're rich. We could live a life of ease."

"It's not the way of my people. I wouldn't know what to do without my work. It's my *life*."

"You said Iri was a jeweler and was going to Home to start his jewelry business again."

"Yes, but I'm an armorer. That's all I've ever been. Pretty ornaments aren't my line." He shook his head, remembering. "I wonder where Iri is."

"Don't start going on about Iri. We're talking about us. Calm down. Let me help you get rid of that tension. See how stiff your shoulders are?"

"Let's get out of here. I don't like this place."

"I'll go anywhere you like."

"Let's go to Jericho."

"All right. Do you want me to pack up again right now?" She leaned over and, with a soft giggle, rubbed her breasts against the back of his neck. "Or can it wait until morning?"

Lingering indoors until well after the city gate closed at sunset, Tirzah and Pepi managed to miss the two real spies Joshua had sent into Canaan two days before.

Pelet, of the tribe of Levi, and Gedor, of the tribe of Manasseh, had been sent behind the enemy lines after the battle of Midian. Although no business could be transacted within Israel during the period of mourning, it was a matter of debate whether the same was true of lands not within the present boundaries of the Israelite domain. And, while the debate was going on among the Levites, Joshua had ordered the two undercover agents across the border.

Pelet and Gedor slipped unobtrusively out of Bethel while the sun was still fairly high in the afternoon sky and arrived at the Jericho wall before the gatekeeper closed the city at sunset. They were making their way down the main street just as a pair of mercenaries sauntered out of a tavern.

Tall, hulking Samlah of Cerar did not make the connection until they were well down the street. "Mehida," he said to his short, stout companion. "Did you see those two fellows in the dark robes back there?"

"*Yes*, one of the bastards almost stepped on my foot." Mehida of Ashdod said. "Why?"

"I think I've seen them before."

"They don't look like soldiers—at least not dressed that way."

"But I have this feeling that they ought to be."

"Well, maybe it'll come to you. Look, I have a fat purse aching to be spent on whores and strong drink. The question is, which should we do first?"

"If we don't get drunk first, we'll have to look at the whores with clear eyes, and we won't like what we see, considering the kind of whores we can afford."

"And if we do get drunk first, the whores will have us thrown out the door before we can do anything. Or, worse, we'll pay our money and then not be able to do anything."

"What about a compromise. Let's go look in on two or three of the whorehouses, we'll have a drink in each, look the girls over, and make our choices."

"Now you're talking. But I haven't been here in a long time. Do you know any of the houses?"

"No, but they all seem to be clustered along the city wall. Let's work our way along the wall one house at a time."

"What are you waiting for?"

In Jericho, several streets away, Pelet and Gedor stopped at an inn, moving into a distant corner of the room where no one could see their faces clearly. The woman who took their order and came back bringing a skinful of cheap wine winked at them. "There are other pleasures to be had here, you know. There'll be dancers coming in soon, and I could suggest other diversions best enjoyed upstairs."

Pelet was embarrassed to find himself blushing. "N-no, thank you. We'll just sit and drink for now."

She moved into the light and let the lantern's glow play on her half-exposed breasts. When she spoke she emphasized her words with an amazingly erotic shake of the hips. "You'll change your minds before the evening's over. Everybody comes into Rahab's Place thinking he's only going to stop for a drink. But changing people's minds is our specialty here. Just call for Rahab. I'll come running—unless I'm entertaining a guest." Her smile was knowing and friendly. When she walked away, Pelet, young and inexperienced, found his eyes wandering to the waggling of her ripe behind.

"Watch out," Gedor said. "We're not here for that. Although, let me tell you, if we didn't have a secret errand, I could think of worse things to do with our time."

Pelet took a cautious swallow of wine. He was unused to strong drink. "D-do you suppose she really owns this place?" he asked innocently.

"Either that or she's got a partner, a pimp, maybe. The Canaanites don't have quite the same view of women as we do, you know. They're an independent-minded lot over here."

Pelet glared at him. "You don't mean to say you prefer their women to ours?"

His friend took a long drink and wiped his mouth. "How do I know? I've never been to bed with any of ours. Too many fathers and brothers to deal with. Tends to inhibit one's passion if you know that rolling in the grass with one of our pure maidens is going to cost you your front teeth or worse. Whereas the women of the conquered lands are quite another matter."

"You mean you've actually slept with—"

"Why, of course! Don't tell me you haven't ever?" Gedor snorted. "You haven't, have you? You're a bashful little virgin. Why, I've half a mind to buy you a first time from little Rahab. She looks like a lot of fun between the covers."

"Gedor, stop carrying on. You're embarrassing me. People are staring at us."

But the wine was beginning to weave its spell, and Gedor chuckled low in his throat. "Carrying on! It's you who ought to be carrying on. For the first time in your life you're free from your priest-ridden Levite kinsmen."

"Don't talk about my family that way!"

Gedor let out a raucous laugh. "Shut up, will you? Shut up and have another cup of wine."

IV

"I thought we were just going to get drunk and bed a couple of girls," Mehida said in a whining voice. "And you have to get into an arm-wrestling match with that big ape from Carchemish and lose nearly everything we had. Samlah, what am I going to do with you?"

"But if you hadn't stopped me, I would have won it all back."

"You would have lost everything that stands between us and starvation."

"Mercenaries like us never need to starve. Jericho's got a garrison. If we go right down there and present ourselves bright and shiny in the morning . . ."

"I don't want to present myself bright and shiny anywhere. I want two weeks off before we sign up for anything again. And look at us. When we've drunk up the little we have left and found a doss for the night . . ."

They had pushed their way into the dirty, crowded little brothel and tavern without even taking note of the sign outside the door. Suddenly Samlah said, "Hey, I know this place. This is Rahab's Place. And there she is. Rahab!"

The diminutive woman turned and was lifted off her feet by a huge pair of arms and spun around so fast that one of her sandals flew off. "What are you doing? Put me down, you big ape!"

But then she recognized the wine-blurred face. "Samlah!" she cried. "Put me down, you overstuffed hippopotamus!"

He set her down, and she bent to retrieve her shoe. "What a way to announce your arrival! Nobody is ever going to housebreak you, are they?"

But he leaned over and stopped her wagging mouth with a friendly kiss. "Is that any way to greet an old friend? A fellow you've bedded twenty times and more? Now fix us a bowl of wine and come sit with us. I've a friend here you ought to meet. I've told him all about you, what a paragon of beauty and grace you are—"

"Nonsense. The only time you ever talk that way, you big water buffalo, is when you've come to town with no coins in your pocket and needing credit. Are you broke? Did you drink up everything again?"

"Again?" asked Mehida, shooting a dirty look at his comrade.

"Come now, Rahab," the big man said. "You can't be serious. Turning us out like strangers. It would be against all the laws of hospitality."

"The laws of hospitality don't operate in a whorehouse," Rahab said, her voice suddenly as hard as flint. "You're old enough to know that. Cash—it's the rule all the way across the Great Sea. If you were Demetrios himself, you couldn't get credit at my place."

"If I were Demetrios, I wouldn't need your place," he said with a laugh. "Come on now, bring us some wine and sit down with us."

He stopped, stared into the dimly lit interior of the big room, and blinked. Under the light of the lanterns a slim dancer, naked except for gold bangles, was undulating enticingly. Samlah screwed up his face, opening first one eye, then the other, trying to focus. "This is interesting. Come here, Mehida, and see this."

Rahab scowled at them and planted her tiny hands on her wide hips. "Don't get any ideas about *her*. There's no one in the world less likely than I am to give you something for free. She turned down a rich sheikh from Moab last week just because she didn't like his looks. She's got

349

some dye merchant from Tyre keeping her. Thinks the old fool is going to marry her and set her up for life."

"I'm not looking at the girl," Samlah said. "Too narrow in the hips. Mehida, look at those two behind her, over in the corner. They're the same two I spotted in the street."

"I guess they are," Mehida said with a shrug. "So?"

"So our fortunes have just been recouped. Because I suddenly remember who they are. Do you remember that stand we made in Bashan? The Israelites beat us coming and going."

"I remember," Mehida said peevishly. "But what's that got to do with—"

"Don't go starting any trouble," Rahab said. "I'll call the city guards if you start a fight in this place. I told you that two years ago, when you and those two Greeks tore the place apart."

"I'm not going to make any fuss," Samlah said. "I'm just going to slip out and call the guards."

"You're going to *what*? Over my dead body!"

"Those two are spies. Israelite spies."

"Spies?" Mehida asked. "But how do you know?"

"Because I spotted those two in Bashan. They were in the second line when the charge came. The older one's an underofficer. He took a swipe at me, nearly took my head off. And the only reason in the world why they would be here is to spy on the city. Everybody knows the Israelites are going to attack us. If I was Joshua, I'd have sent spies in here long ago."

Rahab looked anxiously from one face to the other. "You're sure?"

"You try taking one of them to bed, and you'll confirm the matter. He's been clipped. Easiest way in the world to tell. Besides, I know that face."

"Look, I don't want any trouble. Particularly not with the Israelites."

"Then you should have been nicer to us when we first came in the door. Now it's too late, old girl. I'm about to saunter down to the guard post and collect a nice reward. Come on, Mehida. We're going to win back what we lost and more."

"Please, don't," Rahab begged. "Please." But it was no good. They were out the door.

The disquiet in Rahab's guts turned to panic. Until now she had managed to stay out of politics. She was quite sure that Joshua was going to do exactly what he said he would do. All her sources told her so: men from the caravans that plied the King's Highway from Damascus to Ezion-geber and beyond; men from Edom and Moab who had been forced from their homes by Joshua's campaigns; deserters from various defeated eastern armies who had fought Joshua's hard-eyed young soldiers and knew what fierce warriors they had become; mercenaries like the two who had just left—all of them had told her the same thing. If Joshua made a threat, he would keep to it. If he made a plan, he would carry it out. And he planned to occupy Canaan and have his way with its lands and its inhabitants.

To have two of Joshua's spies arrested on her property would be disastrous for her. She had to prevent it. But how? She bit her lip and looked once more at the two men in the dark robes, in the far corner.

Gedor snickered at Pelet's discomfort. "Can't keep your eyes off her, can you? Not that I blame you. She's a pretty little thing, even if she could use a bit in the hips."

"Doesn't she have any shame?" Pelet asked.

"I don't know," Gedor said with a throaty chuckle.

"When she's finished her dance, let's call her over and ask. I bet she slaps your face. Or she might find the question interesting and stimulating. She might even sit on your lap."

"Gedor, stop calling attention to us. It's dangerous. And put down that wine cup; you've had too much to drink!"

"Look at you, trying not to look at her but sneaking a glance anyway. What a plaguey lot of hypocrites the Levites raise you boys to be, Pelet! I'm going to get you into bed with one of these women before the night is out. We'll book a room here, and we'll each of us have a ripe young Canaanite for the night."

"Gedor, look what you've done! Here comes the inn-keeper woman. Now keep quiet and don't stir up any more trouble."

But it was too late. Rahab, short and plump, bore down on them with the single-mindedness of a hunting hound. "You two, you've got to leave. Now."

"Look here," Gedor protested. "I admit we were getting boisterous, but nowhere near enough to throw us out."

"Come with me, now. This way. It's very important." She looked at the two doors, where she had stationed her two bouncers, big burly Anatolians with bulging arms. Each of them met her gaze and then the one at the front door stuck his head out and made a frantic waving motion. "I was afraid of that. Come with me now!"

Once again Gedor tried to argue, but she tugged at his arm with surprising strength. "Upstairs. It's the only place to hide. The guards are coming!"

"The guards? I don't understand."

"Two of my patrons recognized you as Israelites. They know you're spies. They called the guards. Hurry up the stairs."

Gedor still wanted to argue, but Pelet pushed him up the stairs as the little woman led the way.

Rahab's inn was hardly more than a projection of the city wall, mortared directly onto the wall and abutting the whorehouse next door. When they emerged from the stairwell onto the rooftop Rahab looked around; there was nowhere to hide. She peered over the edge of the roof down into the street. "The street's full of guards. Where am I going to hide you?"

"Can we drop down onto the other side of the wall?" Gedor asked.

"Not a chance. The guards patrol the wall. Besides, this isn't Shechem, with those sloping Hai walls. You try dropping down from this wall, you'll go straight down into the rocks. No."

Gedor caught her looking at a pile of flax in one corner. "No, that won't work."

"It's the only way," she said. "They'll be up here in a minute, and if they catch you you're done for. Hurry up. Down on your bellies, and I'll cover you with flax."

"Ugh! I'd rather—"

"Shut up and do what she says, Gedor." Pelet pushed Gedor down and lay beside him. "Now, ma'am," he said. "We're ready. And thank you."

V

The captain of the guards scowled at the two mercenaries. "Well? You were going to deliver to us two Israelite spies. Where are they?"

Samlah and Mehida exchanged frightened glances. "Sir, they were right here," Samlah said. "I swear it. We both saw them. They have to be here still. Try the rooms upstairs. Try the roof."

"Both areas have been searched," the captain said. "We have yet to turn up any foreign agents. You'd better have a good excuse for dragging out a whole squad of guards."

"Please," Mehida said. "Rahab saw them, too. She can verify that we're telling the truth."

"Don't bring me into this," Rahab said. "I saw no such thing. If I didn't know you were too broke to be drunk, I'd swear you had been tippling nice and hard before you arrived here."

"You know these men, then?" the captain asked.

"A couple of deadbeats from way back. They came here tonight to see if I'd give them credit. Me! Credit!"

The captain chuckled. "True, the house of Rahab is well-known in these parts, but not as a place where the mistress is a soft touch. So you deny there's anything to their claim?"

Rahab threw up her hands. "I saw nobody, Captain. These two are desperate. They probably don't have a place to sleep tonight. My guess is that they saw a couple of strangers and cooked up this plan to have them framed as spies to collect the reward."

"Why, you little liar!" Samlah said indignantly. "Captain, there isn't a word of truth to what she says."

"And what does she stand to gain from lying to me?" the captain asked. "Do you think she imagines there's a reward in it for her for telling me there weren't any spies? No, my friend, the one who has a motive for lying is you." He clapped his hands, and two hulking guardsmen materialized. "Take these two to the city prison. On the way

354

there, acquaint them with the penalties for lying to an officer."

The guards grabbed Mehida and Samlah by the arms, and Mehida winced at the powerful grip on his bicep. "Come along, you scum."

As he was dragged away Samlah called out, "Captain, you're making a mistake. Rahab, you bitch, you'll pay for this!"

Watching the two troublemakers carted off, Rahab felt as if a heavy burden had been lifted from her shoulders. "Captain, I apologize for those two. I do hope you aren't put out with me. Actually, I threw them out half an hour ago. Ordinarily I don't bother with the likes of them. They must have slipped past my guards. Come, have a drink on the house."

"That's very generous of you," the captain said with a smile. "But I'm on duty."

A mischievous gleam lit Rahab's eyes. "Some food, then? Or if you've already eaten, perhaps we can find some other sort of coin in which to pay you for your time."

The captain raised one eyebrow, and she knew she had her man.

"As a matter of fact, on my last day off there was a little wench here from Damascus. She was occupied then, and I had to go away with my . . . curiosity unsatisfied. Perhaps she is available now. I understand she specializes in certain activities not usually offered in these parts. 'Flute players,' they call them in Damascus."

So that's the way the wind blows, Rahab thought. "Certainly, Captain. That isn't against the law, is it? I mean, she hasn't been offering any such thing here, of course, and I wouldn't want to ask her to do anything against the law. But if you can give me your personal assurance . . . you understand I'm a poor woman, unlearned in the ways of the law, and I'd need your word on the matter."

"I *am* the law," the captain said. "And I say it's legal." He winked at her. "Tonight, it is. I served a tour in Damascus, and I rather miss certain attentions the ladies of the evening used to offer. Is she available?"

Rahab smiled. Most men had their price. "Captain, I'll make her available. And let me assure you, you've got quite an experience awaiting you."

It was another hour before Rahab could get back to the roof. At first she could not remember where in the pile of loose flax she had hidden the two spies. Then she tripped over Gedor. He came out spluttering, and she quickly clapped a hand over his mouth. "Find your friend. He must have suffocated by now."

"Here he is," Gedor said, digging through the pile and coming up with an arm. They helped Pelet up and brushed him off. "We're in your debt."

"I'm glad you think so," Rahab said, looking at the two of them. "I risked my neck tonight. I shudder to think what would have happened if they'd found you. I laid everything on the line for you; you owe me something."

Pelet held up his hands, palm up. "Name it. If it is in our power, we'll provide it."

"When you come across the Jordan and take Jericho, protect me and my family. Tell the soldiers to spare the house of Rahab and everybody in it. When the time comes I'll bring my family here."

Pelet looked at Gedor. "Sounds reasonable." He turned to Rahab. "Help us sneak out of town, and we'll swear."

"Done," Rahab said. "I can let you down on a rope over the wall. But not now; you'll run into a patrol. There'll be guards on the walls until dawn. When the guard changes, then you can escape. Wait until one of the caravans leaves. Slip into the tail end; nobody will notice you."

"All right," Pelet said. "We'll wait for the caravan to leave. But what do we do until morning?"

Rahab stared at him, with openmouthed wonder. "You Israelites are a strange lot," she said. "You find sanctuary in a bawdy house and you have to ask what you're going to do to stave off boredom for the rest of the evening?"

In the early morning Pepi and Tirzah began the ride from Bethel to Jericho. Pepi was uncharacteristically silent, so Tirzah reached across the space separating their two mounts to take his hand. "Something is still bothering you."

He squeezed her hand. "The more I think about it, the more I think that with Moses gone, there's no place for me on the other side of the Jordan. Moses was half general, half prophet. The Israelites now need a prophet as well as a general in charge, and they don't have one."

"You think they're going to stray?"

"They've already begun, according to the traders in Bethel. They say the magistrate appointed to rule over Manasseh—Hanniel, I think his name is—is already taking bribes."

"Manasseh! But that's where I lived. That's Bashan."

"Yes. And we were going back to talk to the magistrate to settle our quarrel with Shallum once and for all."

"And you think—"

"I think we have to get back to Bashan."

"Do we?" she asked in a quiet voice, almost inaudible against the sound of the animals' hoofbeats.

But he was not listening to her. He frowned as if in pain and rubbed his temple with his free hand.

*   *   *

Pelet and Gedor slunk out of Jericho in the wake of a caravan. As the long string of pack animals pulled out onto the high road that stretched northward toward Lake Chinnereth, they spotted Pepi and Tirzah riding slowly into Jericho.

"Pelet!" Gedor said. "Did you see them?"

"I did. Pepi in Jericho. And with the Bashanite slut in tow. What do you suppose they're doing?"

Gedor snorted. "Think, man. Remember the stories people were telling about him?"

"You mean about his favoring the other side?"

"Favoring! He's gone over to them. What else would he be doing here, on the eve of our invasion? The Bashanite woman has made a traitor of him!"

VI

Tirzah and Pepi dismounted, hobbled their animals, and hired urchins to guard their possessions before they entered the main gate of Jericho. They moved slowly, following the crowd. But as Pepi walked before her, clearing the way, Tirzah noticed his stumbling walk. She hurried forward. "Is something wrong? You don't look well."

"Leave me alone! Do you have to talk all the time? Can't you ever leave me alone?"

Shocked, she drew back. "I'm sorry."

Pepi stopped. One hand reached for hers; the other went to his head. "Forgive me. My head is killing me. I can't think straight. My eyes keep going out of focus."

"Here, sit by the well. I'll draw some water." She managed to get him to the great rock platform surrounding Jericho's best and most reliable well. He sat down, holding his head in his hands. She lowered a bucket, brought up cool water, and bathed his face. Panic-stricken, she scanned the faces of passersby. Suddenly she locked eyes with a well-dressed, prosperous-looking middle-aged man. "Could you help me, please?"

The man stared at her curiously for a moment, then came forward. A servant stood at his elbow. "What seems to be the matter, my dear?"

"It's my husband," she said. "He's suffered an injury to his head, and now he seems to be having one of his blackouts."

The man looked at Pepi, noting the expensive clothing he had purchased in Joppa. After a moment's hesitation he said to his servant, "Go for the city guards."

"No, please!" Tirzah protested. "If we could perhaps get him to a doctor."

"The guards will be glad to help. Don't worry, my dear. We're not such barbarians as foreigners seem to think we are. You are not from around here, are you?"

Tirzah looked hastily down at Pepi. "N-no. My husband is a—a trader from Nubia. I come from one of the countries of the far north." Suddenly she felt Pepi against her. "Are you awake, my dear? Speak to me."

The stranger knelt by Pepi's side. "He's in a bad way. Doesn't seem to be aware of either of us. He's a trader, you say? Well, we traders have to stick together when these crises occur. My name is Hizki. I'm known here, which ought to ensure a quick response from the guards." He drew closer to Pepi.

"I'm not sure he ought even to be up and around. But he wanted to travel and see Canaan, and he thought he was well enough." She hugged Pepi to her bosom. "Oh, Pepi! I should never have let you come."

Two guardsmen arrived with Hizki's servant. "How may we help you, sir?"

"It's this gentleman, he's had a blow to the head. Where can we take him? He needs a good physician."

"Well, sir, the last time something like this happened, they told me to take the man to the home of the chief magistrate of the city. He has spare rooms for visitors of means."

"Splendid! That's exactly the right thing to do."

Tirzah watched apprehensively as the guards picked Pepi up. He seemed to be unconscious now, and she thanked the gods. What would he think, knowing that, having come to Jericho as a spy for Joshua, he was being quartered in the home of the head magistrate?

A short distance north of Jericho, the ancient road crossed a dry streambed that led to the Jordan. As the caravan dipped into the wadi, Pelet and Gedor took the opportunity to disappear into the underbrush.

"Joshua should be pleased with us," Gedor said to Pelet. "Not only will we be coming back with detailed information about Jericho's defenses, we'll be exposing a spy."

"Are you quite sure of that?" Pelet asked. "We could be wrong, you know. We don't want to accuse Joshua's friend without proof. He's very loyal to his friends. More than once someone has maligned Pepi, only to have Joshua explode in a rage."

"Yes, but Caleb will be on our side. He's been trying to get rid of the Egyptian for a long time."

"Maybe things are changing. When Joshua heard about

Pepi's siding with the Bashanite woman and taking property away from Shallum at sword's point, he was mad. I saw him."

Pelet looked thoughtful. "So you think Joshua is waiting for an excuse to end the friendship?"

"Look, having even one dissenter in our midst as we're preparing for the biggest battle of our lives is dangerous. How much worse when the dissenter is the only foreigner left among us? And highly placed?"

"But Pepi's our chief armorer."

"Who has, I'll remind you, trained a full complement of Israelite armorers who can do anything in the world he can do, except work iron. Who needs him now? Let him go over to the enemy. It won't help them at all. They're disgracefully unprepared. Even if Pepi starts making weapons for them, it'll be too late."

"All the same, I don't—"

"Are you with me in this or not? I'm going to turn Pepi in, with or without you."

Pelet hesitated. He looked at Gedor. He bit his lip. He sighed. "I guess I'm with you."

Pepi came awake with a start and immediately tried to sit up. But pain stabbed through his head, and he fell back on the pillow. "Tirzah!" he called. "Where am I?"

She took his hand. "It's all right. Lie back. We're safe. You've had one of your attacks."

"But where are we?"

She leaned close. "You collapsed just outside the city. A friendly trader helped me bring you here."

"Where?"

"Now don't get upset."

"Upset? Why should I be upset?" He clutched his head with both hands. "This is worse than before."

"All the more reason to stay very calm. Pepi, this is the home of the chief magistrate of Jericho. Don't make a fuss. I told them you were a trader. As long as they don't find out who you are, we'll be safe. Now lie back. They're sending for a doctor."

"But Tirzah, I have to get to Joshua. When we were here before, I noticed cracks in the wall. I didn't pay any attention, but now I understand. Earthquakes! The ground is unstable. That means the walls aren't sound. That's why the Hai replaced the walls of every conquered town with their own great slanting ones. Joshua doesn't know this, but has to. I must get the message to him."

"Quiet, Pepi! Someone might hear you. Lie calmly. You'll be able to get up and around soon enough."

"Soon enough? Time's running out. He needs to know now."

Once again the hand closed over his mouth. "Please," she whispered, "the doctor's coming."

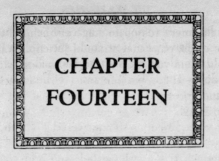

CHAPTER FOURTEEN

On the Great Sea

I

Since Nuhara's betrayal, Theon had not spoken to her or even acknowledged her existence. Once or twice she had addressed him timidly, but he had stubbornly refused to return her greeting or even look at her, and she had crept away.

Now, as the hour for the great raid approached, Theon tried to forget his anger and bitterness by pounding away on the iron sword the Minotaur had ordered.

Except for the ring of pink skin around his neck where they had fastened his chain, Theon was as brown as a berry and rugged looking, with broad shoulders and huge biceps that bulged formidably now as he wielded the hammer. Life as a slave had toughened him and made him half again the man he had been when he had first gone to sea. Nuhara, who had crept out of the cabin, looked wistfully at his powerful arms and tried to imagine them holding her once more.

363

Would it ever come about again? She doubted that he would ever forgive her. How could she explain her actions to make him understand that she had had no choice?

Suddenly Theon became aware of being watched. He turned and, seeing her, scowled. "What are you doing here? Go away."

Her voice broke as she answered. "Theon, don't say that! How can you talk to me that way after—"

"After what? After I trusted you, and you betrayed me? Why should I want anything to do with you after that? I swear if I could reach you, I'd throw you in the sea!"

"Please, Theon, let me explain!"

But he held his hands over his ears. "I won't listen!"

"If you only knew the circumstances—"

"Prodicus!" Theon called. "What atrocity have I committed that I should have to listen to this harpy prating on like a fishwife? Can't you get her out of here so I can finish the Bull's sword for him? There have been enough interrogations already."

"Go inside, Nuhara," Prodicus said.

"But—"

"Leave the man alone. He has work to do, and he hasn't much time to do it in." He made a shooing motion with his hand, and Nuhara, crestfallen, slunk back into the cabin.

"Thanks," Theon said.

"How close to finished are you?" Prodicus asked.

Theon handed the sword to him. "Almost done. Mind you, it's not a sword by Belsunu, but it's an iron sword."

Prodicus hefted the weapon. "I had a Belsunu sword in my hands once. The balance made it seem to weigh about half as much in my hand as it did in the scabbard. There was something magical about it."

"That there was," Theon said with a touch of truculence. "But I can't match that yet, and who knows, maybe neither I nor anyone else in the world will ever match it. Give it back if all you can do is criticize it. I have more work to do."

"Touchy, aren't we?" Prodicus said with a grin. "Here, take the thing. I didn't say it was a bad sword. I just said—"

"I know what you said. And haven't you got something better to do than stand here and insult the slave?"

"Just because your little plot to foil the raid didn't work out . . ."

"I had a mission and I failed. Failed miserably."

"A lot of good men have gone up against the Bull and found that he was more than they could handle. It's no disgrace to have been outsmarted by him."

"This is different," Theon said bitterly. "Lives will be lost." He looked up at Prodicus. "Including your men's."

"Would you mind that?" Prodicus asked. "I'd have thought you would rejoice to hear one of us had died."

"Strange as it may seem, I've found friends here. I'm sorry to see any of you die."

"This from a man who came here to betray us?" He shook his head.

"I was doing a job," Theon said. "But I'd had some hopes of seeing some of you spared when the reckoning came. There are men of honor among you. Including you. And Pandion, how is Pandion?"

"Tromes says he's doing better. He's settled down, grown stronger. It would appear your friend with the red face helped him."

Theon's mouth was set, and his eyes were hard. "I'm glad. But like all the men on the oars and like myself, he'll die chained to the ship if it sinks or burns."

"What did you expect? Those are the ways of war."

"If I'd had my way, Demetrios's fleet would have ambushed you and won without killing a man. You'd have had to surrender or be cut to pieces; I was counting on the Bull's being too smart to fight against hopeless odds."

"He might have been," Prodicus agreed. "But how would you rate the Bull? As a man of honor?"

Theon looked him straight in the eyes. "I don't know what I think. But I would have asked them to spare him."

"And if he wins, will he spare you?"

Theon frowned. "Perhaps to make iron swords. But ask him yourself."

Prodicus wheeled around. "Are we ready, sir? Shall I have the men draw anchor?"

The black-bearded man nodded and looked down at Theon as the mate disappeared. "What's that you have there?"

"Your iron sword," Theon said. He tossed it over, watching the Minotaur's surprise at the unaccustomed weight. "Prodicus has just been reminding me that I'm no Belsunu."

"But neither is anyone else," the Minotaur said, hacking at imaginary limbs. "It doesn't have to be a masterwork to be useful in a fight. It's probably better than you think. You aren't satisfied with it?"

"Far from it," Theon said sourly. "I was sitting here thinking up excuses. The ore. The fact that I'm making it on shipboard, with an inadequate oven. The fact that—"

"It's a good sword." The Minotaur pulled the bronze sword from its scabbard and carelessly tossed it over the side. "So, in an hour or two we'll know how well these men of mine fight, won't we? And who's to rule the Great Sea. Demetrios has built a great merchant empire. I've grown fat and rich stealing from him and sinking his ships.

It was inevitable we'd meet and fight it out. The winner reigns supreme while the loser . . ."

"If only I'd managed to get that message through. We could have taken you without losing a man. And without killing you, either."

"Killing us?" the Minotaur asked. "Killing *me* in particular? Does this prey on your mind?"

"It doesn't matter how many ships you have. Demetrios will have war galleys mixed with the trader vessels, too. And even the traders carry armed complement. He'll fight you to the death. You may win in the end, but Demetrios will get some of you." He looked the Minotaur in the eyes. "I know you too well to suppose you'll be hiding in the rear, letting the front ranks do your fighting for you. Even if you win the battle, you could die."

"So I could. And if they fire the boat, so could you."

"With a lot of good men. Look, it's not too late to turn around. Spare everyone the horror of what's otherwise to come."

"Spare these fellows?" the Minotaur asked, amused. "It's what they live for. If I did that, they'd revolt. They'd take the *Hephaistos* away from me and sail into the harbor with my corpse hanging from the yard." He chuckled humorlessly under his breath. "Ah, now," he said, studying the ships surrounding him. "They're falling into position."

He pulled the iron sword from its scabbard and gave Theon a half-mocking salute. "We've passed the turning point. It's in the hands of the gods. It's me or Demetrios. But either way it'll be a fight." He turned away. "Tromes!" he said in the unmistakable voice of command. "Full speed ahead, man!"

II

The first five ships to enter the mouth of Poros Harbor moved in precise formation, with the *Pylos* in front of the *Gades* and the *Philea* on its flanks. The *Melos* brought up the rear. In the center came the enormous *Hephaistos*.

Aboard each lead ship the *trieraules* was playing the ancient Shinarian dance tune that Theon himself had taught Tromes, and its wail carried out over the water. Many of the strongest rowers in the pirate fleet had been pressed into service in the pits of the four flanking vessels, to allow them to keep up with the flagship's double complement of oarsmen.

The fleet entered the mouth of the harbor at an impressive speed. The pirates, clustered along the rails of the lead ship and armed to the teeth and ready for battle, let out a great echoing battle cry to strike fear into the hearts of the sentinels guarding the harbor.

Theon, standing aft on the deck of the *Hephaistos*, looked back with dismay as the rest of the Minotaur's fleet followed them into the harbor, which, surrounded by hills, looked very much like Home. To the right and left the guard forts let loose volleys of arrows; all but a few fell short. Obviously the attack had caught them unprepared.

Theon's heart sank. If the islanders had been warned, there would have been dozens of small boats firing flaming arrows at the invaders. But there did not even appear to be a full complement of soldiers manning the forts. Where were all of Demetrios's troops?

In despair he looked up to the hills surrounding the harbor. Belatedly, two sentinels had lit the signal fires, and the smoke was billowing into the air. The message was clear: *We're under attack!*

But it was too late.

Suddenly, he saw activity. Two patrol ships had broken away from the wharves and were making their way out across the blue water. Other ships, at anchor only moments before, were being prepared for action. Ranks of oars pointed skyward, then dipped down into the water.

As the *Hephaistos* turned into the inner harbor Theon could see the docks. Every berth was filled. He tried to count the number of ships and gave up after reaching thirty-five. The heart of Demetrios's trading fleet was here. If the pirates were to win, Demetrios's power would be irrevocably destroyed.

The little patrol ships, monoremes unfit for battle on such a scale, advanced bravely. As he watched, Theon's eyes filled with bitter tears. Certainly they knew they had no chance. Yet they went valiantly into battle. He had never witnessed anything so courageous in his life.

He moved toward the rail, to see more clearly, and was pulled up short by his chain. He cursed and tore at the collar.

His tools were stacked neatly on the deck. With no hesitation he reached down and picked up a coarse rasp that was used to work rough-smelted metal into shape. Squatting on the bare deck, he grasped his chain in one hand and began filing. The bronze gave way quickly, and in a moment he was free, a sun-blackened giant naked except for a collar around his neck and the six links of chain attached to it. He leapt onto the rail, then to the top of the cabin, steadying himself with a callused hand.

If the pirates won this encounter Theon did not want to survive. No longer could he live in disgrace. But what could he do? Demetrios's cause was lost.

One thing I can do, he thought, looking down at the file in his hand. His eyes went to where Tromes, stripped to his loincloth, sat playing furiously on his flute at the edge of the rower's pit.

He looked around. The Minotaur and his crew stood by the bow railing, their eyes focused on the vessels coming toward them. Only Tromes remained at his post. Theon managed to sneak past Tromes without being detected. Then he looked back, waiting for a moment when Tromes was looking elsewhere, and vaulted into the oar pit.

It was a leap without looking, and Theon narrowly missed landing on one of the oarsmen.

In midstroke, all the rowers looked up immediately, but Theon signaled silence. The rowers saw the rasp in his hand and grinned. In a minute he had cut through the long central chain that bound them and was hauling it through their leg manacles until the rowers were free.

"Keep rowing," he said. "It's not time yet. Wait for the signal. I'm going to spell Tromes on the flute. When the time's ripe I'll play that Egyptian tune you liked. Do you remember it?"

They nodded. Theon paused for a moment and took a deep breath before mounting the rope ladder. As he emerged on deck he found Tromes staring at him. Their eyes locked. Tromes took the flute from his lips. Knowing he had no choice, Theon hit him with the rasp. Tromes fell heavily to the deck.

The Minotaur's lead ship, *Pylos*, was the first to engage in battle. One of the patrol boats advanced across her path as though intending to ram her; at the last moment the steersman changed course, moving parallel to the enemy ship and, shipping oars suddenly, let its momentum carry it up under the *Pylos*'s outrigger and shear off oar after oar on the *Pylos*'s starboard side.

Screams rose up from the rowers' pit as the broken oars flailed wildly among the oarsmen of the *Pylos*. And as the two hulls met and scraped alongside each other, the pirates on the *Pylos* and the troops on the patrol vessel swarmed toward each other, wielding bronze cutlasses.

Moments later the second patrol boat engaged the *Gades*, outmaneuvering and ramming her. The force drove the little boat deep into the *Gades*'s hull, and water began pouring in through the gap. There were again anguished screams from the rowing pit as the *Gades* began to fill with water.

No matter that the *Hephaistos* had now positioned herself to allow her bowmen to shoot flaming arrows into the two patrol vessels or that the invaders from the *Pylos* appeared to be winning the battle aboard the first patrol boat. No matter that the Minotaur's entire fleet was inside the harbor. For the pirates things were not going with the ease they had expected.

More patrol vessels had separated themselves from the confusion at the wharves and were making their way out into the central harbor. Bowmen aboard the ship that had rammed the *Gades* had turned their attention away from the *Gades* and were firing burning arrows at the *Philea*, which had come to the rescue of its beleaguered sister ships. Some of the arrows dug into the mainsail of the *Philea*, setting it alight. Breezes fanned the flames as they raced toward the deck.

More threatening to the Minotaur were the large galleys that suddenly appeared in the bay, their rails lined with armor-clad mercenaries. They bore down on the pirate fleet from the rear, letting loose volleys of arrows that fell with devastating accuracy.

The pirates were already under attack from two directions when the new force from the docks divided to surround the lead ships.

The *Hephaistos*, under attack from two sides, stood still, her oars shipped at a barked order from the Minotaur, who had not even looked back to see which *trieraules* he was shouting at. Theon stopped playing for a moment, looked around at the bay, and saw what was happening. With no hesitation he crept to the lip of the rowers' pit. The rowers looked expectantly up at him, their oars idled.

Theon smiled as he struck up the Egyptian tune, more lively and spirited than he had ever played it before.

The revolt was on!

III

At the forward starboard rail, the Minotaur watched the vessels bearing down on him. His own ships were firing relentlessly at the oncoming ships, and he saw several of the shafts strike home. One of the flaming arrows caught the middle of a patrol boat's sail. Within seconds the flames had ignited and had begun to spread.

Looking down at the iron sword in his hand, he realized there was nothing he could do now except wait. He counted his own ships again, noting that three of them were out of action. When he counted the enemy, to his surprise he found their number even. And in the bay the smaller boats had a decided advantage.

Prodicus, who stood on the port rail, called out to a smaller ship: "Drop a longboat and pick up the survivors from the *Gades!*" As he turned back, something amidships caught his eye. He focused to see the galley slaves, led by Theon, come clambering out of the pit and swarm up onto the deck. "Mutiny! Mutiny!" he cried.

Except for common implements snatched from the deck—belaying pins, short oars from the lifeboats, and tools pilfered from Theon's forge, the slaves were unarmed. Theon carried a hammer in one huge hand and a length of chain in the other. He was swinging the chain over his head and bellowing with rage as he led the attack.

The Minotaur yelled, "Stop them!"

His men barely had time to position themselves. The Minotaur saw one of his guards skewer a rower, only to have the oarsman continue to come at him, battering him to the ground with the last of his strength. Meanwhile Pandion successfully parried a thrust. Theon struck a numbing blow on someone's forearm with the hammer.

The black slave, taking on an opponent bare-handed, evaded a sweeping cut of the man's sword and moved in to grasp the man's right arm in his iron grip. When the pirate dropped his sword, the black man took him by the throat and choked him until he collapsed. Then he picked him up as if he were a child and threw his body at the oncoming pirates, bowling several of them over. With a shrill war cry, he picked up the fallen sword and charged like a mad bull.

One-eyed Zimrida, his unkempt hair and beard making him look like one of the most ferocious men alive, had hauled his oar up on deck. He charged and caught one of the pirates in the belly with it, then forced him back to the rail and over the side. Swinging his massive weapon he felled three more of the pirates. Finally he dropped the oar, lowered his head, and with a deafening roar, charged the men still standing. One of them stabbed him in the arm, but his momentum carried Zimrida smack into his attacker. With one huge fist he caught the man in the middle of the forehead, knocking him cold. He grabbed the next pirate by the wrist and, with one mighty twist, broke it.

Amidst the carnage Theon found himself face-to-face with the Minotaur. His eyes narrowed as he looked at the iron sword he had made the pirate. Then he feinted a swing with the chain and saw the Minotaur duck. Abruptly Theon changed direction, and the chain caught the Minotaur's free arm. The howl of pain told Theon he had struck an effective blow.

But as he prepared for another swing, the Minotaur shoved his sword in its scabbard, reached out with his good arm, and grabbed the chain from Theon's hand.

With a grimace of pain he tossed the chain over the side and then drew his sword. Empty-handed, Theon backed away. Suddenly he heard Pandion's voice. "Here, Theon!" He glanced to one side and saw his friend toss a sword at him. He caught it with ease and assumed the on-guard position. "Come on," he dared the black-bearded man. "Do your worst!"

Little by little Theon was forced to give ground. He watched for holes in the Minotaur's guard, but there were none. He parried one lunge, diverted another. A disarm motion did not work; his opponent had wrists with the strength of oak. A lunge of his own was turned aside with ease.

"Stand and fight!" the Minotaur bellowed.

Out of the corner of his eye Theon could see Pandion take a thrust in one bicep but still bring his man to his knees. Theon parried, counterattacked, got in trouble again, and once more gave ground. In apparent desperation, he feinted and lunged and, when he saw a mighty sweeping slash coming toward him, prepared to parry, knowing even as he did that bronze would not turn aside iron.

The swords clashed. Theon's bronze sword broke in two. And the blade of the Minotaur's new sword, which had never before been tried in battle, flew off and went spinning through the air and into the bay. The Bull stood there, dumbfounded, the hilt clenched in his fist.

Theon's first reaction was to laugh. "It worked!" he cried. "That'll teach you a lesson: Never attack a man with a blade he made himself. He may very well have a trick—like a sword made in two pieces, and not one."

For a moment, the Minotaur stood blank-faced and shocked. Then he, too, laughed and tossed the useless hilt aside. "I wondered what sort of surprises to expect from you," he said appreciatively. "Now I know. Come, we'll fight bare-handed. You've put on some heft since we last did this! It ought to be a better match."

Mentally Theon gauged how much distance he had behind him. "All right, but you've got the edge on me still. You make the first move."

He planted his feet on the deck, preparing for the Minotaur's attack. But even so, he was not ready for the big man's bull-like rush. He had only the blink of an eye to react as the Minotaur went for his throat. Theon's hands whipped out and caught one of those thick wrists and pulled the pirate forward. He fell over backward and rolled, taking the Minotaur with him. The big man struggled up, tipped over Theon's fallen body, and landed squarely on his own back, knocking the breath out of him.

Theon was instantly on his feet. He jumped onto the Minotaur's belly, landing heavily with both feet. But the pirate was still alert, and he grabbed one of Theon's ankles, pulling him down to the deck. As the Minotaur struggled to his knees and reached for Theon's neck, Theon drew back one rock-hard leg and kicked the Minotaur full in the face, driving his head back against the starboard rail.

Once again Theon lost no time getting to his feet, hoping to take advantage of the Minotaur's groggy condition. He spied a heavy belaying pin on the deck and picked it up. Drawing his arm back, he prepared for the killing blow. Swung with all his strength, the pin, he knew, would shatter the pirate's head like an egg. His body tensed. His heart pounded.

And then he looked up. Nuhara, modestly garbed in an ankle-length robe, was staring at him in horror.

Over her shoulder, near the mouth of the bay, dozens and dozens of war galleys were approaching at full stroke. The ensigns they bore were those of Demetrios the Magnificent. And in the bow of the mightiest of them, looking tall and masterful despite his illness, stood Demetrios.

The Minotaur, seeing that Theon was distracted, snaked out a powerful hand and grabbed his ankle with a grip of iron. Startled, Theon tried to kick free but could not break the Bull's grip. Theon was ready to deliver a vicious kick when the pirate pulled his leg out from under him.

Theon landed painfully on his side and, feeling the Bull's grip relax, rolled away, only to bang his head into the partition that separated the deck from the rower's pit. Groggily, he struggled to his feet, just in time to see the Minotaur, head down, rushing at him. The pirate chieftain drove him backward.

He caught the starboard rail and steadied himself just as the Minotaur came at him once more. This time Theon stood firmly on the deck and drew back his huge fist. It was the most powerful punch he had ever thrown.

It caught the Minotaur in the middle of the forehead. He stood stock still for a moment, his eyes gradually slipping out of focus, then they rolled back, and he slowly fell to the deck.

There was a pause, and Theon felt pain shooting through his hand. To his astonishment, he heard wild applause and turned to see the rowers cheering him on. They had taken control of the ship. The revolt had succeeded.

As other cheers arose, behind him, he wheeled around to see Demetrios's flagship bearing down on him. Suddenly the whole bay was full of Demetrios's galleys. And as he watched, a pirate galley, racing toward the open mouth of the bay, took a flaming arrow in her sail. The canvas blazed, the fire spread, and three of Demetrios's armed ships sped to her side to keep her from escaping.

The battle was won!

In the bow of his flagship Demetrios was smiling. Suddenly Theon recognized the man standing next to him—Iri! The Minotaur had lied to him. Iri had gotten through.

He shook the cobwebs out of his head and looked down at the fallen giant at his feet.

"Shall I kill him?" Pandion asked indifferently. The stolen sword in his hand was covered with blood.

"No, manacle him, hand and foot. Get him up and moving if you can. Demetrios will want to interrogate him."

"Right!" Pandion said, his manner soldierly and efficient. "But have we gotten all of them? Didn't someone say there was a girl here, too?"

"Nuhara!" Theon said. But when he went into the cabin to find her, she was nowhere to be seen.

IV

Subduing the entire pirate fleet was not easy. There were still holdouts, but when Demetrios boarded the *Hephaistos* with his bodyguard of towering soldiers, and Theon's rowers brought the Minotaur in chains to the rail, the last holdouts surrendered.

Theon beamed at Iri as Demetrios, leaning on his cane, approached. "Iri, you made it. They told me you'd been captured."

Iri smiled. "Wishful thinking." He nodded toward Demetrios.

"I wish my brother had told me that the new Home was so wonderful. If I'd known, I'd have gone there years ago." His face suddenly clouded. "But then I might never have met Keturah, and . . ."

Demetrios, joining them, put a hand on his younger brother's broad shoulder. "As I told you, I've heard rumors of a blind woman aboard the boats. As soon as we're done here you can draw upon the full resources of my empire to find her. And you will find her!"

Demetrios smiled at the bronzed young man standing before him. "Look at the two of you! You're made of oak, both of you! Theon—are you the same young scholar I sent out on a mission so many months ago?"

"We're none of us the same as we were when we started." Theon looked around him, as if trying to find someone among the crowd on deck. His eye lighted on the Minotaur, standing stolidly by the port rail and staring out at the wreckage of his fleet. "This will change all our lives. I'm glad that they decided not to fight to the end.

378

I've made a friend or two among them. I'd hate to see them dead."

"They'll be dealt with fairly," Demetrios said. "And the quicker the better. I haven't long, I think. I don't want to spend time away from Rhodope." He looked sharply at Theon. "This chap here"—he jerked his head at the manacled Minotaur—"will have to be tried. If there were friends you made among the crews . . ."

Theon frowned, torn by mixed emotions. "I suppose you're right. Justice, firm and fair and prompt. That's the only way to deal with this. Let's get on with it."

Demetrios's wary eyes never left Theon's face.

The decks of the *Hephaistos* were cleared before the trial of the Minotaur began. The only people remaining aboard the great bireme were Demetrios, his bodyguards and close advisers, Iri, and the little circle of victors who had taken the ship.

One by one Iri embraced Pandion, Okware, and Zimrida. "You're all free, of course," he said, beaming at them. "Okware, I'm going to introduce you to Demetrios. There's sure to be a job in the fleet for a descendant of Akhilleus's. But if the truth be known, you're probably a very rich man now. Akhilleus's estate was beyond all counting. And part of it is yours.

"Zimrida, you disagreeable, one-eyed wretch, start thinking of how you're going to live without any oar master to bedevil you. Whom will you call ugly names now? Whom will you fight with?"

"To be sure, it'll take some adjusting," Zimrida agreed. "I'm not sure where I'll go. There probably isn't a single one of my kinsmen left."

"Then you're free to choose your own home," Iri said.

"And you'll do it with a gift from me, which will allow you to live as you choose. You'll take it if I have to shove it down your throat. It was you who kept me from going mad on the oar, and I owe you more than I can ever repay."

His eye lit on Pandion. "And you, my friend, if you wanted to see the Minotaur brought to justice, now's your chance."

He studied Pandion's face, but it was impossible to read. "Come along," he urged. "Justice is about to catch up with that black-bearded host of ours, and I'm sure none of us wants to miss a moment of it."

As Demetrios prepared to try the Minotaur, Theon's eyes went again and again to the great black-bearded figure at the rail. Finally he could restrain himself no longer. Nodding to the guards, he approached the pirate chieftain. The Minotaur turned and looked at him. His expression, to Theon's surprise, was peaceful.

"I must ask one question," Theon said. "How did we beat you? You'd have overwhelmed any other fleet in the world."

The Minotaur shrugged.

"As a matter of fact, how did I beat you?" Theon asked. "I know how strong you are. I know that there never was a day when I was your master. I still remember how easily you disposed of me. And although I have grown stronger, I'm still not your match."

The answer was another unconcerned shrug, this time accompanied by the faintest hint of a smile.

Suddenly Theon's eyes were opened. "But that makes no sense at all. Why?"

"Things change. There is a time for being young and

a time for becoming a man in his strength. Then there is a time for becoming old. Bodies change. Minds change. Hearts change. Destinies change. The main thing, my friend, is to recognize when a change is due, and accept it. You show signs of becoming a remarkable man, and this is something you must understand."

"You deliberately let me defeat you!" Theon said. "But why?"

Before the Minotaur could answer, the guards hustled him off. Theon watched the big man walk away with them as placidly as a lamb to the slaughter and wondered why the Minotaur had staged his own downfall. It did not make sense.

Someone had brought a chair aboard for Demetrios, who was beginning to show the ravages of his illness. He sat between two of his aides and looked at the prisoner who stood in Theon's old spot before the cabin, flanked by guards.

"My friend," Demetrios said. "You must surely know the law as it applies to piracy. You've disrupted the commerce of the entire Great Sea. No ship was safe, no cargo guaranteed to reach its destination, no sailor's wife free of fear of widowhood. Shall I read the charges?"

The Minotaur shrugged. His eyes were fixed on Demetrios.

"All the charges are punishable by death. If you hang, you will as readily hang for one as for fifty such crimes. Do you freely admit your guilt?"

"I am here to receive justice," the prisoner said, "not to dispute it. You have a reputation for being a just man. If you say I deserve punishment . . ."

Demetrios stared hard into the Bull's dark, unreadable eyes. "Very well, the punishment is death."

The guards were on the verge of stripping the prisoner when suddenly Theon found the words pouring out of his mouth. "Wait, Demetrios! May I speak for him, I, who suffered at his hands?"

Smiling, Demetrios turned to him. "Theon," he said gently. "I have been studying this man's career. Drawing upon my network of spies, I have found out a great many things about him, things I am sure he does not realize I know. Facts he has taken great pains over many years to conceal, even from those who supposed themselves close to him."

Theon ignored him, angry at Demetrios for the drama he seemed intent on playing out. "Demetrios, you must listen to me. Surely some leniency is in order. I've watched him closely all these months. You can't hang him as if he were a brutal and bloodthirsty pirate who kills at random, without any conscience."

"You know the penalty. If I let him go unpunished . . ."

"But he's dispensed justice, and he deserves to receive it! When another man would have called for death, I've seen him be lenient. I've watched him—"

"But the whole framework of trade between civilized nations—"

"Theon's right." To Theon's surprise Iri spoke up. "Demetrios, this is a man who had me whipped, and then ordered twice as many lashes for the oar master who'd bedeviled me. If he's to hang, then half the captains on the Great Sea should hang. In my months as a galley slave I worked for tradesman and pirate alike. Nowhere was I treated more fairly than under this man."

"Let me add my voice," Pandion said. "I came here to kill him. I believed him to be the man who murdered my father. But they tell me that I'm mistaken. Yes, my father was killed by one of the Minotaur's men, but not at his bidding. He ordered my father's killer hanged for his deed."

"Demetrios," Theon continued, "there's good in him. He has skills out of the ordinary. He commands his fleet—he even commits acts of piracy—with minimal violence, whereas another leader would condone or even reward bloodthirsty behavior. There's not a man on the sea who could command these cutthroats the way he does. He rules not by violence but by respect."

Demetrios turned back to the Minotaur, standing fearless and unruffled. "You forget, I have other information that I have not told you about." He turned to the guards. "Prepare the prisoner!"

The guards drew their swords and cut off the Minotaur's tunic. The Bull stood naked before them, broad-chested, massive, his body covered with dark hair.

"Demetrios, please," Theon pleaded.

"Turn around," Demetrios ordered.

As the Minotaur's broad back turned to them, Theon let out a gasp. So did Iri.

Low on the Minotaur's broad back was the unmistakable pattern both men knew so well: the red paw print of a lion.

The Minotaur was one of them. He was a Child of the Lion.

V

Demetrios stared around at his audience, obviously enjoying the moment. "My friends, meet Khalkeus of

Gournia. It has cost me a great deal of time and money to find out who he is and whence he comes, and to learn that he is a distant relative of ours. We share a common ancestor, whose name he was given when he was born."

"I'll be damned," Iri murmured. "Khalkeus! Isn't that the name of that—"

"Yes," Demetrios confirmed. "When our forefather Kirta of Haran abandoned wife and sons to discover the secret of ironmongery across the Great Sea, he wound up as a slave in the palace of Knossos. His overseers renamed him Khalkeus. And it was as Khalkeus that he was eventually freed and became armorer to Minos of Crete and lover to Minos's daughter, Princess Xena."

Theon's brow knit. "But . . ."

"Wait," Demetrios said with a quiet smile. "Khalkeus also became the lover of a girl from Amnesios who worked in the palace. When he escaped the revolt that destroyed Knossos, taking to sea with Xena only to see her felled by a stray arrow from the docks, he had left the girl from Amnesios pregnant. She had the child and named it after its father, Khalkeus. And of course it bore the distinctive birthmark."

"Now I understand the Minotaur's knowledge of the old songs of Ur," Theon said. "They must have remained in the family after Kirta sang them to his lover. And his knowledge of, and interest in, arms making; she would have told her son what his father did for a living."

"And don't forget the very name of his bireme," Iri pointed out. "*Hephaistos*—the Greek god of fire, the patron of smiths."

"My agents have been tireless in tracking down this information. By now we may know things about our kinsman and his family that even he himself does not know.

Although Khalkeus has spent years learning his family history."

He looked at the Minotaur and waited for a response, but the bearded man did not speak.

"Several of these men who have reason to hate you," Demetrios said, "have, instead, spoken up in your behalf, kinsman. I, too, know of your magnanimity in dealing with the crews of captured ships. I also know of the curious covenant by which you reign as head of the pirate fleet. A less remarkable man could not have held together this coalition of cutthroats without becoming a despot. These are remarkable feats. Yet how do I reconcile these with the law of the sea that declares that anyone who has committed piracy must die?"

Now, for the first time, the Minotaur spoke. His deep voice was calm. "I accept my responsibility in this matter. It is your responsibility to render a judgment and execute it. I bow to the will of fortune. Do with me what you will."

Theon looked from the Minotaur's face to Demetrios's. "Demetrios," he said. "Please, take into account—"

But Demetrios held up one hand to silence him. "I have given this matter much thought. I have weighed the factors. I have studied your background, your bloodlines, and your crimes."

"Please, Demetrios," Iri urged. "You can afford to—"

But once again Demetrios held up his hand. This time everyone fell silent. "This is my decree: that you, Khalkeus of Gournia, will come with me to Home."

An astonished gasp arose from the listeners.

"And there, Khalkeus, you will begin your training. I have directed this great shipping enterprise for a long time, ever since Nehsi, son of the great Akhilleus, pulled me out of the streets of Thebes and chose me for the job."

He looked at Okware. "Okware, your own kinsman, Akhilleus, said that the gods chose him, a black slave rowing a foreign galley, to become the richest man in the world. Afterward he decreed that his successors would be chosen by the same procedure. It was his way of ensuring that new people with new ideas ruled his empire. He was a wise man, your ancestor."

Okware smiled and nodded his head. For a long time Demetrios studied each face that surrounded him: "Very well, we understand one another. And now I choose as my successor Khalkeus of Gournia."

No one was more stunned than Khalkeus himself. His eyes opened wide, and his jaw dropped. Demetrios held up his hand again. "You, Khalkeus, will succeed me as administrator of the largest sailing fleet in the world." He smiled. "And what better experience could you have than to have organized and kept peace among the most ill-disciplined men in the world without becoming a despot yourself? And, in fact, remaining, despite the temptations, a just man, compassionate and fair?

"I know you as well as you know yourself. You will come with me to Home to begin your training with the best men in the world. By the time you venture forth once more, I will very likely be dead, and you will be a different man. You will be clean-shaven. You will have a new name; no one will recognize you. We will spread the word that the Minotaur was executed for piracy. None but those who now stand here will be able to connect you with the privateer chief. What say you, brother Child of the Lion? Will you take the commission I offer?"

All eyes went to the Minotaur. Slowly, very slowly his stone face relaxed into a smile. It was a satisfied smile. As if, Theon realized with a start, that is what he had planned all along. Was staging the losing raid the Minotaur's way of escaping the pirate's life, returning to his family, and reclaiming his heritage? Would they ever know the truth? The Minotaur's voice was low when he said, "Teach me. I have much to learn."

Once Demetrios and the man they had come to know as the Minotaur returned to Demetrios's flagship, the ex-slaves gathered on the deck of the *Hephaistos*.

Pandion sought out Theon. "Has the day held enough surprises for you?"

"Enough to last me a lifetime," Theon replied. "I never dreamed I'd hear you defending the Minotaur."

Pandion gave a sheepish smile and shrugged.

"Say, I've learned something important about a friend of yours."

"Friend of mine?" Theon asked.

"The Minotaur's daughter. The one who's so crazy about you. The one whose heart you've broken, you cold-hearted wretch. I found her hiding in the oar pits after we'd won the ship. She told me about everything. She wishes you'd forgive her."

"Daughter?" Theon asked, stunned. "She's his *daughter*? But why? . . ."

"Ask her yourself," Pandion said. "She's standing right behind you."

Theon whirled. There was Nuhara, her eyes red from weeping, but looking lovely. "Can you ever forgive me? I had to tell him. Father had to make sure things didn't get out of hand. He didn't want the raid to turn into a blood-bath. He said it was for your own—"

But Theon did not let her finish. With a great, booming, all-forgiving laugh, he picked her up and hugged the breath out of her, while his fellow ex-slaves cheered.

*   *   *

Iri, Theon, and Khalkeus joined Demetrios aboard his flagship for dinner. "Iri," Demetrios said almost immediately, "I know what is on your mind. Take a ship—mine or one of the captured ones. Choose a crew from my fleet. The pirates will require some retraining before they are trustworthy, and some of them may never be. Draw upon my resources and find Keturah. The Children of the Lion take care of their own."

As an afterthought he held up his hand. "But leave me the *Hephaistos*. Theon and I, along with his shipwright-friend Crantor of Massilia, plan to study it."

"Then you're going to start making biremes?" Iri asked.

"I don't know," Demetrios responded. "Our friend Khalkeus designed this one, and he tells me it's already obsolete; he has ideas for improving it. I may wait until we've perfected the design. The balance of power around the Great Sea is delicate enough without our introducing a revelation like this." He chuckled. "From Theon's expression, I can tell he thinks I'm mad."

Theon shook his head.

Demetrios studied him for a moment. "Your thoughts seem elsewhere tonight, my friend." Theon gave a sheepish smile. "Nuhara and I are just . . . after dinner, I thought . . ."

"Enough, enough. Tell me, Khalkeus, if they produce a child—"

"Gods!" Iri said. "With Khalkeus of Gournia and Seth of Thebes for its grandfathers what a child that will be!" Then his face clouded over, and they could see the thoughts of his own lost child fill his head. He pushed his wine bowl aside. "Demetrios, if you'll excuse me, I want to get an early start tomorrow."

"Certainly," Demetrios said. "Find them. Bring them

to Home. There'll always be a place for you. And don't hesitate to ask for help. You'll find friends in every port. Khalkeus and I have already been talking about changes in the business. We have designated prominent positions in the organization for both Theon and your old oarmate Okware."

"Before I forget," Iri said, "I want to reward Zimrida. He earned it, for helping me and for his part in capturing the *Hephaistos*. May I give him one of our boats? Perhaps one of the captured ones?"

"Tell him to take his choice. The Children of the Lion also take care of their friends. And may good fortune attend your search!"

After Iri and Theon had taken their leave, Demetrios lingered at the table with Khalkeus. "I think," Demetrios said, nodding at Theon's departing back, "that you have found a son-in-law, my friend."

Khalkeus, now clean-shaven and wearing the distinctive tunic of Demetrios's organization, nodded. As far as anyone knew, he had already been put to death by Demetrios's men and his corpse fed to the fish in the bay. "From the first I felt that there was something about Theon that spoke of a change in my destiny. So brilliant and so young!"

"Seth's blood runs strong in him. He has more than a touch of Seth's brilliance. Wait until you see what he wants to do with the *Hephaistos*!" He chuckled. "And wait until you see the city Seth built for me at Home. The most beautiful thing he created was the manor house I live in now, and that will be yours when you succeed me."

He pushed his chair back. "You'll like the job, I think. It's not just the power, and it's certainly not the money. It's the challenge that will require all your wits and resources, day and night." Catching the look of understanding on Khalkeus's face, he went on. "Did you know that your grandchild—and I assume the union will produce one—will have a legitimate claim to the throne of Babylon? It's true. Seth was king of Shinar when it fell; he was married to the king's daughter, and the old king had named him as his successor. If Theon, even today, were to enter Babylon, he'd have to either take the city by storm or dodge assassins. They couldn't allow him inside its walls otherwise." He chuckled again. "You now begin to see what sort of family you're joining."

Khalkeus held his wine bowl up, saluting him. "Consider me a blank slate to be written upon. My life ended today. It begins anew from this moment."

They locked eyes and experienced a moment of complete understanding. And they drank to that, long and hard.

CHAPTER FIFTEEN

The Two Banks of the Jordan

"I don't care what you say, young lady," the doctor said firmly. "I can't authorize your taking him away now. He's a very sick man and can't be moved, not even on a short trip."

Tirzah wrung her hands. "But, I have to," she protested. "He can't spend any more time here. I must get him to where his own people can take care of him."

"Where is that?" the doctor asked. "I thought you said he came from Nubia. Surely you're not suggesting—"

"No, no," she said, trying to keep the desperation out of her voice. How could she explain to him the significance of what she had overheard and her sudden fear? "He has relatives. They have their own doctors. Not that I'm saying they're better than a man of your stature."

"I should hope not!"

"Or even as good. I'm just saying that I think we'll all

391

be happier if I can get him to their place, where he can be looked after night and day. You understand, I'm sure."

"I do; all I'm telling you is that he's sustained a very serious injury, that if you move him now there's a good chance of a relapse, with serious and perhaps lasting consequences. He could die."

"I know all that," Tirzah said. "And I absolve you of all responsibility. I'll also be happy to swear out a statement to that effect, if you're worried about having the magistrate find out that a man receiving care under his roof has been released without his being informed."

He hesitated, and she knew she had found the right key. "It is true," he said, "that these are complicated and vexing times, and the fewer such problems a magistrate— let alone a doctor—has to worry about, the better, what with the foreigners just across the river."

"Draw up the documents of release," she said. "I'll gladly take the whole responsibility and you'll be out of the middle."

He hesitated for another moment, but when she reached inside her garment and shook a purse, letting the coins rattle within, he shrugged and relented. "There'll be a fee for the scribe, of course," he said. "If you give it to me, I'll take care of the matter."

Once she stood clutching the clay tablet, Tirzah hurried down the long hall of the magistrate's house. She had wasted precious time bandying lies with that odious and frightened little bureaucrat. And just when she needed her time the most!

The city was an armed camp crawling with soldiers preparing for the siege everyone knew would come the moment the Israelite army solved the problem of how to cross the Jordan en masse. Technically she and Pepi were citizens of a nation at war with Jericho—or at least, Pepi was. If anyone found out, they could be arrested as spies and thrown into the city dungeons. And when the Israelite army broke down the walls, the wholesale slaughter Pepi had predicted would begin. Either way, they were lost unless she could get them out of the city.

It seemed impossible. The commander of the city guard had ordered that no one was to leave Jericho without authorization. Her paltry clay tablet would do no more than allow her to remove Pepi from the magistrate's house. Now she had to find somewhere safe until she could figure out how to get out of the city.

She knocked at the door, using the special signal they had devised, and hoped he was not asleep.

But he opened the door and ushered her inside, bolting it behind her. "Did you have any luck?" he asked.

"Here," she said, handing him the tablet. "Get dressed quickly. There's no time to spare."

"I don't understand," he said, puzzled. "Can we leave the city?"

"No," she answered. "I overheard a conversation between the guards at the door to the magistrate's office. They were talking about two suspected spies, and of course they could have been talking about someone else, but—"

Understanding dawned on Pepi's pale face. "How do we get out of the city?"

"I don't know. The first thing is to get out of here. There has to be an inn somewhere that'll take us." She began throwing their belongings into bags.

"Forget everything but the bare essentials," Pepi said. "We can always buy new clothes. Take things you can run with, if you have to. We'll head for the thieves' quarter.

People there don't ask questions." The effort seemed to have exhausted him, and he sank back down on the bed.

His words stirred something in Tirzah's memory. "As a matter of fact, I was listening to some of the maids. One of them has a cousin who runs a bawdy house on the city wall; she says that her family will all be safe when the attack comes."

"No, Tirzah, I can't take you to a house of—"

"You have to. Anyone who has a few coins will be able to rent a room. We'll be welcome, and it isn't far. Just ask for Rahab, she said."

Tirzah turned, parcel in hand, looking down at the dresses piled neatly on the bed. "Oh, Pepi! I was raised so poor and to just walk away and leave expensive clothing like this . . ."

"Come now," he said, slipping his feet into his sandals and getting up. "You forget you're a rich woman who can buy anything she wants from now on. If we ever get to Home, I'll show you."

She looked at him now, so weak, so defenseless. *Gods*, she thought suddenly. *Preserve him for me. Don't let them get him. Please! I'll do anything to save him.*

From the top of the promontory Joshua and Eleazar looked down on the valley of the Jordan. Across the river they could see quite clearly, well to the right of the sky blue waters of the Salt Sea, the tall walls of Jericho and the mud huts of the nearby city of Gilgal. But between this position and the cities of the floodplain lay the raging torrent that was the Jordan.

"How are we going to cross?" asked the high priest. "You can lead soldiers across the ford, but how are we to move the Ark of the Covenant? And without it, we are no more than any other army, for all the bravery of our young men and your military expertise."

Joshua's eyes narrowed. "There will be a sign. God has spoken to me, as He used to speak to Moses. He says to wait and trust in Him. And the time grows short. I can feel it. In a few days, a week at most, He will speak to me again and give me the sign."

"Are you sure?" Eleazar asked. "A man has dreams. And sometimes he mistakes them for—"

"This is no mistake," Joshua said. "He says await His word. If I do, if I do not let myself be hurried into desperate and hasty action, we will cross the Jordan on dry land. The great walls of Jericho will crumble before our feet, and we will march into the city in safety."

Eleazar sighed. God had not spoken to him, and he did not know whether to trust this vision of Joshua's. Moses, now there was another matter. When Moses told you God had spoken to him, you could believe him. But Joshua had always acted according to his own will, not that of Yahweh. Was he now to believe that Yahweh— bypassing him, the High Priest, who should be the spiritual leader of His people and who should be the one to whom He spoke in these matters—would suddenly begin to confide in Joshua, a soldier and secular man?

Eleazar did not know what to say. He sighed and stared back down the path toward the camp. "Here comes Caleb. And he has a stranger with him. A rich stranger, from the look of him."

"Caleb!" Joshua called. "Did you give the order to move the encampment down to the river, as I told you?"

"Yes," Caleb answered. "And I've brought someone you ought to listen to. This is Hizki the trader. He just left Jericho on his way to Damascus. Remember the two spies

395

we sent to Jericho, the ones who claimed to have seen Pepi and the Bashanite woman entering the city?"

Joshua nodded. "They claim Pepi has turned traitor. But I'm going to need more evidence before I believe that a man who's spent most of his life among us, who's been faithful through everything—"

Caleb looked exasperated. "In your heart of hearts you know you're just making excuses for him. You're unwilling to believe. But when you hear what Hizki has to say—"

"Something new?" Joshua asked.

Caleb pushed the trader forward. "Tell him, Hizki. Tell him about Pepi's living in the home of the chief magistrate of Jericho. The chief magistrate, highest secular authority below the commander in chief of the army."

Joshua scowled. "Is this true?" he asked. "You saw him with your own eyes?"

Hizki looked at him cautiously, wary of the warlike expression on Joshua's face. "Well, yes—at least he and his wife match the descriptions your officer gave me of Pepi and the woman. He's under medical care there. At the expense of the magistrate himself, I might add. Although that's the usual sort of procedure in cases like this."

"Did you hear?" Caleb asked eagerly. "The chief magistrate! How much more evidence do you need? We've been sold out by our own chief armorer. He's gone over to the other side."

Joshua bit his lip, his face an unreadable mask of mixed, and violent, emotion. "Caleb, if this is true, if I were to believe that Pepi had betrayed us after all these years, for whatever reasons . . ." He pounded his fist into his palm.

Caleb let a small smile steal over his face for a moment. He turned to Hizki. "Thank you. You'll be our honored guest at dinner, of course."

Hizki looked anxiously from one face to the other and was about to beg off as politely as he could when Joshua's anger finally burst out. "Once the army's in camp, turn them out for sword practice. I want them to work out three times a day. I want daily inspections, of weapons, of uniforms, of all their gear. I want them prepared to march across the river and to war on a moment's notice. And I want them to fall on Jericho like dogs on a rat. I want killers, Caleb. Killers!"

"Yes, sir!" Caleb said smartly, standing at attention. "Anything else, sir?"

"Yes," Joshua said. "I want Pepi. A bonus to the man who brings me his head. A bonus *and* a promotion to the man who brings him to me alive."

"Yes, sir!" Caleb said, making no attempt to hide the triumph in his smile.

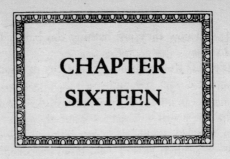

CHAPTER SIXTEEN

In the World of Darkness

When Keturah's birth time came, the women of the slave compound gathered around her. They did what they could, calming her, talking her through the contractions and the last stages; but of course when the child decided to come, nothing could be done for her. She had to bear the baby herself, in darkness and in pain, neither knowing nor caring where she was. She heard her own bloodcurdling screams as if they came from another. Then came the last pain, the one that almost tore her apart, and she thought she would die. And then there was oblivion.

How much time had passed, she had no idea, but she felt gentle hands on her and cool cloths bathing her, and she could hear an angry, high-pitched wail in the distance.

She tried to raise her head from the makeshift pillow but found herself too weak to rise. Sinking back, she said in a gasping, hoarse voice: "My baby, bring me my baby."

"Patience, child," the midwife said. "The women cut

the cord, and now they are bathing the baby. They will bring it to you."

"P-please!" Keturah said. "Is it a boy or a girl?"

"Ah, my dear," the midwife said, "you have a fine strapping boy. A large one, with a full head of hair. He must have been a month or more overdue. No wonder you were so big in your last days." She turned her head and called out to the others. "She wants the child."

They placed him into her groping hands, and she could feel him, and suddenly she did not feel helpless anymore. Her hands could see him, the tiny flailing limbs, the soft little body. She held him to her bosom, and her fingers guided him to the nipple. He sucked greedily. "My son," she said, proud, but exhausted. "He is a beautiful boy, isn't he?"

Suddenly she remembered his father's face and disfiguring birthmark. Her hand snaked out to grasp the midwife's wrist. "Tell me! He *is* all right, isn't he? No disfiguring marks?"

The midwife gently pulled her hand away. "He's a perfect boy," she said reassuringly. "Strong and healthy."

"Then he has no birthmarks anywhere?" Keturah asked anxiously.

"Well, yes, there is one. On his back, just above his little bottom. It's shaped like—"

"Like the paw print of a lion?" Keturah asked.

"Yes, child. How did you guess?"

In answer she hugged the baby to her bosom and found herself weeping tears of joy. She did not know where she was, or who owned her and her son. All she knew was that they were many leagues from where she had been born and that the slavers spoke a language called Greek. And that she had been blessed by the gods who had allowed her to bear a Child of the Lion.

No matter that his father was she knew not where. No matter, even, that their child had been born a slave. None of this mattered now, now that she knew who the child was.

Slave? Chattel? She laughed aloud. With that blood in his veins, he would not stay one for long.

Epilogue

The wind stirred the glowing coals and made them blaze forth again. Above the campfire they could barely make out the old man's face, with its craggy nose, beetling brows, and white beard.

"Thus came the Children of Israel to the borders of Canaan at last," he said. "In the years of wandering they had learned the arts of war, but they had not yet learned wisdom. They stood poised on the brink of victory and of disaster. Over them reigned a man created by God to make war, a fighter fit to stand beside the great warriors of the centuries. But Moses was dead, and with him had gone the voice of a prophet, without which they began to fall into error. What they gained in land they would lose in virtue and in the understanding of the law.

"Tomorrow," said the Teller of Tales, raising his long arms and spreading his fingers, "tomorrow you shall hear how Joshua conquered Canaan and failed to conquer him-

401

self. You shall hear how the breach between him and Pepi, the friend of his youth, widened, and how misunderstanding led to war. You shall hear how Iri sought his lost wife and their child in the lands of the North, and of how his wanderings brought him to the islands of the Great Sea, where fierce and bloodthirsty men amassed a great armada of ships to avenge a deadly insult between nations and set forth in thousands to lay siege to a mighty city named Troy."

A soft murmur from the crowd barely rose above the sighing of the wind.

"Tomorrow," the old man said, "you will hear the endless wanderings of the Children of the Lion, around the four corners of the Great Sea; along the coasts of Achaea and Anatolia, and in the land God gave to Abraham and Jacob, the Promised Land of milk and honey, sought in vain for so many years, and now found.

"Tomorrow," he said, as the fire died, and night fell at last. "Tomorrow."

Read this exciting preview of the next enthrall-ing book in THE CHILDREN OF THE LION Series. Volume Twelve, **THE PROMISED LAND** will be in bookstores and newsstands in Spring 1990.

CHILDREN OF THE LION
Volume Twelve
THE PROMISED LAND

Prologue

It was a night of shooting stars. Across the vast expanse of sky meteors flashed like fireflies. Clustered around a dying campfire the members of the caravan watched with awe. Finally, as the showers slowed, the Teller of Tales stepped out of the shadows and stood tall and commanding before them.

"A night of auguries," the old man said, his voice ringing out into the darkness. "A night of portents. On such a night, my children, might great Joshua, warlord of the Israelite army, have stood looking across the raging Jordan upon the Land of Promise. Looking across into the land of Israel, thinking of Yahweh's command to conquer it and subdue its people to the hand of the Twelve Tribes."

Somewhere in the darkness a child cried, and its mother gave it her breast. The old man looked sharply in her direction before continuing. "So might he have heard the cry of a child among his people, and thought of the wild and raging child he himself had brought forth—a nation of young warriors ordered to face older, more experienced fighters on the battlefield.

"Picture it, my friends," he said. "He was a soldier with only four battles to his credit; on the orders of God, he proposed to invade and conquer settled nations. Was he afraid? Did he question his own competence and courage or the mettle of his young warriors? Or did he have faith in himself and in the limitless power of Yahweh, Lord of All?"

A murmur rose from the crowd. He smiled and raised his arms high, against the dark sky, signaling that the story was to begin. "In the name of God, the Merciful, the Benevolent," he intoned, "hear now the tales of the Children of the Lion. Hear the deeds of these great men and of their endless wanderings. Hear of the great war in Canaan, as Joshua's people prepared to win a new nation—and of a great war far to the north, where in their brief twilight the last of the Achaeans battled brother against brother. And of the men who would create a new civilization from the ruins of their nation, who sailed in from every corner of the known world."

His voice quickened, took on a new edge. "It was a time of change," he said. His words rang out. "A time of auguries, a time of portents. And as the fortunes of men evolved, so shifted the destinies of the Children of the Lion, the caste of armorers who, from nowhere, had come to stand beside the great rulers of the world.

"Hear now," he said, "of the great war for Troy—and of the coming of those who conquered the land of milk and honey to the south—the Promised Land."

Joshua's Israelite army stands at the outskirts of Jericho, poised to begin the offensive that will bring the Promised Land under the rule of the Twelve Tribes. Conquest takes its toll, Joshua's lifelong friendship with Pepi is dissolved in a bitter clash, and the commander begins to lose his grip on his disintegrating forces.

Meanwhile, Iri travels to Greece in search of his kidnapped wife and infant. When an eyewitness to Keturah's death makes his grim report, the bereft Child of the Lion succumbs to his own wish for destruction and joins the mercenaries shipping out against Troy—never suspecting that Keturah is alive and well, and a slave in Troy's royal household.

In the Great Sea, tension crackles between Theon and Nuhara, whose unsuccessful transition from being the Minotaur's daughter to Theon's wife is destroying her marriage.

THE PROMISED LAND
VOLUME TWELVE,
THE CHILDREN OF THE LION Series

(Coming to bookstores and newsstands Spring 1990)

Read this exciting preview of **OKLAHOMA SOONERS,** Volume Two in the bold new saga of THE HOLTS: AN AMERICAN DYNASTY. Look for it in bookstores and newsstands in May, 1990.

Nineteen-year-old Cathy Martin, encouraged by Lucy Woods's success on New York's legitimate stage, runs away from finishing school to seek her own fortune as an actress. Her great-aunt Claudia Brentwood comes to Manhattan to set up housekeeping at the luxurious Waldorf-Astoria Hotel, to chaperon Cathy and her thirteen-year-old cousin, Eden Brentwood. They are joined there by Eden's half brother, Sam, and his wife, Annie, newly returned from their two-year honeymoon trip to Europe.

Friday evening marked Cathy's theatrical debut. Her family could not learn of her performance until after she was a success, an actress. She lied as nonchalantly as she could manage that she was meeting Lucy Woods at the Lyceum Theater, so they needn't worry about her. Somewhat to her surprise, no one made any objection at all. But Cathy didn't think that Aunt Claudia had really been paying attention. And certainly Sam and Annie hadn't. They just glared at each other all through dinner, and Eden looked frightened by their marital tension.

As soon as dinner was over, Cathy decided to go while the going was good. She put on her wrap and picked up her bag with her sewing kit concealed inside it. She had a needle and a packet of pins, which, attached to the tapes she had already sewn inside her dress, would raise the hem to her knees, in accordance with the music-hall producer's specifications. She had bought a pair of black net tights to wear under it and a black plume for her hair, and she felt very giddy and devilish.

If anyone had been paying attention to Cathy, they would have known she was up to something. But Annie had been waiting for two days for a chance to let Sam have it for his infidelities, and Sam, well aware of her mood, had been conspicuously absent from the Waldorf, pursuing his own concerns and returning only when he was sure Annie was asleep. It was Claudia who had bidden him come to dinner tonight. Claudia was the one he wouldn't cross.

* * *

When Cathy had gone, Claudia rose from the table and took Eden off with her to put the girl's hair in curl papers. Tomorrow was Eden's fourteenth birthday, and it was Claudia's wish that whatever Sam and Annie had to settle might be settled now, so as not to cast a pall on Eden's lavish party.

As the door closed behind them, Sam got up too.

"I want to talk to you," Annie said with a suggestion of gritted teeth.

"Going to call me on the carpet?" Sam inquired, grinning at her with saturnine sarcasm. He was furious that there was no way to avoid the confrontation. "Mother dear?" he added.

"I'm not your mother!" Annie snapped. "Even though you've been acting as if you were five."

"Been keeping tabs?" Sam looked rebellious. "Why don't you hire a Pinkerton man?"

"The only thing I need a detective for is to find your conscience; it's that small. Do you think I didn't *see* you, acting like a tomcat with that chorus girl right under my nose? I was just plain mortified."

"And I'm not, I suppose? Coming to you hat in hand every time I want a nickel to spend?" Sam made an obsequious begging gesture.

"You get an allowance. A fat one. And I don't ask how you spend it."

"Shall I confirm your worst suspicions? I spend it on opium. Whiskey and sin. Harlots. I go out and prowl the Bowery every night. I'm just sinking in iniquity."

"Oh, stop it," Annie said. "I know that you bought my Christmas present with it. But why do you have to act like this?"

"Maybe because I'm choking to death on your diamond-studded leash," Sam snapped.

"Well, you didn't mind the diamonds when you married me," Annie snapped back. "And you knew I was going to keep control of my own money. Don't be childish." She looked at his restive, angry face. "Aw, Sam, you know you aren't reliable. I'd be crazy to give you a free rein. You've never managed a business. You don't know how to do it."

"I could learn," Sam suggested. "You ever think of that?"

"Yeah, I've thought of it, and it plain gives me nightmares. You'd put money in every get-rich-quick scheme that comes down the pike, draining off my capital. Before we even left

Virginia City you were after me to put money in that gold mine, and I knew it was salted."

"I knew it too," Sam said, irritated. "But I could have turned around and sold it for a big profit."

"Then you're just flat dishonest." Annie put her napkin down and looked at him, trying to see some steadiness in him and not finding any. "They'd have outsmarted you," she said gently. "I knew those boys from way back."

"Yeah, you always know it all. Maybe sometimes I just want to talk to someone who doesn't know so much."

Annie raised her eyebrows. "Like Sukie, that little chorus girl at the party? A good choice: That tart didn't look as if she had enough brains to give her someplace to put a hat."

"She isn't a tart," Sam said defensively.

"As pure as the driven snow," Annie said acidly. " 'Oh, Mr. Brentwood, you're such a *card*!' "

"Oh, Annie, she doesn't mean anything to me." Sam walked around the table, put his hands on her shoulders, and ran his fingers cajolingly along the back of her neck.

"I expected you'd step out on me some, Sam," Annie said stiffly, "because I've got no illusions about you. But I expected you to behave decently, and I didn't expect you to humiliate me. You've gone too far."

"Oh, now, Annie." He let his hands trail around to the front of her neck and run lightly over one breast under the tight silk bodice. "You know you do something to me that no one else can. You always have."

Annie pushed his hand away. "Stop it. You won't get around me like that. You haven't been home in two nights."

"Maybe I was afraid to," Sam said. He tried to put his hand back.

Annie slapped at it and twisted her chair away. "You aren't coming into my bed out of someone else's. I know you're probably out of money and are afraid of making me so mad that you'll be broke until the next quarter. Well, you stay home and sober a couple of nights. Then we'll talk about an advance on your allowance."

Sam backed off, his eyes blazing, his mood turning defiant again, as quick and unstable as a gas jet. "The hell with you." He turned on his heel and stalked into the parlor.

"Where are you going?" Annie was behind him in the doorway.

Sam snatched his hat off the coatrack by the front door. "Out!"

The Elysian Music Hall, where Cathy was scheduled to perform, looked menacing by gaslight. The customers crowding through the front doors were noisy and seemed half-drunk already, even the women. And the alley by the stage door was very dark. Cathy made her way into the murky light of the backstage passageway, grateful to be inside. Eddie Gamble, who had intervened with the producer to get Cathy the job, was waiting for her by a dressing-room door.

"In here," he said, preceding her into the room without ceremony.

She looked at him with surprise.

"You're late. And your dress is too long."

"It won't take me but a minute to shorten it," Cathy said. There was something different about Eddie: His brown eyes had a glitter that was less friendly and more demanding. She handed him the sheet music. She couldn't raise her hem until he left. "Please give this to the orchestra for me."

Eddie's hand rested on her wrist, caressing it. "You're on in fifteen minutes. They always put new acts on early." He smiled. "We'll have plenty of time to celebrate afterward."

"Oh, I'll have to go right home," Cathy said.

Eddie bent closer to her. "You aren't going to run out on me tonight," he said distinctly. "Girls who get jobs are supposed to be grateful for them. I'm expecting a whole lot of gratitude."

Cathy stared at him. His smile had grown wolflike and hungry. The knowledge that she had made a mistake hit her like a punch in the stomach. She looked around the dingy room, but there was no way out except past Eddie.

He laughed, and his hand moved up her arm. "Now get that skirt hiked up. This isn't a revival meeting."

Cathy pushed at him. "All right. All right. Just go away."

"I'll wait outside the door," Eddie said. She felt his hand caress her buttocks. "I guess I can wait that long."

When the door closed behind him, she looked frantically for a lock, but there wasn't one. Mechanically, she began pulling up the tapes inside her skirt and pinning them. She put on the black net stockings and slipped her shoes back on. She looked into the cracked mirror and, shaking with horror, pinned the black plumes into her hair. There was no way out now except onto the stage.

Somehow she would have to get away from him after the performance.

Cathy looked at the closed door, scared to death of Eddie. *Oh, why did I do it?*

The door opened without a knock, and Swanson, the producer, glared around it at her. "Get out there. You're on next." He inspected the green dress and the sad, silly black plumes. "That damn dress is still too long."

"I can't—it won't—"

"Move!" Swanson pulled her out the door and shoved her at Eddie. He didn't have the sheet music anymore; he must have given it to the orchestra. They led her down the passage, past other dressing rooms filled with performers in various stages of undress. A canvas drop thumped down beside them, and Swanson pushed Cathy out onto the stage in front of it. The orchestra was playing the first bars of her selection "None Can Love Like an Irishman." The curtain came up.

"Ladies and gentlemen, for your particular enjoyment, Miss Catherine Salton, the New York Nightingale!"

The air in the music hall was dim and smoky. The audience, impatiently waiting to be entertained, was a sea of pale faces in the gloom, drinking beer at smeared tables. The orchestra leader looked at her testily. She nodded at him, her teeth chattering.

"The turban'd Turk, who scorns the world—" she sang mechanically, knowing her voice was flat.

The audience began to shift in their seats.

"The gay monsieur—" Cathy lost the beat, struggled frantically to catch it, and stumbled over the next line. She glanced into the wings and saw Eddie watching her, with a grim-faced Swanson. Terrified, she looked out into the audience again. When she saw their angry expressions and heard their booing, she lost the beat again.

She tried to go on singing, but the words wouldn't come. She couldn't remember the next verse. Some of the audience were pounding with their beer bottles on the table tops, and half of the rest were standing up, shouting at her.

"Ask any . . . any girl you happen to meet—"

A piece of a half-eaten sausage bun smacked against the front of her dress, and a beer bottle landed at her feet.

Cathy put her hands to her face and fled, sobbing, stumbling past the canvas drop. One of the tapes holding her hem came loose and straggled around her ankles, nearly tripping her.

Behind her she could hear the audience roaring and the clatter of more bottles on the stage.

"Get the curtain down!" Swanson shouted.

The orchestra wound up the song with a crescendo, and the curtain hurtled down. "Get Mirella out there!" The producer was livid. Another canvas unfurled in front of Cathy's, and Mirella May came out in red spangles and white tights, shedding her kimono as she went.

"Ladies and gentlemen, the management wishes to apologize. . . . Ladies and gentlemen, the miraculous Miss Mirella May!" In the orchestra pit, an all-girl orchestra was taking its place in a flurry of sheet music, while the regular orchestra beat a retreat.

"Damn you!" Swanson grabbed Cathy by the arm and yanked her into the wings, his fist raised. The music started up, but the patrons were still shouting. "You told me you could sing. I'm gonna bust your lying face open!"

She tried to tell him that she could sing, that it was Eddie's waiting backstage, about to prey on her, that had terrified her so; but Swanson wouldn't care.

"Get her out of here, Swanny," the stage manager hissed. "They can hear you in front!"

Swanson started to drag her down the passageway when Eddie Gamble grabbed her other arm and pushed Swanson away. "Oh, no, you don't. You let her alone."

Cathy cringed between the two of them, knowing that this was no rescue. Eddie's next words confirmed it. "It's a shame you were such a flop, kid, but you're still a hit in my book. And you don't have to sing to pay what you owe *me*."

"Let me go!" She gathered her courage to struggle furiously, but Eddie just laughed. He had hold of her by both forearms. "I'll let you go in a while. When we're square." He turned her around and pushed her down the passage toward the stage door. The other performers gave her blank stares, unwilling to interfere. He dragged her out into the alleyway, and she saw with horror that he had a cab waiting in the darkness.

Cathy began to fight him again, and Eddie gave her a backhanded slap across the face that sent her reeling. He jerked the cab door open. The driver looked in the other direction.

"My name's not really Salton," she wailed. "You don't understand!"

"I don't care what your name is. If you're on the lam, that's not my problem. Now get in!"

She clung to the outside of the vehicle, sobbing, and Eddie's grip loosened just for an instant as the sound of running feet came down the alley. Cathy jerked her head around, afraid that it was Swanson or some friend of Eddie's.

With incredulous disbelief, she saw that it was Sam Brentwood. Sukie, the chorus girl he had been romancing, was stumbling after him in her high-heeled shoes.

Sam hauled Eddie off Cathy and swung an expert punch at his jaw. Cathy leaned against the cab, unable to catch her breath.

Eddie and Sam were rolling in the dirt, swinging at each other in fury as Cathy watched, her hands to her mouth.

"C'mon, Sam," Sukie cheered. "Hit him good." Then she turned to Cathy. "We were out front," she explained. "You got rocks in your head, coming here, you know that? And with a guy like Eddie."

"I didn't know," Cathy whispered.

Sukie shook her head. "Jeez, you're green."

Sam twisted away from Eddie and stumbled to his feet. As Eddie got up too, Sam hit him again. Eddie staggered backward and dropped with a thud.

Sam, backhanding blood from his mouth, stalked over to the cab and looked up at the driver. "You get paid to abduct women often?"

"I get paid to drive," the man said. "I don't stick my fool nose in where it ain't wanted."

"Well, you can drive," Sam wheezed. He marched around to face Cathy. "Get in." He pushed her into the cab and got in, too. "The Waldorf," he told the driver.

"What about me?" Sukie demanded as Sam slammed the door shut.

"Oh, Lord, I forgot about you." Sam opened the door again and pulled her in. "Twenty-ninth Street," he yelled at the driver.

"I've never been to the Waldorf." Sukie sounded wistful.

"Well, you aren't going tonight," Sam said.

The cab lurched down the alley. Inside, Sam leaned back and ran a hand through his hair. He had lost his hat, and his dark hair hung limply in his filthy face. His shirtfront was torn to ribbons, and his knuckles were bleeding.

"All right, you putty head," he said when he had gotten his breath back, "what the hell were you doing in that dump?"

"I wanted to sing," Cathy said, sniffling. "And don't you swear at me, Sam Brentwood."

"You could have been raped," Sam said grimly.

Cathy gasped. That wasn't a word she had ever in her life heard spoken aloud.

"All right, he could have taken liberties with your person," Sam said sarcastically. "After what you've been up to, I didn't bother to mince words."

Now that she was in the safety of the vehicle, Cathy was beginning to get some of her spirit back. "What *I've* been up to?" she asked indignantly, with a look at Sukie. "You're calling *me* on the carpet?"

"I wasn't going to be raped," Sam said, chuckling.

"I think you're just horrible!"

"You're lucky I was there."

"Oh? Well, I'll be sure to tell that to Annie!"

"What are you gonna tell your folks?" Sukie asked, interested. "Your aunt's gonna have a fit."

"You stay out of this," Sam and Cathy said together.

The cab rolled to a stop outside the house on Twenty-ninth Street where Sukie had a room, and Sam left her on the sidewalk with a minimum of ceremony.

"It's not your fault, kid," he muttered, "but I don't think I'll be coming around again."

"Naw," Sukie said sadly. "I guess not. Well, it's been fun."

"Look, do you think you could keep quiet about this?" Sam put some money in her hand.

"Sure," Sukie said. "I don't talk." She stashed the currency in her bodice.

"Buy yourself a present," Sam urged. "Consider it from me." He looked up at the driver. "The Waldorf. And see if you can keep quiet too."

When the cab deposited them at the hotel, Sam added another bribe as an aid to silence and handed Cathy down. She quailed a little at the brightly lit street. She had torn the rest of the tapes loose from her dress so that the hemline reached her shoes, but she knew what she—and Sam—looked like.

He pulled her into the shadows and repinned her hair as well as he could. He threw the plumes into a potted tree with a gesture of disgust.

"All right, walk fast and keep your mouth shut." He guided her through the lobby and into the elevator. Its operator goggled at them, but the elevator was quicker than the stairs. Sam slipped him a bill, too. "Sixth floor, and the young lady is not feeling well, so please don't stop for anyone else."

As they got out, Sam took Cathy by the arm. "You're going to have to confess, so you might as well do it right away."

"What about you?" Cathy demanded. "Are you going to confess?"

"Grateful, aren't you?" Sam snapped.

"I like Annie," Cathy defended. "I think you treat her disgracefully."

"Oh, you do? Well, I think I should have left you in the alley."

Sam pushed open Claudia's door, and they confronted a stunned tableau of Claudia, Annie, and Claudia's beau, Howard Locke.

"She was singing at a dump on West Thirty-fourth Street," Sam announced. "They threw sausages at her."

"Oh! Oh, I wish you had just left me there and gone home with that—that harlot!" Cathy screamed at him. She burst into tears and ran from the room. They heard her bedroom door slam.

Before anyone could say anything else, Annie snatched up a vase from Claudia's sideboard and hurled it wildly at Sam. He ducked, and it smashed into the wall behind him in shards of china and sodden flowers. Annie picked up her skirts and ran through the mess, tears streaming down her face, too. Her flying footsteps echoed down the hall, and another door slammed.

Howard Locke took up his hat. "Claudia, my dear, I would stay and help sort things out, but I expect you would rather do without me just now." He bent gallantly over her hand.

"Thank you," she said faintly. "I—it has been a most enjoyable evening, up until this moment. I do hope you will call again."

There was a faint twinkle in Mr. Locke's eyes. "Gracious lady, constantly, if you will let me. When one is my age, one has seen far too much of the world to worry about trifles." He departed with a tip of his hat.

"That is a gentleman," Claudia announced to Sam. She pinned him to the wall with her eyes as if he had been a butterfly in a box. "I am furious with you. By the looks of you I gather that you got Cathy out of a scrape, but you have entirely negated it with your boorish behavior. You are not a gentleman, and I am ashamed of you!"

"Gran—"

His grandmother's violet eyes bored right through him. "Don't talk to me. I am too angry with you. When a man marries, he makes certain vows, and it is despicable not to honor them. To say nothing of throwing it in your wife's face."

"I didn't throw it," Sam protested. "That little devil in there did."

"I'll deal with her," Claudia said grimly. "My advice to you is to go and make your peace with your wife—if she will let you in. If she won't, you may sleep in the hall." She pointed at the door until he went through it.

Claudia decided to ring for the housekeeping staff later; she could hear Cathy hysterically sobbing behind her closed door.

Now or in the morning? Claudia wondered. *Now,* she determined. In the morning the family would be in a flurry with Eden's party. It was a mercy, she thought as she passed Eden's silent door, that the child slept so well. At least Claudia hoped she did.

She tapped on Cathy's door, and when Cathy sniffled "Go away," she went in anyway.

*"FROM THE
PRODUCER OF
WAGONS WEST COMES
YET ANOTHER
EXPLOSIVE SAGA OF
LEGENDARY COURAGE
AND UNFORGETTABLE
LOVE"*

CHILDREN OF THE LION

DON'T MISS
THESE CURRENT
Bantam Bestsellers

☐	27814	**THIS FAR FROM PARADISE** Philip Shelby	$4.95
☐	27811	**DOCTORS** Erich Segal	$5.95
☐	28179	**TREVAYNE** Robert Ludlum	$5.95
☐	27807	**PARTNERS** John Martel	$4.95
☐	28058	**EVA LUNA** Isabel Allende	$4.95
☐	27597	**THE BONFIRE OF THE VANITIES** Tom Wolfe	$5.95
☐	27456	**TIME AND TIDE** Thomas Fleming	$4.95
☐	27510	**THE BUTCHER'S THEATER** Jonathan Kellerman	$4.95
☐	27800	**THE ICARUS AGENDA** Robert Ludlum	$5.95
☐	27891	**PEOPLE LIKE US** Dominick Dunne	$4.95
☐	27953	**TO BE THE BEST** Barbara Taylor Bradford	$5.95
☐	26554	**HOLD THE DREAM** Barbara Taylor Bradford	$5.95
☐	26253	**VOICE OF THE HEART** Barbara Taylor Bradford	$5.95
☐	26888	**THE PRINCE OF TIDES** Pat Conroy	$4.95
☐	26892	**THE GREAT SANTINI** Pat Conroy	$4.95
☐	26574	**SACRED SINS** Nora Roberts	$3.95
☐	27018	**DESTINY** Sally Beauman	$4.95

Buy them at your local bookstore or use this page to order.

Bantam Books, Dept. FB, 414 East Golf Road, Des Plaines, IL 60016

Please send me the items I have checked above. I am enclosing $_____
(please add $2.00 to cover postage and handling). Send check or money
order, no cash or C.O.D.s please.

Mr/Ms _____

Address _____

City/State_____ Zip_____

Please allow four to six weeks for delivery.
Prices and availability subject to change without notice.

FB–11/89

★ WAGONS WEST ★

This continuing, magnificent saga recounts the adventures of a brave band of settlers, all of different backgrounds, all sharing one dream— to find a new and better life.

☐	26822	**INDEPENDENCE! #1**	$4.50
☐	26162	**NEBRASKA! #2**	$4.50
☐	26242	**WYOMING! #3**	$4.50
☐	26072	**OREGON! #4**	$4.50
☐	26070	**TEXAS! #5**	$4.50
☐	26377	**CALIFORNIA! #6**	$4.50
☐	26546	**COLORADO! #7**	$4.50
☐	26069	**NEVADA! #8**	$4.50
☐	26163	**WASHINGTON! #9**	$4.50
☐	26073	**MONTANA! #10**	$4.50
☐	26184	**DAKOTA! #11**	$4.50
☐	26521	**UTAH! #12**	$4.50
☐	26071	**IDAHO! #13**	$4.50
☐	26367	**MISSOURI! #14**	$4.50
☐	27141	**MISSISSIPPI! #15**	$4.50
☐	25247	**LOUISIANA! #16**	$4.50
☐	25622	**TENNESSEE! #17**	$4.50
☐	26022	**ILLINOIS! #18**	$4.50
☐	26533	**WISCONSIN! #19**	$4.50
☐	26849	**KENTUCKY! #20**	$4.50
☐	27065	**ARIZONA! #21**	$4.50
☐	27458	**NEW MEXICO! #22**	$4.50
☐	27703	**OKLAHOMA! #23**	$4.50

Bantam Books, Dept. LE, 414 East Golf Road, Des Plaines, IL 60016

Please send me the items I have checked above. I am enclosing $_____
(please add $2.00 to cover postage and handling). Send check or money order, no cash or C.O.D.s please.

Mr/Ms _____

Address _____

City/State _____ Zip _____

Please allow four to six weeks for delivery.
Prices and availability subject to change without notice.

LE-9/89